JILL TRESEDER's first career was in p: the second in the human side of man work led to a PhD, and eventually, of *The Wise Woman Within: Spirals to V* book for women exploring feminine  ran workshops based on this manual alongside her day job of social research and development projects in the area of child protection.

Since 2008 she has been able to focus on her third career of writing fiction which is what she's wanted to do since she was seven years old. The common theme is exploring how people develop and change.

Her first novel *The Hatmaker's Secret* appeared at the end of 2013. She is currently working on a third about two sisters who escape to England from Budapest during the Hungarian uprising of 1956.

A PLACE *of* SAFETY

JILL TRESEDER

SilverWood

Published in 2014 by SilverWood Books

SilverWood Books Ltd
30 Queen Charlotte Street, Bristol, BS1 4HJ
www.silverwoodbooks.co.uk

ISBN 978-1-78132-258-1 (paperback)
ISBN 978-1-78132-259-8 (ebook)

British Library Cataloguing in Publication Data
A CIP catalogue record for this book is available from
the British Library

Set in Sabon by SilverWood Books
Printed on responsibly sourced paper

To Hugh

1

The sound of my voice gave way to the ticking of the clock, the old station clock Meg bought just after we got married. It was a very satisfactory timepiece – a plain dial with clear roman numerals and a simple brass rim. I liked the snug fit of the trapdoor underneath and the decorated handle of the key. Winding it was a weekly routine and normally its steady rhythm was as much a part of the climate of the room as the books on the shelves and the smell of wood smoke. I didn't even notice it. But today it invaded me. My whole consciousness was hijacked by that persistent beat ticking away our time together. Dropping the paperback on the floor, I crossed the room in two strides, opened the neat little flap and held my finger against the swing of the pendulum until it stopped. I breathed deeply into the silence.

Meg slept. I waited, willing her to open an eye asking me to continue. Nothing. Exhausted by the shared activity of reading aloud, she'd drifted away from me, shrinking back into the cocoon of her illness.

I fetched wood from the stack outside the kitchen door, filled the log basket and lit the stove. A casserole in the oven was already filling the house with aromas of wine and garlic. I knew Meg would hardly touch the food and, God knows, I didn't feel hungry. I shook that thought out of my head. Now was not the time to be bringing God into it. It was the ritual that was important. I pulled the table close to the bed and laid it. Crisp white cloth, her special pewter candlestick and the goblets we bought on our farewell visit to Gubbio. I opened a bottle of our favourite local Chianti, the last of the crate we'd brought back with us, and found a space for it among the cards on the mantelpiece so that it warmed in the heat rising from the woodburner.

I set the wine down next to that photograph. The one Meg gave me for my birthday just after we met. She was wearing her "Lizzie Siddal" dress. It took me straight back to my first sight of her all those years ago when I was working in the library. I'd come up out of the stacks and there she was standing at the desk. A cloud of curls flaming down her back, a swirl of emerald green almost to the floor and orange sequin pumps that matched her hair: a Pre-Raphaelite painting come to life. I must have gasped because she spun round. The dress rustled and green eyes met mine. I was knocked sideways. Literally. Nearly dropped the books I was carrying. She just smiled as if she were used to having that effect on people and said, 'Can I help you?'

I recovered enough to laugh. 'That's what I'm meant to say.'

She laughed too, which was about the sexiest sound I'd ever heard. I don't know how I managed it, but we ended up having lunch together and that was it. She'd been to an all-night party and hadn't been home, which was why she was wearing taffeta at ten in the morning.

Being with Meg was never plain sailing. I knew it wouldn't be. Some people found Meg overwhelming, "heavy-duty" a friend of mine called her once. "Exhilarating" was the word I'd have chosen. I don't think anybody expected it to last. But I'm pretty sure neither of us ever regretted it. I know I didn't. I never understood what she saw in me, but I didn't waste time on that one.

1988, that was, just before Valentine's Day. We were married almost exactly a year later. And now here we were in 2009, and our twentieth anniversary. Our friends didn't know of our plan, but they did know that every milestone was important to Meg, and twenty years was a long time to be married. The doorbell had sounded all morning, but nobody came in. Just offerings left on the doorstep. Flowers, fruit, healthy things. Sometimes I longed for someone to bring take-away pizza and a six-pack of John Smiths, someone who crashed in, laughing loudly. More crazy thoughts. If that person had turned up I wouldn't have known what to do. And I did appreciate the kindness of friends. I really did. Jugs and vases of flowers covered every available surface: lilies, iris, roses and a bunch of anemones from Laura in the special place on the bedside cabinet.

Our decision about Laura still bothered me. But Meg had been adamant. She didn't want anything "confusing" their relationship. She seemed to think that Laura would protest, have some kind of tantrum. I mean, she wasn't a kid any more, but Meg had got it into her head she'd be difficult and she couldn't cope with that prospect. So, when Laura got the invitation to her friend's twenty-first in London, Meg absolutely insisted that she went. 'It's our opportunity,' she said to me afterwards. 'On our anniversary. How appropriate!' And that was that.

She was underestimating Laura. Ever since she dropped out of uni to be with Meg she'd been more of a sister to her than a daughter. We'd been so close, the three of us, such a unit, that it seemed wrong she wasn't here. And it was me, not Meg, who was going to have to deal with the consequences of excluding her. But I could hardly say that to Meg. On the other hand, there was no doubt, it was simpler and calmer with just the two of us. For a start, there was no argument about what music we'd have. It had to be Rachmaninov. "Our" piano concerto. That gentle start and the inevitability, like the tide coming in. I put the CD in the machine ready, tweaked the curtains more tightly shut and looked round the room. The scene was set for our celebration.

Our eyes met as we raised our glasses, Meg holding hers carefully in both hands.

'It's been good,' she said. That truncated form of words to reduce the effort of making sounds. I could fill in the gaps with what she might once have said, but I missed the musical quality of her voice with its trace of a Welsh lilt.

I nodded, able to speak but unable to find the words. The irony wouldn't be lost on her. 'It's been wonderful,' I managed in reply and then lapsed immediately into practicality. 'Shall we eat?'

Meg shook her head and mimicked an expression of inhaling ecstatically. It emerged more as a grimace but it was a familiar shorthand: the smell of food was more enjoyable than the difficulty of eating. And tonight there was no point in eating.

'Are you sure?' I wasn't referring now to the question of dinner and she knew that.

She gave a deep, slow, deliberate nod and gestured for my hands. I moved the table and took both her hands in mine.

She gazed down at them. 'Loved hands al-ways,' she said, pulling one hand slowly out of my grasp and pushing her fingers carefully along the length of mine.

I smiled. 'Silly, you are. Just hands. Ordinary old hands.'

I felt the slightest pressure and appreciated how much effort that cost her. I squeezed back, couldn't bring myself to look up at her. She was wearing that scarf, the one I bought her in Sansepolcro market during the Italy years. That day, the first time she stumbled.

Early spring and the first warm weather after the snow and isolation of winter. The whole world – plants, people, even the stone buildings seemed to be opening up in the sun. Opening to possibilities – bees in the blossom, warmth in the bones, gossip and company.

The market had been in full swing when we reached the square. Meg swooped on the vegetable stall in the corner, gathering fronded carrots, asparagus, artichokes, delighting the Signora with her pleasure in the produce. She kept laughing back at me, holding out a sculptural artichoke, a purple-gloss aubergine, for me to admire. 'Smell this! Just look at that colour!' We wandered on to a stand festooned with scarves which she flicked in the air or held to her face. 'Wow! They're such good value!'

'I'll buy you one,' I said. 'Present to celebrate spring.'

'Ooh, look!' She held up a silky skein of gold and red and black stripes and twisted it round her neck. She was wearing a skinny black T-shirt and jeans and the scarf against the shirt and her hair was sensational. That image of her upturned face, the freckles across her nose, the light in her green eyes, it will always be with me. She was biting the tip of her tongue, such a familiar gesture.

'*Bellissima!*' intoned the man behind the stall. '*Bellissima!*' Like so many young males in this area he was a more robust and muscular version of the Jesus picture in my childhood Bible. With a natural gift for theatre, this Jesus now warmed to his theme, keen on a sale.

I bargained a little and Meg flirted happily while tying the scarf in some clever knot that managed to look entirely casual. We walked on, hand in hand, through back streets smelling of the freshly laundered washing which hung from overhead lines at every other window. Predictably for a market day, we ended up at our favourite ristorante where we always ate a seasonal omelette or pasta dish with a carafe of house wine. That day we gorged on local asparagus.

It happened on the way back to the bus stop. We'd called in at the Duomo where Meg lit a candle.

'I don't know why,' she said as we came out onto the steps. 'It's just a nice thing to do. Kind of symbolic. A thank you to the gods perhaps. I feel so happy. We're so lucky.'

I smiled and nodded and kissed the top of her head.

'I hope you're not being patronising.' She gave me a playful push as she said it, missed the next step and fell sideways. Vegetables rolled and bounced down to the street as I leapt to help her up. An elderly man fielded an aubergine in a surprisingly athletic movement and he and his wife gathered our shopping and carefully repacked our basket, while other people clustered around with exclamations of concern. These were followed by extravagant delight when Meg was able to hobble away on my arm.

On the bus she was subdued and shrugged when I teased her about having too much wine with our meal.

'Are you sure you're okay? Haven't sprained anything?'

She shook her head. 'No. Just a bit sore, and a bashed elbow. It's weird. That step seemed to jump up and bite me.'

She wouldn't talk about it after that. I should have known. Meg was by far the more agile of the two of us. Normally she would have made a good story out of the incident, joked about it, shown off her bruises.

I was never one for introspection. But Meg's illness forced me to reflect. Questions like: why are we here? is there life after death? And the obvious one, should we be able to choose when we die? They didn't seem so out of the way any more. Not that I had any answers. I wasn't acting out of some passionate conviction. I was just doing what we'd worked out we needed to do – Meg and me, at that time, in that situation. I wasn't the crusading type, that wasn't something I understood. Any more than I understood how people could believe in a God when a brilliant, feisty, gifted human being like Meg could be cut down at the height of her powers with a goddam disease like this. I raged all the time inside and sometimes the raging escaped and reached Meg. And she would just shrug and smile. How come she wasn't raging too?

But rage wouldn't serve tonight. Meg made a sound and I looked up slowly. Over the last few months her face had shrunk and become bird-like in the nest of hair. There were still copper lights amongst the grey, but they no longer burned. She had put her fire into living, which she did with passion and intensity. Maybe that was why she didn't need to rage, why she knew when to die, and to do it gently.

'Now,' she said. 'Time.'

I met her gaze and nodded. Time. Time to do what we had agreed.

In the end it was so easy, this moment that I'd agonised over and dreaded so much. It was just our normal routine. The usual pain killers and sleeping drug before I settled Meg for the night. The only difference was the size of the dose. I watched her slowly drain the glass, wanting to steady it, wanting to snatch it away. I did neither.

I held her until she was deeply asleep. Then I drained my glass, poured another and settled with my hand covering hers to wait for the drugs to do their work.

There was a chill in the air when I came to. The fire had burnt out and any residual heat had faded. I raised my head slowly on a painfully stiff neck, slowly, painfully remembering what I was doing. Meg's breathing had changed. That must have been what roused me. It was shallow and intermittent. I watched and listened until it came no more. There was no pulse in her wrist. I stood and kissed her forehead, stroked her hair. I found myself wishing and dreading that her eyes would open, but they didn't.

I don't know how long I stood, paralysed by the silence. I started to sway and my body turned me – out of the door, into the hall, out of the house, where the air felt as cold as I did.

I walked the deserted streets of our city where we'd met and had our child and lived our lives. Once, when we were young, it had represented the suffocating routine of suburbia, and we made our escape to live in Italy. Last year it became the familiar community Meg wanted to return to after her final diagnosis. Was it really only last year? It seemed an eternity ago. 'I can't be ill in Italian,' she'd said. She never did get to grips with the language. She could manage social chat, just, but it was always my role to manage the nuts and bolts of our life. And it became my role to communicate with the health professionals.

The day in Italy when the consultant first told us the diagnosis seemed like the end of the world. Now – leaning on a bridge in Exeter – I'd have given anything to be back there in Sansepolcro with those precious months still ahead of us. A time when multiple sclerosis was still something which affected other people, when pain was a stubbed toe or a cracked rib, when assisted suicide was a concept we simply hadn't registered.

Somewhere a clock struck two. The night frost had penetrated to meet the chill inside me and I was shaking. At home fatigue hit me, an undertow that sucked me into oblivion as soon as I fell onto my bed.

I woke in the transition from night to day when the light is still granular with dissolving darkness. As the furniture gradually materialised, so did my memory of the night before. I'd done it. I expected to feel the stabbing pain of loss, but I didn't. I told myself, *Meg is dead, Meg is no more*, and – more formally – *Your wife is dead*. There was still no reaction from my beating heart so I tried again: *You have killed your wife*. But nothing, nothing except a rejection of the melodrama of putting it that way.

I turned over and tried another tack. It was a relief, I told myself. A relief for Meg certainly, to be out of pain. And a relief for me not to have it hanging over me as it had been for months, the question of how and when and all the careful details to be worked out. But again nothing. No sense of release or freedom from the burden of care. There was just a numbness where the feelings should be, and a rather cold noticing, as if the process might be interesting. What sort of callous person had I become? Was this what happened when you took a life? The thin end of some sinister wedge? Even when the act was one of love and compassion, the last shared ritual?

I kept my eyes closed and searched my mind. I knew I was not this person. There had to be some familiar territory in there somewhere. Meg and me. Me and Meg. I was getting there. Meg and me. This was where I needed to be. Trust. Love. Our plan. A phrase drifted past and I latched on to it. *It was what she wanted.* It wasn't quite what I was looking for, but it would do. It allowed me to swing my legs out of bed.

I found myself walking across the landing, opening the door. That stupid cliché, revisiting the scene of the crime, ran through my head.

There was the table, pulled sideways from the bed and still neatly laid with clean plates and cutlery. The cloth was stained dark where the wine bottle stood and wax had dribbled from the burnt-out candle. I edged my gaze to the anemones still glowing purple and scarlet, but couldn't make my eyes turn any further.

A thin finger of sunlight was striking the crystal hanging in the window, the one Laura gave Meg for her birthday. It was sending rainbows skidding across the walls and they danced in the draught created by my presence.

It was what she wanted. It was what she wanted. I repeated the mantra soundlessly.

In the bathroom I didn't recognise myself in the mirror and turned quickly away. I didn't know what should happen next, except that I had a phone call to make.

The receptionist at the surgery said she would do her best. She picked up on the urgency, my need for our regular GP to come. I could not face a stranger. There'd be too much to explain. They might not understand my motives. That thought made me suddenly chill with fear.

I sat on the bottom step of the stairs, eyeing the door, somehow expecting the bell to ring, knowing it could be hours. Geoff Lewis, our doctor, had become a friend. I trusted him to tell it straight and to do the best he could for me. He was a tall rake of a man, who galloped about but came to a quiet and steady standstill. Meg used to say he listened with his eyes as well as his ears, and he certainly had a useful sense of humour. When we met Geoff we knew coming home had been a good idea.

We received impeccable care in Italy. That wasn't the problem. But it was the language barrier – it meant that we lacked a context for understanding the disease. The consultant we met on that day in Sansepolcro spoke beautiful but limited English. He explained Meg's diagnosis in old-fashioned phrases sprinkled with Italian. We concentrated very hard, but we barely took it in. It emerged that Meg had experienced an episode some time before she and I met, when she almost lost the sight in one eye. It lasted a week or two and her Cardiff GP had put it down to an infection.

I interrupted, indignant. 'How come you never told me?'

Meg shrugged. 'I forgot all about it. It didn't seem important. Not once it was over.' She made a face. 'Not until now, that is.'

The consultant made exaggerated gestures of dismay at this failing and told us that that had almost certainly been the first manifestation of the condition. Nowadays – and in that word he somehow implied *here in Italy* – it would have been diagnosed.

At the hospital entrance I enfolded Meg as if she were a rare porcelain vase in need of bubble-wrap. I felt in need of bubble-wrap myself, some insulation from the world. There was no question of the bus. All that jostling and banter. We took a taxi home, lit the fire and sat huddled together all afternoon, drinking a great deal of wine and remembering a few people we'd known with MS who were barely affected by the disease and led normal lives.

I went on the Internet of course, learnt about the various forms MS can take. But that was no substitute for talking it through with Geoff. He pulled no punches, but his sensitivity and his humour made it possible to do that thing people talk about, to live one day at a time.

When the doorbell did go, it woke me out of a doze. I'd fallen sideways and could feel the imprint of the newel post on my cheek as I moved stiffly to open the door. I was dizzy from having got up too quickly.

'Christ, Alfie,' said Geoff and steadied me with an arm as we went through to Meg's room. I hung back inside the door, leaning on the back of the armchair.

He was busy for a while by the bed. Then he turned and gestured to me to sit down, sat facing me, perched on the coffee table.

'Alfie, you don't need me to tell you that Meg has passed away. You don't need me to tell you that she did not die from natural causes. You maybe *do* need me to tell you that it's obvious. We know what happened here. Yes? I am right, aren't I?'

When I nodded he continued.

'I have to state that Meg's death is an unexpected one, and because of this I am obliged to refer her death to the coroner.'

I could find nothing to say. Silence pressed in on me.

'You're a courageous man, Alfie. Greater love, and all that.' He sighed. 'I guess you probably know just how difficult this could be for you.' He raised a questioning eyebrow.

I shrugged. 'Not really too sure.' My voice sounded odd, not like mine. 'Thought it best not to know.' Truth was, Meg had got the idea that it would all be fine as long as I didn't have to give her an injection. I'd never contradicted her. In fact I'd almost come to believe it.

'This will expose you, Alfie. You will be questioned, gently at first, then more forcefully. If it goes badly you could go down. I say that as a friend, to warn you. But the law's not my job. What I have to do is put aside everything except the medical facts. Meg had what might be termed a terminal illness. But this was not sufficiently advanced to explain what has happened here today.'

I nodded. It was as I'd thought. 'I won't deny it. No point.'

'There's a lot of pressure to change the law of course. You'll get support from the euthanasia lobby. Could work in your favour or not. Who knows? I'll have to say of course, when questioned, that Meg was not capable of preparing and taking the drugs without help.'

'There's a note. A suicide note. She said it was in the desk.'

'But she wouldn't have been able to write the note herself.' Geoff shook his head. 'How...? You didn't...?'

'No. She did it on the laptop. Connie helped, witnessed the signature. So-called signature. You know Connie? Manages the gallery. She's been a rock.'

'Yes, she was here once when I came. In that case, the police will want to interview her, I guess – about the note.'

'I suppose so. Hadn't thought of that. It won't be a problem – for Connie, I mean?'

Geoff frowned. 'I wouldn't have thought... But I really don't know. I'll vouch for you of course, the strong relationship you had. I was well aware of Meg's views. About her increasing dependence. How she couldn't bear the thought of...'

'You've been a good friend.'

He shrugged.

'Everyone knew how she felt. She was very clear about...' I could hear her now, holding forth to friends who had difficulty looking her in the eye.

'That's a good thing – for you, I mean. By the way, where's Laura?'

'Away. She doesn't know.'

'She doesn't know? Uh! No, I suppose not. When's she due back?'

'Tomorrow morning, I think.' I realised I had no idea which day it was. The thought of seeing Laura was terrible to me.

He gave me a long look. 'Are you going to be okay on your own?'

'Geoff, I'll be fine. It was my choice. I'll manage. You really don't have to...'

'Have you got food in the house?'

'Last night's supper. We never...'

'Eat it! And what about Scotch?

I nodded.

'Scotch would be preferable to sleeping pills, but...'

I nodded again. 'Never want to see another sleeping pill.'

'Eat. Then a hefty nightcap and go to bed. Get some sleep.

Sleep round the clock if you can. God knows, you must need it. I'll come by in the morning to make sure you're all right.'

He stood and collected his bag. 'I'll see myself out. You get in that kitchen and feed yourself. I'd better get on to the coroner.'

2

He's a scarecrow of a man. Tall, rangy, with hair like straw setting off in all directions. Big nose and a wide mouth in a face that looks like it's made of broken eggshells. Although when I said that to Joel he said, 'Crazy paving, more like'. Typical Joel. He wouldn't see the vulnerability in Alfie. He must be around fifty, I guess, and he looks like he's taken a battering in life but stayed soft on the inside, though I can't say why I think it.

Nobody knows much about him. He turned up a month or so before me. Taken on at the farm for the lambing, so they say. Then he just stayed on doing odd jobs. Maintenance – and there's plenty of that, it being a ramshackle sort of farm. Mending fences, clearing ditches. And loads of stuff you have to do to sheep, Joel says. I always thought they just got on with munching grass, but I got that wrong. Joel came from London too – Tottenham, so nowhere near me luckily – and he says he's learnt a raft of stuff about farming since he took on the pub.

Me, I'm still learning to cope without a mobile signal. I can just get one if I stand on my bed and wave the phone out the skylight. Even that's not reliable. In more ways than one. I tried that trick the other morning when it was raining. Got my duvet soaked. Joel let me have a fan heater to dry it out. Said it was a damn fool thing to do and did I think it wouldn't rain on me because I was from Harrow? Very funny. Especially as Harrow isn't exactly where I come from. But he's not to know that.

I couldn't believe this village. It's like the lid of a biscuit tin

Auntie Em used to have. Never thought it could be real. Artist's licence, I thought. But here I am living in a biscuit tin. Indoors I feel like Alice when she eats the cake and grows enormous. I feel too big for the place. Outdoors it's like I've drunk from the 'DRINK ME' bottle and shrunk - or is it the other way round? It's like the sky will swallow me up. Alice through the biscuit tin.

Joel says the signal problem's because the village is in a dip. Not that I want to hear from people. For instance, getting that text from Luke this morning. I could do without that, I really could. He's on about my table. I mean, he said I could store it in his flat for as long as I like. So why the fuss? And it makes me feel guilty. I'm taking advantage, leaving the table there.

Anyway, what could I possibly do with a frigging table here? Except, of course, Luke doesn't know I'm working in a pub and sleeping in a cupboard. A fresh start. No getting involved. I could even change my name. Alice, for example. Nice name. Different, but not as different as Esther. Where that came from nobody knows. Nan said, 'Not from the Bible, that's for sure, knowing Carole.' Which was reassuring. Anyway, I'd keep forgetting if I tried to change it.

There's Alfie doing the knife and fork mime that tells me he's ready for his meal. Those intense blue eyes catching mine. They always surprise me when he looks up from reading the paper. He lives up at the farm. They say he spotted a disused barn in the five-acre field, fixed it up for himself and moved in. Don't suppose he can do much in the way of cooking. I suppose the folk at the farm gave permission, but we never see them down in the village. They keep themselves to themselves.

I guess they just got used to him being around. Alfie's like that. He's part of the furniture here at The George. Here most days, and it's nearly always a pint of mild and cottage pie. He's just known as Alfie and he calls me "Girl-with-green-eyes". Ever since he stopped calling me "She-who-never-smiles", after he made me laugh by catching that butterfly. I'll never forget how he watched that flitter-flutter, put down his knife and fork and crept up to the glass. And how gentle he was with those big hands of his. Not that he was gentle with me, ordering me to open the window and be quick about it.

'Can't abide a thing to be trapped,' he said in that deep slow voice. 'I don't know what's so funny, but it's put a smile on your face.' And he pursed his lips and gave me such a look.

It kind of haunted me afterwards. Silly. I couldn't get it out my head. How careful he was with that butterfly.

I know he paints portraits of course. Everyone knows. There's a likeness of Joel behind the bar he did one Friday instead of paying off his tab. Joel was chuffed as a monkey, said he'd make a fortune when Alfie got to be famous. But I still didn't get it when Alfie started watching me. One whole week whenever I looked over to his corner between pulling pints, he'd be watching my every move.

So I'm completely thrown when I take him his meal and he looks up and says, 'Will you come and sit for me?'

Just like that. Says he'll pay me. Says not to worry, it'll only be head and shoulders. I suppose he thinks it would bother me to take my clothes off like models do.

'Okay,' I say. 'Why not? I don't suppose it hurts.'

'You just sit in a chair,' he says. 'It's not like the dentist.'

That Monday, after I've finished changing the beds and cleaning the rooms, I take Joel's bike. A total nightmare. Not a mountain bike but an old boneshaker that everyone uses from time to time. Not worth having your own round here. It's so steep and narrow you spend half your time pushing and the rest diving into the hedge to avoid being knocked over by cars. The going's relatively easy up to the Hannafords farm, but it's a hot day and I'm sweating by the time I get to their track. The sky's a clear blue over the high moor and the air smells of honey. That's a thing I still can't get used to. That perfumed air. The drift of sweetness and pepper in the sun. The fact that rain and grass have a smell. But then I grew up with exhaust fumes, the reek of Indian takeaways and eau de creosote on the garden fences.

The track's just rough stones with grass growing through and holes filled with lumps of rock, so I have to get off and push. There are loads of flowers in the banks on either side, all of them different shades of pink. Foxgloves – I know them - then big blotches of almost red, and lower down tiny crimson stars, with patches

21

of purple every now and then. A funny thing, these colour schemes. I came at primrose time when all the flowers were yellow, what with celandines as well. Then the bluebells came, and now it's all shades of pink.

When I get to the gate into Alfie's field I push the bike through and throw it against the bank, to avoid it being squashed by the Hannafords' tractor. Those brothers aren't too fussy. An odd pair. They've always lived in that farmhouse where they were born and the younger one's said never to speak. People say the place is an awful tip since their mother died last year. I've never been up there and I don't want to, either.

Just at that moment my mobile beeps. So I suppose I must've climbed up higher than the pub roof. I scrabble in my bag only to find it's another text from Luke. He's complaining I never reply, insisting he needs to sort out the table. Sod's Law that he's pestering me, while Auntie Em was nowhere to be found when I needed her. What's got into Luke? It's a simple enough thing, surely, to look after a table.

I turn off the phone and follow a well-worn path across the field to where Alfie's rusting old pickup is parked alongside the barn. I say Alfie's. It actually belongs to the Hannafords and he gets the use of it because he still does work on the farm. I'm expecting his place to be pretty much of a tip too, so I get the surprise of my life when I walk through the door. He's got that barn fitted out like a palace, with carpet on the floor at one end and even a piano in the corner. There's a big squashy leather sofa and a battered armchair with wings and the seat nearly on the floor. So maybe not quite a palace, but even so. On one wall there are rows of books on shelves made of planks separated by bricks. Next to them there's a rack of CDs and a hi-fi, and out of that is coming the most amazing sound, echoing right up to the rafters and back again. It's someone singing but not like I've ever heard anyone sing before.

Down the other end it's all concrete floor, with canvases stacked against one wall, splodges of paint all over the place and a corner of a kitchen with more paintbrushes than cups and plates. The whole place smells of turpentine and a malty kind of tobacco. I've never seen Alfie smoke, but there's a whole collection of pipes on the table next to the armchair and a leather tobacco pouch.

I can't see him anywhere. Has he forgotten and gone off out? I banged on the door but he wouldn't have heard anyway with that music going full blast.

I feel such an idiot when I notice: he's standing right above me, looking down. Looking down my T-shirt most likely. I didn't see there's another floor over the concrete end of the room which stops halfway and he's got his easel, and a bed up there. He grins, and waves a remote at the CD player. It suddenly goes so quiet it's embarrassing.

'Sorry about Puccini,' he says, and swings down the ladder.

Being just the two of us, and on his territory, feels strange. It makes me nervous.

'Coffee?' He's filling a kettle in the far corner. 'You have to have it black. I don't keep milk. But there's plenty of sugar.'

The coffee smells wonderful. I've never been a coffee drinker. I thought it was foul stuff, but then I only ever tried Nescafé. We had PG Tips at home. I heap in three spoons of sticky brown sugar out of a cellophane bag, and it's delicious. We're sitting between the two halves of the room. Then I clock the table. It's an old bare wooden thing like mine, the one my Nan used to have in her kitchen, except she used to scrub hers. It's exactly like the one Luke is currently banging on about. How spooky is that?

Alfie's watching me with that funny half smile.

'I like your table,' I say.

He laughs. 'It was up there in the corner, covered in ancient bird shit.' He nods towards the upper floor.

'I have to leave the window open so they can come and go. Swallows. You know they come back to the same nest every year?'

I shake my head. 'That's cool.' I wonder how the hell they find it. Such a cosy homing instinct doesn't fit with my idea of those wild, swooping creatures.

'I put newspaper down. To catch the shit. They don't seem to take a blind bit of notice of me.'

I don't know what else to say about the swallows, so I ask lots of questions to fill the space, like how does he get the electric to work the hi-fi and the kettle? He tells me he's got a generator out back, and that there's an Elsan out there in case I need it. I've never heard of such a thing so I can only guess and hope I'll manage without. That's before I know how long I'll be sitting there in that effing chair.

It's one of those swivel things like you have in offices, that go round and round and up and down. He picked it out of a skip in town, he says. Thought it would be useful for getting different angles. Trouble is you only have to twitch an eyebrow and the thing goes round. And I twitch a lot more than an eyebrow that first time I can tell you. And is Alfie mad! It's the first time I ever heard him raise his voice.

Blimey, I never thought it was a glamorous thing to do, sit for a painter, even if it is flattering to be asked. But I never realised how tit-achingly boring it would be. I just keep thinking of the money. Not much but every little helps. Look after the pennies and the pounds will look after themselves, as my Nan used to say. And it's true. It's creeping up, the balance in that account. Especially since that nice girl with the rabbit teeth in the building society suggested I move it to a bonus saver account. Saving for a rainy day. That's what Nan would say. Keeping myself safe, that's what I call it. My independence. Keeping off the streets, out the way of the dealers. And if I ever get to go back to uni, well, that would be a bonus.

I wonder if he can find enough people to paint, away up here. 'D'you paint other things? Besides people?'

He gives a half nod and cocks an eyebrow towards the canvases against the wall. 'Landscapes, trees.'

He's concentrating so I keep quiet.

The more I look at Alfie's place up here, the more I realise how weird it is. Or I suppose what I'm saying is that *he's* weird. A farmhand who likes opera. And jazz, I reckon. He's got a whole lot of old vinyl stuff on the bottom shelf under the books. I can't read them from here but they look kind of familiar, like the stuff Auntie Em used to have. And the books. Mostly paperbacks, but some of them are quite grand with leather bindings, but battered. And they all look as though they've been read. They're comfortable books. Not there for show. There's a wine rack under the sink with posh-looking bottles in it. The whisky on the shelf's Johnny

Walker. Black Label, too. Someone asked for that at The George once, a loudmouth from the holiday complex up the road. Joel just laughed. He didn't keep it, he said. Far too expensive for our locals. So altogether I get the impression that Alfie's not short of a bob or two, as Nan used to say. How surprising is that?

When we take a break Alfie shows me all round, telling me about his stuff as if he's introducing friends. It's rather nice. He got the piano from the village hall down at Blidworthy. They'd just left it outside in the rain because the Short Mat Bowls Club said it got in the way. He tells me it needs tuning – holds up the lid and gives a run up and down the keyboard, as if to show me. It could be fit for the Albert Hall for all I know. He's wearing one of those plaid shirts with the sleeves rolled up, and the light's catching the tawny hairs on his forearms. I've never been turned on by someone's arms before. I look quickly away. There's a little box on top of the piano inlaid with different woods and mother-of-pearl. I run my finger over its smoothness and I'm just about to say how cool it is when I feel Alfie freeze. I take my finger away and he moves on abruptly.

He's funny about the wall-hangings. He says they're ancient Egyptian tapestries, although actually I can see they're no such thing. Just old curtains and a couple of tie-dyed sarongs. Then he laughs and says he likes to imagine things like that. He got them from a charity shop and when he lifts the corners I can see they're covering up holes in the wall.

'I'm a magpie,' he says. 'I like finding things people don't want anymore and putting them to good use.'

I laugh. 'I never looked at it that way. I always used to buy my clothes in the Oxfam, but just 'cos they're cheap. So we've got something in common.' When I say that he looks stupidly pleased and I nearly tell him about the table. But that would be making something out of nothing.

'Tell you what,' he says. 'If you sit for another half-hour, I'll buy you lunch at the pub down in Blidworthy.'

That's nice, but I'm wary. 'That's not instead of paying me, is it?'

I come out with it before I think how rude it might sound.

He looks quite hurt and says, of course not. So I say lunch would be lovely, and hope he can't hear my tummy rumbling at the mere mention of food.

He's edgy in the pub, but I'm enjoying my egg and chips, so I hardly notice him go to the gents'. It's some time before I think he's been gone a while. Maybe he went for a smoke. Then there comes an echo in my head and I know I've heard the truck driving away. It's like my ears have been storing the sound until my brain was ready to pick it up. Like you can count the chimes of a clock in your memory and know what time it is, even if it's already finished striking before you notice. I used to do that at Auntie Em's in the middle of the night. Especially in the early days when I came there from the home and I'd wake up not knowing where I was. It scared me the first time because I never knew about striking clocks. But when I got used to it I found it comforting – like a friend saying, 'It's okay, I'm here, you're fine and it's three o'clock'. I was silly like that and I didn't half miss it when I had to leave Auntie Em's.

So he's buggered off and left me here. Shit. What's that supposed to mean? He's bought me lunch – and at least he paid for it. I noticed him get his wallet out of his back pocket and thought what a daft place to keep it. But then again, not so risky round here. Nice neat bum, though. But the point is, he still hasn't paid me. I'm pretty sure that's not why he's done a runner, though. He seemed uneasy from the moment he walked through the door. It's crazy, but the first thought is, I want him to finish my picture. I want to see what he sees in me. And how the fuck am I supposed to get back?

There's a geezer at the bar giving me the eye which is the last thing I want, so I fish my mobile out and peer at it and shake it as if I can't get a signal and then make for the door, purposeful, eyes down on the mobile. Waving the phone about outside allows me to wander round and check whether I'm right without looking like a wally who's been stood up. Sure enough, the truck's gone but the bike's leaning against the wall. Thoughtful of him, huh!

I'm pretty sure the bloke from the bar is watching me from the doorway. I know there's someone there. So I finish an imaginary phone call, climb on the bike and ride past giving him a stony glare.

There's something about the way he looks back that surprises me. I can't put my finger on what it is, but instead of turning left for our village, I turn right. I don't know where the fuck I'm going, but it's my day off. I can go for a bike ride if I want.

I hope he doesn't follow me, but soon I can hear an engine. I'll bet it's that silver Bimmer convertible that was parked under the trees at the far end of the yard. I dive off into a field gateway and crouch in the ditch getting royally stung in the process. That's the trouble with the effing country. I hear an approaching growl and peep carefully through the brambles. He's got the hood down and he doesn't even glance my way. It's not a Bimmer after all, just a souped-up Vauxhall lookalike. I take the opportunity to have a pee. I'll hang on here a bit in case he comes back. He knows I can't have got far. I hold my breath and listen. Spot on. That's exactly what he does. I wait for the dust cloud to settle and the engine noise to fade down the valley. He doesn't stop at the pub in Blidworthy. He'll be driving straight on past The George and I find myself hoping that Alfie's well out the way. Because somehow I know that this guy is why Alfie left so abruptly and that he was only following me to get at Alfie. What the hell am I doing sitting in this ditch for the sake of someone I scarcely know, who's just stood me up and not paid for a piece of work?

I was calm enough when Esther arrived. But my hand trembled when I started painting. She wouldn't have noticed, too busy with the darn chair. Except, how much did she notice? That cool, off-hand manner. Deceptive maybe. Certainly older than she looked. Been around a bit, from what I've overheard at the pub. About twenty-four, I reckoned.

She was just like a kid with that chair. Found all the levers quicker than I ever did. As if she were used to such things, except it was obviously a novelty. She swivelled it round, pumped up and down, tipped it back, with her stick-insect legs swinging up and leaving very little to the imagination in that midget denim skirt. No, I had no inclination whatsoever to do a life study of her. All the interest was in the face.

'Right. You'd better make yourself comfortable.'

Strange. When I said that a shadow passed over her expression and she matured ten years. Remembered what she was there for, I suppose. Her face was such an odd mixture. A combination of deadpan and mobile. A change of mood and almost a different person would appear. She could look like a tart, she really could, when she gave that wry sideways smile as she pulled a pint. Pale, dead straight hair in no sort of style, pushed behind her ear like a schoolgirl. Yet sexy. How did that happen?

'Yes, cross your legs if you like. The main thing is to stay still.'

She could look so serious, intense. With that long straight nose and those fine eyebrows. Like when she was reading that time. She'd just finished her shift and taken a pint of lemonade to the bench outside, to read in the sun. When I said whatever damn fool thing came into my head, it seemed an age before she looked up. Her eyes were glazed over, those great cat's eyes of hers. She hadn't heard a thing. Totally lost in the book. Looked right through me before she kind of refocused and said, 'What? Did you say something?' I said, never mind, and she just shrugged and was right back in her book. I couldn't catch the title but it didn't look like anything lightweight. And she wouldn't leave it lying around, it would go straight in her bag. That was how she was, neat, self-contained, as if she needed all of herself to herself. With some people, you know they're there. They spread themselves, leave their mark. But this one trod lightly, passed through without a trace.

'Try turning sideways, away from me. Yeah? A bit more.'

I wanted that nose almost in profile. I wasn't ready for the eyes, not yet. Although that's why I'd invited her, why I wanted to paint her. It was still too sharp a pain, looking into them: the leap of recognition followed by the deep, dark chasm of admitting they were not the right eyes. They only *resembled* Meg's eyes, but closely enough for me to give myself that torture over and over again. Was it torture or comfort? Or was I slowly trying to dull the pain by continually exercising it?

When I first saw her I'd told myself it would be madness to paint her. I decided against it more than once. Surprised myself when I asked her to sit. I knew she'd come. On account of the money, of course. So now I just had to get on with it. It was only a picture, when all was said and done.

'Now turn your head and look back at me.'

Dear God! What a look that produced. As if she'd seduce me right there and then.

'No. No that's not what I want. Sorry. My mistake.'

Well, it certainly would have been my mistake. Mustn't go there. Mustn't even think it. In spite of being older than she looked, she was young enough to be my daughter. Or put it another way, I was old enough to be her father. Easily.

'Try just turning sideways without looking at me. That's more like it. Now fix your eyes on something, so you can hold the position.'

She took the instruction. That was progress.

She'd flirt with the holidaymakers in the pub, but never with me, nor any of the regulars. She could be quite sharp with people she knew, teasing, but with a hard edge which left you wary. She got on well with Pattie though. You could hear them laughing together in the kitchen. A good sign. Pattie would be a steadying influence. Though why I thought she needed one I couldn't have said. And why should I care anyway?

Good God, could that girl fidget! Mind you, she was always busy in the pub, multi-tasking, as they say. Wiping the bar down, polishing glasses, tidying, straightening. One time when it was quiet she took the coffee machine apart and cleaned it. Not many girls would think to do that.

'Just relax.' Futile. Maybe I was asking too much. 'Okay, we'll do ten minutes and then take a break.'

She was still looking round the room, curious, mermaid eyes flicking sideways.

'And don't move your head.'

Inevitably there was always something she wanted a better look at, just beyond her peripheral vision and the head moved, just a little, but enough.

'I *said*, don't move!'

A pout of those full lips. She didn't like that.

I'd show her round in the break, then she'd be calmer. Thank

God she didn't smoke. Couldn't abide the smell of cigarettes. A pipe, that was a different matter.

She was still at last. Gone into herself. The sketch started to go better, taking shape. Just a beginning, but I wasn't in any hurry.

She seemed excited to be travelling in the pickup. Couldn't think why.

'Glad we're not going to The George,' she said. 'I mean, on my day off.'

As we bumped down the field I spotted the bike in the ditch by the gate. 'Best hop out and chuck it in the back.'

I didn't want to be bringing her back up here. I'd get on with working up that sketch as soon as I'd been out to check the ewes on the high moor. That morning I'd only had time to go round those with the youngest lambs in the enclosure next to the farm.

'I'll be busy this afternoon. Got held up this morning.'

I'd bumped into Tom who'd got on his usual hobby horse about DEFRA and the endless paperwork. So by the time I'd got them fed and watered, Esther was due to arrive.

Blidworthy was a mistake. It was just that bit more on the beaten track than our village.

'Doesn't look too good,' I said as I parked alongside a row of four-by-fours with '08 registrations.

Esther gave me a blank look.

'Whole load of Chelsea tractors. Not a smattering of mud on any of them.'

The occupants were all in suits and open-neck shirts wha-whaing at one end of the bar. Esther was eyeing a Specials' board with fancy writing and fancy dishes to match. We'd be here all day waiting for them to cook that lot.

'All a bit trendy for me. I'll go for a cheese sandwich.' I guess it was a bit pointed, but Esther took the hint and asked for egg and chips. It wasn't that I was being mean. I just wanted to get out of there. Can't stand that sort of place. We took our drinks to a table in the corner of what used to be the public bar. I had a pint and she had one of those J2O jobs. Since when was there anything wrong with orange juice?

'Mind you,' said Esther nodding at the specials board. 'We could do with a bit of trend on the menu at The George. Pattie could...'

She must have seen my face and went on, 'For the tourists I mean.' She tailed off and went quiet. But when the food came she tucked in as if she hadn't eaten for a week.

It was then I noticed him. A guy on his own at the bar, beyond the group of wha-whas. I hadn't seen him come in and he was looking over in our direction. He was in jeans and a black leather jacket, with a diamond stud and a gold sleeper in one ear. It was that combination that rang a bell. I tried to ignore him and kept on chewing, as if I hadn't got a care in the world. But I couldn't swallow and my insides were contracting. I watched sideways, without looking directly that way. He was leaning on the bar talking to the barmaid and they both looked our way. That was it. For all I knew he was looking at a poster on the wall, but I was taking no chances.

I'd placed him now. He was one of the scum who gathered at the front door when I was arrested, who invaded the shop after I came out on bail. He was the most persistent bastard of them all, the Pro-Life fanatic, always wanting to debate the issue of the sacredness of human life. He'd come in to the gallery, asking Connie inane questions about the pictures and the artists. Then he'd install himself on a sofa in the coffee shop area with a cappuccino and wait. Inevitably Connie would be busy, I'd assume he was long gone and he'd catch me and nail me to the wall with his opinions. Everyone's entitled to their beliefs, but I did object to having those beliefs rammed down my throat. Not to mention being told I'd be damned if I didn't agree. He was always far too canny to do anything out of order and you couldn't ban someone for having conversations. That was the whole idea of the place. I avoided him as much as I could and threw the leaflets he left in the bin.

Connie was a star. A tower of strength when Meg was ill, she never wavered when I was arrested. She always was a brilliant manager of the gallery, but she ended up managing our lives as well. Far beyond the call of duty. Protected me from that bastard as best she could. But he just kept on coming. In fact he was probably the reason I was up on the moor, the trigger that made me lock up the house, leave the business in Connie's care and take off. Here he was, invading again, threatening my hard-won peace, my new identity, my sanity even.

'See you in a bit,' I said to Esther and sauntered out to the gents'.

It was a shrewd move, giving him the slip like that. Never gave Esther a thought. Enough that I noticed the bike and flung it out against the wall. I went home pretty pleased with myself.

3

When I wake up next morning I know there's something wrong. Wrong? Or different? I know where I am, okay. But there's something. I hear the weather's broken even before I poke my nose out of the duvet. My squared-off triangle of sky's grey and splodgy. It's a shape like the ones in geometry at school that I could never remember. Most things are skew-whiff in my room and usually I like it, the ceiling coming in on me, the crooked door frame, the floor that runs away with you towards the door. All those odd shapes are homely and make me feel safe. But this morning they make me edgy. Then I remember. Everything used to be simple and straightforward, which is how I wanted it when I came here. That was the whole point. No contacts, not even Luke. Especially not Luke. No mess. No complications. And that wrong feeling I've woken up with is just that. A complication.

I close my eyes and try and make it go away but all I get is the taste of Alfie's coffee and a picture of that table. It's silly, but the table's giving me more of a problem than Alfie. It was just so like Nan's.

It was what was left when she was gone. I sold all the rest but I couldn't sell the table. All Nan's stuff was modern, so it never fitted in and you had to squeeze past it. Should have been in a kitchen with an Aga, but you don't get many of those in a block of flats in Brixton. It had been Nan's mother's, and she was superstitious, didn't like to get rid of it. Not that it seemed to bring us luck. But then you never know how much worse things might have been.

I think of it as an heirloom. Other people get jewellery and priceless pictures. I got an old pine table. And it's sitting there waiting for me at Luke's place. So, sooner or later – sooner if Luke gets his way – I'm going to have to see him again. I mean, it's not as if I can get him to post it on to me.

Everything happened at that table. Nan making pastry, paying bills, the two of us eating meals. My homework with Nan's little radio blasting out Capital FM, all tinny. That's if she was down the bingo. Otherwise it was silence with the fridge juddering and the tap dripping. Always that dripping tap she was going to get fixed one day.

That's what I remember the night she told me Carole had died. We'd just finished our tea and Nan had been unusually quiet. I knew there was something on her mind. Me, I didn't want to know. I was too busy thinking how I could bump into some boy I fancied at school next day. It's all I ever gave serious thought to at that time. Like always, she tapped a fag out of the box, Silk Cut, the ones she smoked when she'd had a few wins. She picked up her lighter, but she didn't flick it.

She held it there in mid-air with the ciggy halfway to her mouth and eyed me. 'Something to tell you.'

And that was it. I didn't know what to say. I mean, I hardly knew her.

'Well, you might say something. After all, she was your mother.' She lit up then and inhaled as if she needed it.

My mother. I never called her that. By the time I could talk we hardly saw each other. The tap went on dripping like it was inside my head, washing away every last word that might have been appropriate.

'Don't even remember what she looked like.' I shrugged. 'At least, I don't remember what she looked like before that day we…'

Nan grunted and flapped her hand to shut me up. We'd made a visit, me and Nan, not so long before, but we didn't talk about that. Neither of us wanted to even think about it.

I left the room then, but not before I saw Nan's eyes brimming over and I felt like some kind of monster because I couldn't stop and give her a hug. But my arms felt like they didn't belong to me.

I felt like *I* didn't belong to me, come to that. I couldn't have done it.

What a cow I was back then. I'd give anything to be able to hug her now. I have to swallow three times to get rid of the image of that table. Then Alfie's face comes floating in to replace it. What's the matter with me? It was just a cup of coffee. And a sitting for a bloody picture. But he's got such a weird way of looking. Sideways, with his eyes half shut as if he doesn't really want to see. Maybe it's just the way all painters look at people. Then I remember the bloke in the pub. And I can't help laughing. Was Alfie ever lucky! With the weather, I mean. I wouldn't have been riding off and jumping into ditches for him if it had been all wet and muddy like today. What the hell was that guy in the car after?

'Good day off?' Joel asks when I make it down to the kitchen. 'You were lucky with the weather.'

It's what they all talk about round here. The weather. Boring or what? You do notice it more than in London, I'll give them that. It's in your face all the time, rain and wind usually. I surprise Joel by having coffee. But it's not like Alfie's, even when I pile in the sugar.

I don't have to do kitchen prep. Marion's supposed to come in on Mondays to give me the day off. But she's a law unto herself and she's coming in today instead. Joel's too much of a wimp to tell her different. Talk about henpecked. No wonder he's always happy to be here behind the bar all hours, every day. Anything to get away from Marion, I guess.

Pattie rolls her eyes at me as soon as Joel goes off down the cellar. 'Maid Marion's on her way, worse luck. I get on faster without her. Coming to lift a finger – until she breaks a nail, that is. I'm lucky if she manages to chop one single onion.'

'Why does she bother to come at all?'

'She likes to keep her eye on things, throw her weight about, and she's got plenty of that.'

Marion's as wide as she's tall and there's not much space in there. It helps being skinny like me.

'Here she comes,' says Pattie when the back door bangs.

Marion rattles with bling, bangles, chains and earrings. All the genuine article, as she's determined to let you know. The only carrots Marion understands are gold ones. Which is another of Pattie's favourite sayings, and she had to explain to me about carats. Now it makes me giggle every time I see Marion.

I'm sent off to clean windows. I give Joel that, he does like to keep the place spotless. I start in the front bedroom, which is how I come to see Alfie striding into the pub yard done up like one of those old pictures of a lifeboat man in black oilskins from head to toe. That's odd because I've never seen him wear a waterproof before. He always says a bit of rain never did anyone any harm. I only know it's Alfie from his walk. He has this way of bouncing up on the ball of his foot as if he's going to jump at every step. I wave, but he doesn't see me. Then he reappears round the corner on the old bike and sets off, head down and peddling as if his life depends upon it. Pickup must have broken down, I suppose. So he's not doing my picture today, then. And he's not coming in to apologise either.

As I watch, a car comes the other way and Alfie can't avoid a deep puddle that's formed just outside the entrance. I can see him brace himself as he skids through it and the water fountains up under the skirts of his long oilskin. I grin to myself as I give the top pane a final polish. He must be drenched.

It's a boring day. A let-down after the early summer weather and an anti-climax after yesterday. The "Caterfood" man delivers and says, 'That was the summer, that was,' and everyone agrees, which is mega-depressing. We have precisely two people in for lunch, a couple of fed-up holiday makers who have ham sandwiches, a half of Best and a glass of Chardonnay, which doesn't exactly stretch me.

Pattie's gone home and Marion disappeared long ago. Joel's doing whatever he does in the cellar, and I'm beginning to regret my impulse to get away from it all and come to the country. At least in town there are things to do when it rains. You can go to a film or hang out in a coffee bar. Even the launderette round the corner from my place was more fun than being holed up in a smelly old pub with no-one to talk to.

We're still supposed to be open so I can't even go to bed

and listen to music. Instead, I slide into the cupboard of an office behind the bar. Joel lets me use his computer and I type "Puccini" into Google. I can't get that music out of my head, or the picture of that Aladdin's cave Alfie's got up there. It's like a magic world, all those books and the paints and the music. Even a piano. A world I've never known, a world I want more of.

There's loads about Puccini online. I'm impressed by how good-looking the guy is, but the rest of the Wikipedia stuff is beyond me. I discover on YouTube that it was *Madame Butterfly* Alfie was playing, but the video gives me goose bumps and I have to turn it off before Joel thinks I've gone all cultural and starts asking questions.

I fetch my book and a big jumper and curl up on the window seat, but I can't get into it today. It's *Sense and Sensibility*, which is a bit of a departure for me. I fell for Colonel Brandon when I saw it on the telly, and I still had my copy from when we did it at school. I'd have thrown it out, but it's one of the things Auntie Em taught me, to keep books. They're old friends, she used to say. I've found that's true and I've been really enjoying the story. I feel as if I know those girls. But today I can't concentrate. I try texting Luke but the signal's vanished again, so I turn off the phone and watch the rain running down the window and the flowers in the tubs being flattened.

The downpour stops suddenly and a haze starts to rise from the puddles in the car park. I'm thinking I'll go out and wipe down the garden seats when this black shape whizzes past. Alfie. I wait for him to come in through the door, ripping off his waterproofs. He must be sweltering in that lot. But he doesn't. Instead, I see him setting off back home on foot after he's parked the bike. He's still wearing the oilskins. What is going on? You can practically see the puffs of steam as he stalks off with the sun glaring on the shiny surface. I'm disappointed, and realise I've been waiting all day for him to come back.

Sod's Law had it that next day I was due to sign in at the police station. Supposing that Pugh guy - I think that was his name – was still snooping? He'd probably been up here covering some piece of rural non-news. What Laura liked to call a "Cow Falls in Slurry Pit" story. It must have made his day to stumble across his local wife-killer. I didn't dare take the pickup to Exeter and risk getting spotted.

What's more, I didn't trust myself with the fellow. If I came face to face with him, I'd probably punch him on the nose for his smugness and his certainties. Just thinking about him got me steamed up. And if I did hit him I'd be done for assault and taken into custody. No, there was nothing for it but to take the pub bike and catch the bus into town.

Thank the Lord for the rain. Blinding, sluicing sheets of water, which meant I had to focus my whole attention on gripping the handlebars, following what I could see of the road ahead. The rain allowed me a disguise. What else could I do, short of shaving my head? I doubt even that would be good enough, with a hooter like mine. Mind you, the disguise brought its own problems. I'd laughed when Tom gave it to me, back when I first arrived at the farm. 'Skirted, you see,' he said, holding out the ancient waterproof with a deal of pride. Eric, the silent brother, was watching and making grunting noises in the background. More animated than I'd ever seen him.

'Father used to wear it,' Tom said by way of explanation.

'Will he mind?' I said and turned to Eric. 'Do you mind if I...?'

But Eric was gone and Tom was frowning and shaking his head as if such a notion had never occurred to him.

They must have had it for decades. It was all very well for lambing of a night. Tom was right about that. But it weighed a ton. And it was no protection against water splashing upwards. My jeans were already soaked. I felt I should have a pistol in my belt, ready to waylay the next stagecoach. Instead of which I was voluntarily heading for Exeter Central police station.

Not that I ever resented that. The law was the law. I could have done without the court appearances where nothing much seemed to happen, but I'd taken a life and there was a price to pay. I accepted that. It was myself I couldn't live with. I used to lie awake making a plan. A packet of pills, a bottle of whisky, up among the rocks and bracken way above where the sheep graze, well off any footpath. It was February back then and I'd have been long gone, stiff with hypothermia amongst other things, before any living being other than a wild pony stumbled across me.

It was the sheep that stopped me, kept me sane. The cold, the rain and mud. The pain and aching sweat of it, an antidote to the craziness going on inside my head. There were no choices. Crawl out of bed in the dark, pull on still damp clothes, get on with it. Unused muscles had creaked back to fitness, sheep became individuals. Some I trusted, some I didn't, but they all had the measure of me. There was no fooling those ewes.

At last. Deadman's Hill. And not before time. A lull in the downpour gave me time to notice a triangle of blue sky, before a pelting of unseasonable hail had me head down once more. At least it was all downhill from here to the bus stop.

Then spring came. And while the sap rose in the plants, what with being out there in all weathers, I felt part of it, felt the sap rising in me too. Felt like a young man again, though – God knows – this bloody bike was letting me know I wasn't. Started wanting things again, made a stupid bloody home, started caring about freedom. To begin with I hadn't cared about going to prison. Now I couldn't bear the thought of it.

It felt obscene sometimes, this new interest in living. I wanted to be free, to start again. And that felt like a betrayal, with Meg only what, three months dead? She wouldn't have thought so. She once said to me, 'Go on, live your life. Mine's being taken from me, and I'll be bloody mad at you if you don't make the most of yours. I'll come and haunt you'.

Once I was on the bus it felt safe to relax. I took off the ridiculous sou'wester and opened the coat – big, old-fashioned buttons and the oilskin sticky with age. I looked like something out of the Ark. But then nobody else was a trendsetter. It was mostly older folk, women who didn't drive, in their tidy clothes for going to town with plastic macs over the top. I sank back into a corner at the back and let the noise drift over me, as the engine shuddered to life and the bus chugged off.

It reminded me of the last time I was on a bus, that God-awful day in Tuscany. The day of Meg's diagnosis. Eventually, when she couldn't hold a camera steady any more, she'd had to tell me. About the dizzy spells, times when her eyes blurred over, not being able to control her fingers. Things she'd been keeping to herself. We went to the doctor the very next day, and he shipped us straight off to the hospital. They kept her in. Tests. Scans.

I took the bus to meet the consultant and bring Meg home. Surrounded and contained, as now, by country people and ordinary lives, the routine of the trip to town on market day we'd always been part of.

On that day the window framed a landscape of yellow and red ochre, raw sienna, olive green. The single digits of cypress trees like exclamation marks, muted earth tones concentrated in a cluster of buildings, the grooved roof tiles echoing the ridged earth. The patterns held my attention, stopped me thinking about what lay ahead.

We passed freshly-tilled soil, clods of burnt umber, their surfaces still shiny from the blade of the plough; three-wheeler farm trucks like toy tanks parked on the verge; a field of sunflowers hanging blackened heads like a defeated army; blousy green of tobacco bunched for drying on the trailer of a tractor. The Tuscan countryside going about its autumn business.

In Sansepolcro I followed purposeful women with sturdy legs across the road, women who probably had much in common with my fellow passengers on this bus in Devon. I was early for the appointment and found myself trailing through the market after an old man in a red jumper. He was carrying a brown paper bag of the sort that might contain nails and string. White hair grew untidily round a conker-smooth bald patch and, as he walked, his free hand flapped backwards. I had such an urge to clasp that open palm and feel its warmth that I had to put my hands in my pockets. He continued across the square and I wished I were he, going home to eat spaghetti with my wife and to get on with mending the fence. Just at that moment I would have given anything to have a job to do involving nails and string.

I was left staring at a group of men on the corner of the square. They'd always been there on that spot whenever we'd come to market. Four squat old guys who'd taken root in a circle. Three were bare-headed. The fourth had a face the colour of truffles, a flat woollen cap to match, eyes like seeds sunk deep in the their furrows. Words passed like chess pieces between them, time-honoured moves on familiar themes. If Lowry had been Italian he would have painted these men. I wished I could join them.

But then the Duomo clock struck. Ten reverberations axing through the chatter of shoppers. I stepped away, out of the sun into a side street. The shouts of the traders faded behind me, as I went to keep my appointment. Life was never the same after that.

The bus rattled over a cattle grid and brought me back to Devon and a grey-cold summer day. We started losing height. The close-cropped grass and wind-flattened thorn trees of the moor gave way to lush banks of bluebells and campion overarched by young beech trees in electrifying new leaf. Flat leaves of pennywort caught the light, and ferns unfurled their scrolls like the cello section in an orchestra.

It might not be Italy, but I struck lucky at the Hannafords'. The moor worked its magic and with spring came the lambing. That wriggle of hot blood in the snow. New life asserting itself in the face of the steel-cold wind. The sweet smell of straw in the barn where the ewes were penned with their newborns. I hadn't lost my touch. Lambing was much as it had been in Dorset when I was a boy helping Uncle Bas. Tougher being up here, no doubt of that, but Tom brought the ewes down to the in-bye land as they came due, so I didn't have to spend nights on the open moor. At the end of the day, sheep were sheep and birthing was birthing.

And now Esther. Everything was simple until she appeared on the scene. Just when I thought I was winning. I was mad to ask her to sit for me. She's nothing like Meg. What was I thinking of? Just those teasing sea-green eyes with their come-hither look. Bloody idiot. I'd finish the picture and be done with it. One more sitting should do it. Stupid thing was, I'd never have gone to Blidworthy if it hadn't been for her. I'd be taking the pickup to Exeter, be on the way back by now. And what the hell am I going to tell her about why I suddenly scarpered?

The more I think about Esther, the worse I feel about leaving her in the pub. Okay, she'd have had no problem getting back. But that isn't the point. Just because she's a youngster doesn't mean it's okay to be rude. Imagine if I'd done that to Laura. I would *never* have done that to Laura. I wouldn't have dared.

Laura who is not speaking to me.

I still shudder to think of her coming home the day after Meg died. There was the usual crash of the front door, the thump of her rucksack and 'Dad?'

I came rushing out of the kitchen and stood in front of the door to Meg's room.

'Come through. There's something to…'

And she followed me through to the kitchen, chatting, full of her trip.

'It was a brilliant party. You'd never believe…'

She trailed away as I turned to face her.

'Dad? What's up? What's happened? You look dreadful.'

'I don't know how to tell you.' My voice shook. 'Mum. Laura, I… She's dead.' My whole body was shaking. I couldn't control it. I put my arms around her and held her tight but she pulled away, peered into my eyes.

'But how? What happened?'

Bit by bit, she dragged it out of me. Our plan. How we didn't want her to be implicated.

For a moment she was quite silent, all colour draining out of her face. I remember thinking that she might faint. Then she screamed. She screamed and hollered and beat me with her fists, like she used to when she was four years old.

Then she went cold. She would come for the funeral. 'Mum would have wanted that. I'll play the piece she asked for. The Vaughan Williams thing. You know. But after that I won't speak to you ever again. I can never forgive you for what you did.'

Just as I was wondering whether it was helping Meg to die that was unforgivable, she added, 'And I can never forgive you either, for not telling me.'

So there I was, doubly damned.

It didn't help that she was there to see me arrested, treated like a common criminal and taken away in the back of a panda car.

She'd have been informed of the charge – murder it was, at that stage – and that I was to be released on bail. But she wasn't there to see me come back home like a regular human being.

Meg would have managed it all so much better, made her see sense, coaxed her. I heard Meg's voice in my head over and over again saying, 'She'll come round. Don't worry. Give her time.' But I wasn't convinced.

If only Meg were here, leaning in, nudging me to notice the odd hat worn by the woman at the front, the profile of the old man across the aisle I longed to sketch. But there was no warm body against mine. I cleared the steamy glass with my sleeve and peered out. No rich colours of Tuscany, but familiar streets. Nearly there.

After I was finished at the police station I went straight to the gallery. Connie was the person I needed.

She gave me a fierce hug that crackled through my oilskin and stood back, running her fingers through the purple spikes of her hair. 'What, in the name of Hades, have you got on? You look like you've stepped out of *The Ancient Mariner*.'

'A long story. Hey, Connie, what I need is a very strong coffee.'

She raised an eyebrow. 'What's that about?'

I creaked out of the coat and folded it over the back of a chair. 'Ought to go back to the house. Fetch the post. But I can't face it today.'

'No need.' She banged old coffee grounds out of the filter holder and filled it with fresh. 'I can drop round there any time. Say, once a week. Then you can pick it up from here. I'll send on anything vital-looking.'

'You're the best. That would be great. D'you know? I think at some level – some deep, totally lunatic level – I always expect Meg to be there. Daft, isn't it?'

She shook her head. 'Not daft. Not daft at all.'

Neither of us said anything for some time. Then she looked up at me. 'You're actually looking better than last time I saw you. Now you've disrobed. You sure you've been on Dartmoor? Looks more like you've been swanning on some hot beach.'

'No swanning, I assure you! Bloody hard work – and outside in all weathers. Windburn most likely.'

She set the coffee down in front of me, and I clasped the cup and inhaled. Just the smell made me feel steadier.

'So what's the long story?'

'That dreadful Pugh fellow's been snooping round. And he…'

'Pugh?'

'You know, the reporter guy. The Pro-Life man. Don't tell me you've forgotten the bastard? No. Anyway, I didn't want him spotting me again, so that was my disguise.' I nodded at the coat feeling suddenly foolish.

'What could he possibly do, though? Apart from be obnoxious?'

'Destroy my peace. Blow my cover. I haven't exactly advertised what I did with my neighbours up there. Didn't seem like the best idea.'

'I get your point.' Then she snorted and covered her mouth. 'Sorry. But that garb really is guaranteed to draw attention. Especially now the sun's out.'

'Not up there, it isn't. It was bucketing down.' I felt needled and gulped at my coffee. 'Any sign of Laura?'

'Haven't seen her, but she did phone. Wanted me to keep her posted about your 'case'. Her word, not mine. I tried to talk to her, get her to see you, but she wasn't having any. Sorry, Alfie. I did my best, but I figured, if I went on too much it would be counter-productive.'

'Thanks Connie.'

We both fell silent again. Then Connie ran her fingers through her hair and I knew there was something coming.

'I know it's tough, Alfie, but… Maybe I shouldn't say this. Just don't take it wrong. No disrespect to Meg, but Alfie, you've somehow *expanded* since she died.'

She was looking at me, or rather, she was looking into me. I didn't want to admit that I knew what she meant.

'You know that wedding photo you've got? It struck me as soon as I clapped eyes on it. There's Meg, okay, she's just a wee thing – but she fills the picture, an explosion of colour and energy and – *je ne sais quoi* – as they say. And you're just a dark line beside her. A strong dark line, for sure. But not taking up any space.'

I didn't know what to say. She'd named something I didn't

want to acknowledge. A something going on deep down. What with the rising sap, it made me feel guilty as hell.

'I haven't offended you have I?'

I shook my head, avoiding her gaze. 'Not at all. Not at all. Put it down to living on the moor, getting out of town. Plenty of space to expand into.'

I could feel her knowing look, her dismissal of my cop out.

'So there's no-one up there? No shepherdess, maybe?'

I laughed. 'You must be joking. No, only Tom and his half-baked brother.'

She gave me another look and cleared our empty cups. 'By the way, when are you going to bring me some of your new work? I need it by the end of the month if it's going in the July exhibition. You have got some?'

Connie, who never takes her eye off the ball, reminding me I still have to make a living.

'Yes, some tree studies. And a couple of landscapes which are okay. Yes, I can do that.' I get to my feet. 'I'd best be off. Thanks for the coffee. And thanks for being here and...'

'Hush. I do what I can. You can count on me. I'll come visit you when you get banged up.' She gave me a high five as I stood to go.

I strode towards the door, suddenly anxious to be out of town, back with my sheep.

'You're forgetting something.' She handed me the black coat. 'If I were you, I'd carry it.'

I took it from her and her eyes were shining. Feisty little Connie with wet eyes. She really believed I'd go down for it. She might well be right.

It's the beginning of the evening and I'm serving a group of tourists, two couples, pleasant, friendly types who ask about the bitter, involve me in their banter. The sort of thing I enjoy most. I see a movement by the door and when I look round Alfie's materialised, looking surly, in his corner. He's slipped in without coming to the bar.

Huh. He seems to be avoiding my eye and doesn't appear

to be here to apologise or explain himself. I don't draw his usual pint. Instead I stalk over and challenge him, careful to keep the whine out of my voice.

'So what happened Alfie?'

He looks up slowly as if taking in my stance, my mood. I hope so. But when his eyes reach mine I see they're looking inward, not seeing me at all. I'm aware of a block of ice where my stomach should be and fold my arms across it, repeating the question.

'What happened?'

'Happened?' He repeats the word as if it was in a foreign language.

'In the pub. Two days ago? You taking off without a word? Leaving me there?' I pause between each phrase, watching for some sign of comprehension, waiting for a response. Finally I add, 'Blidworthy?' and swivel away, ready to return to the bar.

He shakes his head at that. 'Ah, Blidworthy. Yes.'

'Well?'

'Oh, God! Yes, I need to explain that.' He speaks slowly as if he's speaking the foreign language now, figuring out the words as he goes.

'Go on, then.' I'm coaxing now.

'Not here.'

'But there's no-one here. Joel's taken Marion out. I'm on my own.'

He leans sideways and frowns towards the group on the far side of the bar.

'They're only tourists. Anyway, they're yakking away.' Why would they be interested in us, for fuck's sake?

'No. Come for another sitting. And I'll explain.' He's himself again. 'Now, be nice and get my usual.'

Is that it? *Be nice.* Huh. 'I'll be nice, if you'll be nice.'

He looks mystified. 'What do I have to do? I told you...'

'Don't I even get an apology? How private do you have to be to say sorry?' The whine has definitely got the better of me, and I feel like Auntie Em saying "Where's the magic word, then?" when I was a kid and forgot to say please.

'Sorry? Of *course* I'm sorry.' As if it was taken for granted.

I fetch him his pint wondering why he can't come to the bar like anyone else. But then he asks for a whisky chaser. He's never had that before and when he takes the shot glass I notice his hand tremble and suddenly I want to put my arms round him.

Instead I clip out to the kitchen, dig a cottage pie out of the freezer and put it into the microwave to defrost. I turn the grill on high, ready to finish it. Joel hates to admit we use a microwave, but the practicalities dictate it. Personally I don't understand his problem. I'll never forget when Nan got hers. She thought it was a kind of miracle to come in late from work and have a baked potato in five minutes. Joel thinks it zaps all the life out of the food, but it tastes okay to me.

All the time I'm trying not to think about Alfie. What's the matter with the guy? First he scarpers from the pub, then he takes off on the bike in the rain and now he seems to be in a right state. And not a word of explanation. Is he poorly? Is he in trouble? Are we friends or aren't we? Right from the off, with that bloke in Blidworthy, I sensed a mystery. And it seems I was spot on. A loan shark maybe. Do they have them down here? Or a blackmailer? But if so, what's he got on Alfie?

While the cottage pie's heating up I slice wholemeal bread and lay it on the side of one of the large oval plates. I love these plates. White, elegant, such a cool shape. I add two pats of butter from the stack in a box in the fridge. Joel absolutely refuses to have those squares of butter wrapped in foil. And Pattie absolutely complains about having to make the pats, though mostly it's me who does it. It's a job I love. The warm knife blade slicing through a roll of the creamy butter that we get from the farm up the valley. It's almost as good as eating it. Certainly beats Tesco's.

As soon as the cottage pie's under the grill I pop back to the bar to check if anyone needs serving. I love being on my own, imagine it's my pub, I'm juggling all the tasks, getting the timing right so no-one waits long for anything. I'm quick and neat, and when everything dovetails nicely I feel like I'm the orchestra and conductor all rolled into one. It's not great music, more British Legion than Festival Hall. And no mess in the kitchen at the end of the evening. Not like when Joel's in charge. Nan would be proud of me. That's something I learnt from her. *Tidy up as you go along.*

Good old Nan. She never was much of a cook. I was quite rude at first, being used to Auntie Em's garlic and spices. Garlic and patchouli, the smell of Auntie Em. Nan couldn't have been more different, reeked of fags and just churned out the same boring pies and stews – mostly down to my grandfather, I guess.

'Strictly a meat and two veg man', she'd say. Wouldn't have given houseroom to a clove of garlic, any more than he let me, his only granddaughter, darken his door. The bastard. Don't know how Nan stayed with him. Especially after what he did to Carole. I mean, throwing your own daughter onto the street. Nan wouldn't talk much about him. Ashamed, I think she was. But I got the picture bit by bit. Holier-than-thou – which didn't stop him beating her up if he found out she'd been to Mass or if he caught her having a drink. A prisoner in her own home. Never broke out. If only Nan could see me now. She'd be gob-smacked to find me buried out in the sticks like this.

There goes the pinger, and when I set the earthenware pot on the plate the cheese on top is a dark gold and still bubbling. Alfie looks almost asleep when I put it in front of him.

'Grand,' he says and looks up. Then he grabs my hand for a nanosecond and lets it go. 'Thank you,' he says, and the ice in my stomach melts away and I can breathe again.

I'm busy after that. Several regulars come in for drinks and the tourists order food. Alfie's still sunk into himself, eyes down, eating. When there's a lull I'll go over and fix up a time with him. But when I've finished serving and look over to his corner, he's gone.

I sigh without knowing it and old Reg looks up from his pint and says, 'It might never 'appen.'

Without thinking I tell him maybe it would be better if it didn't.

Reg shakes his head. 'Tha's too deep for me,' and returns to his pint.

I gaze at the top of Reg's head, tanned like an Easter egg through the sparse white hair combed across it. He lives in the end cottage of the row close to the pub. Always out there in his big corner plot of a garden, creaking up and down the rows of onions or whatever they are, weeding, digging, poking about with a hoe. Joel buys stuff off him sometimes. Last week it was asparagus. I'd never had it before, an acquired taste, Reg said, and I acquired it. Reg sold us the entire crop, said he can't abide the stuff himself. But he gets satisfaction from growing it. It takes years apparently before you get it to produce anything. Told me all about it, like he was talking about his grandkids.

I realise Reg's said something wise without meaning to. 'Too deep,' he said. It gives me a moment of clarity. He's made me notice I feel ridiculously gutted that Alfie's gone, and that I've been preoccupied with Alfie and his whereabouts ever since Monday afternoon. I can't get Alfie out of my head.

Just don't make a fool of yourself, girl, I say to myself as I clear Alfie's dishes. He's spread the paper napkin over the top of the pie dish and I nearly screw it up, but in the bright light of the kitchen I see he's scrawled on it in biro: *Tomorrow 3pm or Monday.*

Will Joel let me off tomorrow? I sure as hell can't wait until Monday. I stack the crockery in the dishwasher and go back to the bar to check the reservations. All except one table is taken tomorrow evening so there'll be loads of kitchen prep to do. I'll have to get round Pattie to come in early in return for doing her shift on Monday.

Meanwhile a couple of lads from the village have come in. At least I know them and I don't have to go through the ID rigmarole. The drink still goes to their heads, though, and one of them is well away by the time he's downed a couple of lagers. Reg is nursing his glass and watching them. He's usually stumped off home by now.

They're giving me lewd looks and guffawing behind their hands, and I just wish they'd go away. Gary, the taller and less drunk of the two, calls me over. 'Same again for Sean, here,' he says with a smirk that says it might be amusing to see what Sean will do next.

Reg mutters at him not to throw his money around and he reconsiders, adding, 'Make it a half.'

I glance at Sean, who's looking distinctly green, and say I don't think that's such a good idea. The last thing I want is young Sean throwing up all over the place and putting off the tourists.

Sean takes exception to this and lunges towards me, describing in graphic terms what he'd like to do to me, thrusting with his hips in case I'm missing the point.

I cut across him. 'Sorry. I'm not serving you. One more remark like that and you're barred.' I'm on firm ground here. Joel's hot on this sort of thing. I know he'll back me up.

'Oh, yeah! You and whose fucking army?'

'That's enough of your lip, lad.' It's Reg. When I look round I see he's drawn himself up and looks suddenly ten years younger. He glares at the lad. 'Go on. Be off with you. The pair of you. You'm nowt but trouble with that stuff inside you.'

I see a flicker of something in Gary's expression. Not fear, but as if he's just noticed where they are, what they're doing. 'Time to take your friend home,' I say, appealing to that sliver of what I guess is better judgement.

Gary drains his glass and pulls out a packet of Rizla. 'Come on, mate. Fancy a smoke? There's a bad smell around here.' They shamble out the door, Sean lurching sideways and getting a shove from Gary.

'Daft buggers,' says Reg. 'That Sean, he's my cousin Shirley's youngest. Always told her she spoilt him rotten.'

'Thanks for the support. Have another. On the house.'

Reg shakes his head and laughs. 'Nah. Keep me up all night. You did well lass, didn't need my help. Got to nip that sort of stuff in the bud.' He heaves himself off his stool and stretches. 'Best be getting along. Make sure them idiots are on their way and not laid out in some ditch.' He sighs. 'We was all young once.'

Joel warned me that everyone's related to everybody else in the village, and now I've seen it for myself. It's cool how it works. The lads have been stopped from making major fools of themselves. I've seen a different side of Reg and gained an ally. And he's gone off home walking taller. Would Alfie have stood up for me? Would he have got the respect? He's younger and fitter than Reg, but he's an outsider. He doesn't even try to join in.

Some people wouldn't like to live in a village, everyone knowing their business. And right now I bet Sean and his friend are feeling hard done by with family breathing down their necks, cramping their style. They don't know how lucky they are.

4

I pull off the road into a clearing in the gorse and before I've retied my bootlaces Esther's gone. I half expect to see those skinny legs turning cartwheels up the track.

She runs back. 'Hear that bird? What a racket!'

I nod and point to the speck I've just located.

'What? That's it? Right up there? How d'you know?'

I shrug. 'Larks. That's just one of them. They're all over the place.'

'Singing themselves stupid.' She cranes her neck to follow my finger.

I'm thinking of *The Lark Ascending* but I don't mention it, or the nesting habits of larks, because I don't want to feel like teacher today. Esther walks beside me with an annoying gait: stride, kick boot, stride, kick. Birdsong and music drown her out. Notes cascading from Laura's violin strings in the dim church. The way she wouldn't meet my eye. I try to blot that out by thinking how amazingly Vaughan Williams captured essence of lark, but the images of that day are too strong for me: Laura's hair swinging down her back as we followed the coffin; Meg's name on the brass plate down there in the ground; Laura nudging me and hissing 'Dad' when it was time for us to throw in the earth and her bunch of anemones.

That's how it's been the last few days since the sight of that reporter guy and the visit to Exeter. The old life seeping back into consciousness like damp through fresh wallpaper.

Esther's walking backwards in front of me now. 'Is that the sea?'

I turn and point out landmarks – Start Point just visible in the haze way over to the west, the daymark showing the river entrance at Dartmouth, and beyond that, Berry Head. To our left an expanse of gorse-covered heathland rises and falls and drops away into the wooded valley of the Dart. To our right, a similar landscape with a scattering of standing stones and a cluster of larch in the middle distance. Behind us stony outcrops flank the abrupt cliff of the tor bursting out of the bracken.

'You know, it's almost like the birdsong makes the silence bigger.'

I smile. I know exactly what she means. She dances about on the springy turf, intense blue stars of speedwell at her feet. There are yellow ones too. Wish I knew the names.

Esther sends a pile of rabbit droppings flying with her toe. 'I'm going on a bit. You don't mind?'

I shrug. 'Feel free. I'm going the back way, the long way round.' I gesture away to the right, tell her to follow the track. She can't miss it.

'It's just, it makes me tired going this slow.'

I'm stung, an old man in an instant.

'See you at the top!' She lopes away and I'm seeing Laura again, a teenager this time, climbing the yellow road to the hilltop village in Tuscany, always sprinting ahead, ponytail flying. Happy days, before Meg's diagnosis.

Esther's not taking the path I pointed out. She's going for the steep track up the face. She'll be there long before me.

What am I going to say to her? I'm avoiding the issue, coming up here. And for some reason she's gone along with it. I didn't think she would, she was in such a stroppy mood last night in the pub. But she's a good kid. She gave me one of her looks when I suggested a walk, but then she just hopped in the pickup and said it was too nice a day to stay indoors. I didn't want to talk about it there in the barn where I sleep. Didn't want the words flying about, roosting in the rafters, floating down like bats in the night.

But when we get to the top I'm going to have to find something to tell her. If I ever reach the top. She makes me feel ponderous. I kick at a loose stone and send it flying down the slope, swing my arms and lengthen my stride, shaking off the heaviness. There's a voice that says, tell her the truth. The truth would be the easiest thing. But I'm not yet ready for the truth to join me in this new life of mine.

Anyway I mustn't be naïve about this. I know the truth won't stay the same shape when I tell it to someone else. Who knows how it will end up in Esther's mind? Look at what happened with Laura. She made it into a monster. Made me into a monster.

Esther's not involved of course. So it wouldn't be an emotive issue for her. I can see now how huge it was for Laura. Beloved father kills beloved mother. Put like that, you can see the enormity of it. It's the stuff of myth. She chose to overlook how beloved we were to each other, the circumstances and so on. All of which she knew perfectly well. I thought she was mature enough to understand. I suppose if we'd told her beforehand…? But Meg said no, she'd try to stop us. And I agreed, but for different reasons. I didn't want to risk implicating her in any way.

But it did mean she was excluded. And I suppose that's been worse in the long run. It's the last thing she said to me: 'You left me out.' We're both out in the cold, coping on our own when we could have had each other, Laura and me. But it's too late now. And that's beside the point today. Esther is the point. How the hell can I explain why I was so spooked by the appearance of that damn reporter?

Alfie's a funny guy. It's weird. One minute he's like a mate and the next I've lost him, off in his own thoughts, wandering along like a sleepwalker. It drags me down.

I love these stones and this yellow stuff creeping all over them. It looks like you could pick it off like a scab, but I break a nail trying. It's welded on. The rock's so warm. When I lie back and watch the clouds I feel as if I'm floating. I breathe in hot grass and a butterfly lands right near me. It's so cool, the way it opens and shuts its wings. I wonder if it knows I'm here. It's all velvety brown and blue and purple, with that thing like an eye on each wing. I bet Alfie'd know what it's called. I won't move until my butterfly goes.

But I get an itch on my nose, and it's away as soon as I move my hand.

It was a cool idea of his to come up here. I thought he was palming me off for a minute. Sitting there in the pickup with the engine running. Thought he was going to say he had to go out, come again another day. But I guess he thought it would be easier to talk out here. Or maybe he's clean forgotten about the whole thing. You can never tell with him. I'm not really bothered any more. All this sky and stuff puts things in perspective. What does it matter what some git in a pub was up to in Alfie's former life?

I scramble on up the steep path, slipping on a patch of scree. It's further to the top than I thought. Higher up there's a breeze and the view's really ace. You can see for miles and miles and the sky's so blue it makes me giddy. I have a sudden weird thought. Well more of a wish really, except it's too late. I wish Carole had seen this view. I just think that if she had, she'd have been okay. She wouldn't have needed the dope. It wouldn't have all gone down the tubes. She might even have managed to be my mother, a proper mother, capable of looking after me. Silly really. She's dead and that's all there is to it.

I shut down my thoughts, hold my breath and listen. Silence. No traffic noise or drone of planes. No clatter of or shouting or mobile phones. No sirens. Even the larks are quiet. I guess it's the thing most different about being here. That and the dark. I've never lived in a place without street lights before. I guess I thought they just grew along the roads. I found it really scary at first, that blackness. Now I love it. You can kind of rest on it and it covers you like a duvet. Which I guess is what it was always meant for.

A bee buzzes past my nose and heads into a yellow flower at my feet, reminding me of where I am. I scan the bracken where I think the other path is down below me, but I can't see any sign of Alfie. He'd better not abandon me up here. That *would* be really scary. I hope I'm not lost. Sometimes the path is really clear and then it vanishes, like here. I could either go left round that gorse bush or right through that patch of heather and over the rock.

Which is it? But I guess if I keep going upwards I have to get to the top eventually. I keep thinking I must be nearly there, but there's always another bit to go when you think you've made it. Suddenly I come round a boulder and there's Alfie sitting cross-legged at the top of the world, drawing on a sketch pad. Just for a second I'm gutted. It's not that I'm competitive or anything, but I was sure I'd get there first.

He waves and grins. 'Slow and steady wins the race.'

'Except it wasn't a race.'

'Is that right?' He hands me a bottle of water, looking stupidly pleased with himself.

I drop down beside him and glug away while he points out the road we came up and Portland Bill, which he reckons is about a hundred miles away. Wow! That's cool to be able to see that far. I tell him about my butterfly. When I look round he's got tears in his eyes.

'Alfie?' It so takes me by surprise that I forget to look away and pretend I didn't notice. Why do people do that anyway?

'My daughter. She used to love butterflies. We got her a net but she wouldn't catch them. Said she'd done it at school and they had such short lives she didn't want them to waste time in her net.'

'Sounds a cool kid.' I pause and look at him sideways. *Used to love butterflies.* When she was little or when she was alive? 'But why does that make you sad, Alfie?'

'Kids grow up, grow away from you. I don't see much of her now. Just that.'

What's that all about I wonder. A picture comes into my mind – Alfie's big hands catching that butterfly and letting it out the window.

'That anything to do with the guy in the pub?'

'Lord, no. Why would you think that?'

'You've got the same kind of look. You're like, I'd really rather eat sheep shit than talk about this.'

He laughs, but I think I've hit the spot. He's no good at lying.

'That fellow caused me a bit of trouble a little while back. I owed him money. It was a bad time. My wife had just died.'

'Hey, I'm sorry. I didn't know.'

'How could you?'

'No, I mean I didn't know you had a wife.' What am I on about? He just told me about his daughter, so of course he'd have a wife. What I really mean is that Alfie doesn't seem like someone who ever had a wife. Plus I don't want him to have a wife, even a dead one.

'How could you know that either? Anyway it's all done with now.'

'Except he's still after you, that guy. Is he a loan shark?'

'Shark, yes. And I've only ever seen him on his own.'

I groan, though I do actually want to laugh. Alfie's looking so proud of his little joke.

'No, he's not one of those.'

'But d'you still owe him?'

'No. I guess he just thought it would be a good story, finding me up here.'

'A good story? Is he a reporter then? I did think he looked like a reporter.' That or a private detective, but I'm not saying that.

'Well, yes.'

Alfie's not meeting my eye.

'So was it him you owed the money to? Or was he…?'

'No, he was just stirring it up. Like I said it was a difficult time. With Meg…she'd only just died.'

He's not telling the truth, I can tell. He's really shifty. 'What did your wife die of?' I ask.

'MS. She'd had it for years. She was very disabled.'

'How awful. Did you have to look after her?'

'She got very dependent, yes. Nursed her for about nine months at the end.'

'I didn't know you died of it.'

'There's different sorts. And it takes people different ways. It's all very complicated. And I'd really rather not talk about it if you don't mind.'

'Okay, but you still haven't explained what happened the other day.'

'Didn't want to see the guy, that's all. Don't want any more trouble.'

'But if you don't…' I catch a warning look from Alfie and

change tack. 'What about the day after? Why the big disguise, the black oilskins? You looked a total psycho!'

'Oh, you saw that. Well I just had to go to Exeter, and I thought the fellow might still be around. Didn't want to take the pickup, because he'd have recognised it.' He pauses, gives me a look. 'It wasn't that funny.'

'Oh it was, Alfie. It was.' Every time I think of that black figure I get the giggles. 'You going through that puddle! Oh my, oh my, as Nan would have said.'

He does at least chuckle at that. 'I suppose it did have it's funny side. Looking back. But at the time...'

'Couldn't you have put off going to Exeter? Or Joel would have given you a lift.'

'No I couldn't put it off. Now look. This is my business. Not yours or Joel's. And I'd be glad if you didn't mention it to Joel. I don't want the whole pub gossiping. I've explained, and I'm sorry. Can we please just leave it at that.'

I feel really hurt. Hurt that he thinks I'd gossip about him and hurt that he doesn't consider me a friend. Or not enough of a friend to confide in. I've overstepped the mark.

I kick myself for being so prickly and clumsy. That's what comes of not telling the truth. Not that I've actually lied, at least not much, only the bit about the money, but it was the first thing that came into my head. She's wandered off, kicking at stones. I've upset her. I add a few trees to my sketch and wait.

When she's back in earshot I make an attempt at an apology. It doesn't come out too well, but then nothing does today. She just shrugs and sits down beside me.

'It's all a bit raw still. Tell me something about you for a change. Luke, for instance.'

'Luke? What about Luke?'

'Well, you've only mentioned him in passing. Boyfriend, I assume?'

'Not any more. We met at uni. He was a year ahead of me and he was the "welcomer" on my floor.' She makes inverted commas in the air. 'Should have known then.'

'Should have known what?'

'Well, he was always doing the right thing. Being nice.'

'Anything wrong with that?' We're lying on our backs on the prickly grass and I'm watching some clouds blowing in from the west across the blue. People being nice to each other sounds pretty good to me after some of the stuff I've had to put up with.

'No-oo-oo. Only if there's too much of it.'

'Mmm. Yes, okay. Where were you? What did you read?' I shift my position very slightly so that her right breast comes into silhouette against the sky. That wasn't why I moved but I don't regret it. I feel parts of me stir that have been dormant for months, years even.

'Me? Business Studies. Luke was Modern Languages. He was a hard worker. Not as bright as me but he made up for that. He couldn't cope with how I wouldn't work, partied. "Threw it all away" as he put it – and then got star marks for all my essays. Mind you, anyone with half a brain could do Business Studies. But it was always like that. Straight As all through school. How else would a girl like me have got to uni?'

'So what happened?' I'm curious – that phrase, "a girl like me".

'We started going out, and then in my second year he wanted me move in with him. But I didn't want him breathing down my neck, on at me to work harder. Anyway I was sharing a flat with three other girls. We had a laugh. It was the best time of my life, ever.'

'And Luke?'

'He had to put up with it. But it made him mad. He wanted me where he could keep an eye on me. Funnily enough, I didn't cheat on him. Not seriously. Just the odd guy at a party, but no more than what you could do dancing.'

I boggle at the thought of what Esther might be able to do on a dance floor and it causes a minor internal earthquake. I sit up and put my arms round my knees to be sure she doesn't notice.

'D'you still keep up with the girls?' I'm thinking of Laura and her flatmates. On the phone for hours, always getting together.

'Nah. They kind of lost interest when I left. Bex and me met up a coupla times in London, but it wasn't the same.'

'When you left?'

'When Nan got ill I left – to nurse her.' She sits up and hugs her knees as well, so we're both sitting there like two pixies in the grass.

'You left uni?'

'Yup.'

'To nurse your Nan? Your grandmother?'

'Yup.'

'So you didn't get your degree?' What was going on? That she had to be the one to nurse her grandmother?

'Nope. Everyone went mad, specially my tutors and including Luke. I was a dead cert for a first.'

'So why?'

'Couldn't let other people look after Nan.' She rubs her nose furiously on her knee and then leaps to her feet in one bound.

'But why you?'

'I guess I forgot to say I lived with my Nan and she only had me.'

Where's Esther's mother in all this? It only just occurs to me that she hasn't got a mention. 'And your mother?'

'She died.'

'Esther, I'm so sorry. So...'

'But that's another story.'

She's got her back to me and doesn't continue for several moments. 'She'd have had to go to hospital. Nan, I mean.' She spins round, shiny-eyed, challenging. 'You seen those terminal wards?'

'Didn't she have other children? Someone who...?'

'No. My mother was an only one like me.'

'I mean... There must have been another way...' I'm probably putting my big feet in deep, but I can't get over the sense of waste, of her throwing away her chances.

She gives me a look that tells me I've got that all wrong.

'She'd looked after me. Put up with me being a stroppy teenager. We had rows, sure, but that was only when I was running wild, only 'cause she cared. She didn't want me to go the way Car... Didn't want me getting into trouble. The way some kids did.'

She flings herself down beside me again, full length with her hands behind her head.

I'm beginning to see that Luke is probably the least important part of Esther's past. What goes on behind that casual, self-possessed exterior? I slide back down next to her, wondering about that hiatus, the thing she didn't say just then. She changes the subject, not about to enlighten me.

'Is that a buzzard up there?'

I've been watching a pair of them for some time. 'There's another, much higher up.' I point, my mind still on what she's told me, thinking how I'd have felt if Laura hadn't gone back to complete her Music degree. 'I still don't see how you could just chuck it all up. Your future. And a first, that counts for something. And now you haven't got your Nan, which is sad. But you haven't got a degree either. What...'

'That is such a dumb, stoopid thing to say. You don't get it do you? But then you wouldn't...' She's up on one elbow, indignant, glaring at me.

I have to look away and there's a silence in which I listen to the tiny movements of the grass close to my ear. Then I hear a little gasp and an uh-uh sound, and she thumps down on her back again. She bangs her head hard on the ground two or three times, and I feel the vibration in the earth.

'Oh, fuck, fuck, fuck!' She gropes about for my hand and squeezes it tight. 'Well, actually you would know. You looked after your wife... So. Me and my big mouth. I'm sorry, Alfie, I was forgetting...'

'That's okay.' I try to sound unconcerned but I'm glad she noticed. 'You're right. It was a stupid thing to say. But I'd still say it was different. I mean, with Meg I'd committed. You know, for better, for worse and all that. You didn't choose your Nan.'

'She was family. My only family. That counted for something. It mattered more than anything.'

'And your mother? How old were you when she died?'

'Six or seven. Yeah, I was seven.'

'So young. Tell me about her. How did she die?'

'Breast cancer. She was brilliant. Never complained through

all the treatments. But they didn't work. Obviously. I guess they found it too late. She was a fantastic cook, she played the piano, took me to concerts. We had the best time, her and me.'

She's watching me, an almost challenging look that I don't understand. And her whole voice has changed.

'Precious memories, they must be.' What to say? It must have been so hard.

'I was lucky, wasn't I? So lucky.'

Well, not that lucky. After all, she died. Aloud I say, 'How about your father?'

'I don't remember him. He was killed when I was just a baby.'

Dear God! What next?

'He was a bit of a tearaway, very good-looking. He went out on his new motorbike. Came off the road on a bend. And he had no family, no-one to look out for her. Just think how she must have missed him all the while she was making the best of it for me.'

I shake my head and take her hand. We're both quiet as I get to grips with all this. No wonder her Nan was so important to her.

'So then you grew up with your Nan?'

'Well, first of all with Auntie Em in Harrow. Uh...'

'But I thought you said your mother was an only child?'

'Yes. Yes, she was. Auntie Em, she was actually a great-aunt.'

'Your Nan's sister? So couldn't she have helped...? With nursing her, I mean...?'

'No. Well, yes. But they didn't get on. And anyway she disappeared.'

This family is getting more confusing by the minute.

Then Esther adds, 'She was much younger,' as if that explains all, which it certainly doesn't. Only one thing is clear. Her Nan was the only constant in Esther's life.

'So how come you went to this elusive Auntie Em?'

'Nan had her hands full looking after Grandfather. He was in a wheelchair – that was after he fell off a ladder and did his back in.'

I think, at least he didn't die.

'What matters is, I knew I did the best for Nan. She knew I cared. She never did understand about the silly degree. That's why I chose Business Studies. It seemed practical. She could relate to that. She was never happy with me going to uni. I got a place and deferred for a year to keep her happy – got a job and saved up. She was afraid it would change me. It's what she said, over and over. "You're still my Esther".'

'She must have been proud of you.'

She ignores that remark.

'I got a job at first, bar work, waitressing. But I had to pack it in when she got bad. And before you say it, I don't regret a single day.'

'I don't... I didn't...' I'm still watching the buzzards. They're being dive-bombed by a rook trying to see them off. They don't seem to be anywhere near a nest, just minding their own business, riding the thermals – and this aggressive black bird comes out of nowhere to disturb the peace. I'm with the buzzards. I just want to soak up the sun.

'They said, the nurses who came at the end, they said I gave her a year of life. If she'd gone in hospital she'd have died pretty quick. 'Cos they don't feed them, you know. Did you know that?' She glares round at me. 'They say they can't swallow and that means they don't have to waste time spooning it into them, if they won't do it themselves. Not enough staff to do that, you see. A year of life. I'm proud of that.'

I don't say a thing. It reminds me of Meg. The hours I spent witnessing her struggle to eat: her frustration with not being able to cut up her food, the effort of spearing a mouthful on a fork and the spoons she tried to throw across the room. Even that was frustrating. She couldn't throw. They'd just clatter onto the tray, splodging food onto the duvet. Her wry smile, all crooked by then. A kind of pout, with the tears seeping out and a nod that said, at last, I was allowed to help.

'And before you say it, she wouldn't have been better off dead. It was a good year. She did things she'd never done before.'

'I'm not saying any of these things, Esther. I'm not thinking them either. How could I know? She was your Nan. It's your story. You're telling me.'

She rolls away from me, pulls at a stalk of grass and stares up at the sky, chewing it.

After a bit I say, 'Have you ever thought you might go back, complete the course?'

'Maybe. They said I could. But I'd want to do something different.'

'Where was Luke in all this?'

She bites her lip. 'He used to come down. Nearly every weekend to start with. He took us out – she could do that in between the chemo and stuff. Had the time of her life. Said she saw bits of London she'd never seen. Would you believe, born and bred in Brixton and never seen Big Ben? The thing she liked best was going to parks. St James'. Green Park. Best of all she loved the Serpentine. Feeding the ducks. She was like a kid. Luke was brilliant with her.'

'So what went wrong?'

'Got to be too much like… Like he expected one thing to follow another. She'd say "your young man" and he fed her expectations. She thought we'd get married. It was like… I can't explain.'

'She'd have liked to think you were settled, safe. Before she died.'

'Yes, of course. And Luke took advantage of that. Like men do.'

I ignore that comment. 'So? What did you do?'

'I went along with it. For her sake. I told Luke it wasn't for real. But he didn't believe me. He didn't want to believe me. And then when she actually died… Well, he was a star. I don't know how I'd have managed without him. Which made it all worse. I even started kidding myself it was love. Got in all sorts of a mess.'

'So what happened?'

She suddenly grabs my wrist, but it's only my watch she wants to see. 'Hey! Is that the time? Fuck, I've got to be at work in half an hour.'

I watch her scrambling ahead of me down the stony track and wonder how long it will be before she answers my question, whether she'll ever answer it. And will I ever see fit to tell her about Meg?

5

It's Esther's day off and she's come up to the barn early on the promise of coming with me to check on the sheep. My resolve to finish off the portrait quickly and stop seeing so much of her seems to have gone by the board. In fact, it's becoming a habit to go for a walk on her day off. Ever since that day over at High Tor. Something to do with the stuff she told me. Her being so alone.

'I didn't know you had a dog,' she says as we set off.

'Not mine. Tom's. He's got two. This one's always worked with me – from the first week.'

'What's he called?'

'She. Her name's Gyp. She's the mother of the other one. But he's very much Tom's dog. Would never have anything to do with me. They're a law unto themselves, sheepdogs. But this one's got a lovely nature.'

Esther looks dubiously at Gyp. 'But she doesn't live with you?'

'Oh, no. Knows where she belongs. The hand that feeds her.'

'I don't know dogs. Auntie Em had cats. And in Brixton you steer clear – all those macho Rottweilers and pit bulls. What sort is Gyp?'

'Border collie. Most sheepdogs...'

'Did you always have dogs?'

'No, not at all, but...'

'What were you like when you were a kid?' She ambushes me with this question.

Why the sudden curiosity? She's stunned that my father was

a bank manager. Can't think why. But she gets the bit about wanting to escape the boring suburbia that went with that. I tell her all about going to my uncle's farm and the weekends I used to spend up there.

'So that's how come you like sheep,' she says and falls silent.

Warm rain is softly falling and we carry on up the hillside, slip-sliding on wet grass and shiny stones, making our way to find the ewes with lambs. Esther's moved ahead where the path narrows and Gyp is nosing my knee.

As the path widens out again she turns to me and says the strangest thing.

'You talk about your childhood as if you were there. Mine's not like that.'

'How do you mean?' I wonder what we're getting into.

She doesn't answer straight away. In fact I think she's not going to. She's fiddling with her mobile, turning the lock on and off and looking to see whether there's a signal.

'You know when it was the church centenary? And they had that exhibition in the Village Hall? All those photographs of old geezers in waistcoats and hats?'

I'm nodding, wondering what on earth that has to do with the price of eggs.

'That's what it's like. I've got scenes from the past. Just isolated snaps in my head. Nothing continuous. They're black and white, like the life's drained out of them. I can even see me in the pictures but it doesn't feel like me. It's more like I'm the photographer.'

I make a kind of grunt, an *uhuh* sound, and I think it sounds patronising. But she doesn't seem to notice.

'I've got some actual photos too. Not very many. Auntie Em, Nan. And quite a few of me. But I don't remember looking like that. Like I said, it doesn't feel like me.'

'I guess that's all about losing your mother so young?'

A sharp intake of breath, then, 'Yeah, maybe. Yeah, I wondered that. Not quite getting a grip of myself.'

'Have you at least got photos of your mother?' Odd how the mother keeps not getting a mention.

'Oh yes, she was very pretty. They were the Beautiful People, my parents in their photographs. Sometimes I think my mother was too good to be true. Too good for this world, I suppose. When she went everything turned grey for me. She was glamorous, but she was a homemaker too. A real domestic goddess.'

'Did she have green eyes like you?'

She nods. 'She was a natural blonde like me, too.' She tugs her hair. 'It's not out of a bottle, you know. But hers was long and silky. Not like this old string.'

I gesture to her hair, almost stroke it, but draw back. 'Rubbish. Yours just has attitude. And how about your grandfather? You haven't said anything about him.'

'Oh, he was an absolute...' Her voice rises to a crescendo, then breaks off. A pause.

'What can I say? He was an absolute sweetie. When we went to visit with Auntie Em I used to sit on his knee and he'd tell me stories. And then when he was bedridden I'd read to him. Sometimes the newspaper, sometimes the Bible. He was very religious. He showed me where Esther came in the Old Testament.'

I'm thinking he doesn't sound so demanding that his wife couldn't have taken on one little girl. Esther evidently reads my thoughts.

'But of course he was quite helpless. An awful lot of work for poor Nan.'

We're approaching the shoulder of the hill where Gyp's been waiting for us, ears pricked. From there there's a view down into a sheltered fold of land and she's obviously spotted the sheep we're looking for. Above us the vegetation peters out, giving way to rock and scree.

I put my finger to my lips. 'Right now we need to stop talking. The sheep are just over that rise with their lambs and I'm going down to see them with Gyp. You stay here. I don't want them spooked and taking off, so best if you wait here.'

I join Gyp and we set off down the incline. I can see the flock straggled along the remains of a drystone wall. It's a relief, if I'm honest. Just me and the dog and the sheep.

Esther's making me uneasy. Can't put a finger on it, but something doesn't add up. For one thing, she started up about her grandfather with such an edge in her voice. Then she said he was a sweetie, which was the last thing I was expecting. What am I saying? That she was going to say something quite different, and checked herself? But then I guess she would feel ambivalent about him. He was the reason she was farmed out with some great-aunt. Who knows?

The rain's eased and a watery sun begins to break through the cloud. The ewes are all there and in good shape and the lambs are doing well. By now the sun is hot on my back, and I'm sweating when I regain the ridge.

'All present and correct,' I tell Esther.

She's sitting against a boulder with her head tipped back to catch the sun, and steam is rising from the rocks all around us.

'It's like a sauna.'

I stuff my jersey into the rucksack I always carry and add her waterproof. I'm thinking of starting back, but drop down beside her instead.

'You really love those sheep, don't you?'

I look up, surprised. 'Well, yes but…?'

'I was watching you. Just the way you are with them.'

'They're not as daft as people think they are. Really. They're personalities in their own…'

'You cannot be serious.' She shakes her head as if that is way beyond comprehension. 'Phew! Wish I'd worn something cooler.' She lifts the front of her T-shirt and flaps air into it, giving me a sudden view of a silver stud in her navel.

As I roll up my sleeves I have an idea. 'Tell you what, I've got a plan for cooling off. Now it's turned out hot. Do you like swimming?'

She nods and frowns. 'Swimming? Up here? I don't exactly see a pool.'

'Oh, there is one. Well, not up here. But see that bit of wood down there in the valley? There's a fine spot for a dip in amongst the trees. It's a long haul back up but it's worth it.'

She leaps up in one bound. 'Sounds brill.'

' I've even got a towel in here. It's really for the sheep, to wrap poorly lambs in. But it's clean. Fairly clean, anyway.'

On the descent we have to cross a field of heifers. A three-strand barbed wire fence separates their pasture from the moor. Flags of sheep wool hang from it at intervals. I pull some off and hold a clump out.

'Feel that,' I say, rubbing some between my finger and thumb. 'Good for your skin. It's the lanolin in the fleece. What keeps the sheep warm and dry.'

Esther looks dubious. She makes no attempt to feel the wool. The fibres lie on the flat of her hand, then she lets them fall to the ground, and all the while she's glaring at the fence as if it will bite her.

I hold up the top strand and put my foot on the middle one to widen the gap. 'There you go.'

But she holds back. 'Do I have to? Isn't there a gate?'

'It's miles round. You can get through there. Easy.'

She turns away and for a moment I think she's going to walk back the way we came.

Then she grabs my free hand. 'Don't let it touch me.'

'It's not electrified.'

No reply. She bites her lip, screws up her eyes and threads herself carefully through the fence, leaving me to get through as best I can. What's going on here? I don't have time to ask. The heifers are on the move.

Esther moves closer to me. 'Is that a bull?' She points at the largest which is staring, wary of Gyp.

'Young cows,' I say. 'Girls. See the udders? Still pretty small. You'd know a bull if you saw one.' I call Gyp to heel. 'Just take it slowly. They're only curious.'

She doesn't look convinced and makes a dash for the gate when the herd start to canter downhill behind us.

We make our way down to the treeline and follow the sound of the water, Gyp running ahead and stopping to lap at the first stream we come to.

'We can't swim in this!'

'Hardly. It falls into a natural basin further down. It's even got a little pebbly beach.'

It's cooler under the still-dripping trees and we make our way through oak and alder along a dirt path ribbed with roots. Gyp noses into rabbit holes and gets excited at a place where beavers appear to have chewed through low branches.

Esther breaks into a run when we reach the grassy clearing. The water of the pool is black and she stops dead, peering into it.

'Scary. There could be anything in there.'

'Only fish.'

She kicks off her trainers and wobbles on one leg to dip in a toe. 'Delicious.'

She skins off her T-shirt and jeans, hesitates.

'I won't look if you won't.' I concentrate on unbuckling my belt. 'Unless you want wet underwear on the way back.'

'I never went skinny-dipping.'

There's a flash of light as she steps into the pool, plunges forward and shrieks. But she doesn't come screaming straight out. She's treading water, catching her breath and her limbs gleam yellow through the peaty lens of the water. Like Jeremy Fisher's leggings, I think, as she strikes off upriver with a strong front crawl.

I step in after her, electrified by the ice-cold. Gyp whines gently after me but sits on her dignity, guarding my clothes.

We slice through the current, diving and turning. She's a natural swimmer, not afraid to get her face wet like Meg used to be. I keep getting glimpses: a thigh, a breast, a buttock. How come I've never really noticed her breasts before? She turns over into a lazy back crawl and they balloon on the surface. There's no way I can't look.

We float together downstream, gazing up through overhanging leaves. Grey wagtails flit yellow overhead, resting and dipping on ledges in the rock face at the back of the pool.

'What a perfect, perfect place. I never swum outside before.'

'Never? What about the sea?'

'No. Me and Nan went to Southend once, but it was too cold. We went on the pier and had ice creams and came home again.'

'Sea's different again. Waves, salt. More drama. Rivers like this are quieter, gentler.'

'Bet it's not gentle in winter. There's quite a current even now.'

I roll over and manage another eyeful of those breasts before she turns too. 'Race you back,' I say.

She's away and beats me easily. 'That wins you first use of the towel.' I pointedly swim away upstream.

'You don't have to be so polite,' she says later, while I'm towelling down.

I'm not sure what she means by that. 'Well, maybe I just do.' I pull on my jeans and stuff my feet back into boots that now seem hot and heavy.

'You're a nice guy, Alfie.' And she suddenly hugs me. 'That was the best thing I've ever done.'

'Glad you like. It's a special place, I always think.'

Her eyes are shining. 'I never knew that could be so good. Outdoors. Nothing on except water. Better than sex.'

I laugh, wonder for a moment if that's a challenge. But no, she's still caught up in the wonder of it.

There's a splash and we both point together at the silver arc of a jumping fish.

'Salmon. Big one.'

'Wow! To think I was in there with it. It's like swimming with dolphins.'

'Not that big.'

I laugh and she's laughing back, and for a second we're both caught in the moment: the gleam of the fish, the light on the water, the flicker of intimacy in her eyes.

I pick up my rucksack. 'Told you there were fish. Come on, let's head back and see what I've got to eat and you can tell me some more about you. Come on, Gyp.'

As we break out of the trees it starts raining again and by the time we get back to the barn Esther's shivering, in spite of the climb.

'Look, rainbow.' I turn her to see the arch stretching across the valley.

As we watch, the colours intensify. 'Wow! Pot of gold at High Tor,' she says. 'What a day.'

6

'It's my birthday next week,' says Esther one evening at The George as she clears the table next to mine. 'And, guess what? Sod's Law. It's only on my day off. Which means I'll have to find something to do all on my tod.'

I wonder where this is leading. But it doesn't sound like she's angling for anything. No coy looks. She's busy, stacking dishes, wiping down.

'Wondered if you had any ideas? I mean I can't exactly go window shopping.'

'If it's shopping you want, you could get the bus into Exeter.'

'What's the point? I don't want new clothes. Nothing here to dress up for. Anyway, it's no fun on your own.'

I hesitate. But there's no harm in offering. 'I could take you somewhere. I don't do shopping but...'

'But I thought you were shearing? You said next week...?'

'Not till Tuesday. I could take you on a birthday picnic. Nothing fancy. Somewhere on the moor you haven't been. Go for a walk.'

'Oh Alfie, I didn't mean. I really wasn't fishing...'

'I never thought you were. But if you've nothing better to do...'

'Certainly haven't. Are you sure? You're not just being nice?'

I roll my eyes at her. 'What do you think? Just what I could do with before shearing. Early night, mind you. I'll have to be up at sparrow's fart – so no late-night clubbing.'

It's Esther's turn to roll her eyes and I spend the rest of the evening thinking about where to take her. I guess I'm still a bit preoccupied with Esther's story, wanting to compensate in some way. Though, God knows, one not very exciting birthday treat is hardly going to make up for being orphaned so young.

We're lucky with the day. Eventually. As we drive past the prison, rain is sheeting down and it looks bleaker than ever.

Esther shudders. 'What a place! Hope that's not where we're going. Special treat, to visit an axe murderer doing life? Fuck! I bet they never get out of there.'

'Has been known. Tom was telling me a while ago, folk used to leave stuff in a barn. A change of clothes, food, bit of money. When they heard a prisoner had escaped. Not that they wanted necessarily to aid and abet - just to avoid having a crazy convict break into the house.'

'Don't blame them. I wonder how far any of them got? I mean, it's miles and miles to anywhere.'

'And no cover. Wouldn't stand a chance. More likely to die of hypothermia, or fall in a bog. Hey, look at that front coming through.' I point to the light pushing in behind the edge of cloud stretching across the far moor. 'We're in luck. That's the end of the rain.'

'You mean it's going to stop? Is that what a front is?'

She sounds sceptical, reluctant to be impressed. But I'm right. By the time we reach the car park and pull up under the trees the sun is already out.

'So this is it?' Esther looks about her, wondering what's so special about the place.

'Wait and see.' I swing the rucksack onto my shoulders. 'At least it looks as if we've got the place to ourselves. Here, take this groundsheet. It's still going to be pretty wet.'

It's further than I remember to the little avenues of stone we're heading for, but soon enough we hear the burbling water of the leat which leads into the site. Esther's delighted by it and stoops to splash water on her face, jumps across it and back again on the springy turf.

'This is Merrivale,' I tell her when we reach the stones. I sweep my arm in an arc. 'There are standing stones and what they think are the remains of burial chambers all round this area. On a clearer day you can see Plymouth Sound over there to the west.' I place my hand on the pointed upright stone at the start of the first avenue. 'First of all we'll walk the pathways. That's a must. Then we can wander all around and you can choose a place for our picnic. You go first.'

Esther looks mystified but goes along with it. I walk behind her. She's solemn, hopping over the muddy bits, but never leaving the row. When she gets to the circle of little stones in the middle, she glances back at me and then walks all round it before continuing as before, touching the taller stones as she passes and stepping between the gateway stones at the western end.

I point across to the other rows, and she's off, leaping over the leat. As I follow along the northern avenue, she begins to skip, grins at me over her shoulder, and dances to the end. When we both reach the end she takes my hands and swings me round and round until we both let go and stagger about laughing.

She spins backwards and turns to face me. 'So what was that all that about?'

'I was about to ask you the same thing. You were flying.'

'That first path was so serious. It made me feel so sad and heavy. But this one...' She shades her eyes and stares back down the avenue, as if looking for someone. 'It was so, well, fizzy! I just couldn't help dancing. How did that happen?'

I shake my head. Esther keeps on surprising me. 'I couldn't tell you. Whenever I've come here I've always walked the rows. Seemed like the thing to do. A mark of respect I suppose – for the people who put them here – for whatever reason they did it.'

Today I saw no cause to do otherwise – and it was something to do, a way of introducing Esther to the place.

'And do you ever get those feelings? Like I had?'

'No. It's never affected me in any way like that.'

'So who did put them here? What were they used for?'

'Couldn't say. Prehistoric. Bronze Age, they say, whenever that was. I'm not sure anyone knows what the site was used for. Ceremony, ritual. Who knows?'

'Well, if it was me to say, I'd say they walked down that one for funeral processions, and this one here for weddings.'

'As good a theory as any, I'd say. You could write a learned paper. *Rituals at Merrivale: a new look at Bronze Age Ceremonial Behaviour* by Professor Esther Franklin, the celebrated archaeologist.'

She giggles. 'I wish. Except of all things in the world I wouldn't choose to be an archaeologist. Digging people up – it doesn't seem right really. Well, I guess they do a few other things too.' She laughs away the serious moment. 'Hey, isn't it a lovely name for the place? It does feel merry. And even the sad path wasn't sinister in any way. Not spooky, even if it is where they buried people.'

I nod and set off towards the tall standing stone to the south. 'Let's explore the rest of it.'

We take a long sweep around the whole site which takes a lot longer than I expect and numerous stops to fish out the water bottle as the sun climbs higher. Eventually we find a group of granite boulders and settle for our picnic.

I start unpacking it. 'It's nothing grand. Only a few sandwiches.'

'Stop making excuses.'

'I got some home-cooked ham from the shop and some of Reg's tomatoes, so it might be simple but it's certainly tasty. There's apple and cheese to finish.'

'I've never had them together. Hey, that's nice.'

'Mum and I used to have it for lunch.' I don't know why I say that. Just that apple and cheese always puts me in mind of Mum.

'You never talk about your mum. What was she like?'

'Ordinary. Devoted housewife and mother.'

'That goes with being a bank manager's wife, I guess.'

'She sacrificed herself. Not that anyone thought of it like that, least of all her. It was the norm in those days for a woman. But when my father died she suddenly blossomed. No wonder she was so keen on me travelling when I left school. I expected her to want to keep me safe at home. But no. She was all for it. "Go! See the world," was what she said. Just made me promise to send lots of postcards. And she persuaded Father to let me go. He even gave me money.'

'Where did you go?'

'Hitch-hiked through France, bummed around until the money ran out and got a job as a waiter in a place called Sète. Old fishing port turned smart resort. Loved it there, but it was very seasonal. Then I got a train into Italy. Florence, Rome, Naples. Worked in vineyards, saw the sights, learnt the language. But then I had a yen to see Australia. I had a fantasy of becoming a bronzed surfer.'

Esther snorts. 'I can just see it. Well, actually, I can. And did you?'

'Well, I flew to Perth. December it was, by then. High summer. I travelled around a bit. Fantastic beaches, and I did even learn to surf. But in fact I hated it. Oh, it's a beautiful country and I can see why people rave about the lifestyle. But it just wasn't for me. I couldn't wait to get back to Italy.'

'So did you?'

'Not straightaway. I had to earn the airfare first. Then there was this Sheila.'

'They really do call them Sheilas, then?'

'Oh, sure. But it was no contest. Italy won.'

'And were there girls in Italy?'

'No way. Italian families guard their girls. Never got anywhere near. And it wasn't worth the aggro, the risk of a knife in the back.'

'Sounds just like Brixton. I used to see stabbings from my bedroom window. Well, two I saw.'

'Brixton? I thought you came from Harrow?'

She blinks. 'Oh yes. That was with Auntie Em. Well, Rayners Lane actually. But Harrow sounds better. Anyway.' She shrugs. 'It's funny to imagine you miles away in another country. How long did you stay?'

'I was away about a year. To tell the truth I didn't much like travelling. It was Father's expectations I was getting away from. Don't like hot places either. I went north to Umbria. Worked in a vineyard, came home when it got too hot. Best thing was seeing my father's face when I paid him back his money. Sort of thing that goes down well with a bank manager.'

'You didn't like him, did you?'

'Didn't know him. It shocked me when he died. How little I knew him. How little I cared, to be honest.'

An arm comes around me and her head rests on my shoulder. It takes me by surprise. Now I think about it, Esther has been encroaching all the time I've been talking. We started out with the picnic between us, but she's been moving in on the pretext of passing a sandwich or sharing the water. Now all the food has gone, she's got rid of the rucksack altogether and is right beside me. I'm not at all sure about this and start to shift away.

'Don't move. It's so comfy.' She slides down, so that her head is resting on my thigh, and swings her feet up onto the rock.

Her eyes are closed and I watch the shadows move across her face. It makes me think of Laura doing the same thing on picnics in the past. Pretty innocent, after all.

Uncannily, she breaks into those thoughts. 'Did you used to come here with Meg and your daughter?'

'Not here. We usually went to the other side of the moor, it being closer.' I don't say that I deliberately avoid places we used to visit.

'You seem to know it all so well.'

'It was the only thing kept me sane when I first came up here. Hiking all over when I wasn't working. That and the sheep.'

'And now? Do I keep you sane?'

Now what's she on about? I make a definitive move. 'You? You drive me entirely insane. Come on, let's get moving.' It starts off as a jokey remark, but that's not how it ends and she knows it.

'Alfie!' She sits up and pouts at me.

I'm suddenly mad at her. I stand up and stuff everything back into the rucksack, fasten it and sling it on my back, kicking at stones to vent my irritation. I set off at a cracking pace to complete the circuit of the site towards the car park. When I glance back she hasn't moved. Still no sign of her when I get back to the pickup, so I lean on the bonnet and fill my pipe.

Smoking calms me down. She wasn't doing any harm. She probably didn't mean anything by it. It's her birthday after all. And instead of making it a good one, I've been taking my frustration about not hearing from Laura out on her. Not to mention my increasing impatience at not knowing when my case is to be heard.

But it's not just that. I keep coming back to what she told

me about her family. That uneasy feeling that she was spinning me a line. They were all so wonderful. The grandmother a saint, the grandfather so stereotypically doting, the great-aunt saving the day and the mother a paragon. The only negative note was the father who was "a bit of a tearaway" but a dashing and handsome tearaway. But then they've nearly all upped and died on her, so who can blame her if she's gilded the memory? People do that with the dead, don't they? Except just now I'm going through a spell of raging at Meg for landing me in this vile situation. But then that's a bit different.

I'm just beginning to be concerned and to wonder if I should go back and look for her when a forlorn figure appears, trudging through the bracken. She's been crying, by the look of it. I hold out my arms. 'I'm sorry,' I say. 'It wasn't you I was mad at.'

She lets me hug her, but says nothing and we're nearly home before she starts to thaw and respond when I point things out.

Back at the barn I sit her down at the table.

'Surprise for birthday girl,' I say and tie a tea towel round her head as a blindfold. I set out the cake I got Pattie to make and light the candles. When I pop the cork from the Prosecco she rips off the tea towel and tears well up in her eyes.

'Oh, Alfie!'

'Happy Birthday!' I hand her a glass, we chink and she gulps, colour suddenly showing in her cheeks.

I hand her the knife. 'You'd better blow out the candles. And before you ask, twelve was just how many there were in the packet.'

She grins and blows. While she cuts the cake I fetch my present.

'Sorry it isn't wrapped. Not framed either. But if you like it I'll get it framed for you.'

It's a charcoal and wash sketch I did of her early on, one of the few I was pleased with. I've put it in a grey mount which sets it off quite well. She gazes at it, and up at me, and leaps up and hugs and kisses me. The last kiss is on the mouth and I don't respond.

'Glad you like it,' I say and sip my Prosecco. I notice her glass is empty already. I'm thinking she'd better eat some cake, but I refill it anyway.

'Pretty cake,' she says. 'Bet you didn't make it.'

'Pattie did.' She's kept it simple but she's done a good job. Plain white icing with "Esther" written in pink.

'So that's why she was giving me funny looks when she came in this morning. Oh Alfie, and I thought just now, out there on the moor, that you didn't want me. More cake?'

She leans forward and I can see the pale curve of her breasts below the line of her suntan. She cuts another two slices, and looks up under her lashes as she passes one to me on the blade of the knife. It's a look that makes me judder inside.

'Want you?' My voice sounds strange and I take a mouthful of fizz, let it slide down my throat.

'You do want me, don't you? You know you do, Alfie.'

My mouth is dry. My body is telling me that she's right. I do want her. But common sense and caution tell me firmly that I do not.

'You wouldn't go to all this trouble otherwise.'

That remark unlocks me. 'Of course I would. I wanted you to have a nice birthday, that's all. A little celebration.'

'But Alfie,...'

'But Esther. You go too fast. You jump to conclusions. It's a celebration for a friend. We're mates.'

'So you don't want me? I'm no good to you?'

'I do want you, Esther. As a friend...'

'A friend? Just a friend?'

'A special friend, or like a daughter. No, not a daughter, a good friend. Someone who...'

A convulsion seems to go through her from her belly upwards. She does some kind of flip with her free hand and when she turns towards me her tits have popped out of her stretchy top. Those breasts which are so voluptuous compared with the rest of her skinny body. She faces up to me, the knife still in her hand.

'Fuck it, Alfie. I love you. This is how I want you. As a woman. You've already got a daughter. Remember?'

I want to cup those breasts and press my face between them. I step towards her. She hurls the knife down, where it narrowly misses my bare toes and skitters away under the table.

'Shit, Esther!'

For a moment I'm caught in her clear gaze, eyes huge,

translucent with tears. Then she tosses her head, wet cheeks catching the light. Another flip of her top recaptures her breasts and she's gone, scooping up her jacket and bag from the sofa as she passes.

She flings the door open and then stops, hand on the latch, ready to escape.

'You have to make your mind up, Alfie. What d'you want? A friend? Lover? Replacement daughter? A substitute for your dead wife?' She looks back at me. 'Or do you want a real live woman?'

She slams the door so hard that the catch springs out of the lock and I'm left in the sound of it banging, a sharp rattle softening jerkily into silence. I cross the floor listening to the dry brush of my feet on the concrete and close the door carefully.

7

It was a mistake letting her stay the night. The wine was a mistake. And before that and before that, mistakes had just been queuing up to be counted. The whole goddam business about painting her and kidding myself it was Esther I was painting. That was the biggest mistake. Hell, it was really Meg I was painting. Meg as a young woman when we first met. The temptation to have her back was overwhelming.

And now I'm paying for it, sitting on this nasty red plastic chair, being ignored, yet under attack from the noise, the harsh lights, the scud of people all about me and the reek of disinfectant.

The moment I saw her behind the bar on her first evening it became an obsession. That way she had of chewing her lip when she was learning things. A mixture of uncertainty and screwing herself up to do it well. And those glances that flicked out under her lashes. Shy, was my first impression. But later I revised that. Wary was probably more accurate, checking where the next danger might be coming from.

With me she's let her guard down. That's been her mistake. She hasn't seen the danger in me. Not until that last moment when it was too late. I go over and over the last twelve hours but it never gets any better.

My last mistake was the biggest. Telling her about Meg. Telling her something out of context, an event she couldn't possibly understand. There was no excuse. I'd told myself not to do it. Suddenly she must have seen me as a murderer, dangerous. I am dangerous, of course. But not because of what I did for Meg. My crime has been to let her believe I care for her. I suppose she fell in love with that.

I do care about her. But not in the way she wants. It's too soon, too scary. And what future have I got, anyway?

She's been all over me for weeks. I see that now, when I look back. Coming to the studio too often, staying too long. Sitting down at my table in the pub when she came to clear it. There was the birthday incident of course. But she apologised – 'Think I might have made a fool of myself?' What with shearing all day, I hadn't had time to dwell on it, put it down to the alcohol. She thanked me for her birthday treat and wanted reassuring that we could still be friends. In other words, she seemed eager to get back to normal. I didn't notice when she started cosying up again. Or I didn't want to notice. The locals noticed her behaviour in the pub of course. There's been a lot of banter. Joel mostly, making remarks about cradle-snatching. And one time I distinctly heard old Reg say, 'Here comes your sugar daddy,' as I walked through the door. It embarrassed the hell out of me, so I've avoided thinking about it. But she didn't seem to mind. She'd grin and flick me one of her looks. And when we were alone she was always snuggling up to me, leaning on me like a cat that wants feeding. I'm not saying I didn't enjoy it. It was flattering, made me feel young again. I let her. That was the unforgivable bit.

What was I thinking of when I crashed into telling her about Meg? Too late. Or too soon. And back to front. But even so. How was I to know she'd overreact like that? As if I were a mad axe man?

She brought smoked salmon last night. "Liberated" from the kitchen. 'Past its sell-by,' she said, when I raised an eyebrow. She took a lot of trouble preparing a salad, laying the table. It all seemed a bit too domestic until it occurred to me that it was her way of thanking me for her birthday. But she was taking every opportunity to touch me, brush past me, reach across me to take a bowl off a shelf, squeeze into the same small space. It all seemed natural enough in that tiny kitchen corner. Until I noticed.

So when she said, could she stay, I was hesitant. I mean, I could have sent her home, but the rain was sluicing down and she'd had a bit too much wine.

She was teasing me, flicking a tea towel at my back as I stood washing dishes. 'Don't tell me, Alfie, you're bothered about what Joel will think?'

And when I didn't respond, 'I mean, it's not as if we have to *do* anything. I thought we were friends.'

I thought it best not to make an issue of it. 'Of course we're friends. And, as a friend, you can have the bed.'

I took a blanket onto the sofa and resisted her request to tuck her in. Tuck her in. I ask you. How obvious could she get? It would have been easy to fall for it.

Which, of course, in the morning I did. I half expected her to creep in beside me during the night, but she didn't. A relief. And disappointing. I lay in the dark wrestling with the whole thing – about being old enough to be her father, and about how vulnerable she was. But at the end of the day she wasn't my daughter, she was an adult – and no innocent, that's for sure. I couldn't actually remember how long it was since Meg and I had made love, except it would have to be counted in years, not months. And there certainly hadn't been anyone else. A red-blooded male with only sheep for company. I had a God-awful night.

Just got deeply asleep when the sun woke me, shining down from the roof light and there was no turning over and dropping off again because I desperately needed a piss. When I came back in, there she was, putting the kettle on. She was wearing the shirt I'd taken off the night before and she'd left it undone. She turned halfway to face me and that was it. I swear if she'd given me the full-frontal, I could have walked away, told her to button up. But it was that tentative movement, the shy look. I lost it and scooped her up, and that was that. We were up that ladder like a pair of monkeys.

Even now, with the shock of what's happened, my body stirs and fizzes at the memory. I was engulfed by her, those breasts, her thighs. I was afraid I would be all over too fast, but I needn't have worried. It struck me what a pounding we were giving that old platform. I hoped it was up to it, which gave me a focus. But nanoseconds later I was riding high, away from all thoughts, and

Esther's moans had escalated into shouts as we reached a climax together. I never knew a woman to come so quickly.

The second time was slower and lingering, and more delicious for being savoured, but nothing beats the frenzy of that first time.

Afterwards I must have fallen deeply asleep. We both did, I guess, curled into one another. It can't have been more than half an hour, but I woke up feeling I'd had the best night's sleep in years. I just wanted to lie there and bask in the luxury and peace of that. But Esther wanted to talk and touch me and do the sorts of things that lovers do. She wanted to be wrapped in me and I wanted to be alone.

Suddenly it wasn't so peaceful any more. It dawned on me that I'd done something momentous. I couldn't undo it and there was some sorting out to be done. With her, but in my own head first. I needed to do some serious thinking. I thought she'd have to leave, but she just snuggled closer and said she wasn't needed at the pub until the afternoon. So I suggested she sat for me. That's when it really started.

'Why do we need to do that any more?'

'It's what I do, Esther. I want to finish it. It wasn't an excuse, you know. I didn't intend for this to happen.'

'But you're not complaining?'

I laughed at that, kissed her on the top of her head and swung off the bed. But I had the devil's own job to break free as she tried to pull me back.

'I just want to be with you. I don't care about the poxy picture.'

And so she went on. I needed space to know what the hell I'd just done. And here she was, telling me. I'd raised her expectations, just for an impulse. A bold, glorious impulse which left me vibrating with something that might have been joy, if she hadn't been stamping all over it. She seemed to think she owned me. And it was all a terrible mistake.

I suppose I just felt desperate. So I told her. I really didn't have any other excuse. I mean, I guess I'd have had to tell her sooner or later. But I should have prepared her, chosen the time and place and so on. Truth was, I used it. Almost like I knew how she would react. I used it to make her go and leave me in peace.

I said, 'You wouldn't want to be with me. If you knew.'

She giggled and ruffled my hair. 'Why? Knew what?'

I pushed her hand away. 'That I killed my wife.'

That did it. She backed off and her whole body kind of changed. I never saw anything quite like it before. She seemed to shrink and go pale all at the same time. It was like zooming out from a photograph and changing it to black and white. It frightened me.

'Not as in, murdered,' I said. 'It was suicide. She asked me to. I helped her to die. She...'

'Don't give me that. Don't give me *that*!' She leapt up, throwing the duvet aside and holding her hands over her ears. All the time she was backing away from me, as if I might take an axe to her at any moment.

'Esther, Esther!' I started to move round the bed, holding out my hands, trying to calm the billowing sound with my palms. But she only took another step back, glaring at me as if she would turn me to stone. She was too focused on me, forgetting where she was.

That was the moment when I knew what was going to happen. In the seconds before it did, I knew that if I tried to intervene I would only make it worse. At the same time as knowing that I could never cover the short distance between us in time to catch her. 'Stop!' I yelled, but the croak of it was scarcely audible, even to me.

The ladder was to her right but she just stepped on back. It's a fifteen-foot drop and I stood paralysed. Her yells hiccupped into a scream. Arms and legs scissored for an instant and vanished.

Then silence.

She was lying there, a starfish washed up. Rare, beautiful, other-worldly.

I was beside her without knowing how I got there. She lay absolutely still. But breathing. Pulse, yes. Open thighs exposed her woman parts to the world, and I wanted to pull her legs together. But one was at a weird angle. Don't touch, said one inner voice. Keep her warm, came a second. I reached for the blanket on the sofa, floated it over her. I kept saying her name over and over. No response. Again the automatic command told me not to move her. Spine. Paralysis. Don't do it.

As I looked down on her, a tenderness welled up in me that was suddenly all about Esther and the fierce impulse that had landed her there on the concrete floor. It had nothing at all to do with Meg.

I don't even remember the 999 call. It seemed like some kind of miracle when the chopper arrived. All that noise. Couldn't work out what was going on. But when I staggered out the door, there it was, the air ambulance, a big red spider coming down at the far side of the field where it flattens out. And then came the little scarlet aliens, running across the rutted grass to rescue us.

I'd done the right thing, they said. Not moving her. That worried me as much as it reassured me. And I still don't know what's happened to her. By the time I got here, she'd gone for scans. Still unconscious. Christ.

Tom brought me here. Just appeared with the old Defender. Bundled me in. When we got to Exeter I came to enough to ask him if he knew where to go.

'Bin 'ere a few times,' he said. 'Just a few. With Mother.'

We juddered to a stop outside A&E.

'Women,' he said. 'Nowt but trouble.' Then he grabbed my shoulder and half pushed me out the door. 'She's young. She'll be all right.'

There's a warm place still on my shoulder. I lean forward and put my hands over my face to shut out the light and snuff up the smell of sheep shit and wet collie.

'So we meet again.'

They've told me to go home. All I could do was give them the number of my mobile and the landline at the farm. I'm standing outside A&E, considering how to get back. Tom must be long gone, doing my work as well as his own. I'm gazing in a half-seeing way at the smokers, some in hospital dressing gowns, huddled among the cigarette butts. I'm wishing I had my pipe with me when I register the voice at my elbow.

'So we meet again.'

Darren Pugh. I even remember his first name now. How the hell does he come to be here?

'Fancy seeing you. Second time in, what? A week? Ten days?'

I think of walking away but I still haven't worked out where I'm going. Can't even remember what day it is, let alone whether there'll be a bus.

Pugh keeps at it, unfazed by my silence. In his job, with his mindset, he must be used to that.

'A girl, I understand it was.' He put heavy emphasis on the word "girl". 'A girl they airlifted in.'

Of course. The air ambulance. The press get informed. A backhander here and there makes sure they get to cover all call-outs.

'Would that be the same young lady I saw you with in Blidworthy?'

I take a step sideways. People like that make you feel dirty if you stay too close.

'I see I've hit the mark there, then.'

It's as well I've stepped away or I would have hit him. 'What business of yours could that possibly be?'

He gives me the smile of a cobra taking its time, ready to strike.

'We reporters take our responsibility to the public very seriously, Mr Buckland. Justice must be done, Mr Buckland. Questions must therefore be asked. For instance, I understand, Mr Buckland, that the young lady was naked.'

The nasal twang he manages on the word "naked" makes it vibrate on the air like a snapping guitar string.

'I also understand that she had a nasty fall. One cannot help wondering – in the circumstances, Mr Buckland – how those two facts might turn out to be connected. I mean...'

He stops talking when my nose is close enough for me to smell his sour breath, the sickly reek of aftershave. My hands are gripping the lapels of his leather jacket. I draw back, making a piston of my right arm, but before the punch can fly I feel myself gripped bodily from behind and almost lifted away.

Tom has saved my bacon for the second time that day.

'Whatever you'm up to there, won't be doing nobody any good.' He practically throws me into the passenger seat of the Defender, which is ticking over by the kerb.

We drive in silence through the city traffic. The full horror of the way Pugh's mind works is filtering into my consciousness. Only now I see what he must have seen across that bar in Blidworthy. Me and Esther. *The man who murdered his wife with his piece of stuff.* He must have thought he'd struck gold. Suddenly I was much more culpable, much more newsworthy. I see the headline: *Wife Murderer's Floozy in Coma. Did She Fall or...?* No wonder he's still hanging around. I can't believe I'm caught up in his sleaze. About to drag Esther and Joel and Tom through the mud with me.

'Tom,' I say eventually. ' I need to tell you a few things.'

'Don't suppose there's anything I need to know. You'm a good shepherd and I do reckon to know a sound man when I sees one.'

'That's good to hear. But even so. That bloke back there – he's a reporter on the local rag. He...'

Tom makes a fierce spitting sound. 'They folk hear about things before they do happen. And what they can't find out, they do make up.'

'Exactly. That man Pugh's the scum of the earth. But unfortunately he thinks the same about me. For good reason – according to his lights. I'd rather you heard the story from me than whatever sleaze his twisted mind comes up with.'

Tom grunts and I launch into telling him how I come to be working with his sheep.

When I get to my worst fears about Pugh he just laughs. 'The *Echo,* you say? His editor wouldn't risk the libel laws. Never let him publish filth like that. I knows the man. Decent fellow with principles.'

I only hope he's right.

'As to Esther,' I finish. 'I never meant for her to stay the night.'

Tom looks across at me, one eyebrow raised. My heart sinks. He's not liking the idea of "goings-on" in his barn, I suppose. He hasn't said a word about the Meg business. For all I know, he feels the same way as Pugh. He may as well know the whole thing, now I've started. The worst he can do is throw me out.

'But apart from Pugh getting wind of it, I can't say I regret it. I was no bloody saint, I can tell you.'

Tom slaps his thigh. 'Ha! That's the best news I've heard all day.' He changes down with much grunting of the gearbox as we start up Deadman's Hill. 'We'll stop at The George for a pint. Drink to the little lass recovering. On you, mind.'

'Don't we need to get back?'

'Duh! Won't hurt Eric to shift himself for a change. I told him what he had to do. He'm perfectly capable when push comes to bloody shove.'

Joel gives one look at me when we get to the pub and pours me a Scotch which I need more than I realised. News of the accident has travelled fast, but Joel's unclear what's fact and what's fiction.

'Drinks on the house,' he says and raises his glass to Esther.

I no longer feel embarrassed by what everyone seems to take for granted is our relationship. I'm sitting at the bar for the first time, and it doesn't seem a problem that Tom now knows my story. Quite the reverse. I seem to have gained a friend. I guess I'll have to tell Joel, but that doesn't seem so terrible anymore.

'Let's hope the lass makes a quick recovery,' says Tom and places his pint carefully on the bar.

Joel nods. 'She's a fighter. She'll be okay, Alfie.'

I think of Esther alone and unconscious in the hospital and feel bad to be enjoying a drink among friends. She isn't alone of course. Nurses will be monitoring her, even if the machines are doing the work. I was only allowed to see her through a glass partition. So pale and tiny, dwarfed by the cast on her leg.

What if she never recovers? What if she's brain-damaged? What if she's paralysed from the waist down, from the neck down? Will I have to nurse her as I nursed Meg? Has that become my life role? My destiny? Am I to be in the same position all over again, trying to give her a reason for living? Discussing whether she should take her own life? Whether I'll be willing to help her die? I break out in a cold sweat at the thought.

It's ludicrous. I hardly know her. How could we begin in such a situation with none of the history and intuitive understandings that Meg and I shared? How would we communicate? Impossible. Could I really be made to pay that much for a stupid blunder? Then I remember that I might be sent down, and prison seems almost a welcome alternative to a lifetime nursing a paraplegic.

The cold sweat turns to a burn of guilt and shame and I shake my head in an effort to disown the monster I seem to have turned into.

'You all right, Alfie?' Joel's frowning at me, turning to Tom. 'He's gone white as a sheet.'

'Best get you back to have a lay-down.'

I stand up. 'Nothing wrong with me that fresh air won't fix. I'll take a hike to check on the ewes up the top.'

Tom gives me a dubious stare. 'So long as you take it easy. Don't want to be calling the ambulance for you. They'll start charging me. You take it easy. And remember, you can take the pickup any time to go visit the lass. Once you've had a good night's sleep.'

8

I'm whirling, floating in light space.

I'm sucked down in a dark tunnel where I thunder along and creatures I can't see lunge out of recesses to catch me.

I'm slip-sliding out of dreams into the crack behind my eyelids where it's black and red and hammering.

When my eyelids unstick I'm curtained off by eyelashes, and I begin to know it's me when I see the loom of my nose.

I wonder if it's cooler out there beyond its grey shadow, but the light that filters in hurts even more.

A sound hovers high up and far away. It repeats and repeats like a bird call.

I want to spin away again and I'm turning and turning. But something stops my escape. Some powerful thing has hold of the string on my kite. It's tethering me. Pulling me down and down and in and deep.

Pulling me into my body.

I resist and give in, resist and give in. It's alien and familiar and I have no choice.

My body feels heavy. Hot bits and shivers. Disconnected. I'm drawn to my hands and find they are contained by the powerful thing that has brought me here.

It is stroking and squeezing them gently and it makes a sound. It is a deep, hoarse sound, quite different from the bird call, but it has the same rhythm. This sound is repeated too. It doesn't give up. It begins to sound familiar. So familiar that it sets off a waterfall in my head, with tiny pebbles rushing to join the sound to make letters. The letters form a word and the word hovers in the air beyond my eyelids and causes my eyes to open.

Esther. It is my name. It is me. Beyond my name there is a face. And the face is Alfie, although I don't know how I know it.

Eyes rimmed with dark hollows. Lines sagging down into grey stubble.

I want to not see this face so I close my eyes and my hands are squeezed again and the sound of my name comes again. And I know they are Alfie's hands holding mine. I open my eyes again and the face has become Alfie's face and the eyes have come alive.

I say, 'Alfie' and I hear no sound. But he seems to know, because he lifts my hands and kisses each finger.

It's dark when I next wake up. Dark outside – no natural light outlining the blinds. How quiet it is inside my head. Like when a fan switches off and it's only then you realise what a din it's been making. Like when I came down here from Brixton. I had no idea how noisy London was because I'd never known silence.

My head is still behaving itself and I lie here, trying things out, like I'm practising thinking again.

Was that really Alfie? It was. I know it was, and it gives me a warm and peaceful feeling to think of him there, holding my hands.

In the morning a nurse comes and tells me where I am. I mean, by now I've worked out I'm in hospital. But why? She tells me I had a fall and broke my leg. She shows me the plaster and she's jokey and nice, but she won't tell me any more.

Then the doctor comes. You can tell she's a doctor by the stethoscope, but she doesn't look any older than me and she's wearing such a pretty red top. She peers in my eyes and does a lot of tapping and prodding and keeps saying, 'Tell me if it hurts.' Mostly it doesn't and she seems pleased with me. Then she starts asking me questions about how I came to fall, but the questions don't make sense. I think my head's going all wrong again, but the doctor says it's quite normal to lose the memory of what happened and I'll remember soon enough.

I ask how I got here, thinking the pickup would have been very bumpy for my broken leg. And she says, air ambulance. Am I mad to have missed that. I've always been fascinated by those guys. Joel keeps a collecting box on the bar and makes anyone put money in if they use a mobile in the pub. Never thought I'd be the one to benefit.

She says I'm to be kept pretty quiet and not to have any visitors. I ask if Alfie can come and the doctor and the nurse exchange glances and say no, as if they mean especially not Alfie. What's going on?

But then a policewoman comes. She's allowed to see me but only for a few minutes. Just like the doctor she wants to know what happened and I tell her I haven't remembered yet. I just want her to go away. She makes me feel tired. And why does she want to know anyway?

They can mind their own business about the bit I do remember. Me and Alfie made love. I didn't forget that. I never will. It was like nothing I ever experienced. Bits of me seemed to wake up for the first time. Too bad I had to pass out so soon afterwards. It's almost as if I imagined it. I hope not. Luke used to say. 'Don't call it sex.' Was that what he was getting at? Except, with him, that's all it was. Just sex, nothing special. For me anyway. But with Alfie, it was a whole new world. Gentle and fierce all at once. But they're just words. I can't describe it, but I don't have to. I keep it like a precious thing inside me.

I drift in and out of sleep all day, surfacing when the nurses come and look at my machines and write things on a chart. They're all different sizes and shapes and colours. Some of them talk to me and some don't. Some I understand and some I don't, especially one with a Scottish accent I can't get the hang of. I'm in a side ward on my own so it's quiet in between. I'm glad I can't have visitors. I don't know what I'd say to them. There's enough to cope with just being with myself.

I have a visitor but I don't like the smell of him so I keep my eyes closed.

It must be a man. He smells of cheap aftershave. He can't

be staff or he'd have done something by now. They never bother about waking you up.

I must have dropped off because, when I next come to, he's talking: 'And of course we've met before. Well, not exactly met. But we've noticed each other. You and me.'

He puts a slimy emphasis on the last phrase.

'In the pub. Blidworthy? Ring any bells?'

Blidworthy seems like a million miles away. Another life. Wasn't there a bloke in a car?

He mentions Alfie's name. I didn't even know he was called Alfie Buckland.

'I'm sorry to see you in this state, very sorry indeed. And I understand...not able to remember...circumstances leading... unfortunate fall. Now, I understand how distressing...not being able to remember. Very frightening I would say.'

He's right, it is scary. But why should he care? What's it got to do with him?

I must have drifted off again and when I surface he's not making any sense.

'Two possible scenarios...involved from the start in the plot to, shall we say, speed the demise of the late Mrs Buckland.'

What the fuck is he talking about?

'After all, how are we to know how long you have been, shall we say, *involved* with Mr Buckland? It could be weeks, or months, years even.'

What business is it of his?

'In the second scenario you are innocent. In which case you would not go down with him. If only you could be *seen* to be innocent.'

The smell comes closer.

'I do hope you are listening, because in the matter of seeming innocence I do know a thing or two. I pride myself...psychology... useful...in my line of work. I have noticed that a *victim* more easily acquires an air of innocence.'

I'm sinking back down into sleep, but his words still come and go.

'So you see, Miss Franklin...if...remembering, and...wondering and puzzling…whether…a push or a trip…caused you to fall… I mean…where memory or imagination…simply saying…given the choice…shall we say *in your interests*…err on the side of the push.'

I begin to wonder whether I'm awake or dreaming. Then he clears his throat and I know I'm awake. His walks away to the window and I can breathe again.

Even so the weasel voice is beginning to make me want to throw up. 'And of course we wouldn't want anything like that to happen to you again…' He tails off, as if I'm supposed to know what the hell he's talking about. 'I am sure you are fully aware of Mr Buckland's, erm, history. I have no doubt he will have told you…' pause for effect, 'what happened to his wife?'

All this innuendo is making me tired. Of course I know Alfie's wife died. I close my eyes again.

But again the whiff of aftershave becomes overwhelming. I am wide awake now and I open one eye to see what he's up to. Pock-marked skin, a bristly corner of moustache and a worn black collar. One of those cheap leather jackets you get in the market that cracks very quickly. Not that I care about his jacket. It's the shiny gold lapel pin that is horribly familiar.

'I am not sure, of course, whether or not you have taken in anything I have been saying.' I can feel his breath. 'It is indeed as if this conversation had never taken place.'

I have to get rid of him. I might have broken a leg but I haven't lost the strength in my right arm. I bring my fist up sharply under his chin as he leans over me.

He howls. The door flies open and only then I realise, the man must have closed it.

'Why is this door closed?' The nurse is brisk, sounds annoyed. 'And what are you doing here, Mr Pugh? Oh, Mr Pugh, what happened here?'

He stands there with blood running down his chin. He's bitten his tongue, of course – but it looks worse.

The nurse tears off a length of paper from the towel dispenser and hands it to him. 'Nosebleed is it?' She's brisk, impatient even.

'Err, yes, ' says Pugh indistinctly, through the wad of paper.

'You shouldn't be in here. She is not supposed to have visitors.'

'Just doing my job, nurse. Catching up on the latest on this poor young lady.'

'You can get information without seeing patients. As you well know. Can't think how you sneaked past.' She holds open the door.

'Ah, but nurse, there is no substitute...'

'Goodbye, Mr Pugh.'

As he walks away he turns and looks me in the eye. 'You have just made a big mistake, young lady. A very big mistake.'

Mistake or not, it's made me feel a whole lot better.

The nurse is still pink with irritation as she picks up my chart. While she takes my temperature she tells me Mr Pugh is a reporter on the local rag.

'Always stirring up trouble. Always going on about...' She breaks off as if she's saying too much.

'Going on about what?'

'Euthanasia. Abortion. The rights of the unborn child. Who wants to hear that stuff in a hospital? We're here to save lives – and we do. But stuff happens. Who's to say what a person should or shouldn't do? But you don't want me carrying on either.' She puts a hand on my forehead. 'I hope he hasn't got you too worked up. Was he here long?'

I shrug. 'I didn't... I feel...' Tears well up. I don't want to cry.

'What's he been saying to you?'

'It didn't make any sense.'

'It wouldn't. He's a fanatic. Best take no notice, my love. You put him right out of your mind and have a sleep.' She's shaking her head as she leaves the room.

My head aches with a hot, red feeling and that's without thinking about Alfie, without trying to work out what the reporter bloke was going on about. It makes me feel sick. Maybe I don't want my memory back. What the fuck might I remember?

It's just getting light when I surface again. I feel quite different. I prop myself on an elbow and move my head cautiously. No banging. My skull and its contents are no longer moving independently. There's a free feeling round the back of my neck, like when you've been trying and trying to screw the lid of the honey jar on straight and you eventually find the thread and it slides home. Joel teases me that I bother, that I can't leave it crooked.

There's another thing that's different.

My brain has made room for the memories to flow back in. I can picture it all. The scene around the bed. We made love and fell asleep. We were all curled up together and it was like the deepest sleep I ever had.

But Alfie had to spoil it. He kept saying things like, when did I have to go, wouldn't I sit for the portrait? Why couldn't he just *be*? I couldn't really believe he was meaning it. It made me feel cold inside in the place I'd felt so beautiful.

It got worse. It's what happened next that I've been blanking out. And I wish I could unremember it. He said he killed her. His wife, he killed his wife. The way he said it, it was almost as if he wanted to shock me. Like a slap in the face after what had just happened between us. And not like Alfie at all. I knew she died. But for him to say he killed her? Then he backtracked. What he meant was, he helped her to die.

But it was too late. Killed her. Like Preece killed Carole with the dope, is all I thought. Of course you can't say Alfie and Preece in the same breath, and I know that. But then, at that moment, it just flipped something inside me. Everything went black. It had been so good and he wanted to spoil it. He was pushing me away. I just stepped back and back. Wanting to get away from him. Completely forgot where I was. And of course we were up on the platform and I must have stepped off the edge.

The other thing I remember is the look on Alfie's face before I fell. It was the last thing I saw. A raw look of absolute horror, like the skin had been ripped off his bones. He must have realised what was about to happen, that he was powerless to stop it. Yes, it was a look of horror. But there was guilt in there, too. Like, omigod-what-have-I-done?

It's as I thought. Getting my memory back is more painful than my broken leg or the bruised ribs or the sprained wrist. I feel betrayed. The more I think about it the more I have to admit that Alfie was pushing me away. He wanted me to go. It makes me feel so sad and angry that I want to holler and scream and get paralytic on vodka, like I did when I found I was pregnant. I have a sudden picture of that girl, Petra, in the children's home who cut her wrists because she caught her boyfriend snogging another girl. I understand for the first time why she did it.

I've never gone in for self-harming and I don't even get pissed very often. But I just want oblivion so I don't have to face how Alfie didn't want me there, how it can't have meant the same to him as it did to me, how totally unlovable I must be. One minute my body was saying over and over, *Never, never leave me*. That was after we made love. And half an hour later it was saying, *Stay away, don't come anywhere near me*. How could that happen?

I don't holler or scream and there's not a snowball's chance of any vodka, so I pull the sheet over my head instead. In that grey half-and-half place the words of that weird visitor come into my mind. How come he seemed to know that Alfie pushed me away? What was he wanting to protect me from?

I always thought I could look after myself, but look at me now. I do seem to have missed something about Alfie. Trusted him too soon, and look where it's got me. Gave away bits of myself. All that stuff about Nan. Now he's gone off with them. At least I never told him about being in care or what Carole was really like. I never trusted even Luke with that. If I'd told Luke that Carole was an addict he'd have been watching me all the time, looking for signs I was going the same way. Finding another way he could have had me depend on him. Nan always said you should never trust men. So did Auntie Em. You end up like Carole. But I began to think Alfie was different. Since when have I been such a lousy judge of character? And where are you, Auntie Em, when a girl needs you?

There's a lot of tut-tutting when the nurse comes and finds me with the sheet pulled up. Maybe she thinks I'm dead or something. Dead would be good, I think, but actually I'm better. The change in my head obviously shows up on the monitors, because she fetches the staff nurse and when they've checked me out thoroughly she asks me how I feel and tells me I can have some visitors.

'I don't want to see Alfie,' I say and they exchange glances as the staff nurse leaves the room.

'Why's that then, my love?'

It's the same nurse who saw off the reporter guy. Kathy, she's called. She's beginning to feel like a friend and when she says "my love" she sounds just like Auntie Em.

'We're not, you know, an item. I mean, we were friends – but I thought we might... Well, we did, you know. But then we had a row. He was trying to get rid of me.'

'Get rid of you?'

'He'd had enough I suppose. That's men for you.'

'He seems a very nice man to me.'

'They often do.' Something else occurs to me. 'I meant to ask, why did that policewoman want to talk to me?'

'Oh, just routine. Air ambulance, you know.'

I say nothing about remembering. I want to think about it first.

9

Tom and I left The George and went back to the farm. Eric had done his stuff, but he hadn't been up to the high moor.

'That suits me just fine,' I tell Tom.

I call Gyp and we set off. It's good to be outside on the springy turf with the honey scents of gorse and a breeze cooling my head.

I try to focus on each step, like Uncle Bas used to tell me when I got worn out walking the downs as a little lad. One foot in front of the other. Like there was nothing else in the world. It gets me to the sheep and as Gyp gathers them, I watch for any signs of lameness. So far, so good. All present and correct, and the lambs coming on nicely.

But I don't want to go back down. Not yet.

There's a place nearby where once upon a time there was quarrying. Mostly overgrown with brambles and gorse. I make my way to the flat rock on one side under an overhang. I took shelter here once in a sleet storm, way back in February. I was so damned tired I actually fell asleep on this stone platform. Not for long or I might never have woken up.

Since then I've often come here, if I'm in the vicinity. It's a good place for doing a quick sketch and having a pipe, out of the wind. The overhanging ledge curves around like a protective arm and the dark red earth of its walls gives an illusion of warmth. I often sleep here. Ten minutes, half an hour. Never longer, but always deeply. Wake up feeling renewed, so grateful. Never sleep like that in a bed.

Making love to Esther was like being here. Floating in a dark, warm cave. So that afterwards I just wanted to slide away on the wave of it, drifting into oblivion. It wasn't what I expected, that vastness, that healing ocean inside her. Even more surprising than her breasts. Not heavy, but so full and generous on her slender frame, as if she'd stolen them from a more voluptuous woman.

She kept dragging me back, wanting to talk. Oh God, I messed that up good and proper. It was my fault. Entirely my fault. That selfish need to be alone. No matter how anyone else feels. It was okay with Meg. Well, mostly. She needed time to herself for her work, hours in the dark room, which suited me. We suited each other. But Esther? I suppose she was hurt. But why so scared? How could I know she'd react like that? Lose all sense? Forget where she was?

So unpredictable and yet so healing. How does that work? It's a mystery.

I wonder all the time how she's doing. When does loss of consciousness turn into a coma? Gyp puts a heavy paw on my knee, drags it down my leg and repeats the process.

'Okay, Gyp. We'll go down. Time for your supper. I wonder if Tom's got a spare tin of beans.'

Esther's still out for the count. Tom insisted on taking me to see her, but they wouldn't let me in. Something about procedures and "standard practice", but I got the feeling it wasn't for medical reasons. Only got to look through the glass wall again. A motionless figure, barely disturbing the bedsheets, crowded by the busy machines and all those tubes. They said she was stable and shooed me away.

Just as I was going out the door, the receptionist called me back. But it was only to see this policewoman. Apparently she was obliged to interview me. When I asked why, she said, 'Standard procedure, air ambulance', which seemed highly unlikely. I smell Pugh, stirring things up, planting doubts. I told her about the bail. Just as well, as she obviously knew that already. Would I mind giving an account of the accident? She seemed satisfied with what I said. Said she'd be in touch if there were any further questions.

Meaning, if my story didn't fit with Esther's. If only Esther gets to tell her story.

Yesterday I took the pickup, and that's when it happened. After two whole days Esther's regained consciousness. Hallelujah! I was actually holding her hands, willing for all I was worth for her to come round. She's pretty sleepy and they're sedating her, but she opened her eyes and tried to say 'Alfie'. She knew who I was.

Today I'm not allowed in again. They tell me she doesn't want to see me. I might have expected it. They tell me she's making good progress, nothing to worry about. If only they knew.

In an attempt to turn Esther off in my brain, I go to the house to see if Laura is there. It always used to have a peaceful, lively feel about it. Today it's more stagnant pond than still pool. It smells stale and dusty. I sweep dead flies off window sills, clear thickened milk and green cheese from the fridge, put out the rubbish and open windows. There's an unfamiliar stack of sheet music and CDs on the dresser, which shows Laura must have been there lately. I write her a note in case she comes again some weekend, and stick it on the fridge with her favourite Winnie-the-Pooh magnet. It's a relief to slam the front door behind me.

What am I to do about Esther? How come I manage to alienate the people I love most? Love? The word takes me by surprise. Laura, yes, of course. But Esther? Do I love her? My guilty mind wriggles away from the idea. I love her as a friend. That's fine. But loyalty to Meg, fear of Laura, shame about the accident won't let me go beyond that.

I jump on a bus and get off near the shop. Buckland's Gallery. It has a reassuring ring which I like, but which today seems a little surreal. Connie gives one look at me and says she hasn't any brandy.

'Would a very strong espresso do instead?'

She starts the banging and twisting ritual of the coffee machine and turns back to me while it brews. 'So what is it this time? You seem master of the dramatic entrance these days.'

I'd forgotten the visit of the black oilskins. I suppose I do run to Connie when I'm in trouble.

There are no customers. A bad sign, I suppose, but one I'm

grateful for. We sit on the big old sofa in the corner and I tell Connie all about Esther. I tell her what happened, what I said. I don't let myself off the hook.

When I've finished she hugs me to her, strokes my hair, then tugs at it sharply and says, 'Men are such bloody idiots.'

'Hell, Connie. That hurt.' I sit up and rub my scalp. 'Suppose it was meant to. I know I was an idiot. That's half the problem.'

She makes me another coffee, longer this time. 'This lass sounds as if she's all alone in the world. You'll be taking on a lot, Alfie.'

'I'm not sure I'll have the chance. Even if I...'

'Oh, she'll come round. She'll understand – if you talk to her like a real human being, that is.'

'But supposing I don't want to take her on?'

'If you could see yourself, you wouldn't say that. Smitten is what I say.'

'Give us a break, Connie. Smitten I am not. She's...'

'Then why, since the lass has regained consciousness and is out of danger, are you still dragging yourself about looking like you've slept rough for a week?'

'It's not just Esther. It's everything. Laura not speaking to me, feeling guilty about Meg... Yes I know, you don't have to tell me what she'd say, but even so – and it's not knowing about going to court, and the house and that bastard, Pugh. I just...'

'That nutter. What's he been up to?'

'Covered the accident. Got to hear about the air ambulance. Ambushed me at the hospital, making insinuations. Tom was just in time to stop me hitting him.'

'Thanks be to the patron saint of painters and shepherds that there's someone looking out for you. Tom sounds like your guardian angel. Imagine, Alfie! If you'd been done for assault!'

'He just gets seriously up my...'

'Mine too. But even so. He was lurking round here a few days ago. Now I know why. Looking for you, no doubt. But he wouldn't say why. Talked about his "professional discretion". My arse!'

Connie breaks off to talk to a customer and gives her a leaflet about the exhibition. It's good to be here with her. It's familiar and welcoming in a way the house was not. And Connie's down-to-earth approach is a relief. I'm fed up with my broody old head. It doesn't get me anywhere. This place would have gone down the tubes long ago if it weren't for Connie's sound business sense.

True to form, when she returns she's in problem-solving mode. 'Look, let's address the things you can do something about. In order of unimportance – Pugh. He's a speck of dirt, if you see him that way. Not worth wasting time on. Certainly not worth getting arrested for. Walk the other way, Alfie. For Pete's sake, the last time you came here in fancy dress you were talking of nothing but Pugh. He's bor-ing.' She flaps her hand across a mock yawn.

I hold up my palms in surrender. I'm thinking it's easier said than done, and that she doesn't have him trailing after her. But she's already moving on.

'Then there's the house. Not the right time, I would say. What d'you think?'

I shrug. The house and what to do with it defeats me. 'I need to talk to Laura about that.'

'Talk to her, by all means, but it's your decision. And I'd say you can't make it until you know whether you'll be free to live there.'

'Doubt I'll want to. But Laura might. You see it all goes round in circles.'

'That's the most important thing, the one you've got to attend to. Laura. Keep at it, Alfie. She's been in here, you see. Last time she was down. And why would she do that if she hadn't wanted news of you? She's being a bit of a stubborn madam, if you ask me. But you're the adult. You know her number, where she lives. Just keep plugging away with messages, letters, texts, emails, you name it.'

So there might be some hope there? I brush away unexpected tears.

'As to the hearing, you can't do anything about that. The law grinds exceeding slow. And then we come to Meg.' Her voice softens and she touches my arm. 'I understand that. Of course I do. But you know what to do. Talk to her, for Pete's sake. You know what she'll say. You deserve some good in your life.'

The thought is so ludicrous that I have to brush my eyes again. 'Now you're being daft. Just now you said I was an idiot…'

'An idiot, yes, but a fine upstanding idiot. Now, do you want to hear my news?'

I nod. 'Of course. Sorry, I've been blathering on…'

She leans forward dramatically. 'I am moving in with my partner! A little housie just around the corner from yours, as it happens.'

'That's a turn up! You and your independence.'

'Comes to us all. I'm no spring chicken any more. And not to worry, I shall carry on here, come what may. And the move's not happening overnight. But later on you might want to let the flat.'

I shrug. I don't want to add that to my list of imponderables. I manage, 'Congratulations, Connie. Really pleased for you.'

'Now, Alfie. I need to get on with some paperwork. And you need to get back home and do something about yourself. Bath, shower. Whatever you can manage in that shed of yours.'

She's grinning and looking me up and down. 'And shave. Wash your hair. Clean clothes. For Pete's sake, there's no need to go round looking like a health risk. No wonder they won't let you in at the hospital.'

She gives me an affectionate hug and turns me round to face the door. 'Off you go. And if she doesn't want you, then she's not worth it, this Esther. I'd snap you up if I was that way inclined, I'll have you know.'

I walk down the street feeling a million times better than when I arrived. Connie has that effect on people, mostly by not bothering to be nice to them. I've only met her partner once, a shy fair-haired girl with glasses. I was baffled as to what Connie saw in her but then I hardly spoke to her. Can't even remember her name, as Connie always refers to her so formally as "my partner". I hope they'll be happy. Just so long as Connie stays with the business. I can't imagine what I'd do without her. Except sell. At a loss. As to the flat, I'd rather live there myself than in the house. But who knows where I'll want to live, if it's not in a prison cell?

I take a bus out to the Park and Ride where I left the pickup and catch sight of myself in the glass of the bus shelter as I pause, trying to remember where I parked. Connie's right. I'm a disgrace. It's just as well Esther did refuse to see me. It would have put her right off. She seems quite a fastidious person. Not that you'd have to be fastidious to be put off me right now. I probably smell.

I drive back up to the moor on automatic pilot, my head full of pictures of Esther opening her eyes and coming alive again, of Connie's excitement over her move, of Tom shaking his head at me in his battered trilby. I'm rounding the bend at the top of Deadman's Hill when a silver convertible screeches towards me, cutting the corner. It narrowly misses ending up on my bonnet. As I swerve into the bank I get a glimpse of the driver. He's on his mobile, of course, and I swear it's Darren Pugh. He's far too busy trying to steer himself out of trouble to notice me. I restart the stalled engine and reverse out of the ditch, wondering what the hell he was doing up here again. Then I remember what Connie said. Who cares? No business of mine.

10

They all come to see me from the pub, Joel and Pattie and even Marion. Mind you, I reckon Marion only came to keep tabs on Joel. She always thought I was some kind of hussy – that's Pattie's word – and whatever gossip's been going round about my accident won't have done anything to change her mind. Pattie says Marion's always been the jealous sort.

It's obviously got out that I was found without a stitch on, and that's a tad difficult to explain away. I tried to make out I was posing for a life drawing, but of course they all know I stayed the night up at the barn. So that didn't work. Pattie just laughed and said I was a dark horse. Pattie seems to think it's all very romantic. Little does she know. I told her it wasn't like that at all and she kept saying, 'Poor Alfie'.

Joel tells me Reg sent his best. That really pleases me. I've got a real soft spot for Reg, and if he's on my side it'll be a whole lot easier when I get back.

They tell me I can probably go home tomorrow. But I have to wait and see what the doctors say on their ward round. They've moved me into the main ward and got me crutches, and a nice Indian physio came to help me walk. But going home? How will that be? It's not that I don't want to get out of here, but I still don't want to see Alfie.

The policewoman comes back to see me next morning. She tells me her name is Tracy, in case I've forgotten. She obviously never told me. I'd have remembered, because it seems an odd name for a police officer.

'You're so much better, they say you might be able to remember now. Shall we see?'

I tell her I fell off the platform.

'Yes, ' she says. 'We know that. But how? Why did that happen?'

'I forgot where I was. I was upset.'

'You were upset?' She seems to latch on to that.

'We'd just had words. We…well, we'd been close and he was pushing me away. That's how it…'

'He pushed you?'

'Not as in, *pushed*. He just wanted to get rid of me.'

'Get rid of you?'

Get me out of there. I've realised now that's what he meant. By what he said.'

'What he said?'

I'm not about to tell her what he said. 'Well, what he told me made me want to get away from him. Anyway.'

'It's really important that we know. What he said. How he pushed you.'

There's a deafening silence in my head. Like everything went down a chute, leaving it cold as an ice bucket. And in the vacuum there comes an echo of that weasel voice suggesting that I "remember" that I was pushed. So that's what this is about. The police must think Alfie pushed me off the platform. I get goosebumps all over. Alfie! Of all people. For some reason I don't understand, the weasel must want them to think that.

'No!' I almost shout. 'He didn't push me – as in, with his hands. He would never. Never in a million years.'

This is a man who rescues butterflies. What have I said? What can I do?

'It was in my head,' I say. 'It was just that he broke the mood, you know… We'd just, you know. And he wanted to move on, do something else. I was being silly, I suppose. But he was nowhere near. He was standing by the bed when I went over. He was horrified. You should have seen the look on his face.'

She's watching me closely. 'And what was he doing? Did he have anything in his hands?'

'No, nothing. He wasn't doing anything. He was just holding up his hand, like to say stop. But he was too far away to stop me.'

'But you said he was pushing you away.'

'Only with words. You know, shutting down. Going cold on me. It was only what he said.'

'You're absolutely sure about that?'

'Of *course* I'm sure.'

Then a miracle happens. She grins and closes her notebook. 'Men, eh? They just don't get it do they?'

I can't even smile. I feel like crying.

'I thought as much. But we have to follow up. When questions are asked. What we call a routine inquiry.' She's gathering up her papers.

'Is that it?'

'That is it. Don't look so worried. Think no more about it.' I catch sight of a leaflet as she puts it back in her folder. It has "Domestic Violence" zig-zagged across the top.

I'm just about to ask what she meant by questions being asked when the staff nurse comes in to ask her to leave.

She gives one look at me and says, 'I told you not to go upsetting my patient.'

But Tracy touches her arm. 'All finished. If I can just have a word?'

When the doctor does the ward round she says I can go home, all things being equal, and when I can get transport. All things are not equal though. I'm running a temperature again.

Nurse Kathy commiserates and says no wonder, what with police and 'that damn reporter'.

I suddenly have a mental picture of Pugh, his pocked skin, the crackled collar and that lapel pin. 'Hey, tell me. What was it you said he was always on about?'

'He's a Pro-Lifer. Euthanasia. Abortion. That's...'

'The rights of the unborn child. Of course. That's it. Omigod.'

'What's up now? You watch that temperature of yours.'

'I just remembered where I saw his badge before. No matter. It was in another life. It was just bugging me, that's all.'

It certainly bugs me. But I'm not about to tell anyone why. It was just before I had the abortion. That's when I last saw that beastly little lapel pin. It's supposed to be a pair of baby feet. Well, foetus feet to be precise – to show how advanced the baby is at the stage when abortion is still legal. Luke tried to give me one of those pins and I threw it in the river. And wished I could have thrown him in after it. He'd got in touch with those Pro-Lifers. Thought he'd shame me out of it. As if I didn't know what I was doing. As if I'd do it lightly. I knew all that stuff. But I also knew me. I knew I couldn't look after a baby. I didn't want to go the way Carole went.

Kathy's leaning over me. 'You all right? Here, drink some water and don't go upsetting yourself.'

As she's leaving she steps back into the room. 'By the way, that Alfie, he's come every day you know, even though he couldn't come in. Came back twice yesterday in case you'd changed your mind. Just thought you might like to know.'

Poor Alfie. No wonder he ran from that reporter. What a rotten trick, using his job to get to people like that. Why can't people have their opinions and keep them to themselves?

When I think about it I can see that me and Alfie did quite a similar thing, ending a life. In fact, you could say that what I did was worse. At least his wife wanted to die, but I didn't have my baby's consent. If it had known, it sure wouldn't have wanted me for a mother though.

The more I think about it, the more I'm ashamed at how I overreacted up there in the barn. Like I'd never done any growing up. Like I never had any therapy, never spent half the night talking through Carole's death with Nan when I had nightmares. No wonder Alfie wanted shot of me.

But Kathy said he's been coming here. I wonder if he'll come this afternoon.

11

'Who'd have thought it? That we'd be sitting out here in style with Joel waiting on us hand and foot?' And who'd have thought we'd be an "us", says a voice in my head -which evokes the image of Connie, grinning and repeating the word "smitten".

Esther smiles dreamily and gazes up through the branches of the ash tree. She's lying back in a lounger with the plaster cast making her good leg look even more stick-like than usual. We're in the back garden of the pub, not the one the punters use, and Joel has just brought us a tray of drinks and ham sandwiches.

'I never thought a tree could be interesting,' says Esther. 'I've been watching it for ages, and so much *happens* in a tree.'

I nod.

'I mean, even without the birds. I don't make them out. They hop about or stay still for aeons but there's no rhyme or reason to it all. But it's the leaves. The patterns against the sky. And the way they go matt or shiny when the wind blows. Blimey Alfie, who'd have thought I could ever spend half a morning watching a tree?'

She's changed since the accident. There's something quieter about her. She's not so sharp and we're both gentle with each other. Being careful, with a lot of explaining still to do. We've had the first conversation. That happened in the hospital with the visitors at the next bed ear-wigging. It mostly consisted of us both saying sorry over and over and competing to be most at fault. We fell over each other to say we'd misjudged, misunderstood.

She claimed to be childish. I said I was selfish. But it was what we didn't say that was more important.

When it came to taking Esther home, Tom ran me in and I hired a taxi for the return trip. Neither of us thought the plaster cast would fit comfortably in the Defender or the pickup. So we drove up to The George in style. The welcome was not what we expected.

Marion stood in the pub entrance with her legs planted firmly apart. I remember thinking she had shapely legs for a woman of her size. She got less shapely as the eye moved upward. And she'd chosen to swathe herself in lurid pink roses, which didn't help.

'You're barred,' she said as I paid the driver.

Her voice was tight and shrill. I didn't really think I'd heard right, so I carried on opening the door to help Esther out.

'And she's fired,' continued Marion, pointing a scarlet finger-nail at Esther with a rattle of gold bangles.

'And we're so pleased to see you too, Marion. What's all this about? What's Esther supposed to have done?'

'As if you didn't know.' Her face gleams an unhealthy shade of orange in the sun.

'Well, I don't know. That's why I'm asking.'

'Oh, we know your dirty little story. Thought you could pull the wool over our eyes. Thought we were just country folk who wouldn't notice. Folk with no morals who wouldn't care? Is that what you thought? Was it? Was it?'

Her voice was verging on the hysterical as the driver took the bag from the boot and I helped Esther with her crutches.

'And you, you'd better wait,' Marion shouted at the cabbie. 'You'll be taking them right away again.' She was sounding more confident, getting into her stride.

Esther stood there, leaning slightly forward and stared at her. 'What the hell are you on about? There was none of this when you came to visit in the hospital, nice as pie.' She was speaking quietly but I could sense the suppressed fury. 'How can I get fired when I was just lying there? Okay, so I can't work. Not yet. But that's nothing to lose your rag about. And what's it got to do with Alfie?'

'You little hussy! How you have the nerve to stand there and even look at me!' Marion was almost foaming at the mouth.

Esther hopped over to the nearest bench and sat down, and Marion turned her attention to me.

'As to you. To think I let you sit in my bar with that poor wife of yours hardly cold in the ground... The thought of it. You conniving murderers.'

Another voice came from inside the pub. 'What the hell's going on here?' Joel emerged and looked from Marion to me to Esther.

He crossed to Esther and kissed her on both cheeks. 'Welcome back. Good to see you on the mend.' He spun round to me and shook my hand. 'Well done, mate. Got her back here safely. Sorry about the reception.'

He turned to his wife. 'What have I been hearing? I was down in the cellar. How dare you? These people are our customers, our staff, my friends. They are welcome. And just in case there's any doubt, this is my pub, I'll have you know. I don't think your name appears above this door.' He pointed up at the inscription on the door frame as if Marion might care to look.

Esther and I stared at each other open-mouthed. Was this really hen-pecked Joel who always let Marion have her way?

Joel meanwhile had crossed to the taxi driver, pulling out his wallet. 'There is no need for you to stay. This is for your time and to ensure that events here go no further.'

As the driver reversed and drove off, Esther got to her feet again. 'Marion, you've had a visit from a reporter, right? A fellow who works on the local paper?'

Marion's mouth dropped open. She glared at Esther with a mixture of fear and disgust.

I was gazing at Esther with something like awe. My knees had been shaking since Marion started, but here was Esther, just up from her sickbed, unsteady on her pins, yet apparently unfazed by Marion's attack. And she seemed to have turned psychic into the bargain.

'I knew it!' Esther was saying. 'Fuckin'ell, Marion. I didn't think even you would be so brain-dead as to believe that toad.'

'Don't you "F" me!' Spit bubbled at the corners of Marion's crimson mouth. 'Here I am... In my own... I'll have words with you later, Joel Kingsley.' Then she recovered herself. 'And remember, she's not staying. It's her or me.' She turned abruptly and disappeared.

Joel put his head in his hands. 'I don't know what to say. "Sorry" doesn't cover it. Come on, let's go inside and get ourselves outside of a drink. I know I could do with one.'

'So how did you know?' Joel asked Esther when we were settled at the window table with drinks.

Esther grinned, enjoying the mystery.

Joel went on, 'A fellow *did* come here. Weaselly bloke making outrageous insinuations. Marion was lapping it up, but I had no idea she really believed it all.'

'Pugh,' I said and groaned. 'So how the hell *did* you know, Esther?' I remembered the close encounter with a silver convertible two days earlier. So much for Connie's advice to ignore Pugh.

'He visited me in hospital. I mean, I didn't know who he was until afterwards. I was half asleep. But he said some weird things, something about me and Alfie plotting. I think he was trying to influence my memory – which still hadn't come back at the time.' She paused for a drink. 'Anyway just now, sitting on the bench, I started putting two and two together. Shit, has he got it in for you, Alfie.'

'He has that, all right. How dare he get at you! Christ, Esther, what a mess. I am so, so sorry.'

Esther waved away my protests. 'Don't worry. I got my own back. I hit him. Made his tongue bleed.'

'You *what*?' say Joel and I in chorus.

She just cackled.

'I thought you said you were half asleep?'

'I woke up. It did take him rather by surprise.'

She looked so pleased with herself, but I was thinking it was no wonder he came up to the pub. He had to have his revenge.

'Can't we get him for libel? If he's a reporter?'

'Oh, he'd never print any of that stuff. He keeps the professional and the personal strictly apart, so he says. That's not how it feels but, technically, he keeps himself safe.'

'Clever bastard. Of course, he never actually said you *did* x or y. All just hints and nudge, nudge, wink, wink stuff. But it was enough for a very stupid person – like my wife – to pick it up and run with it. I'm disgusted with her, I really am.'

'And did she run with it! Crumbs, that was some reception. No, no, don't apologise. Not your fault. But it should be good for a free drink or two. Seriously though, you've got a problem there.'

Joel shrugged but I could see he was pretty churned up.

'So what happens next?' Esther looked from Joel to me. 'Do I have to move up to the barn – until I can make other arrangements, that is?'

I noticed how careful she was not to presume.

'Certainly not. Your room is still here.' Joel broke off, looking embarrassed. 'Unless you two…?'

'No, no. Esther couldn't possible manage up there. She needs a few mod cons and a decent bed and so on.'

'Right, yes. You can't work, obviously, Esther. But we've got a girl from the village to help out and Pattie's doing extra hours.'

'But Marion gave me the sack. She won't let me stay under this roof.'

'You are staying. If she means it's her or you, then it's you. And that's final.'

'What happened Joel? Did you…'

'You mean did I get a personality transplant? About time. It was that man Pugh. I saw red. And to see that woman prepared to lap up that rubbish and turn on good folk like you. Scales fell from my eyes, as they say. If she wants to stay, things have got to change, big time.'

The evening turned into a kind of impromptu party for Esther's return. The two of us were set at the corner table, Pattie served us cottage pie, Joel opened a bottle of fizz and Reg bought us both drinks when he came in, as did several other locals. Yesterday Marion took off in her Volvo sports coupé, and Joel would have had another party if Pattie hadn't drawn the line. 'Too much work, not enough profit. And in very bad taste,' she told Joel. 'I can see I'm going to have to keep you in order.'

According to Esther, Pattie knows that the pub depends on Marion's funds even if her name isn't over the door. Joel seems not to have remembered that yet. Meanwhile he's everybody's friend and can't do enough to make up for Marion's insults. Which is how we come to be lounging in the garden being waited on.

Now Esther sits up to sip her lime and soda. 'What would Marion say to this?' She puts on her Marion voice. 'That hussy being waited on under my roof!' A gurgle of laughter. Esther can't hear Marion's name without collapsing into giggles. 'Wow! What a home-coming that was.' She grins across at me. 'I thought she was going to explode right out of that gruesome dress, I really did.'

'Well, she's gone now. Wonder what Joel's going to do about that.'

'Doesn't have to do anything. He's well shot of her.'

As we eat the sandwiches Esther puts on her serious look.

'There's some things you should know about me. Starting with why me and Luke broke up.'

'Okay. Go ahead.'

'You won't like it. It's not very nice. You might...'

'Spit it out,' I say. 'It can't be that bad.'

'I had an abortion. You see, it *is* bad.'

'That must have been tough.'

I've always avoided thinking about the whole abortion issue – if and when it should be legal and so on. Never got beyond thinking that the Catholics miss the point, giving God a role in the decision-making. Surely it has to be down to the woman, the circumstances. It's her body, after all.

'Was it Luke's baby?'

She nods. 'It was tough. Not the actual operation. That was the easy bit. But deciding to do it, and Luke making me feel like a murderer. An unnatural woman. D'you think I am?'

I shake my head. 'Not at all.'

'You're not shocked?'

'Why should I be shocked? Shit happens. It was your body, your decision. I don't suppose you took it lightly. And Luke... It wasn't going to last with him from what you've said, so not the ideal...'

'Oh, Alfie! You're a star. Come here.'

Raindrops interrupt us. They are so fat and heavy that at first I think grubs are falling from the tree.

'How come it's raining out of a blue sky?'

'Look that way. This is only the start.' I point to the dirty grey cloud looming over the pub roof. 'Come on. Mustn't let that plaster get wet. You go on in.'

I help her up and hand her the crutches. Off she goes, step, swing, step, swing. I hold the door open for her.

'You said there were some *things* you were going to tell me. Things plural. What else?'

'Did I? Yes, well. I tell you what, I'll show you some of my photos. We'll go up to my room. Can you bring my stuff?'

I start to gather her things. A paperback, a battered whodunnit from the pub shelves, and the cotton floral bag she keeps everything in, that goes everywhere with her. It seems strangely intimate to be handling it.

Esther greets me upstairs, leaning on her crutches. She swings across to a tiny bookshelf, pulls out a grubby little volume and tosses it onto the bed.

It's a tiny, irregular room with painted floorboards. Just a bed, one upright chair and a chest of drawers, with a curtain across one corner for a wardrobe. It's neat and bare. Apart from the books, the only signs of Esther are a hairbrush and the sketch I gave her propped on the chest. Must get round to framing it. As I close the door I notice a Mickey Mouse T-shirt hanging on the hook.

'You sit on the chair. I'm better on the bed.'

It's more a scrapbook than a photo album and on the first page two cut-out figures have been pasted in.

'My Mum and Dad' She runs her finger over the picture of the woman. 'My handsome Dad and my beautiful mother.'

Surprised at the change in her voice, I give her a sideways glance, then peer down at the couple. The man's face is familiar. A celebrity, the sort of thing you get in a Sunday colour supplement. I look more closely. I'm not much good on film stars but even I know this one.

'That's a picture of Tom Cruise.'

'Well spotted. Yeah, I didn't have a picture of my Dad when I made this book. He's in another album.'

'But it is your mother?'

'She nods. 'I told you she was beautiful.'

I make a non-committal noise. The girl is quite pretty in a nondescript sort of way. Beautiful she is not.

'Here I am with my mother.' Again that sugary note.

'And these are Nan.'

A series of shots of a white-haired woman – on a park bench, in a paper hat pulling a cracker, with birthday candles alight on a cake. Every album has them.

'And this is Auntie Em and me.'

A fuzzy-haired woman is looking down at a little kid. Esther's half-turned from the camera, looking back with a defiant glare. Recognisably Esther, but she looks... I can't pin it down. Urchin-like, almost feral. She doesn't look like a kid whose mother played the piano and took her to concerts, though I kick myself for falling into stereotypes.

'She's the only person I have and I can't find her. She moved away. That's why I came down here. To find Auntie Em. The people where she used to live said she'd come to the West Country. Cornwall, actually. But now I'm here, I realise it's a daft idea. It's not like London.'

'One of these days,' I say, 'I'll take you to find Auntie Em. That's a promise.'

She squeezes my hand but I don't think she believes me.

We come to the end of the book and she turns back to the beginning, holds up the collage of her mother and Tom Cruise.

'I told you, Beautiful People.'

This is getting difficult to take. I like the gentler Esther. But since when was she syrupy? About anything?

'Let me look again.'

She passes the book to me and I examine the young woman. She has short, spiked hair and an elfin face. Okay, so people cut their hair. But, unmistakably, her roots are growing out and she has large brown eyes. What was it she said? *Natural blonde, silky hair. Got the green eyes from her.*

'Any photos of your grandfather?' I ask.

She slams the book shut. 'No. None.' A pause. 'He didn't trust cameras.'

She puts the book on the bedside table and eyes the shelves on the opposite wall. Am I going to be treated to the photo album as well? Hopefully not.

But she jerks her head away and looks up at the skylight. 'Still raining.'

I feel a pang of guilt for my lukewarm reaction and lean over and kiss her.

'Thanks for showing me. Special pictures.'

'I know what we should do now.' She shifts over on the bed. 'Come on, Alfie. Of course there's room.'

'But what about...?'

'It's only my leg that's broken. The rest of me works.'

'I'm scared of hurting you, causing damage.' But I remember our first time. I can't resist.

She wedges the leg with the cast against the wall and giggles. 'Just be gentle.'

It's a tricky manoeuvre. Gingerly, I lower myself and enter her. She shifts position. We find a way. It's good to have her home.

12

'You should be in training for the Paralympics,' says Joel.

Which is probably the most PC comment you'll hear in the bar about my accident. 'Here comes the cripple' is common enough from Reg, who usually calls me "Polly Peg-leg", and Joel won't have me behind the bar on account of four legs cluttering the place up. But to give him his due, underneath all the banter he's determined I don't mess up and put weight on the thing before it's ready.

I must admit I'm getting to be pretty ace on the crutches. They give me a challenge. Like, every day I have to try to do something I didn't think was possible. I found a bag with long handles and I sling it round my neck so I can carry things. Except not a plate of food or a mug of coffee. I haven't solved that one yet. But my arms are getting stronger and I can make it to the village shop without getting too knackered.

Today I got as far as Reg's garden and I managed to get a whole bundle of rhubarb into the bag. I asked what it was, more from something to say than anything. I was gobsmacked when he told me.

'I bet youm thinking, yuk, school dinners,' Reg said and I nodded.

Roobarb'n'custard. Those brown bits managing to be slimy as well as hairy, ruining a decent splodge of custard. And here it was growing like a tree on the corner of Reg's potato patch.

'This'll be different, just don't overcook it.' He pulled it out of the crown and I loved the way it came away all white and clean at the end of the pink stem. He took out his pocket-knife and sliced off all the leaves. I was disappointed. They were so dramatic. But he said they were poisonous and piled them on the bonfire, a heap of leathery parasols.

I put the rhubarb in the porch to take up to the barn when Alfie picks me up. When Pattie saw it she teased me about Reg being sweet on me. She told me how to cook it and to use plenty of sugar. She even picked out a dish from the kitchen and put half a bag of flour and some butter in it, saying, 'I don't suppose he's got any sort of larder up there.' I only hope Alfie likes it.

I asked to go up to the barn to see how the accident happened and get that over with. I didn't want Alfie's place to be somewhere I'm afraid to go. It's a relief to find it's still the haven it always was. It hasn't lost its magic.

Alfie treats me like I might break. He can't believe I can cook and brings me a chair, but it's much easier to stand on one leg and have a lean on the table from time to time. When I start cutting up the rhubarb I quite expect to see letters appearing, it looks so much like the rock Nan bought me that time at Southend. I suppose up here it would have to spell out Widecombe-in-the-Moor as that's the only touristy place around. But it's not exactly snappy – you'd need jumbo-size sticks of rock for that. Alfie wonders what I'm blathering on about. It's just ordinary old rhubarb to him. It looks so appealing I try nibbling a bit. Blimey! Is that sour! No wonder Pattie said about the sugar.

Trouble is, I get carried away with the pleasure of cooking. It's so satisfying, putting the dish in the oven. It's such a domestic activity. Comforting. I wipe my hands and go and make some silly remark about imagining living up here with him. I even mention getting a decent cooker to replace his ramshackle calor gas stove with the oven door that doesn't fit properly.

It sets us off on the conversation about how staying together would be a recipe for disaster. I mean, he's talked about how the age gap wouldn't work before, but this time he starts going on about having kids. He's never done that before.

'You're young,' Alfie's saying. 'You'll want children, a family.

I'm too old to start all that over again. A pensioner with teenage kids. I don't think so.'

'No!' I shout. 'Absolutely not. I'm never having kids.'

It's only when I see how startled he looks that I realise how fierce I must have sounded.

'Hold your hair on. I was only saying what anyone would say. If they saw two people like us planning to get together.'

He tries to grab my hand. I know he only wants to calm me down but I can't bear to be touched. He sits back in his chair and reaches for his pipe. I watch him unroll the leather pouch of tobacco and tease out the strands, poking it down into the bowl with his finger. I like the fact that Alfie doesn't have a whole set of fancy tools to play pipes with. Just the pipe and his fingers and a box of long matches. Every now and then he scrapes out the bowl with an old screwdriver.

He gets the thing going and puffs away. It's almost as soothing, looking on, as having a smoke myself. Not that I've done that for a few years. He's watching me as if I were a difficult sheep he needs to get into a pen. I feel kind of stupid now, to have got so worked up about something I thought I'd coped with.

'So what's going on here?' He says it really gently. And he's serious. He's not laughing. He's not patronising me, either. Which is why it's really easy just to tell him.

'It all started one day at school. I'd have been about eleven or twelve. A group of us discussing having babies. At least, the others were discussing. I was just listening and my skin started to prick all over when it begun to sink in. Someone had a sister who was pregnant and she'd put her hand on her sister's tummy and felt the baby kick. Oh shit! All the others went "Ooh!" and "Aah!". They were really enchanted, but it made me feel ill. And I said I'd never have children. It horrified me, the thought of something growing inside my body. They all stared at me as if I was some kind of freak.'

'But you were only a kid yourself then.'

'I never once felt any different. I completely freaked when I missed my period and tested positive. Total panic. It never occurred to me to go ahead and have the baby. And it never occurred to

Luke to get rid of it. Nightmare. He went on about my body being a sacred vessel. I ask you! I told Luke I felt more like a rubbish bin. Regretted it as soon as it was out of my mouth. He didn't deserve that. It was the beginning of the end.'

I've never said this stuff out loud before. I tried with Luke but he wouldn't listen. And when I told Alfie about the abortion I was scared to say any more in case I couldn't stop. Makes me really shaky. I swing over to the sofa and sit down.

Then I remember Pugh and his lapel pin. That feels like safer ground.

'Did you ever wonder what made me hit that Pugh geezer in hospital?'

'Perfectly natural reaction. I want to hit him every time I see him. No, actually I did wonder, but then you're not known for your tact and diplomacy.'

The teasing grin fades from his face as I describe the lapel pin Luke tried to give me.

'Pugh was wearing one of them. There it was right in my line of vision. I didn't even remember what it was until later. But it triggered something. I mean he'd been pretty fucking creepy, anyway. I just brought my fist right up under his chin.'

'Highly satisfying that must have been.'

I nod. 'It was.' I remember the moment of connection, the elation. 'It was the look of sheer fucking surprise on his face as much as anything. Anyway, as I was saying, getting the abortion was really quite easy, once I cut Luke out of the equation. I mean, I suppose it was hard on him, but it was my body. It took five minutes for him. It was going to be nine months for me and that's just for starters.'

Alfie nods.

'I just thanked my lucky stars it didn't happen when Nan was still alive. I could never have told her. A good Catholic, you see. Would have gone right against her faith, the sacredness of life. Not that she behaved like Pugh's lot. It just would have upset her so much.'

I'm just about to tell Alfie how I felt afterwards in that sterile white room at the clinic, when he interrupts.

'No wonder you're upset. I wouldn't know of course, but I'm told that an abortion's the worst possible thing a woman can go through. And here's me saying I don't want any more kids, and you're thinking it might happen again.'

He's entirely missed the point.

'Alfie, you don't get it. The termination – good word – it's just what it felt like. The termination was the best thing. I felt clean again. Empty. Whole and free. My own body to myself, like before. But with a terrible warning that I never, *ever* would let that happen again. I wanted to get sterilised, but they said I was too young. I'd change my mind. But I won't. I haven't yet and I never will.'

Poor Alfie. He looks baffled. He's staring out the window, frowning and puffing at his pipe – but it's gone out, so he uses the whole ritual of relighting it to regain his equilibrium. I have a cold feeling in my stomach that creeps upward as I wait for him to say something. Eventually he looks round at me.

'Yes,' he says slowly. 'You're right. I didn't get it. I had missed the point. I've never come across anyone who felt like that. You mean, what you're saying is, you couldn't stand the idea, the feeling of something growing inside you?'

I nod. He thinks I'm a monster. An unnatural woman. He might not want any more children but he won't want to be with someone like me.

'D'you know, I'd never thought about it like that before. I mean, men…we don't have to face it I suppose. It's a pretty weird thing when you really think about it. I mean, we just plant the seed. And you, you women, you're left with it. All those cells dividing and multiplying. Limbs developing, becoming recognisable.'

I shudder. I can hardly listen to this. It gives me the creeps. Even now. But I mustn't interrupt. He's doing his best. He's making sense of it.

'The miracle of life.' He puffs on his pipe and looks at me, still thinking.

'Yuk,' I say and wish I hadn't. Saying the word makes me want to gag and I sound like a kid with a plate of stew. But Alfie doesn't take any notice.

'And it gets pretty big, of course. And kicks and all that. Such a weight to drag around. I remember that. Did Meg's back in. The birds have got it right. Damn sight easier sitting on a nest. Having all that stuff going on inside the egg. Now you say it, I'm surprised more women don't think that way.'

I'm stunned. That's the thing about Alfie. He really does listen. I'm not being made to feel like a weirdo. 'Well, I've thought about that. I reckon a lot more women than let on think like that. They just don't say so. They say they're career women, or they can't conceive. Maybe they see to it that they don't, or maybe they really can't. Their body refuses for them. Who knows?'

Alfie doesn't say anything, just nods and looks at me thoughtfully.

I'm fired up now. It's almost as if it's gone to my head that Alfie's not slagging me off.

'I mean, women have a raw deal all round,' I say. I'm thinking of Carole, of course. Carole and Preece. When he wasn't invading her with his effing penis or selling her to other men to do it for him, he was doing it with a hypodermic.

Alfie raises an eyebrow and I hesitate. There's no way I'm telling him about Carole. Let alone Preece. He'd never want to touch me again if he knew there'd been that kind of scum in my life.

He takes the pipe out of his mouth and waves it at me. 'Go on then. What else?'

'Well it's not just babies that do the invading. Women get it all the time. Being invaded. By men, I mean. Like we're programmed to take it lying down. Literally, most of the time.'

I laugh. I'm on a roll. As well as the stuff about Carole, there's all the resentment about Nan not being able to stand up to my grandfather, though I can't say that.

'But not just sex. All the time. Getting walked all over. Being available, taking what's thrown at us. Saying "Okay" when we mean "Bugger off". Swallowing everything they give us. Drugs, insults. Like men were gods or something.'

Alfie's looked away as if he's trying to shut out what I'm saying.

I tail off. 'No boundaries. You've got to draw the line.'

I've lost Alfie. I make an attempt to grab him back. Explain. Justify. 'I guess I draw that line closer in than most.'

Too little. Too late. It sounds feeble, even to me.

I want to tell him how Carole never knew how to draw the line, nor Nan. Tell him how they were walked over. But I dare not.

Alfie's standing up and slowly walking towards the door. He kicks off his sandals and stuffs his feet into boots.

'Going out. Need to walk,' he says. 'Remember to take the crumble out. Smells like it's cooked.'

His footsteps fade away and I'm abandoned. It's like being given a huge compliment and then being told it was meant for someone else. Just gone, without a word. When we were having such a lovely day. I want to howl, but I won't. I've a good mind to let the crumble burn. But that would be a waste of all my efforts and I want to see what it looks like. I kick the chair aside. It's tricky getting it out standing on one leg but I manage. It's golden brown and pink round the edges where the juice has bubbled out. Smells wonderful. I take the edge of a spoonful out of one corner and scald my lip. Shit! But what I can taste is a lovely mixture of tart and sweet, crunchy and soft.

I wander outside. I'm not really looking for Alfie, but I see him up there on the hillside and he waves. Which is something.

As soon as I go back inside I start listening to myself. I've messed up. Ruined everything. All that soap-box noise, but I always leave out the most important bit. It's what I don't say that matters. Can't do it. Can't be nice. I've never told Alfie how good it is. None of that invasion stuff applies to Alfie.

It's like I open to him. I invite him in, except that sounds like a tea party. My body just does it. Like petals opening. It never happened before. But Alfie doesn't know that. *Because I haven't told him.* It's all stayed inside my head.

And right now he's thinking I feel invaded by him. And he must be thinking I'm a right cow. He's probably thinking, the girls who cry rape really are asking for it, or something like it. Can't blame him.

Trouble is, if I try and explain now how I really feel with him, it'll look like I'm just making it up to make him feel better and so he doesn't chuck me out of his life.

I wish I hadn't shown him those photos. It makes me feel more of a fraud than I really am. And it's only going to make it harder when it comes to telling him the truth. "Oh, what a tangled web we weave", as Nan would say. Or was it Auntie Em? I'm even confusing myself.

Alfie deserves the truth and sooner or later I'm going to have to come clean. All those stupid photos. What must he have thought? It was just a bit of teenage make-believe. Tom Cruise. Puhlease. But back then I used to fantasize about famous people. Anyone could have been my father. Tom, Dick, Harry or Tom Cruise. It kept me going at the time. At least the pics of me and Miss Coomber beat the hell out of the one, the only one, of me and Carole. Miss Coomber looks like she could be my mother. Alfie obviously swallowed it.

I'd like to write him a note. Try and explain. And leave. Trouble is I can't leave. Fucking crutches. Or could I?

I find a sketch pad by his chair. I've got a pen in my bag. I keep it short and simple and then I write "I love you" very small at the very bottom. I've never written it to anyone before. I leave the note beside the crumble and take another spoonful now it's cooler. Even better.

Then I set off across the field. There's no sign of Alfie up there on the hillside. He must have gone up onto the moor. Probably checking his beloved sheep. It's hard going over the bumpy grass, and I have to lean on the gate before I'm ready to go on.

13

I slam that door and stride away.

Christ, she's a weird kid. What the hell am I supposed to make of that lot? She's like two people really. Ninety-nine percent of the time so cool, so self-contained. Then come these storms suddenly bursting out of her. And it makes you wonder how she holds it in the rest of the time.

I clamber over the gate on the far side of the field and drop down on the other side, taking the sheep track that meanders between boulders up onto the high moor.

I was getting the drift of what she was going on about, all that stuff about being pregnant. Seemed quite understandable really. But then the worm turns and suddenly I'm under attack, along with every other bloke in the universe. I really can't stand that sort of thing. So now she thinks she's being invaded, does she? Well, I sure as hell won't be imposing on her one moment longer. Christ! She's been throwing herself at me. So it's a disaster, is it, for her? You certainly wouldn't think it, the way she is in the sack.

Doesn't she stop to think for one single minute what it's like for a bloke? Trouble is, it's not something I can put into words, even if I thought she'd listen. Well, to be fair, she would listen. But how could I make her understand?

All the usual clichés go through my mind. There's panic in there, underneath the sheer abandon, a kind of primitive deep-down fear. Of being swallowed, never coming back. A whole lot more clichés that I've never bothered to analyse. Don't want to either. Where's the joy in that? But she's confronted me with her side and it's like I feel I've got to meet her with mine.

I've made my escape and I'm puffing, what with climbing so fast and feeling so angry. There's enough distance between us now. Not that she can follow of course. Psychological distance. What they call space these days. I sink down onto a rock and look back. As I watch, Esther emerges from the barn and swings out. She's wearing a lime green dress and she looks like a lost grasshopper as she leans on her crutches. I feel an involuntary surge of tenderness towards her and censor it immediately. She gazes all round and up towards my perch. I freeze. But it doesn't really matter whether she sees me or not. I find myself waving. The sun glints off her crutch as she raises it in reply.

With Meg sex was never so – dramatic? Fraught? Whatever the word is. It was wonderful, sensuous. Oh yes, it was good, but I never felt threatened or beside myself as I do with Esther. I was never overwhelmed. No, that's the wrong word too. That's what other people or events do to you. This is being caught up in something bigger than that. A kind of mystery, I suppose. But I daren't tell her that. She might stamp all over it.

I'm not sure Meg would understand all that stuff of Esther's about being pregnant. Meg *was* a sacred vessel. Sounds pretentious when you say it like that, and we never did. But she changed when she was carrying Laura. She had a serenity that we both recognised. It was beautiful, it really was.

And what's going on in Esther? Is she just neurotic because of her past? That feels a bit of a lazy answer. Maybe it means she's more raw, more intense.

Just thinking about it makes my brain hurt.

Better go on up and see the flock. Wish I had Gyp with me. But at least I can check none of them have fallen over or got stuck. I make a fair attempt at a count and they all seem to be there. None are obviously lame, and I set off home with the excuse that they'll all be rounded up for drenching in a couple of days. Tom's worried about ticks and fly-strike now it's got so much warmer. Just focusing on the animals calms me down and gives me a sense of perspective.

Up until now I've just thought of Esther as a bit scary – if I thought about it at all. But in fact she's even more heavy-duty than Meg. And in a totally different way. I'd be taking on a lot if we ever got together. That's what makes me wary. Nothing to do with our ages.

The light's changed and it's clouding over from the west. Rain on the way, a storm even. We'll have an early supper and eat the damn crumble and then I'll get her back to The George before it sets in.

Trouble is, no doubt, I'm fond of the girl. More than fond. But I'm getting tangled here in something when I've no business to get tangled at all. In a few weeks I may not be around. It's no good kidding myself I can fill that time with a casual affair. She's worth more than that. That date at the end of the month is creeping up. Halfway through June already. In fact, if I really want to help her find this aunt-person, I'd better get on with it. In case I go down. But, at the same time, I must make my position clear.

There's no sign of Esther when I get back. Not on the sofa, not out back in the privy. No crutches. I even climb up to the platform, in case the crazy cow managed the ladder. She tried it earlier and it seemed impossible, but I know how she takes things like that as a challenge. But she's not there.

Then I spot the note beside the crumble. Funny how she was so insistent on cooking that rhubarb.

Dear Alfie,
I'm an idiot. I NEVER feel like that with you. But I never told you. Double idiot.
   I got carried away. Stupid soap box.
   I'm sorry.
Esther
<small>*I love you.*</small>

I pick it up and read it again. Rub my eyes. Dear, silly girl. *Got carried away*. I fold it into my shirt pocket and head for the pickup.

She's only half way down the farm track and she leans into the bank away from me when she hears the engine. I jump out and hug her to me as the first drops of rain come down. I help her manoeuvre past the door and into the seat and drive on down the track.

'Where are you taking me?' A forlorn voice.

'Back for supper? Crumble? Looks good.'

She manages a smile.

'And we need to talk.'

She grunts but there's no protest.

By the time I've turned round and we get back up to the barn the rain is stair-rodding down. I scoop her up and carry her in. Even with the plaster cast she's lighter than I expect.

I set her on a chair to grate some cheese for an omelette, while I cut bread.

'You read my note then. Did you understand? You see I never did tell you...how special it is. With you. Like never before.'

My stomach lurches and I resist the urge to do more than kiss the top of her head. I want to talk about the mystery of sex. Because, of course, it's right in there at the core of all those deep thoughts I've been having. But she might think I'm crazy.

I start whipping up eggs for the omelette.

'I do understand. And I'm glad. But there's a few other things we need to get straight.'

Stay with the practicalities, our situation. Don't seduce her with mysteries.

'To me you're a special girl. But let's face it, Esther. As I've said before, what on earth do you want with an old man going grey. Look!' I bend my head forward tugging my hair and pointing at the increasing amount of grey I've noticed lately.

'It doesn't even show in your hair. I don't care about age. What the fuck does that matter?'

'But there's other reasons. I'm drawn to you. Love you, dammit, for who you are. But for a long time – until very recently in fact – it was because you remind me... Not all the time, but in a certain light, with some gestures, an angle, an expression. And your eyes. Eyes mostly. Meg, when she was your age – when we first met.'

'I know all that, Alfie. What's new?'

'But you deserve more than that. More than a lover who's imagining he's got his wife back.'

'If you want her back you shouldn't have bumped her off in the first place.'

'Ouch, that was below the belt. 'I didn't "bump her off". You know that. Don't try to...'

'Okay, sorry. That was out of order. I've still not got used... And I do believe you 23-7.'

'And that other hour? Every day an hour of doubt.' The oil starts to smoke and I turn down the gas, pull the pan aside and stare at her.

'Well, I wasn't being precise. Might be only a split second on a good day. Because you're Alfie and I trust you. Might be several hours in the middle of the night, though. You know, that time in the small hours when you imagine everything is the very worst it could be. After all, I've only got your word for it.'

I can't hope for more than that. I tip in the eggs, ruffle them through. 'That's what the jury will think. Hey, stop eating the cheese and pass it over.'

'Will you really go for trial?'

'Oh yes. It's a waiting game. And that's another reason – I may well go to prison. Could get as much as fourteen years.'

Her mouth drops open. 'As much as that?'

She goes quiet, chewing her lip. It's sinking in. She'll be making her plans without me now.

'But it doesn't make sense. You, of all people.'

'It's the law. And it's what a lot of people think should happen to people like me. It's not just maniacs like Pugh. You did yourself...'

'But I don't think that any more. That was just all my shit. I understand what you did. I do. I've been getting there.'

'I suppose that's as much as I can ask.'

I fold the omelette, cut it and slide half onto each plate. We munch in silence, and I'm thinking that the stuff about prison struck home. I won't tell her the date. Best not. I'll just slide away. She won't want to be visiting an old man in clink. Christ, I could be a pensioner when I come out.

'It was huge, wasn't it? What you did?'

I nod. 'It was huge, between me and Meg. Obviously. But I didn't realise how huge in the eyes of the world. Murder, it's a big word.'

'Murder? Is that…?'

'That's what they charged me with. Initially. Then it was changed. Reduced to Assisting a Suicide. Section 2 of the Suicide Act 1961, in case you're interested. I couldn't have pleaded guilty to murder. It wasn't. It just wasn't.'

'God, that must have been terrifying. Sorry I said that earlier. Bumping her off, I mean, being glib. I do that. When I'm scared.'

'It's not…'

'What was she like? Your Meg? You've never said… Or maybe you can't?'

'No, I can talk about her. At least I think I could. But where the hell do I start?'

'Beginning? I mean, where did you meet? I assumed art college.'

'She was an art student, yes. It was just before I got in. I was working at the library. Saving up.'

I give a version of my first sight of Meg but Esther's never heard of the Pre-Raphaelites so I don't elaborate.

'Very romantic. So was she a painter too?'

'No. She switched to photography. She had a real talent.' I don't want to talk about Meg after all. 'Let's try your crumble.'

She grins. 'Brilliant omelette. But my crumble's going to beat it. Did you compete, the two of you? Your paintings against her photos?'

I laugh. 'Meg used to. And she was a good critic. In fact she'd have been a better painter than me. If she'd kept it up.'

'You do a brilliant likeness. What more do you want? If it looks like someone, that's a real gift. Hey, it's *my* crumble. I get to dish it out! Hope you like.'

The rhubarb's good, better than I expected, and we both prefer it without the custard.

'I still haven't heard anything much about Meg. When did she get ill?'

'While we were there the second time. In Tuscany. We came home, you see, for Laura's schooling because she was starting to think she was Italian. Once Laura was off to college, we went back. But not for long. When she got ill Meg couldn't cope with not being able to communicate with the doctors and so on. It made her feel helpless.'

'So how did you decide…? To do what you did? How does anyone come to that?'

'It was always her idea. It wasn't so much the pain. She was amazingly stoical about that. But she couldn't stand the idea of being dependent. Of course she was dependent, but it was all a matter of degree, and she…she drew a very firm line and asked me to help her not step over it.'

Esther's looking at me, taking it in, still wondering.

'Look, I've got some photos. They probably give a better idea of why.' I clear the dishes and fetch the inlaid box from the top of the piano which I rarely have the courage to open. The first one I pull out is of Meg dressed up like Lizzie Siddal, which she always loved to do for parties.

'Wow! She was so beautiful! But she doesn't look anything like me. I don't understand.'

'Thought you'd say that. It's all about the eyes. I told you she had green eyes like yours. And something you do with your nose, gestures. It was never that you looked alike.'

Esther stares at the photo, holding it up to the light. 'She looks very feisty, very…like she might jump up at any moment and do something crazy, like dance with no clothes on or climb a tree in that dress. Something totally unexpected.'

I laugh and nod. 'Got her in one. She could be a total nightmare.'

'But you loved her to bits.'

'Yes, I'd have done anything for her.'

'You did.'

I can't say anything for a moment. I just pass Esther the next snap.

'That must be Laura. She looks like her mother.'

Laura's about six and they were holding hands – doing some sort of dance, I seem to remember.

'Yes. Equal nightmare. Not talking to me because of what I did.'

'Oh Alfie, that's awful.' She looks back at the photo. 'That is so sad. Such a waste.' Her voice cracks, but she carries on. 'Meg was still beautiful then.'

We'd all been grape-picking in our landlord's vineyard and Meg's in scruffy trousers and an old T-shirt with her hair scraped back in a rubber band. I never remember her looking anything but beautiful. Except near the end.

'Then came her illness. See what it did to her. She made me take this. She wanted people to understand – what it was like.'

The last picture shows Meg propped on pillows as I last remember her, shrunken, grey-haired.

Esther gasps when she sees it. 'But you can still see her spirit – her eyes are still the same.'

I nod. I want to show her Meg's poem, but I haven't shown it to anybody. Maybe it's too intimate. Maybe it would be a betrayal of Meg. But I want Esther to understand how it was between us. Esther's told me about her past and it's only fair to reciprocate. So I take that out of the box too.

'Meg wrote this for me. It was just before she died. When I say wrote – she got Connie to actually write it down. Left it with the suicide letter.' I spread it out and look at it. 'I'm so grateful she did. I haven't got her letter – that was considered evidence. The police have got that.'

I wonder whether to read it aloud but I'm not sure I'd get through it. In the end I just hand it over.

For Alfie

Through the ear of a raindrop, butterflies dance on my grave.
Waves crash on the shore to the rattle of shingle falling, falling
through forests of seaweed that give me vertigo as I float
Looking down the tall fathoms.

The wind roars through branches, washing my dreams,
rivalling pain and the hammer of rain on window panes.
And now the calm after the storm, the rock of a boat,
solid, wooden, clinker-built, smelling of tar. Old varnish
in amber blisters is smooth to my touch,
hard as the winter sun.

Trees billow down to the water's edge like a shaken duvet,
and a pair of egrets watch from the white bones of
    a skeleton ash.
You lean on the oars and the rowlocks join the silence all
    around
as I ghost through the bottom of the boat.

I drift on the tide of my being which has flooded for the
    last time,
ebbing me steadily out to join the ocean where I will
    become
the smallest drop.

Where I will fall as rain next time around?
Which stream of droplets will I join? How will I flow?
Will you be there?

Alfie, my darling, this seems to be a kind of poem which
bubbled up in the night while you slept, exhausted, in
the chair. It is for you, my dearest, and I will get Connie
to put it with the formal letter where you will find it.
I thank you, my love, from the bottom of our ocean of
tears and joy, for all you have done and will have done
to make this life so full and blessed.

A sniff makes me look up and Esther's face is wet with tears. She wipes her cheeks with her palms. 'That is so beautiful. Thank you for showing me. That's, like, it's the best thing you've ever done. Like you trust me, I guess.' She pauses looking back at the poem. 'It's funny, sometimes I think I know things and sometimes I think I'm mad. This poem's like that. It doesn't make any proper sense. But it does. It touches something, I don't know, it...'

'It touches a mystery?'

'Yes! That's exactly it.'

'Funny. I was having some thoughts – up on the hill. About what you said about being pregnant. There's a...'

'Don't let's get back to that, Alfie. Please not.'

'Another time maybe.'

She ignores that, folds the poem and hands it back to me. 'You're still very much in love with her, aren't you, Alfie?'

'I suppose I am. If it's possible to be in love with someone who's dead.'

'I'm sure it's possible. I guess that's part of the mystery.'

'Which is another reason you wouldn't want to be with me. You'd be living with a ghost. That's an awful lot of reasons.'

'Alfie, do you ever feel it? The mystery, I mean. Or whatever you call it. When we're together. When we're making love?'

I nod.

'That's what I never said. Should have said. Instead of all that other stuff.'

'Me too. You see, I'm no good at saying these things either.'

'I guess I was too scared to say it. In case you didn't. Feel it, I mean.'

I put my arm around her and kiss her hair. 'But it doesn't alter the situation. It doesn't alter any of those reasons.' I pull myself away, ignore her protests. 'Now I'm going to make some coffee, while you convince yourself.'

'Alfie, why don't we just take one day at a time?' She raises her voice over the sound of water drumming into the kettle. 'I mean, you don't have to swear to love me forever.'

I light the gas, set the kettle to boil and turn back to her. She doesn't say any more. She's just watching me with her cat's eyes. I feel my resolve run away like water through sand.

'You've done your best to put me off and I'm not. Wouldn't you miss me?'

Of course I would. My look tells her that.

'And what would Meg say?' Her voice is tight and she looks away.

'She'd say, "Get on with your life".'

'So what's the point of being miserable when we could be enjoying it?'

I can't argue with that.

136

14

Alfie turns up in clean jeans and a white shirt instead of the tatty plaid numbers he usually wears. He looks so clean.

I give him a big hug and whisper in his ear that he looks even more fanciable than usual. All he does is natter on about sheep. But I can tell he's pleased.

'You never even came to the pub in the evening.'

I've missed him so much and it seems much longer than two days, but all he says is that he was too tired and starts explaining about treating and cleaning the sheep.

'Too much information,' I tell him. Stuff about sheep's bottoms really doesn't do it for me.

'Has to be done. Otherwise...'

I do lots of fake yawning, but in the end I have to put a hand over his mouth to shut him up.

We're off on the trip he promised. We're going to find Auntie Em. The thing I came down here to do. I've been back to the hospital and, at last, I'm allowed to put weight on the leg. Joel has been totally brilliant and loaned us his Jeep Cherokee. I was gobsmacked but he insisted. Couldn't bear the thought of me rattling about in the pickup. He brushes it off by saying he has to invest in his workforce.

'I need you back at work. You're costing me money, my girl.' Then he adds, 'Doubt that rustbucket of Tom's would make it that far anyway.'

'A holiday!' I lean over and kiss him as I fasten my seatbelt.

'I can't believe we're off together. Posh car, leather seats. Good old Joel.'

'I feel like a gangster,' says Alfie as we set off through the village.

But I love Joel's shiny great Jeep with all its chrome trim.

'You're lucky it isn't Marion's, with leopard print seat covers. Hey, that reminds me. Marion's coming back. Probably. They've been speaking. He reckons she's bored without someone to boss around, and I reckon Joel misses having someone telling him what he's got to do next.'

'Good luck to him,' says Alfie, concentrating on the gears.

It's so exciting to be going off on a holiday, let alone with Alfie. But Auntie Em? I'm shit-scared. I never thought he'd really take me to find her. Should I come clean? Or should I risk it? I mean, Auntie Em's not exactly discreet. It might come out, and then he'll know I was just a kid from a home. I regret lying about my mother now that Alfie and me have got so close. But it was always such a habit. You have to invent something, something respectable that puts an end to the questions. And quite apart from all that, I'm really, really nervous about seeing Auntie Em again. Excited too, though.

I'm pretty sure I've located her in Port Boscoe, a tiny village on the north coast of Cornwall. It only took about five minutes on Joel's computer.

Alfie asks why I hadn't done it before and I have to confess I did – weeks ago.

'I was too scared to ring her.'

I also have to admit there's a Mrs E Miller in St Ives, Penzance and Truro.

He's quite short with me about that. 'Oh, come on, Esther. We can only stay away a couple of nights. We can't do the grand tour of Cornwall. You'll have to phone them, find out which one is Auntie Em.'

In fact every time I start to say, 'About Auntie Em. There's something I need to tell you…' he interrupts and tries to get me to phone her. In the end I think, what the hell, I'll take the risk.

I don't want to ring ahead. I really couldn't face it. I just want to turn up, but I have to work hard to convince Alfie. 'I've got a feeling about the Port Boscoe one. It's the sort of place she'd go to. Not a big town. She'd like to be a big fish in a small pond.'

He wants to know how she managed to be a big fish in Rayners Lane. I can't explain. But she did. Everyone knew her. He says it's a far cry from Rayners Lane. Of course it is. Anywhere west of the M25 is a far cry from Rayners Lane. In the end I have to agree to phone the others if we draw a blank in Port Boscoe.

Alfie shrugs and points out a pair of buzzards riding a thermal, and I think how much part of the place he is and how amazing it is that we two ever met. I wonder aloud about how he came to be here on the moor.

'How I come to be here?'

'Yeah. I mean I know why, what you were getting away from. But why exactly the Hannafords' farm?'

'Well, it wasn't by design, that's for sure. I got here by following old Tom's Defender. It was such a classic – old as the hills, covered in mud. There it was, strapped onto a trailer on the back of the pickup.'

'So what made you...?'

'I was in a kind of daze. Fed up with people I knew who were all trying so hard to be normal around me. Fed up with the dreaded Pugh. Heading out of town. I just got comfortable with this ramshackle outfit bumbling along in front of me. I liked the number plate. OAF. Suited me and how I felt exactly. I wasn't really taking much notice. Following it saved me having to make decisions. And everyone pretty much backed up in the lanes to let us pass. So when it stopped I just thought it was waiting for some guy to find reverse gear. But we were in the farmyard.'

'You mean, you didn't notice going up the track?'

He shakes his head. 'Sounds crazy, I know. But that's how I was. A bit crazy really.'

'But didn't you just turn round and go?'

'Well, no.' He laughs, almost to himself, as if it only now strikes him as odd. 'Me and Tom got talking. He didn't seem that surprised to see me. Tom doesn't let on much. He was more concerned about getting the Defender off the pickup – and here was help at hand. As I say, we got talking. He had some problem with one of his ewes. I must say he was a bit knocked back that I turned out to know something about sheep. I hadn't done any farming since I was seventeen, but sheep don't change. I think he thought it was some kind of act of God that a potential shepherd had followed him home, when his own shepherd had upped and died just in time for lambing. It all got a bit biblical for a bit.'

'What happened to your car?' I'm trying to picture the scene.

'Oh, it fell apart. It was an ancient 2CV. It used to be Meg's car. A few weeks of rattling up and down the track and bits were falling off it like there was no tomorrow.'

'Bet it was red.'

He's surprised at that, but I'm right. It's obvious Meg's car would have been red.

'So how did you get all that stuff up at the barn?'

'Didn't live there for a while. Stayed at Tom's place. But I was never very comfortable with that. When I fixed up the barn I just dropped by home with the pickup a couple of times after I signed on at the police station. Picked up my paints and a few books, and some music I missed.'

We don't say a lot after that. That's the nice thing about Alfie. You don't have to talk all the time and it never feels uncomfortable. There's loads to see, dropping down off the moor to places I've never been. Alfie points things out and I sit there feeling like a queen. I like watching him sideways, the concentration, expressions on his face. I do so love this guy. So why can't I trust him? Every now and then he looks across at me and grins and says, 'Okay?' And I am *so* okay.

Except for the way my stomach keeps reminding me: he's so trusting and I'm deceiving him. Suddenly I can stand it no longer.

'There's something I need to tell you'

'Yeah?'

'Before we get there. Something big.'

'Go on then.'

'And I'd rather you heard it from me.'

'Esther, I'm listening.'

'It's about Auntie Em. I haven't been straight with you.'

'Okay.'

'Well, I told you she was an aunt, a great-aunt even. Like, Nan's sister?'

'Mmm.'

He's giving me some sort of a look but I keep staring straight ahead watching the white line on the road disappearing round a bend.

'Well, she wasn't. She was actually a foster-mother. You see, I was in care. I was placed with her from a children's home.'

There. I've said it. And what do I get? Silence.

'Alfie?' I make myself look round at him. 'Say something. Please.'

He raises one eyebrow and shakes his head slowly. Then he blows out as if he's been holding his breath. Shit. I guess I've just ruined our little trip. He'll be looking for somewhere to turn round.

'I don't know what to say. So many things. Things falling into place. Things that didn't quite make sense, like your Nan, how important...'

'But Alfie, just say. Tell me what you think... Are you...?'

'I'm trying to tell you. Of course your Nan was special to you. Trying to imagine... What it was like for you. I mean, what a culture shock, to go into a children's home. Not that I have a clue...'

'But are we still going? Aren't you going back?'

'Going back?' What the hell are you talking about? Of course we're still going. What difference does it make?'

'But aren't you mad at me? Don't you hate me?'

'Well, I'm pretty mad at you for telling me stories. And for making her a great-aunt. I mean, aunts are two a penny. A loose term. I had several aunts who were no relation. But a great-aunt!' He actually laughs. 'It's not so much I'm mad at you, actually. I just don't understand why you did that – made it up.' Then he looks suddenly serious and he says, 'But hate you? Why would I hate you?'

'For being a snotty kid from a home.'

'Snotty? Were you snotty?'

'Alfie! Don't tease. Please. Just tell me.'

'Sorry, but you said it. Hang on a minute.'

We've been going slower and slower and now he pulls over into the entrance to a lane. Oh, shit.

'Been looking for somewhere to stop. This'll have to do.'

He turns off the engine, turns to face me and takes my face in his hands. It gives me goosebumps all over.

'Of course I don't hate you. I wish it didn't have to happen to you. But you've told me why. Your mother dying, your grandfather, your father already gone. It must have been a shock – to move from such a sheltered life into a home. I just wish none of that was true. But it wasn't your fault. You couldn't help being all alone in the world.'

Suddenly I find I'm crying, tears pouring out my eyes as if someone turned on a tap back there without even asking me. And Alfie's undone his seat belt and he's leaning over and hugging me and trying to get his hanky out all at the same time. He mops my face and the hanky smells of malty tobacco and wet dog and Alfie and it makes me cry even more. And I so hate to cry. And I so don't ever do that. What's going on?

'And your grandmother? She couldn't do anything? Couldn't have had you?'

I shake my head. That at least is true. My grandfather would have gone berserk if she'd tried. But my "sheltered" childhood. Don't make me laugh. That makes me feel guilty all over again.

There's a loud croak from behind and a tractor's come up the lane wanting to get by.

'Crikey, better get a move on.' Alfie buckles up and starts the engine and I'm left clutching his hanky and thinking he's the only person I know who would say "crikey" and who uses proper men's handkerchiefs, even if they are grey rather than white.

Once we're back on the road Alfie reaches over and squeezes my hand and we're quiet for a bit. Then he starts talking about other things. I'm really grateful. I can get a grip of myself and it feels like he's saying, okay, that was that and it's no big deal, carry on as before. But at the same time I can almost hear the cogs turning inside his head. There's not much traffic and he's gunning along the straight, thinking about it all. I know he is.

Soon we're in Cornwall and driving along a sort of ridge.

Alfie says, 'See those trees? Compass trees, I call them. You can always tell where south-west is if there's one of those around.'

They're a funny shape but I don't believe him. 'You're pulling my leg.'

'Would I? Prevailing wind. They grow that way because the wind never gives them a chance to do anything else.'

'Aah.' I see what he means. 'It's cool the way they're flat on top, like a table.'

After a while he points up ahead. 'There's the north coast of Cornwall. See where the light changes? That's the sea. Hey, I'm beginning to enjoy driving this monster.'

I just can't get my head around how such a feisty person as Esther, with everything going for her, can carry around such a sense of shame about going to a foster-mother when her mother died. Not her fault. Obviously. Just a rotten deal to lose both parents. Were there really no relations around? A thought that sets off a whole raft of questions about the grandmother. You'd move heaven and earth, wouldn't you? To keep a kid in the family? Surely... That's still all going nowhere, like ants on the brain, when we get to the Port Isaac turning.

'This is where we're stopping for a bite. Think you'll like it.'

We sit on the quay and Esther's eating her first real Cornish pasty.

'They're just the same as Devon ones.'

'Course they are,' I say. 'Just don't let anyone hear you say that.'

I'm curious about Auntie Em. Strikes me the woman must have done a good job.

'Will you tell me about Auntie Em? She must have been pretty good news. Otherwise how come you've turned out so normal?'

'Normal? Am I?'

'Well, what's normal, come to that?'

'Alfie, you're not taking the piss?'

'I wouldn't take the piss, Esther. Well, I would, but not about that. Go on, tell me about this Auntie Em before I get to meet her.'

'Well, she was just a star. A real earth mother I suppose. Like you wouldn't believe. All home-made bread and cakes, finger paints, paddling pool.'

'One up on a home. Sounds more like your…'

'Definitely. The home wasn't bad but she was, like, mine. She was big and colourful and she adored kids. All too good to be true, as it happened.'

'What happened?' So this isn't going to be a happy story.

'Well, it was all right while it lasted, but then I had to leave her. This is what *I* think happened. Which isn't what it said in the records. But I'll come to that later'

Esther chews, swallows, take a deep breath.

'I was twelve, nearly thirteen. I came home from school one day, a Friday it was. I remember I had my period so I rushed straight up to my room to get myself fixed up. Had the shock of my life. My stuff was all packed up. Suitcase on the bed. Carrier bag with all my U2 posters rolled up and stuffed in with Pink Panther. I turn round and crash right into Auntie Em who's steaming up the stairs. She goes on about having meant to catch me in the kitchen, but then the phone went at the wrong moment and she missed me. I mean, what difference would it have made? My stuff was packed up and that was it.

'I shouted at her, what the hell's going on? My Nan was downstairs, she said. Waiting in the front room. That's what was going on. You're going to live with her, she said. She was crying then, and hugging me, and suddenly I felt better about it. Because until that moment I thought Auntie Em had betrayed me. You know, ganged up with that fucking social worker. But I could tell, she was just as shocked as I was. It wasn't something Auntie Em could have done. She didn't collude. And she always talked everything through. Talked it through to death, I used to say. "Just tell me what's what", I used to say. "Shit happens".'

She breaks off and laughs. 'Well, no. I guess I didn't used to say that. Not then. But it's just, I was used to my life being full of shit and Auntie Em never quite believed how much I could cope with. Shit always happens to kids like me. It certainly happened that day.'

I don't know what to say. But, once again, something doesn't quite stack up. Wouldn't she have been pleased to be going to her grandmother? And what's this shit she's talking about? I'm not saying that having both your parents die isn't dreadful, tragic even. But to refer to it as "shit"? I suppose the home made her into the tough little kid I sometimes see in her.

At the same time it's all hitting me in that guilty place somewhere behind the solar plexus where I keep my feelings about Laura. The way Meg and I got it wrong at the last, most important, moment. How, in Laura's eyes, we broke trust with her. Because that's what Esther's telling me, that the trust was the most important thing.

Esther's watching me, unsure. I guess she knows she's lost me.

'So was it all a big mistake? You didn't have to go, did you?'

'It certainly was a big mistake – but not in the sense you mean. And yes, I did have to go. You can't fight the system. Well, Auntie Em did fight, but it didn't do any good. She sat me down on the bed and asked me where I wanted to live. With her of course. I was used to her. Plus there was school. I had mates, and I was doing okay. So then she got on the phone. Told me to listen in on the extension in her bedroom. Fuck knows what my Nan was thinking while all this was going on. But she can't have expected it to be that easy, I guess. I mean, it wasn't going to be like picking up a load of stuff from Tesco's. Except it almost was.'

There's the faintest crack in her voice and she breaks off and she chucks the last of her pasty down the beach to the waiting gulls. Part of me wants to cuddle her up and tell her how much better she is than a load of groceries, but I can't move.

She clears her throat. 'Anyway my so-called effing social worker wasn't available, sneaky bitch. She should have met me from school, lazy cow. Too afraid of a scene, or that I'd run under a bus to get away from her – or that she'd break a finger nail. Anyway Auntie Em got to speak to her supervisor. And she gave her hell. I've always treasured that call. That someone cared about me that much. She really meant it. She wanted me to stay. And then came this awful voice.

Esther pinches her nose and in any other circumstances I'd have laughed at the twang of officialdom she achieves.

'But, Mrs Miller, how can you say it's a shock and surprise? It's

been part of Esther's care plan since she came to you. As soon as the opportunity arose, she was to go to live with her grandmother. And the opportunity has arisen. You have done a wonderful job with a very difficult and needy child, Mrs Miller, but, as an experienced foster-mother, I know you will appreciate the importance of maintaining links with family. The sense of identity...

'Blah, blah, blah-di-blah. Auntie Em went on till she was blue in the face about continuity and the school syllabus and the fact that I could well have walked past my Nan on the street and not recognised her. But the Voice kept on about the care plan and how it was all on file that the usual preparation had been done. What a load of hooey.

'But, trouble was, God knows why, Auntie Em swallowed it. She came back upstairs looking all hurt and asked me why I hadn't told her. Did she really think I'd have gone sneaking off on visits to my Nan without telling her? I told her no, and she said it was okay, she believed me. But I wondered. Daft really, because of course she knew she would have been part of it all if anything had been properly planned. That's what they were supposed to do. Have a case conference with all the people involved, including me. Bloody awful, they used to be. And you knew they kept what they really thought about you until they got out to the car park. But at least you got to know what decisions were being taken about your life.'

'So did they ever explain what had gone wrong?'

Esther rolls her eyes. 'Did they hell. No, I reckon the stupid cow social worker was just as afraid of Auntie Em as she was of me. Thought she'd kick off. Which she might of. Decided the element of surprise was the best way out. She didn't last long, that one. I had a new one when I went to Nan's, and I heard the old one left under a cloud. Suppose that's some consolation.'

'So what happened? Did you go? Then and there?'

She nods. 'Oh yes. I knew when I was beaten. You see, there was one thing the Voice said that made Auntie Em go very quiet. She said that if I stayed, with my...with me growing up, they couldn't let Auntie Em have little kids to foster any more. And Auntie Em just loved the little kids. Couldn't bear it if the house was empty when I went to school.'

'Why wouldn't they let her? Were you getting into trouble?'

'Uh? No. Just getting older. I suppose that was it. Mind you, it made me think, well, if they think that's what I'm going to do, I might just as well do it. So I did give Nan a bit of hassle. It was like, so you think it's that easy, to get a granddaughter? I'll show you.'

Esther shakes her T-shirt to dislodge flakes of pastry.

'What made me mad was the lies that cow told. When I saw my case file...'

I frown. 'Case file?'

'Well, you were allowed. You know, the record of everything that ever happened to you. You had the right of access – when you got to be old enough or when they thought... Oh, I don't remember. But I heard you could, so I went and demanded to see it. I mean, that was a few years later. After I left school.

'So this was written up in there?'

'Oh yes. Everything's in your case file. Anyway, that day at Auntie Em's, the stuff they said. Rubbish. Dunno what that cow was up to, saying how she'd "prepared the ground". Said she'd discussed it all with me. Discussed it with Auntie Em. Encouraged my Nan to visit more often, get to know me better. Taken me to visit her place. I couldn't believe it. Pages of write-ups of visits she was supposed to have made to Auntie Em's. And bits that said: *Met Esther after school and took her for a coffee. Issues and feelings discussed.* She never did, of course. Wouldn't have dared. But that would have been my word against hers. Nobody could check up on it. Cunning.'

'So you really didn't know your Nan? I thought you said you used to visit?'

Esther doesn't miss a beat. 'Oh, that was ages back. I was supposed to remember her from way back then?'

She runs her fingers through her hair, tugging at the ends. As if she wants it to hurt.

'She was supposed to have made a plan with Auntie Em, this Miss Effing-What's-her-face. And it was perfectly clear on that day Auntie Em knew fuck-all about any plan.'

She looks up with an air of finality, as if there's nothing more to say.

I stand up, ready to go. There's a limit to how much I can take of this.

'Fuck it. I'd give anything to go in the sea.'

She looks so forlorn, so I fetch her crutches from the car. 'You can paddle with one foot, but for God's sake don't get the other one wet.'

That was such a sweet thing to do. Alfie stands right close in case I wobble. The water's really cold, but not as cold as the pool on the moor. My other foot is screaming to join in.

Then he spoils it by having another go at getting me to phone Mrs E Miller of Port Boscoe.

But I don't give in. 'Best to just rock up.' Anyway, there's no signal.

It feels weird when we set off again. One foot's tingling and the other's all dry and hot. And I'm *so* nervous. Will she have changed? Will she recognise me? Will she even be the right one?

It's such a small place, Port Boscoe, not big enough to be called a port. Just a sheltered cove with two fishing boats pulled up on the beach. It doesn't take long to find where she lives. There's a tiny shop in the front room of a house on the quay and we go in there to ask. Bay Tree Cottage doesn't mean a thing, but then I say 'Mrs Miller' and that her name is Emma or Emily. Funny I never actually knew what Em was short for. Light dawns on the lady's face.

'Emmylou, you're meaning. Oh yes. Go back up the hill, take the first right. It's narrow, mind. Hers is the last on the right. Yellow gate. You can park. It don't go nowhere else.'

Just as we go out the door she calls us back. 'If she's not in the house, she'll be in the garden, up opposite. In her veg patch.'

The Jeep only just fits down the narrow track. We park between two yellow gates beside a row of runner beans. It reminds me of hot summer days in Rayners Lane, when I would hide in the green tunnel and Auntie Em wouldn't be able to find me. She was pretending, I guess, but I didn't know that then. Anyone, of course, can have a row of runner beans on poles.

Alfie spots her as soon as we get out the car. 'There's someone up there. Is that her? Is it the right one?'

I stare anxiously. It could be but I don't want to make a fool of myself with a stranger. She's got her back to us. A flowing cotton dress in a pattern of rich reds and ochres billows in the wind. Brown legs with thick ankles in sturdy leather sandals straddle a row of carrots as she bends to thin the feathery tops. A frizz of hennaed hair showing grey at the roots is held back with an orange scarf and hooped silver earrings catch the sun. She turns and stands as we approach, shading her eyes with an earthy hand glittering with rings. A weather-beaten, but otherwise familiar face.

She suddenly drops her trowel and comes galloping towards me. I only hope she can stop. It's Auntie Em all right. She wraps me all around in a cloud of sweat and patchouli. Later Alfie tells me I completely vanished when she hugged me.

'Esther, my girl,' she says eventually, standing back and looking me over. 'Skinny as ever, but just as pretty. How on earth…? What on earth…? How did you get here?' She points at my plaster. 'And what the blazes have you done to yourself?'

We're both laughing and crying and falling over ourselves and it's only when I introduce Alfie that a shadow crosses her expression.

As we go past the Jeep she asks, 'Is that thing yours?'

'Is it okay there? No, it belongs to my boss. He lent it…'

'As long as it's not blocking the footpath. Ugly great gas guzzler. Men like that sort of thing.' She glances at Alfie.

'Oh, Alfie hates it. But it was very generous of…'

'Don't have a car myself. There's a bus once a week. And otherwise I can get a lift with my neighbour. Now, let's see about a cup of tea.'

She leads the way through a small garden rampant with roses, hollyhocks and weeds – wild flowers, she calls them. The door opens straight into a kitchen-living room. The sink is stacked with dirty crockery, the table piled with papers. Auntie Em clears chair seats and fills the kettle, talking all the while.

'Fancy you turning up like this. After all these years. And finding me…'

'There's so much to tell you.' I settle into a chair in the corner where I can stretch out my leg.

'After you went nothing was the same. Oh, I know I saw you a few times, but it was always awkward. No, it didn't work, did it?' She reaches for a cake tin and opens it. 'Oh dear, thought I had some biscuits but they seem to have got eaten. Never mind. So where was I? Oh yes. I carried on taking children. I had some lovely little kids. But they were never with me long. They came and went and my heart wasn't in it any more.'

The kettle screams and drops into silence as Emmylou turns out the gas.

'But Auntie Em...'

'Please don't call me that any more. Call me Emmylou. Everybody does.'

'So how come you moved here?'

'Oh, you'll never guess what happened.' She breaks off, hovering the kettle over the three mugs she's set out. 'I had a call one morning. A solicitor – all formal. Anyway, to cut a long story short, my aunt had died. You remember the one I always used to write to? She'd left me this cottage. It seemed like a message.'

She draws breath for long enough to ask if we take sugar and hands out the mugs.

'I mean, I'd lived twenty-five years in Rayners Lane. All my friends had moved away. All the shops changed. You'd never believe, nearly all takeaways now. Every cuisine in the world you care to mention. I used to think, doesn't anyone cook anymore? What was there to keep me there?'

She turns to me. 'So here I am. And here you are. How come?'

'I went to see you. And the people there thought you'd gone to Cornwall.'

'You went to find me...?'

'Yes. I was having a difficult time. I...'

'And I wasn't there. Well, well. And yet you found me in the end.'

'Thanks to the Internet and Alfie.'

All this time Alfie has been minding his own business and sipping his tea, letting us get on with it. Auntie Em's been ignoring him but I suppose that's just because we're catching up.

Now he smiles. 'What's it been like, coming here after Rayners Lane?'

I can't help noticing that she doesn't look at Alfie when she answers.

'It's been wonderful. Such a community. And you know what a gardener I am. Stuff grows like weeds here and I've got so much space. And of course with the Internet I can do all the things I used to do just the same. The campaigning, I mean.'

'So you're still doing that…?'

'Yes, I can still carry on. No problem. What with that and cooking for my neighbour and doing a turn in the shop, there are some days when I hardly get out in the garden for more than half an hour.'

We finish our tea and I get to tell Auntie Em all about Nan and her illness while good old Alfie does a mountain of washing up. I didn't see how anyone could cook supper otherwise and Alfie wouldn't let me stand there that long.

'So you gave up on your degree. But you'll go back and finish? They'll let you I imagine?'

'I want to. But a different course. I haven't asked about that yet, but I'm saving up.'

Alfie looks round at that and raises an eyebrow, like it's news to him. Of course it is. I've decided I want to do a proper degree – like English – and study literature, but I'm too scared to say so. Like maybe he'd laugh, think it was beyond me. The sensible part of me knows he wouldn't and that he'd be a real help. Even so.

Auntie Em doesn't even ask what I want to change to. She's going on about Nan.

'That poor woman! What a God-awful life she led with that monster of a husband of hers.'

My stomach turns to ice and when I slide a glance at Alfie he's raised both eyebrows this time. Omigod-thank-you-very-much, Auntie Em. But I can't say a thing. I'm certainly not letting her know just how not-quite-honest I've been with Alfie.

But Auntie Em's not done yet.

'Mind you, I always thought, I'd never have let any man do that to a daughter of mine, no matter what she'd done. I hope he's rotting in hell and she's on a cloud having a rosy old time.'

'Okay,' says Alfie. But it's not okay. His voice is loud and harsh. And then nothing. He turns back to the sink, pulls the plug and there's a gurgle of escaping water. He squeezes out the old-fashioned mop and bangs it on the draining board to fluff it up. Then he's busy with a dishcloth wiping down. I'm frozen, sitting there as if I'm watching a play. Auntie Em's on hold too, looking baffled. Maybe he's ignoring what's just been said, after all.

But no. He looks around for a towel, dries his hands slowly and deliberately and leans back against the sink, thumbs hooked into his belt.

He gazes steadily across at me. 'So just what sort of cock and bull story about your sainted grandfather and all the rest of your family have you been telling me?'

I can't meet his eye. I can sense Auntie Em ruffling in her chair as she looks from one to the other of us. She can't keep quiet.

'You mean you haven't told him? About that mother of yours? Oh my, the state that baby was in!'

Alfie turns his head so sharply I hear his neck crack. He's frowning at Auntie Em with a look of complete bewilderment.

She speaks to him for the first time. 'I suppose you don't even know I was her foster-mother? How I...'

'That I knew.' Alfie holds up a hand and she splutters into silence. 'Esther?'

He's not ranting. He doesn't even sound angry. I can't gauge his mood. He's being inscrutable. He's teasing me. He's laughing at me. They both are. Auntie Em's certainly not helping. It's like I'm on trial here. The snotty kid caught out in a lie. The wet pants. The missing dinner money in my school bag. The cheese I nicked from the fridge, smelly under my pillow.

This hasn't happened to me in so long that I don't recognise it until it's too late. Like there's a point when there's nothing you can do to stop the milk boiling over. Except this isn't boiling. More deep freeze. It's my dry ice meltdown.

That's what they used to call it in the home. When I kicked off, which was rarely. I never did know whether the dry ice bit was more to do with being a drama queen or the way I went dead white and ended up afterwards in a heap, shivering myself to pieces. That was after I'd done a fair bit of damage.

But this time it's different. When I go to get up, ready to lash out, smash stuff, I can't move. The plaster cast is like an anchor. So I scream. Even I'm scared by the noise I make. Not clean enough to shatter glass, but the walls might come tumbling down.

Auntie Em arrives in a whirlwind of scarves and slaps me right in the face. I suppose she thinks it will calm me down. But it has the opposite effect and I lash out at her. I never connect. Because Alfie's right there. He's pushed Auntie Em aside and he's pinning my arms to my sides and holding me close. He's saying, 'Whoa, whoa there,' like I was a difficult sheep. When my teeth start chattering he stuffs his hanky between them so I won't bite my tongue. It smells of him and it brings me to my senses quicker than anything. That's different too.

There's another thing that's different. Though it takes me a while to admit it. I've been "behaving" according to a formula and deep down I know it. Before, when I was a kid, I really was out of control. This time, I could have stopped at any point, but it was the only way out I could see. Alfie being so gentle makes me feel ashamed.

Auntie Em's chuntering on. 'Just like when she was a kid. I remember she did that a couple of times, soon after she came to me. Then it didn't happen any more.'

Alfie goes 'Hmm.' And then he says, 'Got any brandy? Or Scotch?'

'Can't afford that stuff. But I've got some "Rescue Remedy".'

Typical Auntie Em. She always went for alternative things. She burrows around in a bag, makes me tip back my head and squirts liquid on my tongue from the glass dropper. She was always taking it herself when we were out and she got het up about something. It actually does seem to make me feel calmer. Or maybe that's because Alfie's stroking my hair and all the anger seems to have gone out of him. I mutter into his shirt something about being sorry and he says not to worry, that we'll talk about it all tomorrow when I'm feeling better. I doze off a bit because that's the easy thing to do, while Auntie Em starts "rattling a skillet" as she always used to say when she started cooking.

Dinner is a heap of pasta with a red-hot tomato sauce which

was always Auntie Em's standby and a favourite of mine. There's a huge green salad full of rocket and herbs, all from the garden. The kitchen may be a tip, but she hasn't lost her touch. I start off thinking I can't eat a thing. But the spicy sauce warms me up. It's really comforting. Auntie Em's rabbiting on about green living, her latest campaign causes. Alfie hardly says anything. He doesn't need to. I let it all wash over me.

As soon as we've finished Alfie gets up and pats his pocket.

'You okay if I pop out for a spell?'

I nod and he says he'll leave us "girls" to talk. The last thing I want to do with Auntie Em just now.

As soon as he's gone she says, 'Well, what was all that about, young lady?'

'I don't want to talk about it. Anyway, pretty obvious, isn't it?'

'I'd have thought you'd have grown out of all that by now.' She tut-tuts. 'Kicking off like that.'

I say nothing. What is there to say?

'What sort of friend is this Alfie, anyway? He's not just the driver, is he?'

'Oh no. We're together. An item.'

'What does he do?'

'He's a painter. And just now he's...'

'Bit old for you, isn't he?'

'Auntie Em, that is none...'

'Emmylou. Please. No. You're right. It's none of my business. But it seems you don't trust him...'

'Of course I trust him. It's just that...'

'Not enough to come straight with him. And now of course, he doesn't trust you.'

Talk about stating the obvious. I'm not getting into that one.

She looks at me and sighs when I don't respond. 'At least it makes the sleeping arrangements easier. There's just the one spare room and it's got a double bed.'

She pauses and looks back at me. 'You said you came looking for me? In Rayners Lane. What was that about then?'

'I was in trouble. Thinking about having a termination. Wanted to talk it through with someone I could trust. But...'

Auntie Em's leaning forward, glaring at me. 'An abortion? You were going to have an abortion?' She looks like she'd happily throttle me.

I nod. 'That's right. I wasn't...'

'You litle murderous...' She breaks off. 'But did you? Did you go ahead?'

I shake my head. There's no point in going through all the stuff she's about to throw at me if I own up.

'And the baby? What about the baby?' She looks round wildly, as if I've been concealing a child in my bag.

'Miscarried,' I say.

'But you wouldn't have...?' She's still glaring.

'I guess not.'

She still carries on about the wickedness of abortion, all the things I know so well. As if I hadn't thought it through. I close my ears to it all until I realise she's asking me a question.

'Was it his?'

It takes me a while to realise what she means. 'No, it wasn't Alfie's. I had a boyfriend in London. At uni. It was his.'

She jerks her head towards the door. 'He's not from round here is he?'

'Alfie? No,' I say. 'Why?'

'Oh, no matter. He just seemed vaguely familiar. Thought I might have seen him somewhere.'

'Why don't you ask him?'

'Oh, no, no. He's got enough on his mind. Now, I'll just go up and clear the junk off your bed. It gets full of my clutter up there.'

I'm left staring at the dark window. It's all a mess. And not how I imagined meeting up with Auntie Em. She was supposed to be impressed with how well I'd done. I even thought I might come and live with her for a bit. Huh! That's a laugh. But right now all I care about is what Alfie's thinking.

The coastal path is only a few yards from Emmylou's garden gate. I check I've got tobacco and turn right towards the village. Cloud is covering the moon and all I can see is the pale snake of the shaley track. Bracken brushes against my legs and brambles snag my jersey. By the time I reach the cove my eyes have adjusted, and I walk out across the rocks to a ledge where I can lean and light up and feel alone.

My head throbs as if it's still dealing with the God-awful noise Esther made. Like an angle grinder in the hands of a madman. Now I know what it means to jump out of your skin. What the hell was going on there? Why not just say, okay there are a few things I didn't tell you. Apologise. Put the record straight. Why such a big deal?

Seems I was right about the grandfather. Esther's been lying through her teeth. Cats leaping out of bags all over the shop. What did he do to the daughter? And what had the daughter done to deserve it? Mysteries every which way. There's going to be a lot of explaining to do when we finally make our escape.

Jesus, can that woman talk. And when it comes to hobby horses and soapboxes she's in a league of her own. I'm pleased for Esther that we've found her. Not the most auspicious reunion, mind you. Maybe it was seeing her Auntie Em set her off. Turned back the emotional clock or some such. Who knows? But dear God, I hope we can leave in the morning. Could have done with a stiff drink to help things along, especially after that little drama, but not even a bottle of wine in sight. And what the Dickens is "Rescue Remedy"?

It's peaceful out here. And quiet. The squat houses of the original fishing community in their fresh white paint loom above me. They face inland, away from the sea, damp probably in winter, but that won't bother the incomers who have done them up for summer living. Don't suppose Emmylou's fazed by a bit of damp.

Looking across the bay it's difficult to tell where the cliff overhang ends and the inky water begins. Only an oily rocking of the tide marks the boundary. Not a breath of wind, the black ocean lapping the dark land. Washing away all those words. All that passionate intensity.

I don't know what to think about Esther. How can I trust the girl? To have got to where we have, and to find we're on shifting sand – it makes me wonder. What else hasn't she told me? Will she ever be straight with me? Does she really care about us, me?

Just how unstable is she? It takes the edge off the fun of coming away with her. She was so excited, being in the car, seeing places. Thought she'd burst into "Yellow Submarine" at any moment, but then I realised I was thinking of Laura. Still no contact there. I relight my pipe to distract myself from the sharp pain that still gives me, wonder what she's doing, how she's coping.

Esther's easy to be with. When she calms down. And she does care about people. Doesn't she? The way she looks at Emmylou, listens to her, insisted on cleaning up her damned kitchen.

There comes the whisper of a mini-wave from the beach, followed by the faint throb of an engine. The noise grows steadily and the shapes of two fishing boats round the headland, dark against the dying light. The tide must have turned – they'd be coming in on the flood. The engines cut as they approach the beach. Traditional boats, with a pretty curve running aft from a high prow, Padstow registered, both in need of a lick of paint. One's blue, the other green, with a name I can't read painted on the bow. The two fishermen jump out into the shallows and one strides up the beach, turns on a floodlight and comes back dragging stuff behind him.

Esther would love to see this. She must still be listening to that Emmylou carrying on. I bet that woman's giving her the third degree. Getting the low-down on me, no doubt.

The men set about a well-rehearsed routine of rolling the boats up the beach with the help of a pulley. As far as I can see, each boat has a loose framework made of poles and chains to act as a kind of flat cradle. Their great-grandfathers probably did the same thing a century ago, but without the floodlight. They work as a team hardly exchanging a word. First one vessel, then the other. As soon as the boats are beached and secure, each skipper leaps back aboard, busy sorting the catch, cleaning the deck, tidying up. Their yellow oilskins catch the light as the dusk deepens around them.

I'd pop into the pub if there was one. Bet there were several once upon a time, judging by the size of the church huddling in the valley. That's where the locals are living now – in the ugly new bungalows we passed on the way in, strung out along the only road. Away from the weather, double-glazed, modern, convenient.

Chimes from the church clock shudder through the darkness. I count ten. Better go back. At least it's late enough to go to bed. As I pass, I nod to the fishermen who are now stowing their catch in a battered white van parked on the edge of the beach.

15

When I wake up in the morning Alfie's sitting on the window seat reading something. As soon as I move he slips a sheet of paper into one of the boxes beside him.

'What's that?'

'Oh, nothing. Lovely morning.'

'What d'you mean? Nothing? Tell me.'

'Just Emmylou's campaign stuff, I guess.'

It's only when I hear her name that I remember what happened last night. Shit. I made a prize idiot of myself.

'Fuck, Alfie, I'm surprised you're still here. You must think I'm a total psycho.'

'Not really. Emmylou got on to me last night – when I came back in. Wanting to know whether you did that stuff often.'

'And you said…?'

'What do you think? Christ, I wouldn't be around if it happened every day, I can tell you. But she was worried. Obviously. I put her mind at rest.'

'Thanks. God, she gave me such an ear-bashing about abortion last night when you went out.'

'How come?'

'I made the mistake of telling her why I went looking for her at her old house.'

'Why did you? Don't think you ever said.'

'Wanted someone to talk to – to talk through about having an abortion. I just wanted to be clear. Jesus, did she lay into me.

Lucky she wasn't there that day, she'd probably have locked me up to stop me. Can't say I really want to see her this morning...'

'Take no notice. She obviously gets bees in her bonnet.'

'Sure does. Like green energy. She was a Green before they were a party. Always said she was ahead of her time. Before that it was Greenham Common. She always had a cause. What was it last night at dinner? I wasn't really listening. Was it harnessing the tide she was on about?'

Alfie rolls his eyes and lowers his voice. 'And plastic bags and supermarket packaging and labels on individual apples and making fuel from chip fat and electric cars and wind farms and solar panels and composting toilets and recycling bathwater and – anything I forgot?'

I'm giggling by the time he finally draws breath. 'She always was a bit OTT. I mean, she's right of course, but...'

'I'm surprised she didn't ask me to go pee on her compost heap.'

'She would of, if you'd hung around.'

'I needed a bit of quiet, after...'

I nod.

'Hmm. Talking of which... When do I get to find out who you really are?'

He says it so quietly. No ranting, no accusations. What have I done to deserve this guy?

'Not here. I can't talk about it here.'

When I come back from the bathroom, he's gone. I get dressed and pack my bag and look out at the bay and the rocks and the endless sea beyond. So much of it, so deep, all the way to the horizon and on and on all the way round the world and back again. It makes me feel tiny. Me and my pathetic stories and my stupid idea that I could leave the past behind.

As I turn away I spot the paper he was reading. A Pro-Life flyer. Stuff about abortion I guess. I pick it up, look underneath. Fuck me, the whole box is full of Pro-Life paperwork. Publicity, minutes of meetings, agendas, e-mail printouts and newspaper cuttings.

I make my way downstairs looking for Alfie. No sign of Auntie

Em. Alfie's leaning on the far gate staring into the runner beans.

'She's already gone out. There was a note propped against the kettle. Said she'd forgotten a meeting. I left it there.'

'How odd. Not to say goodbye.'

I write a goodbye note on the back, remembering to call her Emmylou.

As soon as we're out of the village Alfie pulls off the road.

'Right. Spit it out. I'm not going anywhere until you tell me. And I want the truth, the whole damn truth and nothing but the truth.' He looks across at me. 'And before you say it, I don't hate you, but I do need to know where I stand. Where *we* stand. In my book, if you have something going with someone – like I thought we had – that's built on trust. No dark secrets. You are who you are. And if that's not how you do relationships, then it's no good for me. It can't go on. So tell me.'

If only he knew how much I want to do relationships that way. Specially this one. 'Oh, Alfie, I just wanted to be someone else. I'm sorry, I really am. And then yesterday, when she said that stuff, I felt cornered. Like a kid all over again.'

'Never mind about that. Just tell me.'

'She dropped me right in it. Good old Auntie Em. Not that I blame her. Oh, fuckin'ell Alfie, what a mess. Where do I begin?'

'Your grandfather? Didn't sound like the sweet old gentleman you made him out to be.' His voice is very level, as if he's got the words on a short lead.

'No, there was no sweet old gent. I never met him of course. No visits with Auntie Em either. Sorry Alfie, I made all that stuff up.'

'Stop apologising, will you. Just give me the facts.'

I grip my thumbs to stop myself shaking and take a deep breath. 'My grandfather was a total bastard as far as I can make out. A teetotal Methodist bastard who wouldn't even let Nan go to Mass. I think I told you she was a Roman Catholic? Nan didn't like talking about him, but I did gather he used to knock her about. Said he was beating the evil out of her – just because she liked a drink occasionally.'

'So what did he do to your mother? And what did *she* do, come to that?'

'She got pregnant when she was only fifteen. Still at school, big disgrace. And this precious Christian father of hers chucked her out the house – as in, put his own daughter on the street – and wouldn't let her "darken his threshold" ever again. I didn't know people really said that stuff. But he did, according to Nan.'

'Good God. Very Dickensian.'

'Which is why I never met him. He wouldn't let me in the house either. Pretended I didn't exist. Which is the real reason I never went to live with Nan sooner.'

'So not because he was disabled?'

'Disabled? Oh that! He wasn't disabled, there was no ladder. I invented that. It was all I could think of.'

'Why Esther? Why? Why all these lies? What is it about me that you couldn't tell me the truth? Christ Almighty.'

Abruptly he starts the engine and we drive on in silence.

I'd planned to splash out. Give her a treat, a surprise. Stay in a hotel, show her St Ives. But the whole thing's turned a bit sour. To say the least. She's told me the truth now. At least I think she has. There's the rub. How do I tell? How will I ever know? We've both gone into our shells. Both hurting and we both know it. Looks like neither of us can see a way out. I certainly can't. Can't see a way back to what we had. Or what I thought we had.

In the end we checked into a B&B just down the road in a one-horse town with no decent restaurant. I got indigestion from eating greasy fish and chips and had an awful night in a lumpy bed. I must have gone deeply asleep around six and now I've been woken by a load of seagulls cackling on the roof.

I slide from the bed and leave Esther sleeping. There's a pale wash of a morning moon as I step out and the cold is fresh and damp on my face. People are on their way to work, bending against the wind. One woman reaches after an umbrella that turns inside out as if it will fly her to that ghost of a moon.

I climb out of town into the dark tunnel of an inky sky, its arc framed by a complete rainbow. I wish Esther could see it. Seconds later I'm regretting the impulse to walk. The deluge is blinding, my eyelashes washing my cheeks as I blink away water. Sight gives way to sensation: needles on the skin; the trickle of the drip that always finds its way past collar and hood; the flat slap of trousers plastered to legs; the cold basting of puddles lobbed for good measure by passing cars.

But it's better than tossing and turning in that damn bed. Esther can sleep anywhere. She'd hardly moved, neat and vulnerable. I made such a big deal about her lies, but she wouldn't defend herself, just shrugged when I kept asking why. I never even got round to asking how her mother coped. I guess it was a bit of a shock to the tearaway boyfriend, but I suppose he must have found them somewhere to live and looked after her. Before he went and wrapped himself round a tree, that is.

I'm so wet there's no point in turning back. On the brow of the hill I come out on the other side of the tunnel, leaving the darkness and the houses behind. A blur of far hills appears behind the skeletons of crone-like trees and the sky is once more a source of light.

I grope in my pocket as I feel my phone vibrate. A text from Esther. 'Where r u?'

I text back, 'Lets get out of there soonest. Be back in ten.'

She's packed up and dressed by the time I get back and check out.

We're in the Jeep before she notices the state of me.

'Crumbs Alfie, you're soaking. Why didn't you change.'

'Couldn't stand that place a moment longer. Certainly didn't fancy their breakfast.'

She doesn't say anything. Disappointed, maybe – or just wary. We're circling round each other. I decide we'll head for St Ives after all. At least we can have a decent lunch and still get back to Cadstone by evening. On the main road I spot a breakfast van just in time and screech into the lay-by. I change my shirt, the sun comes out and bacon butties never tasted better. Life begins to look up.

'About the lying, Alfie,' she begins when we set off again. 'It's partly because I'm ashamed…'

'Ashamed? What's to be ashamed of? Your mother did a good job in spite of everything. I was going to ask – how did she cope? You know after she was…'

163

'I'll come to that. But I do feel ashamed. It's how people react. They either don't want to know. Or – and this is much worse – they feel sorry for me, want to look after me. So I stopped telling the truth. As I said, it got to be a habit.'

'That I understand. But I still don't see...'

'Before you go on. I need to tell you. Carole never did look after me.'

What's she going on about now? 'Carole? Who's Carole? I thought you were going to tell me about your mother.'

'Well, it's not like I told you. I never knew my mother. Not in the way people mean. I didn't even call her my mother. I called her Carole. I knew who she was, and I knew she'd looked after me from time to time when I was little.' Esther buzzes her window all the way down and halfway up again. 'Even that's not right. I lived with her, on and off. But she didn't look after me. That was the problem. She hadn't a clue. She didn't know how to look after herself, let alone a baby.'

More fiddling with the damn window.

'I was watching some ponies the other day. A mother and a little foal. Such a pretty one, honey colour. She was so protective when a car came down the road. You see, *they* can do it. But she couldn't.'

'But I thought... You said... That was her in that photo you showed me?'

'Huh. No it wasn't. That was one of the housemothers at the children's home.'

'That figures.' At least that accounts for the hair and the eyes. I've been assuming that some of her story has to be true, but I'm now beginning to wonder.

'And your father? The Tom Cruise lookalike? He looked after her when your grandfather chucked her out? Found somewhere for them to live?'

'You must be joking. He didn't exist. I haven't got a father.'

'You haven't got a father? How...?'

'Not even a putative one. That's why there was no photo.'

'Putative?' I'm trying to work it out but my Latin isn't up to it.

'It's what they call the father when it's not certain. And the only thing that was certain was that Carole didn't know. Or wouldn't say. I guess you don't have those any more, what with DNA testing.'

'So which do you think it was? Didn't know or wouldn't say?'

'Didn't know. I mean, why would she keep it secret? To protect someone? Him or herself or me. An alien concept. She was totally incapable of protecting anyone.'

We come up behind a lorry and I'm glad to drop back, slow down. 'Must be strange. Not to know.'

She shrugs. 'You get used to it.'

'Did you ever try to find out?'

'I thought about it, but there was absolutely nothing to go on. I think she used to just get paralytic and go with anyone. Probably several at once for all I know. Or care.'

Her voice says she does care and I change the subject, trying to find a way into the bleak landscape she's outlining.

'So how old were you when...?'

'Six, seven weeks when I first went into care. NAI. Non-accidental injury.'

I must have looked a bit blank.

'That's what they call it when your parents knock you about. Looking back I can see I was lucky. I could have been a Baby P. I mean, I could have died. Neglected by her and knocked about by her bloke, whichever one it happened to be. But someone in casualty spotted the signs, took action. They took out a "Place of Safety".'

'A what? What's that?' I can hear her trying to make light of it all. Dear God. I keep thinking of Laura's childhood, running wild in Italy, adored by all the adults around her.

'Oh, it's some order they have to get. When it's an emergency. So they don't have to wait to go to court. I went to Auntie Em. She was my place of safety – in more ways than one.' She's suddenly silent and her jaw is clenched. When she speaks again, the bravado's gone out of her voice.

'Every now and then there'd be a new social worker and she'd have the wool pulled over her eyes by Carole and I'd go home on trial. Home! That's what they called it. What a joke. It's all there in the notes. And then I'd either end up in A&E or the social worker would find me yelling in a filthy cot, with my mother out cold and syringes all over the shop.'

'So if you went to Auntie Em, how come the children's home?'

'She was often full. And anyway, when it came to be long-term she wasn't allowed. She was supposed to be short-term and so…'

'But that's terrible. If you knew her…'

Esther shrugs. 'It's how it was. They weren't exactly queuing up to foster kids like me. But eventually – you know, after she'd had me a few times – she made a fuss and in the end she got approved and I went there permanently. They did their best really. I was lucky. Some kids were much worse off.'

'If you say so. But I find it difficult to imagine.' I reach across and give her hand a squeeze.

'So now do you see why I told lies? Imagine, Alfie, you're a kid at school. In the playground. I mean, who wants to tell their friends, my mum's on the game? Oh and by the way, she's a smack addict.'

'I guess there's no answer to that one. Except you're not in the playground anymore.'

She shrugs. 'I'm doing my best.'

'So, your mother, when did she actually die? I mean, is she…?'

'Yeah, she's dead. I was fifteen. But I'm not talking about that now. Please, Alfie.'

'Okay. But another time? Promise?'

She nods and next time I look across she's fast asleep. Christ! No wonder she reinvented her childhood. I feel bad about banging on about lies and trust, but how was I to know? I don't suppose I've heard the half of it.

It's after a bottle of wine in a shiny restaurant in St Ives that the tears come. Once I'd have been embarrassed, but now I don't care anymore. I just cuddle her and stroke her hair. She's weeping for them all, I guess. For the mother she never had, for her dead Nan and for Auntie Em – who promised well but must surely be a disappointment. Going on about abortion, and then buggering off like that. When we move outside to the sea wall to sit in the sun I find my eyes are wet too. Not just for Esther, but for Meg and for Laura.

'What a right pair we are,' she says.

We share a handkerchief and swing our legs over the wall. Esther has to lift the heavy cast. Why is that so funny? We both double over at the same moment, tears turning to laughter, helpless. We cling together, mop our faces, subside into silence.

Esther is first to break it. 'Auntie Em,' she says. 'You know, that person who's turned into Emmylou?'

'Ah. I was wondering what you…'

'Bit of an anticlimax. I mean, it was good to see her. But she's moved on, got another life. They say you should never go back.'

The difference, I suppose, between a real mother and a foster-mother, or an Emmylou at least.

'Anyway, Auntie Em always used to say you should have a safe place. Someone, something in your life you can hang on to. That would always be there, come what may, even if you only go there in your head.' Esther flaps her hand in front of her face as the tears threaten again. 'And of course Auntie Em was mine – I told you that. "Place of Safety", remember?' She gives a half smile. 'Then for a while it was Nan. But when she died… That was why I needed to find Auntie Em.'

'Now you feel as if you've lost your safe place.' This doesn't surprise me. I feel selfish for having a moment of panic. Half my motivation for this trip was to find someone who'd be there for her. So it wouldn't just be me. 'What about Luke? Was he ever…?'

'No!' Suddenly such passion. 'He was never… Could never…' She pauses. 'Do you know? I never thought of that. But as soon as you said it I knew he never was. Bex – she was my flatmate at uni, so she saw quite a bit of Luke – Bex used to say he wanted me in a cage. That wasn't quite it. Not that bad. Just like people clip the wings of their hens so they can't fly off and lay their eggs some place else.'

'I hope I don't clip your wings.'

She laughed. 'No way! How could you think that?'

I think of Meg and what Connie said about Meg taking up all the space. 'It can happen without anyone noticing.'

She looks at me, the laughter falling off her face, draws breath but looks away, out to sea. I don't want to pursue it. I don't want to talk about Meg. Just thinking about what Connie said feels more of a betrayal than being with Esther.

'You don't clip my wings, Alfie. You show me how to fly.'

For a moment that sounds such a cliché I think she's trying to make me feel better, but she's not smiling and her eyes are alight, greener than the sea.

'What about when I paint you? Sometimes people feel trapped, like I've set them there forever.'

She shakes her head violently. 'No, it's not like that at all. Every time you paint me, you paint something different, you see. Another me. It's exciting. Scary though.'

I know what's going to come next. It doesn't come immediately. Not until we're on the way home.

'Alfie? Alfie, can I ask you something? Will you be my safe place?'

At one level I want to say yes, of course. But at another, deeper and probably more important, level I'm so damned frightened of the commitment. I'm ashamed of the fear. I want to care for this beautiful, tough, fragile flower that is Esther. But a warning voice is telling me that I ignore the fear at my peril. Or her peril, more like. Because I won't be able to follow through. I'll be like Luke, or Emmylou. Weak, selfish, call it what you like, but needing to live my own life. I'll let her down.

Esther speaks into my hesitation. 'I know it's not easy. Not for me, neither. I've never asked anyone before, you see. I always just kind of borrowed that person's safeness without asking. And I was thinking, maybe that's where I went wrong. So this time I thought I'd ask you first?'

I glance across at her. 'You choose your moments, I have to say. Here I am driving this tank through the narrowest lanes possible, and you come up with what seems like a life-changing question.'

'Don't think it has to be life-changing for you, Alfie. Though it would be for me. I'm not asking you to marry me! I just want to borrow your safeness when I need it.'

'Okay, I understand that...'

'And – if I'm honest – I suppose I'm asking for you to be there for me when things get tough.'

Exactly. Well, at least she's being upfront about it. What can

I say? What can I say other than what's on my mind.

'Esther, I actually feel really honoured. And I wish I could say yes entirely without any reservation whatsoever. I care about you, I really do. I want to… But what if I let you down? For a start, what if I go to prison? And if I don't get sent down, I might want to up sticks and take off to – Australia or somewhere.'

This is so goddam unlikely that I feel ashamed as soon as it's out of my mouth.

There comes a giggle from beside me as I brake hard and back up for an oncoming tractor.

'I'm not stupid. I know all that. You can be a long-distance place. I don't have to, like, *sit* on you.'

At least she's not saying she'll come with me. At least she's still got her sense of humour. Maybe I'm overreacting, over cautious.

I laugh but I'm still wary. 'And the other thing – which I have mentioned once or twice before – what about when I die? Seeing as I am, after all, twice your age?'

'Oh, Alfie! Give me some credit. Don't you think I might have done some growing up by then? It's not as if you're going to pop off tomorrow.'

I grunt and swallow the impulse to tell her that if she's going to issue an invitation, then she should let a person decline. It feels like there's only one acceptable answer to this question of hers. In that respect she reminds so much of Meg. I hear Meg's "We-need-to-talk" voice. *I want to live as long as I can, Alfie. But if I can't work, and if I can't talk to you and Laura and if I can't feed myself and if I get incontinent… Then I won't be capable of taking my own life.* It was the first time she mentioned it. I was shocked to the core. But she didn't let up. *I need to know how much you'd be prepared to help. Would you be willing to give me the drugs? Think about it. But I need to know. If you can't, I quite understand. But in that case I'd need to make plans to do it myself, and sooner rather than later.*

I never could see that there was more than one answer to a question like that. Yet I always maintained and I still believe that Meg was not manipulative. She always gave you a clear choice. To which there was only one possible answer. To Esther I say, 'Seems like you'll probably use what you call my safeness whatever I say...'

'That's not fair. After I take the trouble to ask you.'

'What can I say? Be my guest, but just don't blame me if my safe place turns out to have a leaky roof.'

I feel worn out by all this. I just don't want to talk any more. 'How about some music?' I'd brought a clutch of CDs from the barn, some Mozart, Bach, Dylan, Eric Clapton – just the discs on top of the pile, grabbed as an afterthought as I headed out the door. Without looking I pick one from the door pocket and push it into the slot. It turns out to be Puccini arias. The sound system's superb and it fills the vehicle and my head.

At the end I take a look at Esther to see if she liked it and the tears are streaming down her face. My heart sinks. I think it's about her Auntie Em again. I pull over onto the verge.

'That was so beautiful,' she says. 'That music, what is it?'

When I tell her she says, 'You never play your music when I'm round your place. Not since that first time. That was Puccini too.'

I'm amazed. She remembers. She likes it.

'I wish you would. Play it, I mean. What was he saying? What's "Me key armo?" It gave me goose bumps.'

'"Mi chiamo"? It means, my name is... He's fallen in love, he's remembering how she told him her name. Manon...'

'Is that all? Sounds a lot better in Italian. Come here.' She grips my arm, pulls me to her and kisses me.

'Christ, Esther.' It wasn't just any old kiss. I want her so badly, but we're up on the open moor. No cover at all.

'In the back, Alfie. Now.'

'But your plaster... And the road. Someone might...'

'Yeah, it's Piccadilly, right? We can manage. But put the music on again. I want to make love to that music. Just that last track.'

I fiddle with the CD player. 'I'll have to call you Manon.'

'I don't think so. No, don't fancy that. Sounds too much like Marion. I'll stick with Esther.'

I whip off my jeans. It's a bit of a struggle to work out whose legs go where and we end up laughing, which is no help whatsoever. But Esther's urgency cuts through all that. We both have it now – that frantic need. The musky smell of her is driving me wild and

I'm hard as a hammer. She cries out as I slide into her wetness, and we're locked into one another, locked into a rhythm which joins with the music and sets the whole Jeep rocking. When we drive on there's one thing I'm sure of: *Manon Lescaut* will never be the same again.

16

The weather shifts around again. It's cold and dismal by the time we get back to Cadstone and the barn. It must have rained a lot. I empty the bucket under the leaky roof, make a pot of coffee and set it on the table between us. It reminds me of the first time she came here. How differently I see Esther now. So much water, so many bridges.

Her face is pinched and pale, the happy, sexy mood eclipsed.

'Here, get yourself warmed up. It's been a bit of a roller coaster, I guess.'

The ends of her fingers are white as she wraps them round the mug.

'It's just stirring up all that shit. You've been a star and then there was Puccini and – everything, but… Yeah, it gets to me.'

'I don't know how the hell you deal with stuff like that.'

She takes a spoonful of demerara and holds it against the rim of her mug allowing the coffee to seep in, just enough to darken the sugar. She puts the spoon in her mouth and sucks on it before continuing. I notice that this habit of hers doesn't annoy me any more.

'I used to have a way to deal with it. There was this shrink I used to see at the Child Guidance Clinic. Doctor Mo, she was called. She taught me to use different names for myself for the different times in my life. The early bit, I used to call that Some Baby. Like it wasn't really me. Then Doctor Mo said I should look after Some Baby. So I put her in a shed at the bottom of the garden. This is all in my head of course.'

She breaks off, staring away. 'Hey, Alfie, you won't tell anyone?'

'Of course not.' Who the hell would I tell anyway?

'Anyway, after that, whenever I remembered something horrible it would go in the shed. And Doctor Mo, she'd help me go in the shed and unwrap the things and look at them and wrap them up again – until they weren't that scary any more. And one day I said "Baby Esther" instead of "Some Baby" and she said that was a breakthrough. Like I'd let her be me, I'd owned her.'

I make encouraging noises, pour myself some coffee.

'I stopped seeing her then. But it wasn't like you got it, had a breakthrough, and then you could always cope. Stuff kept happening.'

'What sort of stuff?'

She hesitates. 'Well, when I went to live with my Nan... She was a Roman Catholic, right?' She looks at me, frowning. 'Promise you won't tell anyone?'

'Promise.'

'And you won't laugh?'

I shake my head. I doubt I'll want to laugh. Cry seems more likely.

'Nan took me to Mass on Easter Friday. Which is a big occasion. And the kids were taken off at one end to do some kind of play-acting, well not play-acting, but hands-on stuff. So the little ones would understand what it was all about. And they'd made a crown of thorns. Someone had just done it with wire, barbed wire.'

Her voice goes hoarse and she pauses. 'They'd painted it green. Well, they passed it round. So you could feel it. Like it would hurt. You know, if you had it on your head. And I totally freaked. Just started screaming. And Nan was called out. And then I fainted. And she had to take me home. And no-one could figure out what got into me. Nor me, neither.'

'That must have been...' I have a flash of Esther on that day we went swimming, staring at those strands of barbed wire like a horse about to bolt.

'You're thinking of me with that fence that time. Yeah? Exactly. Like I bet you thought that was a bit freaky.'

I had thought it was weird, but I just nod. 'Yeah, I remember. You didn't like it. The barbed wire. Did you ever...?'

'Years later I found out. When I read my case file.' She swallows more coffee and wipes her mouth with the back of her hand. 'Oh, fuck, Alfie. I half wished I hadn't. If it hadn't had my name on the front, I'd have thought it was someone else's life.'

I steel myself and wish I'd poured drinks instead of coffee.

'It was all typed up on this thin yellow paper with the typewriter making little holes in the tissue at every full stop.'

A pause while she pokes in the air at an imaginary key with her index finger. I picture a teenage Esther hunched up over this file in some grubby little office.

'You could fall through those holes. I remember thinking that. I certainly fell through some hole. It wasn't my story I was reading.'

She covers her face with her hands and I think she's going to cry again.

'They should be more careful, how it's done. There I was, on my own in this room with these piles of papers, trying to cope with what it said. Okay, some of that was just down to the language they use. But then I really started to pay attention. I found out all sorts of stuff no one ever told me about Carole. But that's another story.'

She gulps at her coffee as if it will give her strength.

'One of the things it said was this. When they busted the flat one time looking for my Mum's boyfriend – he was a dealer – they found this baby chair. I'd been taken into care again – the day before, I think. From the clinic. It's a miracle Carole ever got me to a clinic, but I wasn't feeding and was losing weight and the health visitor got on to social services. Anyway there was this baby chair they found at the flat. It had barbed wire fixed to it instead of a baby harness.' She takes a deep breath. 'Then they understood the marks I had on my arms and legs. They'd known they weren't cigarette burns but they hadn't been able work it out.' She stops abruptly and sucks at her mug.

I'm dumbfounded. I can't believe what I've just heard. That there are people in the world who... It doesn't bear thinking about. And she's so deadpan, like it's nothing.

'Hell. Hope you're still talking to me?'

'Why wouldn't I be?'

'You might not want to know me any more. And you didn't say anything.'

'Just stuck for... I mean. Jesus. I don't know what to say. How the hell can anyone ever do that to a little kid?'

She breathes out as if she's been holding her breath. 'So of course it wasn't rocket science to realise why the crown of thorns in the church that time freaked me out. And I'd never had to climb a fence of the stuff. Not before that day we went swimming. So you see...'

The cool manner collapses into shaking shoulders. I scoop her up, half carrying her to the sofa where I cuddle her against me and stroke her hair. After a bit she breaks free and runs into the kitchen. She tears off a length of kitchen paper, blows her nose fiercely and stamps her feet several times as she throws the paper in the bin. She walks slowly back, placing her feet very deliberately as if completing some ritual.

'Sorry about that.'

I start to say it doesn't matter but she interrupts. 'I *hate* to cry. And I keep doing it today.'

I think she'll stay distant, but she sits right back down and leans against me. I just hold her tight to my side. It's all I can think to do. I can't even frame the questions in my mind and I keep thinking of Laura, of what a sheltered childhood she had. I try to imagine what it must be like to rely on a case file to piece together your life. But I can't get past what it would be like to have a case file, full stop.

'You'd think, if you didn't remember something like that, it wouldn't affect you. But Dr Mo used to say that your body remembers. "Cell memory", she called it. Which is weird, isn't it? But it explains a lot.'

'Suppose it does. Blimey, what a God-awful story. I think you need a drink. Purely medicinal.'

I pour her a slug of Black Label and cut it with a splash of water. She shudders and chokes a bit, but at least it gives her a bit of colour. She'd gone quite ashen.

'You think it was that bad?'

'Well, of course I do.'

She goes quiet for a moment or two, sipping from the glass. 'You see, I always kind of thought it was pretty normal. I'd been moved about a lot. Backwards and forwards to Carole's in the early days, children's home, Auntie Em. I guess I thought it was business as usual. Having you react like that... Well, it tells me I had something to cope with... Yeah, maybe I'm not as hopeless as I sometimes think I am.'

'You're about the least hopeless person I know.' As I say it I realise I really mean it.

She rolls her eyes at me, but snuggles closer. 'You're a star, Alfie. It may sound daft, but sometimes, you know, I feel as if I'm not really here? Telling you all that stuff, knowing you know and you haven't walked away – well not yet, anyway. It helps, kind of. Makes me exist. Does that make me a total headcase?'

'Why would that make you a headcase? You can't help what life threw at you. I tell you what, you look really whacked. Why don't you just lie right there and have a nap?'

She stretches and yawns. 'Wonderful.'

'What time d'you have to be at the pub?'

'Not till six.'

'I've got to see to the sheep, check in with Tom and so on. But I'll come back and wake you.'

She doesn't say another word, just reaches out her glass for me to take and curls up like a kitten as I lay a rug over her. I drain the whisky she's left, refill the glass and take it out onto the doorstep.

I feel knocked out, as if someone's been hitting me over and over and only just stopped. As if something momentous has happened that's nothing directly to do with Esther's story. I'm clear about one thing. I need to get in touch with Laura. What the hell am I doing accepting her refusal to speak to me? She's out there somewhere, she's hurting and feeling abandoned and it's up to me to do something about it. What a bloody waste if I don't.

I'm distracted by a great twittering in the hawthorns behind the barn. They're home to a whole bird book of finches and warblers, as well as blackbirds, thrushes and wrens. As if to emphasis my thoughts of Laura, a family of pheasants emerges. The brown hen leads two youngsters with the colourful cock bringing up the rear. I watch them processing in single file along the bank to the bottom of the field.

But there's something else going on in my mind which isn't so obvious. I need to figure it out. It's a phrase Esther used. *It makes me exist.* That's what she said. *Makes me exist.* The words keep repeating in my head until eventually I say them out loud.

'Makes her exist. Makes Esther exist.'

That's what's happened. I've seen her, at long last, for the first time. Of course she meant that it made her exist in her own eyes. But all this has opened my stupid eyes, too. I've seen Esther for real. Not as I remembered Meg, not as some ghost from my past. But Esther as she is.

17

Esther was edgy on the way down to The George. I swung round in the car park ready to drive straight off, but she didn't get out.

'Alfie, there's something else. I want to get it all over with. Floodgates and all that. Would you come down? Later? And I can tell you when I knock off?'

I was drawing breath to say no, and she knew it.

'Alfie, please. I know you're tired, but it's all come churning up. I can't...'

'Of course,' I said then. 'After all, I did ask for it.'

I kissed her goodbye and drove off, wondering what I'd got into.

So here I am in her room again, bracing myself for the next instalment.

'It's about Carole.'

'You never did say how she made out, what happened after your grandfather threw her out. I assumed that her boyfriend found them a place to live, and then it all fell apart after you were born. But...'

'There was no boyfriend, remember? I made him up. Seems some school friend took her in for a bit, but then it went from bad to worse. The parents couldn't cope with her, said she was a bad influence. So she was kipping on people's floors, sleeping rough. Then a hostel for girls with babies, bed & breakfast places. You name it. I don't know the half.'

She climbs on the bed and sighs. 'Leg's a nightmare tonight. Really aching. Anyway. I've been wanting to tell you this ever since the accident. But I couldn't bring myself to do it. You see, it explains why I went so ape and lost the plot when you told me what you'd done to your wife. I know it was entirely different, but in the moment I couldn't see that.'

'Okay, go on.'

'I need to start with Preece. He was Carole's bloke. He got her drugs, he was her pimp. He controlled her life. He used her for years. And in the end he killed her.'

So matter-of-fact. Words that I've rarely used, and yet they're part of her history. I wonder again what that feels like.

'She was sick, the heroin would have had her sooner or later, but he didn't wait for that. He had no further use for her. Tried to make it look like a suicide pact.'

I nod slowly, beginning to see the connection.

She takes a battered book from the bedside table, holding it like it's a Bible. 'This was Carole's, my mother's. The police found it after she died. There are all sorts of bits written in it, like a kind of secret diary. He never found it. Preece, that is. He'd have burned it if he had, but I don't suppose he ever looked in a book.'

She takes a deep breath.

'I guess this is the closest I ever came to Carole.' She opens the book and passes it to me.

It's a copy of Gibran's *The Prophet* and someone has written closely in biro at the end of the passage on dying.

A rare lucid day. not many of those now. My life is like being down a mine, going deeper and darker with fewer and fewer candles, and knowing you'll never come out. He's killing me, and not so slowly any more. I know and I don't care. He's got no use for me any more. He wants me out the way so he can go find another poor girl to prey on. I wish he'd go down for it, but they'll just say it was an overdose and he'll be free to do it all again.

I read it slowly, getting used to the handwriting. Then I read it again and look up. Esther is staring at me.

I nod, understanding seeping into my brain. But I'm only half understanding. How did Carole get involved with Preece? Who or what was he? Esther is holding out her hand for the book, turns to another page and hands it back. This time the writing is in the margin all round one of the pages on children.

> *My life has been an utter pathetic waste. Except that if my Esther is up there in the world, out in the sunshine, maybe I did something right. I hated them when they took her away, but it was right. It kept her away from him and it kept her safe from me. I was never the stable bow, but she is the arrow that flies.*

When I look up again Esther's eyes are swimming in tears. "'My Esther". She calls me "my Esther". I know it's not the same way a real mother would say that, but to know that she thought it, even if it was only once or twice.'

I'm choked. I can't speak. I hug her in a clumsy kind of way but it's not enough. Nothing will ever be enough.

'I didn't have this for ages after she died. The police found it. It was evidence of a kind, I suppose. She'd have been so pleased, so proud that writing this helped to send him down. He didn't get to do it to any other girls.'

I take up the book and read the passage again. 'She must have been a remarkable person.'

'She would have been,' corrected Esther.

'No. She was. In spite of the Preece man. And you take after her.'

Esther makes a face, half grim, half pleased. 'There were some photos I got, too.'

She starts to move off the bed and I jump up. 'I'll get them.'

'At the far end of the shelf. The album.'

It's a pathetically thin little plastic folder with snaps slipped into transparent pockets. Esther flips through it and holds out a colour photo of a young woman sitting at a table with a child standing beside her.

'That's me with Carole. It was her birthday and my social worker took me to visit. She was clean and she was living in this

180

kind of commune, and the plan was that I should go and live with her. On trial at first, and then permanently if it worked out.'

The girl Carole has the air of a ten-year-old. She's wearing a pink dress that shows anorexic collarbones and her pale blonde hair is held back on one side with a butterfly slide. The little girl Esther looks more self-possessed than her mother, but the resemblance is striking. She's wearing a green gingham dress with a pink cardigan that appears to have shrunk in the wash. The look she is giving the camera is disconcertingly streetwise.

On the opposite page, Carole is blowing out the candles on a cake stuck with Smarties. It looks like an illustration for an old-fashioned children's reader.

'How old were you there?'

'About four, I think. Well, let's see. It was her twenty-first so I must have been nearly five. She had me when she was sixteen.'

'What an occasion!'

Esther gives a short laugh. 'It ought to be my best memory. Me and my Mum at a party together, but I only remember one bit. The rest all came from my case file. The fact that she'd been in rehab and she was living in this so-called supportive environment.'

'What's the bit you remember?'

'Two bits, actually. The door, when we went in. The place was in a huge converted warehouse way over Dalston way. It was like a foreign country from Brixton. The idea was, she'd get away from the bad influences. Like hell she did.'

Esther took a breath.

'Anyway, what I remember. You went up these smelly stairs and there was a huge thick steel door like it was a prison. You can see from the photos it was just one big barn of a room with like cubicles curtained off where people slept. And this great big table in the middle. But it's the door I remember. The other thing was that she got given a Pink Panther and she gave it to me.' Esther reached behind her and pulled a scruffy stuffed creature with dangly legs out from under her pillow.

'So what went wrong? You never did go to live with her, did you?'

Esther shook her head. 'Preece is what went wrong. He turned up in the commune, infiltrated. He was cunning as hell. Seemed like a squeaky clean guy to start with, apparently. He homed in on Carole. "Grooming" you'd call it now. Bought her presents, then started giving her stuff to smoke. As soon as they found out she was using again she had to leave the commune. That was their only rule. And he stepped in like a knight in shining armour and took her to his flat. Said he'd look after her, see her all right. He was her minder, pimp, jailor, supplier, you name it. Murderer, eventually. He controlled her life. And her death. But he used her for years before it got that bad. Nan used to go to see her. Carole would be all dressed up and she'd give her tea with a cup and saucer and say she was happy, but Nan always knew Preece was in the next room, listening. Like he'd told her what to say.'

Esther pauses, clears her throat. The only sign she is finding this difficult.

'Then it started to be that Preece wouldn't let Nan in when she visited. He'd say Carole was out, or that she had flu or a migraine. Nan got in touch with the social, but they said there was no reason for them to go in. They couldn't do anything. And Nan couldn't make a lot of fuss. It was all in secret. If my grandfather had found out she was seeing Carole there'd have been hell to pay. He'd have beaten Nan up.'

Again the throat-clearing.

'Nan only ever took me there once. I'd got in with a bad crowd at school. I was about fifteen. So about the age Carole went off the rails, got pregnant with me. She said I ought to at least know who my mother was, but actually I think she did it to scare me. It certainly scared me all right. And it scared the hell out of her too.'

She pauses, but this time it's for dramatic effect.

'Preece opened the door. He was an ugly looking bastard. Shaved head, these very thin lips and eyes that just bored into you. Black shirt and drainpipes and this huge silver belt buckle with a death's head on it. He started to say we couldn't come in, then he noticed me behind Nan, and he looked me over like I was a piece of meat he was thinking of buying and ushered us in. Nan took hold of my hand. I guess she noticed the way he looked at me too. And we went through to a room at the back, more like a cupboard it was. And there was this creature like a skeleton on a dirty mattress and splashes of blood on the walls and on the ceiling, like I'd seen in public toilets where addicts hang out.

'Nan went and shook her and kept saying, Carole, Carole, but Preece just stood in the doorway and said there was no use shouting, she wouldn't be round till about five o'clock and then he'd be cooking her something tasty for her tea. I never heard anything more unlikely. God, it was creepy.'

She looks across to see how I'm taking this. 'Fuck, it was scary, Alfie.'

'What happened?'

'Nan was quick. She asked him to fetch her a glass of water and while he was in the kitchen she bundled me back down the hall and out the door. He yelled down the stairwell after us, but Nan and me kept running. In the street we had a bit of luck. There was a black cab going past and Nan shot out in front of it with her arm up and it stopped. I couldn't believe it. Nan was always so careful with money and here she was stopping a taxi! Turned out it was only taking a short cut and not for hire. Cabbie said he never stopped round that area, it was far too dodgy, but he took pity, poor old Nan looked so desperate. We climbed in and she just hugged me so tight and we were both shaking.'

She pauses, breathless, as if she was still running in the retelling.

'She said afterwards, Nan I mean, that she was afraid Preece would set someone to follow us if we hung around at a bus stop. We struck lucky with that cabbie, too. Nan just told him to take us down to Hackney Road where we'd get a bus and the guy stopped the meter half way and only charged us a couple of quid to cover his diesel. I remember Nan said to him, "If only there were more people like you in the world."

'Carole died soon after that. We couldn't even go to the funeral. Nan was too scared he'd come after me. But the great thing was that the police got on to Preece. They'd had an eye on him for some time, but they'd never been able to pin anything on him. But it seemed he went to pieces about Carole. I even think he loved her in a weird and warped kind of way. Apparently he tried to make it look like a suicide pact which he'd survived. But he lost the plot and nothing was very convincing. They couldn't do him for murder, but he did go down for manslaughter and dealing.'

Esther looks wiped when she stops talking.

'No wonder you're so tough,' I say, stroking her hair.

'Am I? I don't feel it. It all used to make me ashamed until I got that book of Carole's. But does it help you understand? Really?'

I nod. 'Certainly does.'

'You know it's funny. When you think, all that's still going on, dealers, drugs, people going under. And here I am, in this place. With you. And Joel and Reg, and people who leave the car keys in the ignition and don't lock their doors at night. Sort of surreal. It kind of feels like cheating somehow.'

'About time, I'd say. That you had something different, someone to look out for you.'

'I did have Nan.'

'But you ended up looking after her.'

'And Luke. Except...'

'Ah, yes. Luke.' I often wonder about him. 'Where's he?'

She shrugs. 'Don't know. Don't much care. Past history.'

I smother a yawn.

'Go on, Alfie. Go home to bed. I won't make you try and share this with my leg.'

Thank the Lord for that. I feel knocked out and I guess she is too. 'I was hoping you'd say that. Not that I don't...'

'No worries. I haven't got the energy to clean my teeth, let alone...'

I'm glad not to meet Joel on the way downstairs. All this emotional stuff. I need space, lots of space to unpack it, to let it all find its level in my mind. It'll be good to get out on the moor early in the morning. Just me and the sheep and the sky.

18

I've just got a letter from Auntie Em. Emmylou I should say. This big brown envelope arrived covered in flowery handwriting with circles dotting every "i" and a flower drawn in pink felt tip on the back. I was a bit embarrassed to be honest when Joel handed it to me, but I think maybe she's wanting to make peace. She wouldn't go drawing flowers otherwise, would she?

She starts off by apologising for typing the letter. Which I couldn't care less about. Then she says we parted on a 'wrong foot' – talk about understatement – and she might have said things she didn't mean. Maybe I was upset. Upset! I'll say I was.

She goes on to say that there are things I don't know that would help me to understand her point of view. I really, really don't want to understand her point of view any more than I do already. But I read on. We need to meet up, apparently, and she's going to a conference on green energy in Totnes, which she thinks isn't far from Dartmoor. Will I come and meet her there?

She ends:

I was so thrilled to see you again and to have my Esther back that I would be very sad to lose you again just because harsh words were spoken. With fondest love, Emmylou.

The signature is even more flamboyant than the envelope. I put the letter up in my room and think about it all day while I'm working. It's a changeover day and there are three rooms to do, not to mention kitchen prep with all the tables booked for the evening. It's amazing how quickly my leg's recovered once the plaster came off, but I'm still not as fast as I used to be.

I'm not sure how I feel about meeting up. I've been busy putting Auntie Em out of my mind and here she is, resurrecting herself. But then again, she's all I've got. A person who knows who I am. Knows all about Carole. Understands about being "in care". Or "looked after" – the current label, as Emmylou was quick to remind me. Why do they go to all the bother of changing the words? As if the life of the kids will change as well? Bet it costs a bomb for some consultant straining their brain. Money you could use on staff in children's homes. Then you might really feel "looked after". But none of that helps me decide whether to meet her or not.

I'm glad when Alfie turns up late in the evening. I knew he wouldn't be eating, not when we're so busy, but I've been willing him to come down to see me. I fetch the letter and push it across the bar with his pint.

He's sitting outside waiting for me after closing time. 'Well, what d'you want to do about it?'

'Can't decide.' I tell him how confused I feel.

'I'd be dubious. Don't want you getting all upset again. Opening it all up and finding another can of worms.'

'But she's trying to – you know – make peace. And she's my link with the past, Alfie.'

He makes a face as if to say, why would I want a link with that past? But I do. It might not be a great past. But it's mine. I suppose it's all about identity. I try to explain and I realise I'm talking myself into going.

'Well,' says Alfie. 'If you do decide to go, that date she mentions, it happens to be a day I have to go to Exeter. I could drop you at the station and you could get a train to Totnes.'

'Well, in that case, I must be meant to go.'

He shrugs. 'That sounds like something Emmylou might say.'

There aren't many people on the train and I get a window seat. Watching fields of cows gives me space to wonder about Alfie. He was so quiet this morning. And smart! I've never seen him in a suit before. Wouldn't say what he was going to be doing in Exeter. I kept getting the feeling he was going to tell me something, but he never did.

Wow! The sea. I didn't expect that. All those red cliffs and the feeling you could fall right into the waves. It's a real shock. I didn't know we went along the coast. Dawlish, the lady opposite tells me, and it's got a problem. The line's under threat from storms in winter. I think it would be really cool to be snug inside with waves breaking on the carriage windows.

Emmylou's given me directions to walk from the station. Alfie said Totnes is an old market town, full of quaint architecture. But this bit certainly isn't like that. When I get to the bridge I see a café right by the river and I think that would be a lovely place to sit and talk, but it's not the one. My map takes me across the road and I see the yellow door immediately. It's the same colour as Emmylou's gates.

I order a cappuccino and I've hardly sat down with it when Emmylou bursts through the door, kisses me, greets the lady at the counter like she's known her all her life and asks for an apple juice.

She fans herself with a table mat as she sits down. Today she's wearing a purple tunic with white trousers, which anyone knows a woman of her size should never wear. But Emmylou looks magnificent. Her hair is piled on top of her head and secured with a colourful collection of clips and slides and combs. She jangles as much as Marion, but the look is more car boot than Cartier.

She dives almost immediately into a tote bag embroidered with elephants, sequins and mirrors and produces an envelope.

'I made a copy. But I thought you should have the original.' She pushes it across the table and watches as I open it.

It's a photograph of me and Auntie Em in the garden at Rayners Lane with lots of roses in the background. It's such a surprise that tears well up and overflow before I can do anything to stop them.

Emmylou tosses me a tissue. 'Bet you forgot about that!'

I shake my head. 'But I *remember* that day. It was Double Figure Day! You said we had to celebrate because I'd reached double figures. It was my birthday. I was ten. You made a cake. And tied that silly bow in my hair! And we played hide-and-seek. And that nice Mrs Warren came in and took the photo. And she gave me a cardboard doll with lots of different sets of paper clothes.' It all comes out in a rush.

'And then what happened?'

'And then…' I hesitate, taking myself back in time, into that garden, through that kitchen door. 'Oh yes! You cut your finger really badly and Mrs Warren came in to babysit while Mr Warren took you to casualty. And they stitched it all up, and you had your arm in a sling.'

Emmylou sits back and laughs. 'So you do remember.'

'Of course I do.'

We both go quiet and sip our drinks.

Then I say, 'Why did you want me to come? After the things you said?' I don't want her to think she can seduce me with memories and get away with it.

Her face clouds. 'I guess I wanted to say I'm sorry. And I am. I get carried away with ideas. It's a great fault of mine – to get caught up in "isms" and lose sight of the person. I've always done it. That's what the campaigning's all about. It's almost like an addiction. I wasn't listening to you, to your story. I'm sorry, Esther.'

That's it, what I've been waiting for. What I came for. An apology. She reaches out and touches my arm but I don't take her hand. 'Thank you,' I say. Somehow her apology doesn't make me feel any better about her. It's like it was just words. Words she'd practised.

'I do have something to tell you. About the abortion issue, that is. But I'll come back to that. I'm worried about you and that man of yours. For a start, he's far too old for you, he won't want children, he'll be a pensioner before they're grown, he'll drop dead just when you need him most and…'

I hold up a hand. 'Hey, I thought you were supposed to be apologising, not getting off on another rant.' I eye her as I spoon froth off my coffee, irritation bubbling up. 'Do you imagine we haven't thought about all those things? That we haven't discussed them? D'you think I'm still ten years old? D'you think it's any of your business?'

Emmylou puts her hand over her mouth, but she keeps right on talking. 'He had a funny look about him – and then he kept going off on his own.'

'Hardly surprising, the way you ignored him, hardly spoke to him.' I'm beginning to wish I hadn't come. Maybe Alfie's first instincts were right.

'Oh dear, you haven't changed. You always were a fiery one. Such a temper, you used to have. Okay, I was out of order – again. But if you'd just simmer down and...'

'Sorry, Auntie Em. I mean Emmylou.'

'Just tell me what you see in him.'

I suppose I have to give her a chance. 'Well, he's gentle and sexy and funny. He listens. And, come to think of it, he likes the same things you taught me about. Books, music... He's not your conventional...'

But she's not listening.

'He's still a man,' she says. 'And I don't do men. You see, it's all part of the story. I'll tell you. But I think we should be ordering lunch.'

Emmylou orders roasted vegetable tart and I go for the spicy carrot and coriander soup with spelt bread, which I've never heard of, but which Emmylou says is better than bread made with ordinary wheat flour. I don't take in why, because I'm really too caught up with our conversation to want to bother about food.

'It was Mr Miller, you see. He seemed such a good kind man when I married him. He was quite a catch. Steady job in the city. He wouldn't live in some poky flat. Only a proper house with a garden was good enough for his bride. Three bedrooms! Fancy! And a bathroom upstairs, where you want it. We saved up for decent furniture and I ran up curtains. All those windows – and that big bay in the front rooms.'

She's gone quite misty-eyed. Anyone would think it was a mansion she was describing. I did used to think it was grand. I got a shock when I went back last year and there it was, an ordinary little semi.

'I was so house-proud in those days. Polished the windows with newspaper and vinegar like my mother used to. Dusted every day. Imagine! And always had his tea on the table when he came in. I was good at budgeting too, could make a meal out of nothing.'

I'm wondering whether she wishes she was back in Rayners Lane and when we'll get on to Mr Miller – and whether he has a first name and whether I care.

'He, Mr Miller, that is, was keen on being a family man. Which suited me. I was considered quite a beauty in my time. You wouldn't think it now. I've what you might call gone to seed. An overblown rose.'

She's so caught up in herself. Auntie Em was never like that. Or was she?

'So, yes, I was good-looking and I was bright – but I was never interested in a career. Children were what I wanted, and a home and a husband. Not quite the thing these days, but then I look at how these career girls are run ragged trying to be all things to all people... But I mustn't get off on that one.'

Emmylou draws breath as the food arrives and I examine my spelt bread and wait to hear about Mr Miller while she munches on her vegetable tart.

'That's better. I didn't know I was so hungry. Didn't fancy the breakfast. Where was I? Oh yes. Mr Miller. Everything went swimmingly to begin with, but then we were trying and trying to start a family and nothing was happening. And he got more and more moody and in the end he started blaming me. I said we should go and seek help and advice and he got very angry at that. Out of character it was. Seemed he was dead set on founding a dynasty. Yes, he had very grand ideas. Imagine, a dynasty in Rayners Lane! Ridiculous really. But it was his whole aim in life. So one day he just upped and offed, and I never saw him again.'

'He just vanished?'

She nods and attacks her tart again. 'Went to find a woman who could give him kids, I suppose.'

I sip my soup, which is yummy, and tear off lumps of bread and dip them in it.

'The irony of it was that he'd hardly gone when I missed my period and tested positive.'

'Did he come back?'

'Didn't know where to find him. I tried hard enough. But he had no family, nowhere I could start. Only a brother in America and he never answered my letter. As it turned out, it was just as well. I had a miscarriage, you see.'

Emmylou pours water from the carafe and takes a gulp.

'That's when it all started. My horror of abortion. They let me see it, you see. That little foetus was a miniature baby, a tiny human being. It broke my heart.'

She stops again. More water, more tart. I remember now. Whenever Auntie Em was upset she would eat. Anything that was in the fridge, and failing that, cornflakes. Comfort eating, she called it. Me, I'm the opposite. Can't eat a thing if I'm worried. I just hope she's not going to go on about the stages of foetal development.

'And that's where my distrust of men started, too. He'd seemed such a reliable man. Everyone said so. Mind you, he did his bit financially. I suddenly found the mortgage was paid off. And money arrived in my account. Only for a year, mind you. I realised I was better off on my own. But there I was, high and dry and unable to have the one thing I really wanted in life. Children. I mean, you can imagine how angry I got when I heard about people having abortions. It wasn't just the taking of a life. To me, every abortion was a baby I could have loved and looked after. So I started fostering.'

I nod. I don't feel angry any more. It all makes perfect sense. It's hard to imagine, but I guess I might even feel the same way myself. If I wanted children. I won't attempt to explain the way I feel about that. I don't think she'd understand. Even if she listened. It's like we come from different planets.

It's funny to think that I owe that good bit of my childhood to Mr Miller. And however much she annoys me or says outrageous things or doesn't listen, I'll always be grateful to Auntie Em for giving me that.

Emmylou has coffee and a slice of lemon polenta cake – another unknown. I taste it and it's lovely, but I wouldn't want a whole slice. While she eats it I tell her a bit about Alfie.

'He cared for his wife for years until she died. She had MS. They loved each other, that's plain to see. He still loves her. He's been very straight about that.'

I don't say how Meg died of course. That's Alfie's business. Nor do I mention the painting, she'd get the wrong idea. I can see Emmylou gets the wrong idea very easily. As it is, she's frowning and looking thoughtful and I don't want her asking questions so I carry on.

'He's a shepherd, and he comes down to the pub where I work. Maid of all work. Lovely people I work for.' Joel, that is, and Pattie. I don't mention Marion and all that drama. Altogether too many wrong ideas to pick up there. 'That's how we met. Serving him cottage pie and bitter. Dead romantic!'

'And his daughter? Do you get on?'

She doesn't say 'being of a similar age' but it's written all over her face.

'I haven't met her yet. As I say, it's only a month or two since Alfie and I met and we're out in the sticks up there on the moor.'

I've no intention of saying any more about Laura, my accident, Pugh or any of that stuff. That's Alfie's business. Alfie's and mine.

Emmylou seems satisfied – in her tummy and in her mind. She makes no attempt to give me any pamphlets or to sign me up for anything, which is something I dreaded. She even insists on paying for my lunch and we link arms and wander up the High Street together, looking in the boutiques and health food shops. Everything's organic this and environmentally friendly that.

Emmylou was hoping to find one of the town's famous rickshaws to take us up the hill, but there's no sign of one.

'You really mean you've never heard of them?' she puffs. 'Powered by recycled cooking oil. It's all part of this "Transition Town" thing, you see.'

I've no idea what she's talking about but I know she's about to tell me.

'It's all about being less dependent on oil. And they've got the Totnes pound and garden sharing…oh, that's a pretty frock.'

I don't see what the Totnes pound can have to do with oil, and the dress she's pointing out in a charity shop window is hideous. No, I don't want to try it on.

'People think they're a load of pot-smoking, born-again hippies, these "Transition" folk. But that's not what the real Totnes is about. They're a very sensible, hard-headed lot. I mean, I'm not a good advert. I have to admit, I can look a bit daffy. But they're not. Not in the least daffy.'

Two days in a place and she thinks she's an expert. Aloud I say, 'I don't know why you don't come and live here. It seems just your sort of place.'

She laughs. 'Couldn't leave Port Boscoe. I belong there now. I was lucky. Aunt was such a well-loved person and I've kind of inherited some of that, I suppose.'

By this time we've reached a shop selling organic vegetables and Emmylou raves about 'proper muddy' potatoes and cabbages with caterpillar holes. I grin to myself to think what Pattie would say if Joel produced veg like that for her to prepare.

Then it's time for me to catch my train and we set off back down the hill. It certainly is a pretty town. I'd like to come here with Alfie. I find Emmylou's doubled back to buy some bangles I rather liked. She presses them into my hands as we say goodbye. We say we'll meet again, but I wonder how long it will be before we do. The thought gives me a pang as I walk away and I turn back to wave. But Emmylou's already crossing the road back to meet her conference cronies. I feel sad watching her. We've settled our differences, but she's Emmylou. She never will be Auntie Em again. She only exists in my head. As the purple and white figure disappears I realise I don't need her to be Auntie Em any more. It's the most grown-up I've ever felt.

Alfie and I have arranged to meet at his gallery. It gives me a funny feeling to see the name "Buckland Gallery" picked out in gold on dark red above the window and to know that's Alfie. I mean it's not in lights or anything. But it gives him a kind of special place in the town. It's no ordinary picture gallery either. The moment I step inside I love it. The wooden floor, all the pine shelving, old leather chairs and the smell of coffee. I could spend hours looking at the pictures, especially Alfie's, and picking out books from the shelf of second-hand paperbacks in the coffee shop.

Alfie's head to head with a woman with pinky hair. He's told me about Connie and how brilliant she is managing the place and how much she helped when Meg was ill.

He leaps up when he sees me and says, 'This is Esther I've been telling you about.' He puts his arm round me and brings me to the table and it feels like he's kind of proud of me.

I like Connie immediately and after we've said hello I tell them to get on with their talk. Alfie wants to know how my meeting went, but I tell him it'll wait and wander off to explore the place. It feels peaceful and special. I've been admitted to another part of Alfie's domain.

As I'm falling asleep in my crooked little room that night I look back over the day, and that's been the best bit. That, and the way Alfie introduced me to Connie.

19

Ever since the court appearance I've been having a recurring dream. It's only a scrap of something bigger I can never recapture, but it keeps on coming. I'm standing on the edge of a vast tract of moorland, wild and desolate, and the wind is blowing rain in my face. I feel a mixture of elation and dread. There's something behind me I have to escape, but my feet won't move from the spot.

What an anti-climax. The trial didn't happen. No pathologist to give evidence, so the whole thing was adjourned. The judge just set another date and renewed my bail. All those people gathered for nothing. What a waste – time, money, effort. But at least it didn't matter that I hadn't told Esther. And Connie thought the delay was good – because of some case she was going on about which has gone to appeal.

The dream reminds me of a hike I made when I first came up here. I followed a stream and took a path uphill to an ancient forest where the enclosing bank and the twisted trunks completely cut out the sound of the brook I'd just left down in the valley. It was windless in there, as if time stood still. I made a couple of tree sketches to work up later, and sat against a moss-covered oak under green-bearded branches, soaking up the stillness. If I risked falling asleep it might be for a hundred years, so I clambered on and up, over furry boulders to the far side.

There I emerged, as in the dream, on the open moor. Clouds raced, a north-easterly cut through my jacket, needles of rain turning to hail peppered my face. It was exhilarating, then terrifying. No hiding place. I imagined how it would be for a convict from the godforsaken prison down the road, trying to make an escape. Then the visibility dropped to a few yards and I lost my nerve. I thanked my good instinct that had made me bring a compass and headed back to the nearest road. I hitched a lift with a vet on his way to a farm beyond Blidworthy, who clearly thought that a shepherd out walking for pleasure must be off his head.

Another thing's happened since Cornwall – I've started painting Esther again. So far the results are dramatically different.

Esther gives one look and says, 'Wow! That's cool. It looks like she might talk. Is that really me?'

But I can see she knows it is and that she's beautiful.

'I have to say, I didn't ever say, but – apart from the sketches, like the one you gave me – I never liked what you did before. The pictures always looked a bit, kind of, dead. Is it me that's changed, or you? To make that happen?'

I know it's me and I know what that's about, of course. I'm not trying to paint a blonde version of Meg any more. But then again, perhaps Esther's let me behind the mask.

'Could be either. Or both. It could be that what's between us has changed.'

She kisses me when I say that. I hope I haven't said too much. But it's true. There's a trust that wasn't there before. Deep down I believe in us. We're in love, although I still tell myself I have no right to be.

Esther seems to have taken the "in-love" bit in her stride and she's moved on to the commitment part long before I'm ready.

Today, for instance. It isn't even her day off but she's up here as usual, slotting in to my sheep routines, playing records and reading while I'm out. Her plaster's long been off and the leg's good as new. She's restless and we end up in bed sooner than usual.

Afterwards she starts on about the fact that her job is coming to an end. I'm rattled. Christ! Is she about to disappear?

'When's that then?'

'I told you. When the children go back to school. Next week. Can you believe it's September next week? I mean, we're slack already. The tourists have mostly gone home. We've got nobody staying. I wouldn't be up here today otherwise.'

I zip my jeans and start down the ladder, wondering how to respond.

'I have to make plans. Can't stay at The George, especially with Marion coming home.'

'What about uni? Your plans to go back?'

'Too late for this year. Didn't get round to it in time. I'll try for next year.'

There's a hesitation in her voice and I wonder how much she really wants to go back to studying. I should have paid more attention, taken an interest.

'Anyway, Luke's back from his travels. He's started texting me again about Nan's table. I need somewhere to put it.'

She hasn't mentioned Luke for weeks. I'd forgotten all about him. I peer into the tiny mirror over the sink as I fill the kettle, and wonder what Luke will make of me and Esther.

'Have you told him yet? Told Luke where you're…?'

We're interrupted by a shout from the door. It's the postman, a rare visitor. Apart from the police, only Laura, Connie and my lawyers know my address here. Laura doesn't communicate, Connie uses texting and my solicitor's letters arrive in white envelopes. This is one of those.

I stand in the doorway watching the postman's weathered legs stride back to the red van as I tear it open.

'Anything interesting?' Esther's come down to join me.

'Looks like there's going to be another adjournment.'

'Adjournment of what?'

'The trial date next month.'

'What? Trial? When? Why didn't you *tell* me?'

'24th. I didn't want it hanging over us. Especially after last time. Why get worked up for nothing?'

'What d'you mean? Last time?'

'In June. It was adjourned because the pathologist wasn't available.'

'Alfie! Are you saying what I think you're saying? I wondered what you meant – "*another* adjournment". You went for trial in *June* and you didn't tell me?'

I nod. How could I have done that? 'I'm sorry. I couldn't… I was confused. And then the Emmylou thing came up. You know, when she wanted to meet up in Totnes.'

'It was that day? Of course! The suit. *That's* where you were going! You were in such a mood. Oh Alfie…'

She flings her arms round me, and it feels like I might be forgiven.

'I wonder just how long it would have been before you told me about this one – if this letter hadn't come. Come on, you'd better explain it all.'

'Donald says it's a bit different this time. If the Crown don't apply for an adjournment – which they almost certainly will – then the barrister will. He encloses a copy of her letter. Thing is, there's been a landmark case and now these new guidelines are due. She seems to think they could make a difference. And a barrister ought to know, I suppose.'

'I'm coming with you. I can get the day off.'

'No! Absolutely not. I don't want people knowing. Especially as it's just going to be adjourned. No point.'

'But Alfie…'

'I promise I'll tell you when it's for real. Except you'll be back in London by then.'

'Why the fuck would I go back to London? With you down here?'

'But, suppose I'm banged up?'

'I'd stand by you anyway. I would.'

I wait for the "if" that I can hear in her tone. 'You would? You would if…? If what?'

'I didn't say "if".'

'You implied it. Otherwise you'd have said, I will stand by you.' I'm not usually pedantic but I can feel her reservation.

'You're splitting hairs. It was just a way of saying.'

I raise an eyebrow at her and say nothing.

The whistling of the kettle intervenes. She swears, as she always does, at the scald of escaping steam when she pulls the whistle off the spout, and raises the kettle high over the coffee pot as she pours.

We drink our coffee in silence and then she says she has to go. 'There'll be people in for lunch. See you tomorrow, maybe?' I nod.

I wonder if she'll come tomorrow. I reread Donald's letter and fold it away. It takes an effort of will to go out on sheep patrol and I have to make myself trek up to the farm to give Tom an update.

'Just so long as it don't interfere with tupping,' he says. 'I'll not be putting the ram in before Guy Fawkes'. Don't want to be caught out with late snow for lambing.'

'But Tom...'

'But me no "buts".'

I appreciate his confidence but it fails to lift my mood.

'Go on, ye daft bugger. Go and be miserable, then.' And Tom stumps off inside.

Back at the barn I pour a tumbler of Scotch and pull out the notes I made at the last meeting with Donald. I never saw him so animated. He reckoned there were changes in the pipeline since that Debbie Purdy won on appeal to the House of Lords. Got mad at me when I said, 'Debbie who?'

'Christ, Alfie! Aren't you following this?'

I'd heard of her. Of course I had. Just forgot the name. But follow it? How am I supposed to do that with no telly and no Internet? I hardly ever see a paper unless someone leaves one behind at the pub. And I'm happy with it that way. Which was a mystery to Donald.

Apparently the Director of Public Prosecutions was due to make a statement. 'Fingers crossed,' he said. 'New draft policy from the DPP. The Prosecution will have to reconsider their position.'

'Draft, though,' I pointed out.

'Sure, but still significant. Final policy due early next year. They're not hanging about.'

Will this statement come in time? And how much difference will it make anyway? Will it benefit someone who's already being prosecuted? I asked him about that and he said he was cautiously optimistic. 'It's going to affect the whole climate of opinion, influence the thinking of judges.'

So he says. Which means, an awful lot depends on the judge.

Sod's Law says I'll get landed with a dyed-in-the-wool reactionary who's having a bad day. It doesn't bear thinking about.

I might have known Connie would be following all this stuff online – the Purdy case and all the debate since then. She sent me a cutting from the paper – all the relevant bits highlighted. She even phoned me.

'You're in with a chance, Alfie. Have you even read the stuff I sent you? For example, Meg let people know she wanted to die. Plus she wasn't going to recover. Oh, Alfie…'

I refused to get excited. Empty words, I told her. Won't apply and doesn't apply to me anyway, I added. Connie cut across me then. 'For crying out loud, Alfie! Don't go allowing yourself a glimmer of hope. Oh go on, then *don't* be pleased.' And she put the phone down. Later she texted that she understood but it wasn't going to stop her thinking lucky. Good old Connie.

I wish I could talk to her now. I'm hungry and I wish Esther was here, but I can't face the pub. I push the papers aside and cut some bread and cheese, but the bread's stale and dry. Then I have a go at finishing the landscape on the easel. But I'm not in the mood and in danger of ruining it. So I finish the Scotch and climb into bed to bury myself thoroughly in self-pity.

Esther bounces in next morning and stamps all over my hangover.

'Did you know it's Widecombe Fair next week?'

Of course I know. Tom's showing cattle, reckons he's got a couple of prize-winning heifers this year. He's entered a couple of ewes he wants me to show and one of this year's ram lambs. 'So what?' I say.

'So Joel closes the pub. Tradition, he says. And we all go. Pattie will be there with all her family. And Reg and his lot. Most of the village, in fact. It's a regular do, they say.'

'I guess so.'

'You're in a cheerful mood, then.'

'So would you be, with that date hanging over you.'

'All the more reason to do stuff. So you don't keep thinking about it.' She picks up the whisky bottle and waves it at me. 'Not the only thing hanging over, I see.' She grins. 'How about going up to High Tor and walking it off? Then we can have a sandwich in Blidworthy on the way back.'

It's afternoon before she comes back to our conversation of the day before. I assumed she'd forgotten all about it.

'You were right. Yesterday. It makes me mad that you know me better than I do myself sometimes. I did have an "if". I guess I meant I'd stand by you if you and me... If we were going somewhere. If we were a proper item.'

'I thought we were.'

'Except you don't tell me about absolutely effing critical events in your life. Except you absolutely refuse to talk about the future. That's what I meant by making plans. Maybe moving in together, getting...'

'How can I make plans? With a trial hanging over me?' I swat at a fly and miss. 'It would be crazy to move in together. What's wrong with standing by me as a friend?'

'But you're not just a friend.'

'Not "just" a friend. A special friend.'

'Oh fuck, Alfie. You know what I mean. We've been here before and I thought we'd got past all that shit.'

Of course I know what she means. Dear God, I want to give in and have her there for me. But to bind her to me? It would destroy her. All that youth and energy wasted on an ageing con.

'I can't drag you through all that. It wouldn't be fair.'

'Isn't that for me to decide? Can't I have some responsibility in this too? Why can't we talk about "what if" – like "what if you get off" or "what if you don't"?'

'I can't even go there.' It's true. I just don't want to think about what might happen. I'll meet it when I come to it.

'There you go again. Calling the shots. What about me?'

Maybe she's right. Maybe I try to be too much in control. Though God knows, I haven't been in control so much of the time. Maybe I'm trying to be the father figure, when that's precisely what I'm afraid she sees in me.

When I try to explain that she says, 'But of course you're a father figure. I'm not that blind. It's no great surprise I'd be on the lookout for one of those. But that's only part of it. It's not the whole story. I mean, don't you think we met for a reason?'

'Meaning?'

'I don't think it was just chance. We were meant to meet. Why can't you accept that we're just two human beings in a muddle, a bit lost, who have found a life together? Like we've been unravelling each other?'

'Unravelling. That's what I'm afraid of. I've unravelled your life.'

'What's wrong with that? I mean we've been sorting each other out. Haven't we?'

'Is that what you mean by unravelling?'

She nods. 'Undoing the knots. Untangling the string.'

I take her face in my hands and kiss her. 'Nothing wrong. I love you. It's just that I absolutely don't deserve you and you are not, repeat not, going to ruin your life for me.'

She sighs and goes quiet, messing around with CDs, trying one and then another.

I turn away and stand in the doorway, looking out across the field. This view has always calmed me. The barn stands at the interface of farm and moor, of the tamed and the wild. It's sheltered by trees, while the moor undulates away towards the outline of distant tors. I can paint it over and over because it changes constantly. The activity is all between light and rain, sun and wind. A group of Scots pines, stencilled onto the sky, marks the edge of the cultivated land. Rabbits hop about on the scrubby grass in the early morning and evening and the occasional pheasant stalks past. Insects fly inside, fly around and fly out again if I don't interfere. It leaves me free to stretch my mind on the silence and space.

But today the view brings me no peace. As I watch, rain sweeps across, blotting out the moor, matching our mood. It was cosy pretending Esther was Meg, a kind of buffer against commitment. But now I'm shocked to discover I'm in love with Esther herself. It's wonderful, and I'm terrified. I suppose it's the 'no hiding place' of my dream. I never thought I'd find love again. Not such a love as this. The most I might have hoped for would have been companionable affection, like a nice cup of cocoa. But this is full-bodied, red-blooded and astonishing.

202

Esther breaks into my thoughts. 'Alfie, what I reckon is, you're a commitment freak. You won't even do "what ifs". I can't cope with being in limbo like that. And anyway, I've got washing to do.'

No tantrum, no storming out. She just gathers her things and kisses me very sweetly on the cheek and wanders out the door. Maybe she's hoping I'll call her back. But I'm not that much of a hypocrite.

Limbo is exactly where I don't want her to be. Not now, not for the next few weeks and not for the next God knows how many years. I know what that's like. I've been there long enough.

20

I can't get over how busy and noisy it is. Like the Elephant and Castle only with animals instead of cars. Except there are beat-up Land Rovers all over the place, towing horseboxes and sheep trailers. You can't hear a thing over the loudspeaker system if you're anywhere near the sheep, they're bleating so loud. I spot Alfie and wave, but he doesn't even see me.

Joel was determined to have a lie-in, so he's not coming up until later. I wanted to see Alfie's sheep being judged so I got a lift with Pattie and her husband and her younger son, Martin, who still lives at home. She thinks it would be nice if me and Martin got together. Not that she's said anything directly. She's got nothing against Alfie but I'm sure she thinks he's too old, just like everyone else. Martin's at the other extreme – only nineteen, much too young for me. Plus he's terribly shy and blushes every time he looks at me.

Alfie and Tom were going up at dawn, according to Alfie. Anyway there wouldn't be room for me, what with sheep and cattle and Eric and his ferrets. Apparently he's a star when it comes to ferret-racing. Or his ferrets are. How surprising is that? I've never even seen Eric – and I've never seen a ferret, come to that. Alfie gave me his wry grin when he told me, watching my reaction. As if to say, that's given you something to think about. It certainly did.

People speak as if Eric's a bit simple, a "shilling short in the pound" and that sort of thing. But that can't be right because Alfie says he gets the *Telegraph* in the post every day and does the big crossword, and can add up any figures in his head quick as a flash.

Pattie says it's people he can't get on with, apart from Tom.

Martin and his father vanish as soon as we arrive, Pattie and I head for a coffee, and I can't resist a bacon bun.

'It's the best smell in the world,' says Pattie. She pats her stomach and won't have one because she's on one of her diets and she's wearing her best frock.

By the time we've finished our coffee they're announcing the livestock judging so we make our way to the ring. I'm amazed to see all the animals looking so clean and all those tough-looking farmers brushing and combing blooming great bulls as if they were in a poodle parlour. I see what Alfie meant when he said I'd know a bull when I saw one. Blimey. To say the least. I nudge Pattie and she tells me to behave myself, but she's grinning too.

Tom wins second prize for one of his heifers and walks away with his rosette looking proud as punch. Then Alfie gets a second for one of the ewes.

'Don't ask me which one,' I say to Pattie. 'Two teeth? Four teeth? How would I know? He told me all about it, but it's a mystery to me.'

It seems an odd way to describe a sheep when you can't see their teeth anyway. But I'm just a townie. Which is probably what Pattie is thinking. No doubt she understands it all, but she just smiles and says nothing. She's not one to be a know-all.

'Oh, look! Here he comes again.'

This time it's the ram lamb. I can tell that because it's much smaller. The judging takes ages. At last they select three, but the judge keeps going back and forth between two of them. Obviously there's not much in it. Finally it's Alfie winning the first prize. Pattie and I clap like fury and as he walks out of the ring he looks across at me. He's got his lips pursed up like he does when he's pleased with himself and thinks he ought not to show it. He's chuffed to bits. He's been in such a grump all week that I almost thought he didn't care a fig about the show. Except he's so daft about those sheep.

Alfie's the other side the ring now, watching the next class of sheep. He's discussing the animals with an old guy with hardly any teeth at all, so they won't be judging him. After a bit Alfie comes round and joins us. I like the black-faced sheep best but that's obviously the wrong thing to say.

'Enough,' he says. 'These aren't so interesting anyway. I could do with a beer.'

The sun's warmed up the day and the beer tastes so much better outside, even in a plastic glass. We wander round the side-shows and I spot this geezer with a spectacular white beard sitting on a matching horse.

'What's the old guy doing on the horse?'

'Oh, that's Uncle Tom Cobley.'

'Uncle who?'

'You know, the song. He's all ready – on his grey mare. They enact the whole thing at some stage.'

'Alfie, just *what* are you talking about? And by the way, the horse is white. In case you hadn't noticed.'

Alfie grins. 'I see you need educating.' And then he only starts singing – if you can call it that. How embarrassing is this? But it gets worse. A whole lot of people round about start laughing and joining in. The story seems to be that a whole load of old farmer types get on a horse to come to the fair and the horse dies. Sometimes I do still find country folk weird.

By the time the song is over I'm doubled up laughing.

'Omigod, Alfie. I nearly wet myself. I thought you said it was your father that couldn't sing…'

'And just for the record,' he says. 'If a horse is white, it's a grey.'

That sets me off all over again, but Alfie grabs my hand. 'Look here!'

He pulls me over to a flatbed lorry where two girls dressed as pixies are pulling this contraption back and forth between them.

'Uncle Tom Cobley model. With moving parts. It's an automaton.' Alfie's fascinated. 'Isn't that something else.'

I must say it is quite clever. There are all these guys in hats squashed up on the horse, seven of them altogether and each one a real character. As it rolls along the horse nods and opens it's mouth, Uncle Tom waves his hat, and there's even a little dog jumping up behind. Took some geezer two years to make, exactly fifty years ago. It's really cool that it's been restored.

When we move on I spot the Hammer Striker and fancy having a go. I can only shift it up a few feet and even Alfie can't hit the bell. It really gets him going and he pays for a second go. Eventually, on his third hit he manages a faint 'ding' and comes away shaking his head. He's brilliant on the coconut shy, which cheers him up. Wins me a coconut. I'm not too grateful.

'Gee, thanks! What am I going to do with that all day? It weighs a ton!'

'We'll put it in the pickup and you can see Tom and Eric.'

When we get over to where their animals are penned, Tom's talking to the farmer with the single tooth and Eric's hovering in the background. When Alfie introduces me he gives a half nod and vanishes behind a horsebox. Alfie joins in the conversation with Tom and the farmer, but I honestly can't understand a word they're saying.

Tom and Eric won't be staying for the evening disco in the marquee. They will take the animals back, and me and Alfie will get a lift with Pattie or Joel. I'm looking forward to the disco. I wonder what it'll be like dancing with Alfie.

We meet up with Joel for lunch of a pasty and more beer, and after that we watch the ferret-racing final – not the most exciting sport I've ever seen. All these big men looking like it was Aintree, and fussing over these little furry creatures nosing about in tunnels. In fact, I get the giggles and Alfie has to nudge me to shut up. He'd rather die than offend Eric and Tom. Eric wins, as usual, with his prize animal. He's so animated when he talks to his ferret. You wouldn't believe he can't look a person in the eye.

Then Alfie wants to see the vintage machinery. 'It's fascinating seeing how these things developed, the early combines for instance…'

I give him a big yawn. 'I think I'll give that a miss.'

'Ferrets were as much as you can take? Okay. See you in a bit.' He laughs and strides away.

I wander off to look at a jewellery stall I spotted earlier. Pattie's there too and takes me off to join up with Reg and his clan. He's watching Gary having a turn on the Hammer Striker affair.

'My nephew,' he says with pride. 'Turned into a fair young man these days.'

He speaks as if recommending a car I might like to test-drive. Oh, no. Not Reg as well.

At least there's no sign of Gary's cousin Sean, the lad I turfed out of the pub. Gary's a big, muscular guy and not bad-looking either, I'll give Reg that. The bell's clanging every time he swings the hammer, and he ends up winning a teddy bear for making a record score. Then the weirdest thing happens. He turns round in a victory pose, holding the bear in the air and suddenly sees me. He comes loping over and gives it to me. Gives me the bear. I don't know what to say. I don't want the thing. It's a hideous pink, but what can I do, what with Reg looking on and Pattie saying "Aah"?

'What have I done to deserve this?'

Gary shrugs. 'You best have it.' And he blushes through his tan.

Omigod. He fancies me. How embarrassing is that? And where is Alfie when I need him?

After that, I keep finding Gary shadowing me. He doesn't walk with me. But he hovers. When I go to buy an ice cream he steps in with the right money, while I'm rooting around in my bag for my purse. I don't enjoy the ice cream at all, because he's standing there just watching me. I say I'm going to the toilet and at least he doesn't follow me there.

It gives me the chance to go looking for Alfie. He's not at the vintage machinery – which looks as dire as I thought it would. At last I find him leaning on a wall, smoking his pipe and watching a juggler.

'There you are!'

We both say it at once. I run up and kiss him, but he doesn't kiss me back quite like he usually does. He kisses me, but there's something missing. Like the fun of the morning never happened.

'I've decided to go back with the sheep. It's a bit much to handle for Tom and Eric on their own.'

'But you'll come back?'

'Sure.'

He strides off. I watch him go, with a bad feeling in the pit of my stomach.

The bad feeling gets a whole lot worse ten minutes later. I'm trying to find Pattie or Joel and avoid Gary. And I'd kill for a cup of tea. I peer into the beer tent, thinking Joel might be there. No Joel. Gary's there with his back to me, and at the far end of the bar I spot Pugh, the journalist. Omigod!

I shrink back the way I've come and nearly knock the glass out of Joel's hand.

'Steady there!' He puts his arm round me and kisses me affectionately on the cheek. He's happily pissed.

'I've just seen Pugh in there. You know, the newspaper guy who conned Marion into her great showdown?'

'Well, yes, I suppose he'd be here. Sort of thing he'd cover. Where's Alfie?'

When I tell him Alfie's gone he says, 'You just stay with Uncle Joel and I'll look after you. Until the lucky Alfie gets back. Best he's out the way. That bloke, Pugh, won't stay long.'

He fetches me a shandy. It's not tea but it's wet. We sit on some hay bales and watch the donkey derby of pantomime horses and laugh ourselves silly.

'You're a good girl, young Esther. Good company.' He puts his arm round me again. 'Marion doesn't go for this kind of thing.'

I snort. I cannot imagine Marion setting foot on the show-ground. 'When's she coming back?'

'Next week. She's off on a cruise with her sister. Mediterranean. Much more…'

A voice cuts across him. 'I see Mr Buckland's floozy's putting it about a bit today.'

I move my neck so fast, I hear it crack. It's Pugh of course.

'That's the third *gentleman* I've seen you with today. I was hoping to see Mr Buckland but he is elusive. While the cat's away… as they say…'

Joel grabs at me as I leap to my feet. But before I can reach Pugh a large lady wearing an official badge sweeps between us.

'There you are Mr Pugh. I need you now, right away. I have the winners of the garden produce all lined up for photographs in the marquee. Wonderful onions this year, I think you'll agree.' And she carries him off as fast as his short legs will carry him.

'Phew,' says Joel. 'I'm afraid I wasn't much use there. Bit slow on the reactions.'

Gary emerges from the beer tent and I duck, but he's got that glazed look and he doesn't even see me. I watch the marquee until Pugh comes out again, camera in hand. Joel's right. He sets off towards the exit, and I step across the road and wait in the shadow of a big oak until he's disappeared round a bend in the road. I'm standing at the entrance to the school, except you'd never know it if it didn't say so. It could be anybody's regular house. Imagine, going to a school like that.

I wander off down the lane. I'm hot and sticky and my head's throbbing. I've had enough of beer and men who are half-pissed. I want Alfie and I wish I'd gone back with him. Then I remember how he left and I know he didn't want me to. The middle of the village is pretty, what with the old smithy and the tree with steps all round where you can sit. I go through the lychgate and up the path to the church. It's called St Pancras which is weird, here in the middle of nowhere. But then, I just thought of him as a station. Never occurred to me he was a proper saint like Matthew or Mark. It's cool and peaceful inside.

Up the front there's a banner with pictures for all the churches around. I like the angel with all the rich colours, but Alfie wouldn't think much of that leery sheep with the flag. My favourite has a flagon and a fish, still alive, with bubbles coming from its mouth.

The pews in the choir stalls at the front are wider, and one even has a cushion. I lie down and look up at the vaulted ceiling and wonder how they built it all those hundreds of years ago. There are little coloured carvings where the beams intersect. Lots of creatures and faces peering out from leaves, looking down at me.

What have I done to upset Alfie? We were having such a great time. Surely nothing to do with not going to look at old tractors with him? Nah. Alfie's not that sad. You never know with him. Which reminds me of that awful phone call from Auntie Em, Emmylou.

She said that. *'You'll never know with him.'* I still feel hurt with how excited she sounded, full of having remembered why Alfie looked familiar. It all fell into place on her way home from Totnes. Sod's effing Law that the time she was involved with

Pro-Life just happened to be when Meg died. Trust her to have a newspaper cutting complete with photograph of Alfie.

'Murdered his wife.' That's what she said. But she sounded so – well, triumphant. And then 'You'll never know with him'. And I've just thought that too. Except I don't mean he might murder me. Bugger Emmylou. The worst thing was, she sounded so disappointed that I knew about Meg and how he helped her die. Which tells me she doesn't really care about me at all. Not any more. But what the hell. I don't care. I certainly never want to speak to her again. I didn't tell Alfie she'd rung me. Didn't want to upset him, and now he gets in a mood. That's all the thanks I get.

I put one of the kneelers under my head. That's better. I'll just stay a bit longer and give the headache a chance to lift. Those faces up there will watch over me. They're really cool. I give them a little wave.

When I wake up, the light is dim. I wander back up the side aisle and look at the leaflets set out on a table. One booklet has a piece on St Pancras – he's only the patron saint of headaches! How spooky is that? No wonder I feel so much better. The door creaks open and I step out into a warm twilight. Down at the field there are fairy lights, and I make my way towards the sound of the disco music, to find Reg sitting at the entrance to the marquee.

'Joel's been looking all over for you.'

'Have you seen Alfie?'

'Nope. Don't look so worried. He'll be along.'

I spot Joel dancing with Pattie but neither of them has seen Alfie.

Joel lunges towards me and plants a kiss on my cheek. 'Where have you been, darling?'

'Asleep in the church.'

'Well, that beats the lot. D'you hear that Pattie? She's been asleep in the church.'

Pattie giggles. She's as well away as he is. I'll have to find Alfie on my own.

But I don't find Alfie. I scour the whole showground. I see a load of things I don't want to see, like Gary throwing up behind

211

the beer tent, blokes pissing all over the place, and a couple making out in the long grass between two vintage tractors.

But no Alfie. I hear that 'sure' that he said as he left. I listen to it over and over in my head. He never intended to come back. I think of texting him, but of course there's no signal. What am I supposed to do? What got into him?

I drag myself back to the disco tent. Reg tells me his stock phrase.

'It might never 'appen.'

'But it has. Alfie's only stood me up.'

Reg pats the seat beside him. 'Twill be summat to do with they sheep. He'll have to stay and look to one of them. Now, do an old man a kindness. Go get us both some of that hog roast. The smell of it's fair making my mouth water.'

'Proper job,' he says when I come back. 'No sign of Gary, I suppose?'

I shake my head and say nothing. We munch on the pork, which is the best I ever tasted, and I sit with Reg until Pattie's husband, Alan, appears. He's probably the only sober man for miles around. He drags her away and asks me if I want a lift home.

I shift in my seat as we approach the track to Hannafords' farm and Alan says, 'Best not go up there tonight. Sleep on it, whatever 'tis.'

His flat tones are kind of reassuring and I don't protest. Pattie squeezes my hand as they drop me at The George, and I make my way through to the back garden and sit on the wooden bench. It's probably the last time I'll come here, and it reminds me of the happy times with Alfie when my leg was in plaster. I'll have to leave at the end of the week, especially as Marion's due back. Where on earth will I go? The YWCA in Exeter is probably my best bet. At least until Alfie's trial. I'm not leaving the area until I know what's happened to him, even if he never speaks to me again.

It's a starry night and I lie along the bench to look at the sky. I never noticed the stars in London. Couldn't see them anyway with all those sodium lights. But here the sky's dark as velvet and each star blazes like a ring in a box. They're looking after me like those ancient faces in the church. I wish I knew which star was which. I had all those constellations on my bedroom ceiling at Auntie

Em's. Not just glow stars, but a proper map of the heavens that kept on shining long after the light went off. Auntie Em would lie down beside me and try to teach me, but I always fell asleep. Which was maybe why she did it.

Bet Alfie knows the stars. He can probably find his way across the fucking moor by the stars. But he couldn't make it back to the fair.

I'm wide awake but I'm shivering, and I want to be well out the way before Joel comes rolling in. I let myself in through the kitchen and climb up to bed thinking how much I'm going to miss this creaky old building and Pattie and Joel. It's come to feel like home.

Next morning I'm well into my second mug of coffee before Joel appears, still in his dressing gown.

'Shit! You look like death. Not even warmed up.'

Joel groans. 'No comments please. Nothing a few magic pills won't fix.'

He scrabbles around in the medicine cupboard, muttering about a Bloody Mary until I find him his pills. He downs them and I try to make him drink the rest of the water but he shakes his head.

'Christ, that was a mistake.' He holds his head carefully on either side and looks at me as if for the first time. 'There was something. Wait a minute. No. It's a Bloody Mary I need. Just wait there.'

He shambles off into the bar still holding his head and I can hear him opening bottles and swearing. He comes back with a tumbler of dark red liquid.

'Wonderful stuff. Secret formula. Works every time.' He takes a gulp and sighs deeply. 'Hits the spot. Mind you, don't let me have another. That's the mistake people make. Just the one. Now, a little toast perhaps? With honey. And some coffee to follow.'

'At your service.' I sigh and put bread in the toaster. It's not as if I'm feeling exactly great myself this morning. He hasn't even asked how I got home, let alone whether I ever found Alfie.

'Now where was I? Oh yes, there was something for you. You see, it's working already. An envelope. It was on the mat when I came in. You see, I wasn't quite as rat-arsed as you might think. Now, where did I put it?'

I want to shake him. Not a good idea though. Instead I tip the grounds out of the coffee pot and make fresh, then press my nails into the palms of my hands as I watch the glow of the toaster and wait for the bread to pop up.

It's as if Joel wants to be sure of his breakfast before he tells me. I fetch a plate and a mug, put the toast and coffee down.

'I remember,' he says. 'I thought I needed a nightcap. A wee dram for bed. Big mistake. That envelope, it'll be behind the bar. I know, I put it on the till where you'd see it.'

I'm gone and I take the envelope right upstairs to my room before I open it. There are two sheets of paper inside, heavyweight stuff torn from one of Alfie's sketch blocks. One is closely and neatly written, the other a scrawl. I read the scrawl first.

Dear Esther
I wrote enclosed letter after you left the other evening and then I lost my nerve about giving it to you.
Tonight I did a lot of thinking and I'm giving it to you after all, because it makes things clear. And today they didn't seem at all clear.
I didn't come back to the disco because I thought you'd have a better time with all those young lads without me hanging around with two left feet. I thought you'd be glad.
Then I thought you might be mad at me.
Then I realised I was jealous. And you can certainly do better than that nephew of Reg's or whoever he is, however hunky he might be.
The more I think the more confused I get. So I decided to give you the letter because I wasn't confused when I wrote that.
Love Alfie

I gaze at the note in disbelief. Alfie jealous! I giggle to myself when I think of the pathetic Gary. How come Alfie could possibly be jealous? Gary didn't even summon the nerve to touch me, and I certainly kept my distance. But he was hanging round me for

214

quite a while. Alfie must have been watching it all. And there was the teddy bear – which I must have left in the church – and the ice cream. I take a deep breath and spread the other sheet of paper.

To my very dear girl-with-green-eyes...

He hasn't called me that for months. And 'very dear'. I like that. Somehow it's nicer than all the 'darlings' and 'sweethearts' Luke used to use. I read on.

> *You were right of course. But so was I.*
>
> *You're right because I probably am a commitment freak. Not by nature – God knows, I think I have a track record there – but because of all that's happened. And all that might soon happen.*
>
> *As I said, there's no way I'll commit to you – or let you commit to me – before the trial. And that's where I'm right. Nothing will change my mind about that.*
>
> *After the trial – IF I GET OFF – is a different matter. I love you, Esther. I want you. I love being with you. But I admit I am still afraid. For all the reasons you know so well. That you could do so much better. That you'll get tired of an old man. And so on and so on...*
>
> *And if I go to prison – which as I keep saying – is highly likely, I CANNOT BEAR the thought of you visiting and WAITING for me. Visit occasionally by all means. AS A FRIEND, a special friend. I would love that. Just so long as you are getting on with your life and loving someone else. I want you to promise me that. Otherwise I'd feel so bloody guilty.*
>
> *I'm sorry to get you into such a mess.*
> *Your Alfie*

'Your Alfie'. I like that, too. I kiss the letter, which is such a naff thing to do, but there's no one to see, and fold it carefully and put it back in the envelope with the scribbled note – which is just as precious in its way. I put the envelope under my pillow and race downstairs.

Joel is clutching his empty mug. 'Just in time to make me some more coffee.'

I roll my eyes at him but put the kettle on. 'Can I take an hour and nip up the farm on the bike? Please, Joel? Pretty please?'

'No way. Not the way I feel. I am totally incapable of getting ready to open. Gotta be open by eleven. Prepare for lunches. Nice day I notice. Could be walkers.'

'Joel, surely if...'

'Sorry girl, you gotta earn your keep today. Extra day off yesterday. What more do you want? Affairs of the heart, all very well. Alfie'll keep. You can go after lunches. After two. So long as you're back by six.'

I make him a mug of instant coffee.

'I'll take this up and get showered. Put new life in me. Hope that Pattie shows up.'

Joel staggers off upstairs and I open all the windows in the bar and fetch the bucket of cleaning materials. I'm suddenly full of energy.

21

I am on the pavement outside the law courts. Donald is at my elbow, propelling me forward. A great crowd of people is milling around. Who are they all? I feel cut off from them, from Donald, as if I'm looking through the wrong end of a telescope. The focus is sharp, but they're too far away. Meg and I went to the ballet once, a seat in the gods. The dancers were tiny and I got vertigo. That's how I feel now.

Donald steps in front of me. Cameras flash into action, microphones target him and a shout goes up from people waving banners in the background. He's making the customary lawyer's statement to the press on my behalf.

It all happened as Donald predicted. In September the prosecution asked for an adjournment. They needed to consider their position in the light of the DPP's interim policy guidelines, which had recently been announced.

Donald's optimism became less cautious, and it turned out to be justified. Today, minutes ago, the Crown prosecutor stood up in court and announced that the Crown was dropping the case against me. *Will not be calling any evidence to support the charge.* There was an audible intake of breath from the gallery. But I was still holding my breath. *Would ask Your Honour to enter a verdict of "Not Guilty".* Only then did I breathe again.

Not guilty. It feels surreal, after all these months, to be a free man. Not that the bail conditions restricted me. But, when I walked the streets, I was always aware of it, conscious of not being free as those all around me were free. Now that shadow has lifted. So why do I not feel like leaping and whooping with joy and relief? Why do I feel cut off?

I keep hearing those phrases Donald used in our recent discussions, the same ones that Connie highlighted in that *Guardian* article. *Clear, settled and informed wish. Indicated unequivocally. Motivated by compassion.* So she was right to get excited. They aren't just empty words. They're words not just with meanings, but with meanings that exactly fit what Meg wanted and what I helped her to achieve. These words have set me free. Common sense and compassion seem to have prevailed over fear and suspicion and it feels like a miracle. But, like a miracle, it feels unreal.

The statement is quickly over, the police clear a path. Donald's on one side of me, Tom on the other. Walking me away.

Suddenly I hear a yell of 'Dad!' and there's Laura. She stands in front of me and we stare at each other for a full second before she throws herself at me and I hug her close. Nothing ever felt so good. She's sobbing into my neck. 'Dad, Dad. I'm sorry, so sorry! I've missed you so much.' A young man in a broad-brimmed black hat appears and pulls her gently away as a car draws up and I'm pushed inside. It accelerates away abruptly. I put my head in my hands and find I am weeping.

Next thing I know I'm in a hotel, a lounge with a bar. Tom is handing me a glass and telling me to drink. It turns out to be neat whisky. I cough and grin and gulp some more. I see Laura and the black-hatted young man approaching the door from the lobby and lift a hand in welcome. And then Esther is at my side.

'Alfie!' She's vibrating with excitement. 'We ran all the way. Joel and me, chasing your taxi.' She reaches up and pulls my face down to hers and kisses me, full and hard. I close my eyes and inhale the good smell of her.

Joel is there, slapping me on the back and pumping my arm and Tom comes back with a refill. I look round for Laura. The doorway is empty. There's no one else in the room. I stride across the floor. They are in the foyer. The young man has Laura by the arm, waving his hat in my direction and trying to pull her back. Laura is resisting and shouting, 'How can I? That tart! You saw! She's the same age as me!'

218

She sees me advancing on her. 'No, Dad! It's disgusting. She's only a kid. Couldn't you wait? It's not even a year – since Ma,' she hesitates, 'died.'

She turns to the young man. 'No, Ed. I will not. I cannot. Take me away.'

I stand watching from behind the revolving doors as my daughter walks away down the street with a stranger's arm protectively round her. I turn to see Esther standing in the doorway. Her face tells me she has seen it all.

'Will she come back – if I go away?'

'You're not going anywhere. She'll just have to grow up.'

'Alfie!' There's a shout from Joel. 'Come on, we're trying to have a party here, and the star player's gone AWOL.'

He's standing drinks all round, Connie's ordered a platter of sandwiches and Tom can't stop slapping me on the back. More people arrive – Donald, friends and neighbours and Geoff, whom I haven't seen for months. How did they know? Who's arranged all this? But there is no chance to ask the question. People can't stop hugging and kissing me. I am absolutely not permitted to be sad. I force myself to join in, to smile – and when Esther stops looking worried every time she looks at me I know I've succeeded.

When the sandwiches arrive and everyone gathers round to help themselves I stand back at the bar, trying to make myself feel real. How is it possible to be feeling such joy and such pain all at the same time? Joy that Laura came, that she hugged me. Pain that she has gone again. Joy that I am free and pain that I've lost Meg. Joy that I have Esther and pain that I've lost Laura.

Esther comes across with a plate of sandwiches for us to share, but I can't eat. I already have too much to digest.

There's something going on in my head apart from the Laura stuff. Something that doesn't add up – as Father would have said. And what's Father doing, sticking his oar in? It's about freedom. And Esther. I have no right to them. Okay, I'll argue myself hoarse for Meg's right to be helped as I helped her, for people like her to be sure that people like me won't be prosecuted. But, after the event, another rule kicks in. You take a life, you are punished. An eye for an eye, and all that.

Maybe I would have felt better if there had been a trial, if the issues had been aired in court, if a judge and jury had weighed the evidence and told me I deserved to be free.

It's not that I don't value the freedom. Yes, the freedom I could cope with. But my picture of freedom is of a void. A vast desert. No oasis, no sunlit uplands. No reward. No free gift. No Esther.

I've been cheating up until now. Escaping into spring, summer. Into new life, new love. That no-man's-land up on the moor. I look back on it and it seems unreal, obscene even. Like putting a chocolate-box picture of lambs and primroses among the sombre headstones in a graveyard. And Laura, underneath the needy child and the drama queen, she's thinking the same way. Yes, I can understand that.

Connie is suddenly at my side. 'What dark thoughts are you having?' She holds out her mobile, takes my arm and walks me over to the window. 'I've just had a text from Laura. Oh, Alfie, I'm so sorry, I saw what happened.'

I shrug. So Laura's texted Connie rather than communicate with me. Back to square one.

'I just thank your lucky stars that toad Pugh wasn't here to witness that little scene. He'd have made much of it.'

I still don't take the mobile. I'm thinking that maybe Pugh had a point. What's come over me? I shake myself out of it. 'Was he there in court? I didn't see him. I'd have liked him to see me discharged.'

'I heard he got the sack from the paper. Letting personal beliefs getting in the way of professional judgement. Something along those lines. It figures.'

I shrug. 'So what does Laura have to say? You tell me. I don't want to read it.'

'She was going to be staying at the house tonight – with you. I imagine that's where you'll stay?'

'I guess so.'

'But she says she's on the train back to London, and to tell you,' Connie hesitates. 'To tell you she'll speak to you when you come to your senses.'

'Big of her,' I say, and I think, maybe I do need to come to my senses.

'Oh, and I put some groceries in the kitchen. Milk in fridge and so on. Just so you know. And Alfie,' she hesitates and puts a hand on my arm. 'Don't let Laura spoil things. You know. You're a free man. And there's Esther. She's a lovely girl. Pure gold. And you deserve her, you really do.'

She hugs me and leaves to reopen the gallery. Donald is next to leave, followed by Geoff, rushing back for a surgery, and my next-door neighbours. But Joel has gathered a hard core around him who show no sign of giving up. Tom's leaning on the bar on his own, making his pint last.

Esther leaves the group and I watch her coming across the room towards me. She smiles. A shy little grin as if she's not sure – of what? Of me? She slips her hand into mine. It's cool and dry. 'We don't have to stay,' she says.

I'd rather just talk to her, but Joel is calling us over. I squeeze her to me, feel her warmth, inhale the everyday smell of her – shampoo, something lemony, something musky. What's the matter with me? I push away the dark thoughts. 'Come on,' I say. 'It's our party.'

'Your party,' she says. 'The first day of the rest of your life.'

It seems like hours before the celebrations break up and we're on our own in the hotel foyer. It's as if we're expected to have some sort of honeymoon. We've both left our jobs, so what's to stop us?

Esther links her arm in mine. 'So what's next? Where do we go?'

I think of the house and the groceries purchased for Laura and her man – and for me, if I got off. And I remember the night we never had in a posh hotel in St Ives.

'We're going to stay here for the night. Hope you brought your toothbrush?'

Esther shakes her head. 'I didn't want to tempt providence. Thought I could borrow yours?'

I hug her close and we book in to a grand room with a four-poster bed. I'm deep asleep before Esther's finished exclaiming about the gold taps and the towels and the minibar and the curtains.

'So this is your house.'

We're standing in the little hallway. I've promised Tom I'll be back to keep my appointment with the ram, but I've insisted he look out for another permanent shepherd. After all it's seven months since I was taken on for a few weeks for the lambing. There's no way Esther would spend a winter in the barn, and in any case the planners are bound to get wind of it sooner or later.

When I said that to Tom he laughed. 'They've already been up here. Reckon as that newspaper bloke put them on to it. But I put them off the scent. Told the fella it was just used as a shepherd's hut and that you had your quarters in the farm. Offered to show him – but then, see, Eric popped out of the shed over yonder with one of his ferrets. And I just gives Eric a nod and a wink and he starts to act a bit strange. Jerkin' about and that. You know how he can. And happen he comes between the fella and the gate and the dogs start getting restless. Put the wind right up him, it did. He were off sharpish.'

'Even so,' I said. 'They'll be back. And anyway, I've a business to see to and Esther needs to get a job.'

Esther's been in touch with her old university, but it's all taking a while. One step at a time. Moving into the house seemed the obvious first step. Now I'm not so sure.

'Well, aren't you going to give me the conducted tour?'

Meg's bed has gone thank goodness – it belonged to the NHS – but the room still needs rearranging. The mattress I slept on in the back room is still there but otherwise there's nothing to remind me of those last months. But everything does remind me.

We both assume we'll sleep in the double bed in the front bedroom where Meg and I used to sleep before she got too ill to go upstairs. But when it comes to it, neither of us can cope with that.

'It's only a bed,' I say.

'No, it's not,' says Esther. 'It's *the* bed.'

I take the mattress from the back room back up to Meg's studio where it used to be, and Esther makes up Laura's bed. I wonder what Laura would think of that, and I'm sure it occurs to Esther too. We drink the wine thoughtfully provided by Connie, but still we can't sleep. Eventually we drop off in the early hours, curled into each other on my old mattress. But I wake early in a cold sweat, disentangle myself and leave Esther to sleep on.

A shower is what I need. The hot water fizzing into my skin is sheer luxury, and one that I've missed in my primitive barn. I turn the temperature gradually higher until it's no longer bearable and then switch to cold until I gasp with the shock of it. I creep about finding warm clothes and my pipe, and pad out to the seat by the back door to watch the dawn.

I'm still not ready for this house. I can't sleep here. I can't live here. Coming back has returned me to the source of the pain. Maybe that's no bad thing. I guess it has to be faced. I feel as if I have a well inside me. It's dark and deep and there's a heavy wooden lid on it. Coming here has lifted the lid. I'm in danger of falling down the black well. It feels like I'm desperately searching for the womb of my family. What a strange phrase. Where did that come from?

Esther stops me from falling. She's like those springs on the moor, bubbling up through the grass where you least expect them, light and effervescent. Like she's always laughing, seeing the funny side. Like the stream in the leat at Merrivale. That water, too, must come from a deep, dark underground source. And in Esther's case, I now know that it does. But with her you wouldn't know it. She's visited the dark places and survived. Do I need to do the same? Is it necessary? Do I have a choice?

I do have a choice about living in the house. When I put it to Esther, she comes up with the obvious solution.

'Didn't you say there was a flat above the shop? Couldn't we live there?'

I ring Connie. She doesn't sound surprised. The flat is still empty, and I suspect she anticipated something like this and hasn't made any effort to find a tenant. The woman's psychic.

Esther loves the flat and I realise she was finding the house as difficult as I was.

I set down our bags and stride to the window. 'It's much bigger than I remember. Mind you, what with my mother and all the baby clutter, there wasn't much room.'

'Your mother lived here?'

'Oh yes. When Father died she got herself a bungalow near the sea. But then Laura arrived. That was just as Meg's photography started to take off. So Mum helped us buy the place and moved in here to babysit. It was all a bit of a squash. The café was actually her idea. It brought people in. She really got the whole place going. She was in her element. It was all too good to be true.'

'So what happened? Did she go back to her bungalow when Laura grew up?'

'No. She got stomach cancer. A tummy bug, she kept saying until I persuaded her to go for tests. She was gone by the time Laura was two.'

Esther puts her arms round me. 'And you still miss her.'

'Not really. But it was like I only got to know her properly in those couple of years. And it was only then she really got a life. She was a different person without Father. She just *laughed* so much!' I shake the memories out of my head. 'Sod's Law, but at least it happened. She had that time. We had that time. Now, where do we start?'

22

It's uncanny. The moment we move into the flat and get it straightened out, Luke starts texting me again. I've scrubbed the whole place and rearranged the furniture – even thrown a few things out, to be honest. Mostly Alfie agreed with me. A few items went when he was out. There was some rubbish stuff. Can't think how Connie put up with it. One day we both look at the kitchen-cum-living room and say, 'We need a table.' Alfie can't remember what happened to the old one, but Connie tells me later that it was riddled with woodworm and she took it to the tip.

I bring up Luke's latest message on my mobile and pass it to Alfie. 'Would you believe? Good timing, or what?'

He peers and reads out, '"When can I off-load the table?"' and gives me a dubious look.

'But we need a table, right? And I've got one.' It seems a no-brainer to me. 'And I do want it. If you remember it was…'

'Yes, your Nan's table. You told me.'

It's Luke of course, not the table, that Alfie's dubious about.

'Alfie! There is nothing, repeat nothing, between Luke and me – except a table, that is. And the sooner that's sorted the better.'

'Fine, fine. You go ahead. But I'm not sure I want to meet him.'

'Okay. No prob. I'll find out when he can come.'

So finally it's time to let Luke know where I am. I mean, I suppose it's odd that I've been so secretive. But I know how tricky he can be. And it isn't as if we parted friends. If it hadn't been for the table, I'd never have spoken to him again. It's like sharing custody. Just with no kid. Imagine what that would have been like.

His texts go a bit mental when he finds out I'm in Devon. He's got a friend with a van and it seems he thought it was just a matter of taking it across London or something. I grin to myself and tell him I'll pay for the petrol. He comes right back and says, diesel. Typical Luke. Puhlease.

With all this going on, it's a while before I notice that Alfie's in a bad place. I expected him to be over the fucking moon about getting off and having his life back. I guess he did too. But it's not like that. He moons about. Gets up late. Stinks the place out with his pipe. I never noticed it up at the barn with that high roof, and anyway he mostly smoked outside there. I can see it wouldn't be exactly relaxing standing outside on the pavement, puffing away. He moans about not being able to have a smoke in his own shop any more, and then I discover he's sloping off to sit on a bench near the cathedral along with all the down-and-outs. I nearly tripped over him when I went out exploring.

'Fuckin'ell Alfie! Shall I get you a bottle of cider in a brown paper bag to take with you next time?'

Said he didn't want to upset me. That's rich.

'Alfie, you are such an ace idiot.'

'Anyway, I don't like to be cooped up – and you meet some interesting guys round here.'

'I dare say. But you've got a home and a business to look after.'

He just ignores me and carries on. 'I've been sitting here thinking. Discovering things. One thing I've discovered is, you can't mourn someone until they're dead. Sounds so obvious, but it isn't.'

I snap my big mouth shut. Listen to yourself, carrying on just like Nan used to. And all the time... I might have known something was going on in that scarecrow head of his.

'You see I lost Meg, the real Meg, months before she died. But that part of her, that person, was still there, inside her somewhere, hidden from me, hidden from her too, I guess. So I couldn't do it. The grieving, I mean. And people, friends and so on, go through the motions – but really they think you should be glad, or relieved at least... Is this making any sense?'

I nod. It was the same with Nan. 'They show respect, but next thing they're saying, what a relief, she's out of her misery and you can get on with your life. Not quite in the same breath, but…'

'Yes, that's it exactly. And with what happened – the way she died – there was another layer to it all. I still couldn't do the grieving before I knew what they'd do with me. Selfish really. I was just too preoccupied. I've only just realised, that's really why I went to the moor. That man Pugh was an excuse. I wanted to escape – because it was too complicated. Can you…?'

'Yes, yes. It's what I was doing too.'

Alfie nods slowly. 'The same with your Nan.'

And Luke, I think. The abortion and losing Luke, losing a friend, straight after Nan died. I had layers, too. But I don't want to talk about Luke. I don't want to spoil it, this close feeling.

'So we were both playing a part.' Alfie looks at me and gives a dry laugh. 'The Shepherd and the Barmaid, the Artist and his Model.'

The warm feeling turns cold and spreads slowly in my stomach, as if I know what he's going to say next.

'And now we've stepped off the stage. And we're just Alfie and Esther.' He puts his head in his hands. 'The real world now. Just plain Alfie and Esther.'

He's saying the magic's gone. And although we make a game of thinking up famous pairs – from Antony and Cleopatra, to Beauty and the Beast and Bonnie and Clyde – and although he holds my hand as we make our way back to the flat, it no longer feels like home. And although that night he lets me hold him, I feel him sobbing as we fall asleep and I know he's still wedded to Meg and I can't reach him.

I'm even relieved when Tom calls.

Alfie turns to me. 'Is it okay for me to go up to the farm? Tom could do with some help getting the ewes ready – worming, and so on.'

Of course, I say. Alfie's grinning like the old Alfie when he comes off the phone. He sets out on Saturday with his old rucksack and a spring in his step. Tom's going to meet the bus.

I miss him in bed. It's not just the sex. I'm all at sea without his warm, safe body curved in my back. On the other hand, I feel positively light-headed to wake up in the morning without his heavy cloud hanging over me.

Connie notices immediately. 'You've perked up. Don't worry, I know what he's like when he's in a bad place.'

I focus on the computer screen. I'm helping her computerise all the gallery records and she's teaching me the system. 'Just a bit gloomsville. I guess he's fed up with me.' I try to sound jokey. 'Now we're together all the time.'

She brings another bundle of files and dumps them beside my keyboard. 'Don't be daft. Nothing to do with you, and hardly surprising either.'

'Laura, you mean?'

'Yes, Laura. But not just that. You may not want to hear this, but I guess he's only just now coming to terms with losing Meg. After all he's been focused on the trial all this time. Plus he's been up there with the animals. Now he's back in the old life. Can't face the house, you see. There's your clue.'

I say nothing. It's just what Alfie said himself, but I'm still afraid it's me.

'Look how he cheered up when he was off up to the moor. Away from here, you see.'

Connie's doing her best, but that only means he prefers sheep to me. Maybe Alfie was right and we aren't meant for each other after all. I like Connie and we've hit it off from the start, but it does bug me that she knows Alfie inside out. Better than I do. Trouble is, she's been through so much with him. I grin to myself. At least there's one side of Alfie I know better than she does. That keeps me going.

Alfie rings that evening and says they're not quite done. He won't be home tonight. There's a hole in the roof of the barn to fix. I'm surprised he slept up there. I thought he'd be staying in the farmhouse, but I don't have a chance to ask. He's giving me news of everyone at The George, and I suddenly feel choked. He's there without me, and I'm suddenly jealous and homesick. I don't even know who to be jealous of. Alfie or all the folk at The George. Why didn't he ask me to go with him? Why didn't I ask?

I wander into the bedroom and take out Carole's copy of

The Prophet. I have to be careful with it because the pages are all coming unglued and falling out. In the back I keep Alfie's letter – the "Widecombe Fair" letter, I call it. I spread it out and read it again. *I love you, Esther. I want you. I love being with you.* That line I read over and over again. Did he really mean it? Does he still mean it? *You never know with him.* Shit. Life's a bitch.

I wash my face with cold water, make some coffee and sit on the window seat with my mug, having a serious think. Life and the universe, Bex used to say. We'd sit up half the night in the old days in the flat, just talking. Not that she's any help. Last I heard she'd taken a job with an American company and was off to New York. I need to make plans, get a job, save up. And, for now, I'd best get one here in Exeter. Whether or not things work out with me and Alfie, I don't fancy going back to London. Either way, I need to be independent. I'm interrupted by a commotion in the street – banging and shouting. It's a quiet enough area in the evening so I peer out to see what's going on and find myself looking down at Luke.

'You certainly know how to hide yourself away,' are his first words as I let him in through the coffee shop.

'Sorry, yes. There's no bell for the flat.'

'No front door either. I've been hammering away for hours.'

'You could have called or texted.'

'Wanted to take you by surprise.'

He's certainly done that. Lucky Alfie's not here. I'm about to lead the way upstairs when Luke says, 'Stop. Turn around. Let me look at you.'

I look back at him, taking in the familiar flop of dark hair over his forehead and the less familiar tan.

'You're looking good,' he says, as if he's surprised.

'Why shouldn't I?' I shrug and climb the stairs. 'Coffee? I just made some.'

'You never used to drink coffee. I'd prefer tea if...'

I fish out a tea-bag and drop it in a mug, switch the kettle back on. He's looking good himself but I'm not about to tell him. Any more than I'll tell him how pleased I am to see him. That's a bit of a shock and I'm glad to be able to focus on the kettle and dibbling about with a tea-bag. I even remember how he likes his tea.

'Well, how's tricks?'

He listens while I tell him about The George and life on the moor, the village.

'So how come you've tipped up here? Although I'd say it was a bit more you than a pub full of yokels in the back of beyond.'

That gets me miffed straight off. He's out of order, but it's probably how I'd have described The George a few months ago.

'Seasonal. End of the summer, no more tourists, no more job. And I love this gallery, and the café. The manager's training me up.'

'So where does he live?'

I can see how Luke's mind is working. I haven't mentioned Alfie and I don't want to. I know only too well what Luke will say when he discovers how old he is.

'She. Connie Parker. She used to live here, but she's got a house now.'

'Lucky for you. So why "Buckland's Books?"'

'Oh that's the owner's name. So where have you been globetrotting? Somewhere hot I can see.'

He falls neatly for that one, tells me all about his summer in Barcelona.

'You see before you a fully fledged TEFL teacher.'

'Teffle?'

'English as a foreign language, T for...'

'Yeah, yeah. Why? What's the idea?'

'Another string to my bow. Got up to speed with Spanish at the same time. Two birds with one stone. Puts me in line for head of department, if I've got three strong languages under the belt.'

'But you've only been there a year.' Luke's been teaching at an independent school in Hertfordshire. I teased him rotten when he got the job. Didn't quite fit with his ambition to bring modern languages alive in the inner city.

'Have to look ahead. Strategic. I want to get on. I've got a nice apartment now, but I'll want a house before long.'

So he's fallen for the middle-class dream he used to be so scornful of. All ready for the two point four children and a Labrador.

'So shall we get this table in?'

Luke brings his van round to the front and we somehow

manhandle that table up the stairs. It gets jammed at one point and I can see we should go back down and turn it, but Luke forces it. One leg makes a bad mark on the wall but he's not bothered.

'This whole place needs redecorating, anyway.'

Hello? It's none of his business but I button my lip. At least I've got Nan's table back, and it looks great in the living room.

'Perfect! Just the right size. I said it would be.'

'Can't really see why you were so keen to keep it. Okay, sentimental value – but well, everyone to their own. I'll go park the van. I'm assuming it's okay to stay tonight?'

It never occurred to me he'd want to stay. But how can I turn him away when he's just done me this big favour? It would be horribly inhospitable, unfriendly.

'Sure. It's a really comfy sofa, long enough, even for you.'

'Why don't we go for a pizza or something? I'm ravenous after trailing around tracking you down.'

I avoid Alfie's favourite Italian and take him to a tapas bar round the corner. We relax a bit and play "Do you remember when?" I even tell him about finding Auntie Em. It's kind of comforting to talk to someone who knew Nan and knows where I come from. No questions asked, no need to tell. He gives me news of people I've lost touch with and tells a few funny stories about the staffroom at his school.

When we leave the restaurant he puts a hand on my shoulder, but I move away and he doesn't attempt to put it back.

'So this is a café as well as a gallery,' he says, looking round while I fix the locks and bolts.

'Internet café. It's pretty popular.'

'Funny mixture. The rest of it's so old-fashioned.'

'I think that's what people like. I certainly do.'

'Pretty bleak, these landscapes of the moor.'

I look round. He's standing in front of one of Alfie's pictures, a favourite of mine.

'There's a lot of weather up there. It's not all pretty ponies, you know.' I don't trust myself to say any more.

As we climb the stairs he says, 'You're not really going to make me sleep on the sofa, are you?'

My stomach jumps. 'Certainly am. I can't believe you just said that.'

'For old time's sake? Oh come on, Esther. One last glorious...'

'No, Luke. Friends is fine. But no more. Not any more.'

He shrugs and goes off to the bathroom while I find some bedding for the sofa.

When he comes back his mood has changed. 'Who is he then? I thought you were living on your own. Who's got his shaving kit in your bathroom? Why didn't you tell me?'

'You didn't ask. You just assumed. He's the owner – Mr Buckland. Alfie, his name is.'

He gets it all out of me of course. Bit by bit. And he goes quiet. Looks for a moment as if someone's kneed him in the groin.

'So where is he now?'

I tell him about the farm. 'It's how we met. He used to come into the pub.'

I can practically see the wheels turning as Luke tries to imagine a painting shepherd, and I have to grin inwardly.

'He does portraits so I sat for him.' I catch his cynical glance. 'Not what you're thinking. Head and shoulders. And he never took advantage.'

Luke raises his eyebrows, as if to say he's not such a fool as to believe that.

'Think what you want. But it's true.' I speak quietly, and maybe he does believe me. In any case he changes tack.

'You mentioned a daughter. This fellow's got a kid? How old is she?'

I guess he's wondering how I will cope. A stepdaughter, me bringing up a child.

'She's at college. Royal College of Music, so she'd be...'

He comes to life then. 'What? Hardly younger than you, then! This Alfie must be old! Old enough...'

'To be my father.' I finish for him and sigh. 'You are not the first person to notice that.'

'Oh, come on, Esther. I can cope with you saying you've fallen for a bloke your own age. I could lose you to someone who'd give you a life. But...'

What does he mean, lose me? He hasn't had me to lose, not for six months or more. 'Who says Alfie can't give me a life? And anyway I wasn't yours to lose, remember?'

'Oh, I remember, all right. Our baby would have been due any day now. I haven't forgotten anything.'

'That didn't make me yours.' I start to feel mad, but he's staring at the floor looking really sad. 'Well, it didn't, Luke. But I'm sorry about that. Not that I regret it. It was horrible, but it had to happen.'

He looks up. 'Well, there's a turn-up. It's the first time you've... Well, put it this way, you didn't seem to give a damn.'

'Oh, I did, I can tell you.' I say no more. I was giving a damn about me, not about the baby, not about Luke. I don't feel guilty about the baby, but I do feel bad that I didn't even consider Luke's feelings. The thing was, I couldn't afford to.

'This Alfie, he probably won't want more children, at this stage in his life.'

'No, not that it's any business of yours.'

'That's dreadful. And if he did, it would be dreadful too. He'd be drawing his pension before they were teenage.'

'No, it's not dreadful. It's a huge relief. I haven't changed my mind, Luke. I never will.'

'Wait till that biological clock...'

'Shut up, Luke. I'm tired. Time for bed.'

But he suddenly drops to his knees in front of me and takes my face in his hands. 'Esther, I can't let you do this. I can't let you sacrifice yourself to some old fellow who's somehow fooled you into...'

I pull away. 'He's not an "old fellow". Alfie hasn't fooled me into anything. Quite the...'

He pins me into the chair by my elbows as I try to get up. 'Esther, no. Listen to me. I love you. I always have. I messed up. I understand that now. Look at what I can offer you. A secure future, a decent home, a good life. Not living in a shabby flat, working in a shop and widowed at fifty. And that's if you're lucky. You might be nursing a sick old man for years.'

'Just get off my case, Luke. And let me fucking get up. You're talking rubbish.'

'I'm asking you to marry me, Esther.'

Oh, fuck! What have I got into here? How can he possibly imagine...? He's stark, staring bonkers. Yet there's something in his eyes that softens me. He means it. I suppose I have to accept that in his own weird way the idiot loves me.

I'm cornered, stuck in the chair listening to him blathering on about what he can offer that Alfie can't. It dawns on me that I'm part of his strategy for the future. Luke and Esther in green wellies walking the Labrador. Oh fuck. I take a deep breath.

'Luke, I can't possibly marry you. I don't love you. I don't want that life, and even if I did I wouldn't marry you for that. You're worth more than that.'

'You would grow to love me. I know you would. Remember how we used to be? We know each other. I know your past. I knew your Nan. We're old friends. It's a good basis.'

He's really thought about this. He knows which buttons to push. And yes, we were good friends until he started thinking he could run my life.

'It wouldn't work, Luke. We were good friends once, but people grow apart. And anyway, I'm in love with Alfie.'

'Ah. "In love." That's different. How long will that last?'

Maybe it's already over I think, remembering the bear-with-sore-head person who left yesterday. 'Please Luke. Drop it. I know what I'm...'

'Okay. I'll drop it. But first tell me. What is it you see in him? Why Esther? Tell me.'

It's no business of his, but he still won't let me move. I take another deep breath. 'He's funny and sexy and honest and practical and creative, and he takes me as I am. He's gentle and tough and thoughtful. And he doesn't fit into any boxes – which makes him hard to describe.' I pause, thinking it's not enough. It nowhere near captures Alfie. I want to say, it's the way his hair sticks out, the way he grins with his eyes. And that look of his. I never knew what "quizzical" meant until I met Alfie. But that's all too personal. I don't want Luke knowing stuff like that.

'Certainly doesn't fit into any known category. I'd say...'

'Anyway, you can't just say what you see in a person. That's the attraction, sure. But after that it's all about what happens between you.'

I can see he doesn't like that. He shrugs. 'Seems like a jack of all trades. I mean, where the hell do the sheep fit in?'

I've had enough. 'Like I said, none of your business actually. You said you'd drop it. And now I really do need to go to bed.'

He lets me go and stands up. Which is a relief. I never really thought he'd come on heavy, but you never know.

He reads my thoughts. 'It's okay. I won't try anything. I respect you too much for that. But I'm not giving up either. Just think about what I said. My offer.'

He's unlacing his trainers as I go through to the bedroom and I wonder what he means by not giving up. I know what my answer is and always will be. I don't need or want to think about it. But it keeps me awake for hours. I can't even go and make myself a drink, in case he thinks it's an invitation.

23

Tom drops me off in Exeter just after nine on his way to see a man about a ram. We worked late last night to finish treating all the ewes. Nightmare in the dim light of Tom's barn. I was sad to see that, even in the short time I've been gone, some of their feet had been neglected. This morning I got up early to fix the barn roof. It needs a slate but I managed to make a temporary patch job.

My head's still full of animal talk as I walk up the street. Then I see them. Esther and a guy with dark hair at the entrance to the gallery. She's standing on the doorstep and he's out on the pavement, but he's still much taller than her. The thought flashes through my mind that they look so good together. I can't help it. Young, attractive, *right*. It gives me a pang to think how different – how not right – we two must look as a couple.

As I watch, he takes her by the shoulders and is obviously speaking very earnestly, looking into her eyes. What the hell is this? Then she nods, and he kisses her – on the mouth – and steps away. He waves but she's already disappeared into the shop. On the mouth. He kissed her on the mouth. Did she return that kiss? She looked kind of casual, but I was too far away. I can't tell.

The man starts walking towards me. I slow my pace and take a good look. Six foot three, medium build, dark wavy hair, deep-set eyes, probably brown, horribly good-looking. A slightly Latin look or possibly Jewish. An easy, confident stride. Blue jeans, black jumper. By the time he's ten yards away I could describe him to the police. He doesn't seem to register me, but why should he? I'm just wondering whether to stop him and confront him when he swings off down a side street.

I stand on the corner and watch until he disappears.

'Any news? Anything happened?' I ask when I get to the gallery.

Connie shakes her head. She's only just walked through the door ahead of me.

'No visitors?'

She frowns. 'No. Were we expecting anyone?'

'No. Not at all.' I leave her looking puzzled as I take the stairs two at a time.

Esther's loading the washing machine.

'Wow, Alfie! That's a surprise. I wasn't expecting you so early.'

'Seems not,' I say. 'Who was the fellow?' I can hear the anger in my voice.

She looks up sharply.

Then I notice the table. Of course. It must have been Luke. Shit. I came close to making a total fool of myself. And shit again, because Luke is not at all as I imagined him – as some rather weedy, God-bothering schoolteacher.

'It was Luke. Who else? Did you meet him? No, obviously not. Or?'

'I saw him leaving. It must have been him. I was down the street.'

She says nothing. No explanation.

'So he stayed over?'

'Well, yes. Couldn't very well turn him out. He didn't find me until late.' She waves at the table. 'What d'you think? Doesn't it go well there?'

I look, but I'm not seeing the table. I'm still seeing that exchange, that kiss.

She straightens the sofa cushions and looks up at me and grins. 'Don't worry Alfie, he slept here – on the sofa. In case you were wondering.'

'Of course I was wondering. After what I just saw.'

She flings her arms round me then and kisses me, and the tight knot in my stomach begins to loosen.

'I saw him leave, Esther. I was watching.'

'Yeah?'

'He just seemed a bit, shall we say, intense. I was some distance away, but the way he kissed you.'

'Oh, that's just Luke. He still feels responsible for me.'

'So the table wasn't the only thing between you then?'

'Alfie, he's an old friend. Well, okay, an old flame. But there's nothing. Not any more. I told you all about it. He was just, you know, looking out for me.'

'Wants to be sure I make an honest woman of you, or…?'

'Something like that. Anyway, how did it go? Up at Tom's? I was dead jealous when you rang last night. Seeing everybody. Being there without me.'

I'm reassured. I put Luke out of my mind. The table business is done and that's that.

Meanwhile Esther seems positively energised by the arrival of the table. The missing piece in her jigsaw, she calls it. She's got plans. I tell myself this energy has nothing to do with seeing Luke.

'How's about I redecorate your house?' she says that evening at supper. 'Paint it from top to bottom, so it feels completely different? Would that be awful? Like sacrilege? Or would it help? What d'you think?'

I'm touched that she's thought about this and come up with the idea. It might even work. 'Okay. We could give it a go.'

'Right. Just give me the money and I'll get on with it. Better if you don't help. So long as you promise not to go join the winos. You can have the place to yourself, here. Paint pictures while I paint walls. I'll do it white, neutral colours. Or you could come and choose.'

She reckons she can get it done in a week. It's only the walls need painting. The ceilings are in good shape and all the wood-work's stripped. The only dark colour that will need a few coats is in Laura's bedroom. Laura's room. I wonder about that. She still uses it sometimes. But I decide to say nothing.

I feel cut off from Esther. I don't understand why I can't break out of it. It's almost as if I'm punishing myself for upsetting Laura. Punishing myself by not being close to Esther – as if that would solve anything. Plus Meg is all around in a way she hasn't been for months. It's as if she slides in between us, intercepting an exchange.

Not the warm generous Meg who would wish us well, but the Meg who was sometimes hijacked by her illness into mean moods and twisted thoughts.

It brings me back to those feelings I had after the trial. Getting off. It wasn't meant to happen. I should be banged up, paying the price. And, as to me and Esther – we're just cheating the system. When I talk to Connie in this vein she shakes me by the shoulders, says, 'You weren't supposed to die as well. Meg wouldn't have wanted that.' But it isn't about what Meg would have wanted.

Old friends get in touch. Some are wary, some over-hearty in their greetings and others very straightforward. All of them remind me of times we shared that can never be again. However kind they are, I simply don't want to reconnect. I can't face them.

Esther isn't helping either. She's not trying to engage any more. It seems she's painting the house and that's it. She has this way of melting away if we meet people in the street. Like on the day we go out to buy paint. I turn to introduce her and she's gone.

'I reckon you'd rather talk to them without me,' she says. 'I don't mind if you want to go round there, see them on your own. Then you can invite them back and they can meet me then – when they've had time to get used to the idea.'

'I don't want to see them. And don't even think of entertaining.' I can barely keep the snap out of my voice. What the hell is she thinking of?

'Okay, okay. I just thought… Oh, never mind.'

She puts out a hand then, but I move away. I don't exactly shake her off. But I feel scratchy. Irritated, with her, with myself.

I do try painting, like she suggested, but it leaves my mind too free. Every inch of the flat conjures Meg and Laura. Pacing the floor with Laura as a baby to get her to sleep, the bedroom crammed with baby paraphernalia, toys all over the place. Meg tousled in a T-shirt at breakfast after another broken night, moaning that she'd never work again. Mum sleeping on the sofa. God, it was cramped with the four of us here. How we jumped at the chance to move out when Mum gave us the deposit for the house.

And then came the guilt when I first clocked how ill Mum was. I'd been so busy playing house and happy families that

I never noticed how thin she'd got. Meg was getting her work focus back and got miffed when Mum said she was too tired to have Laura in the afternoons. Even then the penny didn't drop. When I eventually tumbled to the fact that Mum was so ill, Meg never stopped beating herself up for being so selfish.

My pictures sicken me. That's never happened before. It's as if I've been doing art therapy, not art. The dark thoughts have found their way onto the canvas, sombre and muddy.

I miss Meg like a physical pain. Esther finds me bent double in the kitchen one day and she begs me to go to the doctor. But I know what it is. It's grief. And I don't want to say that to Esther.

'It's just a tummy ache. Stop fussing.'

'Alfie, if only you'd talk to me. Trust me just a little bit?'

But I won't. I can't. It's like there's a trapdoor in my throat. But how can I explain that? How can I explain why I keep moving the washing-up bowl because that's where Mum used to keep it? Why I won't throw out that moth-eaten blanket because it used to be Laura's cot cover? Laura, who has still not been in touch. Trouble is, when there's one thing you're not saying, it stops you saying anything at all.

I don't want Esther to feel jealous of a dead person, to feel she's not enough. The truth is, Esther's too much. She seems to have boundless energy, while I just feel exhausted all the time.

My heart is no longer in the business. I can't get excited about the exhibitions Connie's planning, and I've nothing new of my own that's worth hanging. There's not enough to occupy me anyway, because Connie's so efficient and likes to do things her way. I can't blame her for that. She's had a free hand for so long. Let's face it, my heart's not in anything anymore.

One day I try taking a walk. All round the city and out along the river. It's not the open moor, but it's better than being cooped up inside or sitting on a bench. I observe the people – the high-heeled secretaries clipping down Southernhay at lunchtime, shoppers laden with glossy carrier bags queuing for the Park and Ride bus, bulky old women feeding the ducks and the pigeons. I survey the prison and wonder what the hell it's like in there.

I'm shocked that you now have to pay to visit the cathedral.

So different from the Duomo in Sansepolcro – where people would drop in with their shopping bags to light a candle and kneel for a moment or two as part of the daily round. That sets me off thinking of Meg again, and I wish I hadn't started that train of thought.

How warm it will still be in Italy at this time of year – just that bit more heat left in the sun on your skin. Will I ever bring myself to go back there? Strikes me, as I plod through a light drizzle, that I might as well be desolate in a better climate. But could I be there with Esther?

I'm playing with that idea on my way back home when I spot Luke. He's unmistakable. He's skulking in the doorway of the key cutting shop opposite the gallery and he's gazing intently up at the flat. I freeze. There's no doubt, he's watching our windows. This is no joke, no ordinary concern for Esther. I start to cross the road but a bus lumbers past, obscuring my view. By the time I reach the other side he's vanished. I look up and down, walk to the corner. No sign of him. Maybe he spotted me. If he's been watching our comings and goings, he probably knows who I am by now.

I don't mention it to Esther. She's so fired up by her painting project. And I want to bide my time. I wonder if he's followed her to the house. Does she know? I pour a neat whisky to burn that thought out of my brain.

The next day my walk takes me down our old street. I'm just in time to see Luke get into a van and drive off. Has he been with her at the house? Was that what gave her the painting idea? Is that what's giving her all this energy? It's all too much of a coincidence to ignore.

Deep down a voice tells me, trust her. But there's another voice tells me, she's lied to you before. Don't be made a fool of. But inventing a past – that was different. She's not really a dishonest person. She wouldn't two-time me. Or would she?

Esther gets in before me that evening, announces that she's very nearly finished the work. 'Only one more coat on Laura's room. At least I think that will do it. That bottle-green's a pig to cover and it's still shadowy. It may need two, in which case I'll have to go back Saturday morning. I'll ring if I finish, and you can come and see.'

So, she'll ring me, will she? We'll see about that.

'Aren't you pleased? Alfie?' She looks round from the sink. 'I guess it's a bit scary. It'll be okay, you'll see.'

Next morning I give it an hour or so and set off to our neighbourhood. The white van is parked in the next street. There's no one in it. I let myself in quietly, and hear voices coming from the kitchen.

24

I'm concentrating so hard on slipping into the house unnoticed that it's only when I reach the back room that I breathe again, inhaling the harsh tang of fresh emulsion. The voices are animated – raised, in fact. One of them is Laura's.

Not Luke at all. So much for my suspicions. What on earth is going on?

Esther seems to be in control. 'Now look, Laura. I understand how you must feel. About your mother, I mean. But think what Alfie feels. About losing you, I mean, as well as her.'

'He wouldn't be losing me if it wasn't for you, you cow.'

'That's not quite true, is it? I mean, he lost you for months until the trial. And he didn't even meet me until April. We didn't get together until about June time.'

I'm impressed at how Esther is keeping her cool.

'So fucking what? He's still disgusting to be dating someone younger than me.'

The venom in Laura's voice takes my breath away. It doesn't sound like her.

'Not younger, as it happens. For the record I'm twenty-four. Not that it makes any odds. Why does that make him disgusting?'

Laura flounders. 'It just is. A man of his age. I suppose he painted you and you got your tits out and he couldn't resist.'

There's a pause and I wish I could see Esther's face. 'He's an attractive man, Laura. I guess you don't like to think of your father like that, but he is. And it wasn't like that at all. Seems to me, the disgusting bit is all in your mind.'

Still that calm, even tone. If it weren't for that, I can see myself having to break up a fight.

Laura tries a different tack. 'I suppose you think you're on to a good thing. Freeloading off a man with a business and a house – someone who'll look after you. I suppose that's why you're busy tarting up the place. Ruining my fucking room – my *home*.'

I can understand Laura's dismay. The house has lost that comfortable scuffed fit of an old pair of slippers. It feels different. But that was the idea.

Esther drops her voice. 'As it happens, Alfie's not been able to stay here – because of the memories. I'm painting it to see if that helps. If you stopped thinking about yourself for five fucking minutes, you might get a handle on what it's been like for him.'

'But what about me? I lost my mother.'

'I know that. But what am I supposed to do? I can't make it better for you.'

'He didn't have to do what he did.'

'I'm not getting drawn into that one. It's not for anyone else to say, none of my business.'

'None of it's your business. But it sure as hell is mine! I just wish you'd get the hell out of our life.'

Another pause, then Esther again. 'As a matter of fact I just might…'

My stomach hits my boots. She's thinking of leaving me. So there *is* something in the Luke business.

'In fact, I would – if I thought it would bring you two together. You see, Laura… Laura? Are you listening? I know how much you mean to him. More than me. But Alfie says no. Your father won't see you on those conditions.'

Laura is silent.

My stomach climbs uncertainly back into place and I find I've been holding my breath again. I inhale, and look about the room for the first time. She's done it a soft mushroom. It's restful and I find I can't remember what colour it was before. It was an "everything" room – Laura's playroom, the TV room, music room, homework space and eventually my crash pad. Esther's a good painter. No spatters on the woodwork.

Esther's breaking the silence in the kitchen. 'And, Laura? Do you know what? I think it's the most terrible waste in the world to have a father and not to be in touch, to let your shit get in the way of, well, loving each other.'

'How the hell would you know?'

'Oh, believe me, I know. I'm not about to tell you how. But I do know. And I know about losing mothers too. Just you fucking think about it. Or you'll regret it.'

On the shelf right next to me, a square tin with an electric pink lid shrieks against the anodyne walls. It fits into the palm of my hand, and I shake it to hear the contents thud snugly against the sides. *Daddy, Daddy, now can we do the quiz?* Laura's childhood voice competes in my head with the rant coming from the kitchen. A long-forgotten ritual from the days when the "Amazing World Quiz" used to be a part of Sunday evenings. I slip the box into my pocket and wonder where that Laura has vanished. Is she still reachable? How would she react if I went in there and gave her the box? Likely she'd throw it at me.

They're both silent and I wonder whether I can slip out again unnoticed.

Then Esther again. 'It's funny, you know. I had this fantasy that you and I would get on. You know, be good mates, cook together. Go shopping. Stuff like that. How fucking wrong can you be?' She pauses. 'But that was when I thought you were a grown-up.'

'Gee, thanks!'

While Laura's exploding and lighting another cigarette I creep into the hall, open the front door and slam it. Then I walk through to the kitchen.

Esther leaps up. 'Alfie! I was about to phone you. When Laura turned up. I finished, you see. But...'

'This – *person* – threatened to tip paint all over me. This cow's completely fucked up my room and then the bitch sat me down and yakked at me. I'm not...'

I raise my hand sharply and let it drop slowly to my side. 'If I didn't think you would run from the house I would slap you, Laura. I will not have you speak to Esther like that.'

Laura takes a long drag on her cigarette while she stuffs belongings into her bag with her free hand. 'I'm out of here.'

'Oh no you don't.' Esther pushes her back down into her chair. 'I'm the one who's going. I'm done with you. I'm done with the house. And you...' She makes the "you" sound as if she's addressing a spider she's just found in the bath. 'You are going to stay right here and talk to your father.'

Esther squeezes my arm as she sweeps out, still wearing her paint-spattered T-shirt.

'I suppose you're going to run after your t...' Laura pauses and seems to think better of the word she was going to use. 'Girlfriend.'

'No. I'm staying right here with you.' I gaze steadily at her as I take out my pipe and pat my pockets, hunting the tobacco pouch. I haven't needed a smoke so much since the night Meg died.

'I'm not about to pass up the chance to get to know my daughter again. But I'm not staying to be insulted – or to listen to Esther being insulted.'

I sit down at the table, wait for Laura to speak and start the business of filling my pipe. Of course I want to talk to Laura, but it's all I can do not to follow Esther and have it out with her, once and for all, about Luke. That was the conversation I was running through my head as I walked here. For all I know she's rushed off to meet lover boy.

My priorities are hurtling round inside my head. It's clear that I owe it to Laura to be there for her. But am I prepared to sacrifice my relationship with Esther? That would be allowing Laura to run my life. I'm her father, not her lover. It feels like I'm on a tightrope.

The presence of Luke may mean my relationship with Esther is over, of course – which would make life simpler for me as a father. There's actually relief in that. But that is none of Laura's business.

Laura hasn't moved, which is something. She clears her throat and I glance up. She's furiously stubbing out her cigarette on a saucer.

I strike a match and draw the flame down into the pipe. 'Would you be happier if we went somewhere else? Not here in this house?'

'No. *I'm* perfectly comfortable in this house. It doesn't surprise me you're not. Anyway…' Her hostile tone falters. 'I feel close to Mum here.'

She shakes the last cigarette out of the packet. As she scrabbles for a lighter, I see tears making dark splodges on the leather of her bag. I strike a match and hold it out. She accepts it and we both inhale.

'So where do we begin?'

She shrugs and wipes her eyes with the heel of her hand. 'Dunno. I did know, you know, before… Before *her*.'

'Let's leave Esther out of it. She's got nothing to do with you and me.'

She makes a face. 'Dunno about that. But, as we're here, what I really want to know is *why*? Why then? Why when I wasn't there?' Her voice rises to a crescendo. 'I couldn't even say goodbye to Mum, for fuck's sake!'

I groan. 'I know. I know. It was a dreadful mistake. Didn't Mum say anything about that? In her letter to you?' I've never known what was in the envelope marked "To my darling Laura" which Meg left alongside my poem.

Laura shakes her head.

'I guess she wrote it before we decided when. It was a pretty last-minute decision in the end. You see, Mum was afraid you'd try to stop me. I should have insisted. Your mother wasn't making good decisions. And I was afraid you'd be dragged through the courts with me. She had no idea I'd be prosecuted.'

'And you knew?'

I nod and relight my pipe. 'Thought I'd be put away. Could have been as much as fourteen years.'

'Oh, Dad.'

It's the first time she's sounded like Laura.

She sniffs. 'She was right, of course. I would have tried to stop you.'

'I could have talked you through it. Should have trusted myself, trusted you. You see, she couldn't bear the thought of getting worse, of becoming…'

'Yeah. She explained all that. I *knew* all that.' She squashes another half-smoked stub into the heap on the saucer. 'But I was selfish enough to want her to stay alive and suffer. She was my mother. She had no business dying. I needed her.' She fishes out a crumpled piece of tissue and blows her nose. 'Pathetic, isn't it?'

'No,' I say. 'Not pathetic at all. Normal and natural. I've been angry with her, too.' I reach her hand across the table and she gives it to me. 'It was what she wanted, but I was angry with her for wanting it.'

'Isn't it really bad to be angry with someone who's dead?'

'Is it? Well, if it is, then we'd better be bad together. Because it isn't something I can stop happening. It just wells up. Not so often these days, but even so.'

'Is that because of her? The "not so often"? Because of Esther?'

I eye her, appreciating that first use of Esther's name. 'I don't think so. I think it's time. Coming to terms.'

'Ed says I'm always angry. He thinks I should see someone. I told him the only person I needed to see was you.' She breaks into deep sobbing at that, and I put my arm round her and we cling on to each other.

We end up going round the corner to our old local for a pub lunch. There's no sign of Luke or his van, and I find myself wondering if he gave Esther a lift home. Or if he's just driven her out of my life.

Laura tells me about Ed. He's a cellist in the year above her, the year she would have been in if she hadn't interrupted her course to be with Meg. They're planning to move in together. So she's allowed a relationship and I'm not? I have to silence that protest. It's different. I know it's different.

'Any chance of meeting Ed?' I'm wary of asking, afraid I haven't earned enough favour.

'Sure. Actually...' Her eyes well up again. 'I've really been wanting you two to meet. To somehow make it more real? Is that totally, like, crazy?'

I grin. 'Not crazy at all. I know what you mean. In fact...' I take the risk of a little humour. 'I felt the same way about Esther. But it turned out to be a little bit too real.'

She manages a twist of a smile. 'You didn't hear what she said to me. She wasn't nice.'

'Why would she be nice to someone who called her a tart before being introduced?'

Laura actually laughs. 'Before being introduced. That's cool. Sometimes, Dad, you can be quite funny.'

'I wasn't meaning to be funny as it happens. But let's not talk about Esther. When can I meet Ed?'

'Tomorrow? He's driving down early. We could go up to Finger Bridge and walk.'

That childhood name of hers for the local beauty spot. The thought of the three of us. Me and Meg swinging Laura by the arms – "One-two-three, whee!" It's always been her favourite outing, walking through the woods, playing Poohsticks off the bridge.

I swallow hard. 'Sounds okay to me. Should be spectacular. The leaves have turned and the colours are particularly good this year.'

'We'll pick you up. About eleven? Just you, though. Not her.'

'Sure. Just me.' Esther would love the place, but never mind. One step at a time. 'Will you stay at the house tonight?'

She nods. 'But I can't sleep in my room. It smells of fucking paint.'

'There are other beds. Mum's studio maybe?'

A shrug.

'You could try telling her exactly what you think of her for going and dying. She'd probably listen.'

She makes a face and shrugs again, but I can see she's giving it thought. I wait while she buys more cigarettes at the bar and we walk together to the corner. I watch until she turns in at the gate and returns my wave.

Esther's waiting at the window when I get back. She flies at me and buries her head in my jumper. The teapot's on the table, the one she got in the market because it was like her Nan's. There's some game show on the box.

'I'm so proud of you.' As I say it, I realise just how proud I am that she thought it was worth doing all that with Laura.

'What do you mean? Proud of me?' She grabs the remote and douses the television.

'All that stuff you said to her. How did you manage? You were so damn calm.' I laugh at her puzzled face. 'I was listening. Eavesdropping. Wicked, wasn't it? You two never heard me come in. So I hid in the back room.'

'But how come...?'

'Yeah. I slammed the door, so you'd think I'd just arrived. Cunning, eh?'

She punches me in the chest and the colour comes back to her face. 'Alfie Buckland! I don't know what to say.'

'So how did you do it? I have a sneaky feeling you impressed her, in spite of herself. Though she'd never in a million years admit it.'

'I pretended in my head that she was a lager lout I was going to bar from my pub if she put one more foot wrong. It was the only way I could handle it. We had training you see. When I did bar work in London.'

If only Laura knew it. One day, just maybe, they might be able to laugh about that. But I'm jumping the gun, several guns.

'But anyway, how did it go? After I left? Did you talk? Is she...'

'Good. We're back on track – thanks to you. We talked some, and then we went to the pub. In fact, I'm going to meet Ed – that's the boyfriend. I hope you don't mind. Tomorrow. And she didn't want...'

'Didn't want me along? Oh, fuck no. Time enough. In another million years or so. Anyway, I could do without seeing her for quite some time, I can tell you.'

Esther opens the fridge and takes out a hunk of cheese. 'I'm ravenous. Couldn't eat a thing when I got back. All very well for you, having pub lunches.' She cuts off a wedge.

It's now or never. I take a deep breath.

'Esther, there's something I need to ask you. It's actually why I came over to the house. What's going on with Luke?'

Her head comes up and her mouth falls open. 'Luke? What d'you mean?'

It's such a natural reaction, I'm suddenly sure she doesn't know. I tell her about the number of times I've seen Luke or his van.

'Fuckin 'ell! I had no idea. He's kept well out of my sight. Are you sure? That it was Luke?'

'He's not someone you forget, once you've seen him.'

'Suppose not. I never really thought about it.'

'What I want to know is, *why*? What's he up to? Is there something you haven't told me? Or is he a nutter? Or what? I don't know what to think. Should we be getting on to the police, for instance?'

'Hey! Hey! Steady on. This is Luke we're talking about, right?'

'Sure. He might be your old friend but he's not exactly behaving normally. Or like a friend, come to that. I'd have had it out with him by now if he hadn't been so slippery. In fact I fully expected to find him at the house with you today.'

'You what? You mean you thought I was carrying on with him? You didn't even trust me?' She drops her cheese onto the table.

'Esther, I didn't know what to think. I thought he might be stalking you, that he might be a danger to you. Or... Well, I didn't want to think of what else he could be up to.' I tail off lamely. 'At best, I thought he might be helping with the painting.'

She's turned away from me. She's crying. She's hurt, angry. Oh, Christ. What have I done now? Just as things were going so well.

'Esther, I'm sorry. It wasn't that I didn't trust you. I just saw him and you together that time. There he is, good-looking, successful, young...'

'And totally boring. Alfie, how the fuck did you think...?'

'Because you looked like couples should look together, young, attractive – just, kind of right.'

'I don't believe I'm hearing this. Why should you...?'

'Because he was hanging around. What was I to think? Why was he here? Why, Esther?'

She speaks quietly now. 'He said he wouldn't give up. That must be it. I wondered what he meant. It's his half-term. He said he was going to the coast. But he obviously didn't.'

'What do you mean, "wouldn't give up"? Give up on what?'

'Well.' She hesitates. 'Well, if you must know, he asked me to marry him. He thought I was throwing my life away.'

'You see?'

'No, I don't see. Just listen, will you? He didn't seem impressed that I didn't want him and his precious lifestyle. Wouldn't take no for an answer.'

'Ah.'

And he'll keep on at her, I think. Wear her down until she sees the sense of it.

That night as I clean my teeth I look long and hard in the mirror. What was I thinking of? When I get into bed with Esther, for the first time ever, I can't bring myself to make love to her.

25

At this moment I am perfectly content. I notice it and hold on to it. A cracking autumn morning for my birthday. Not that anyone knows that, which lets me – and them – off all the tedious business of cakes and buying drinks all round. I'm standing in the yard with the sun on my back, holding the pot of blue raddle waiting for Tom to bring in the ram. Eric stands by to hold him steady, while Tom and I get the colour on.

'Plenty of it, mind,' says Tom. 'We needs to be quite certain.'

Eric cackles as the ram kicks up.

'That should do the trick,' says Tom. 'Let him through then.'

I lift the hurdle and release the ram into the field of ewes.

'Off you go, have your wicked way with 'em. Mind youm do your stuff. We'll be keeping track of they blue rumps.'

Tom had summoned me back up to the farm to help with tupping.

'Reckon as it'll be peak time,' he said. 'And my knee's playing up. Bloody nuisance it is too.'

Esther couldn't see why the sheep couldn't get on with it by themselves. She wouldn't let me explain. All part of the edginess between us. Connie was wanting time off to soak up some sun in Tenerife with her partner, Anne, and Esther jumped at the chance of looking after the shop. Suited me. It didn't seem to occur to Esther to come with me, and I didn't ask the question. Whether Luke comes back on the scene is up to her. It gives her the chance.

I don't want to think about Esther. She thinks I'm just up here for a week or two. But I'm not going back. Leave the field free for the younger man, I tell myself. See how long it takes for Luke to win her over. Connie will let me know what happens. Or will she? She used to be my ally, my prop all through Meg's illness. But now? She gets on so well with Esther. And that used to please me. It still does. But it means she'll feel loyal to Esther. So it wouldn't be fair to ask her. Connie would never turn spy.

Esther texted Luke that day. The day I confronted her about him hanging around. Something along the lines of *Get lost. Alfie's thinking of calling the police.* Or so she said. He sent a message back that he was on the way home. So, not a nutter. At least, I suppose he has to be given the benefit of the doubt. And who can blame him for wanting Esther?

I haven't been managing to be so philosophical of an evening. And I wouldn't be sleeping it weren't for the whisky. I tell myself it's for keeping warm. But it's for swamping the longing for Esther. In Exeter Meg got in the way, came between us for the first time. But here, it's Esther who haunts me. Every pore in my body screams out for her. I pour a glass and try to conjure Meg. I read her poem over and over but it doesn't touch me in quite the same way. In fact it makes me angry. All very well for her to drift away. Leaving me to the turmoil. And that makes me feel guilty and I pour another shot.

I look at the sketches of Esther and turn them back to face the wall. I can't imagine ever painting again. That compulsion has left me. I play Puccini and wallow in self-pity until I disgust myself and grab the bottle again. I've been falling into bed in a stupor, waking with a thick head, to drink a gallon of water and swear I won't do it again.

During the day, working with the animals, I know where I belong. And Esther certainly doesn't belong up here on the moor in winter. I tell myself it suits me, and Tom's glad to have me. There'll be muttering at The George but no-one will be that surprised it didn't last – the young girl and the old man. I'll have a drink or two tonight with Joel. No Esther, no complications.

Tom breaks into my thoughts. 'How's that lass of yours?'

I tell him Esther's fine.

'Surprised she didn't come with you. Beautiful weather like this.'

I'm non-committal. 'She's busy with the café, holding the fort.' I know Tom's not one to push a person.

But Joel's a different matter. There's a card for me at The George. He hands it over between sneezes and watches me open it. 'So it's your birthday! Drink on the house then. Scotch? I'll have one, too. Fix this bloody cold.'

It's from Laura and I'm stupidly pleased.

'From my daughter,' I tell Joel.

'None from Esther then? Or did you do all that before you came away?'

'She doesn't know.'

'You cannot be serious! What's that all about? How is she anyway?'

'Oh, she's fine.'

Joel's face clouds and a question surfaces in his eyes, but he thinks better of it. He covers his confusion in another sneezing fit.

I tell him about Laura and meeting Ed and how she wants to bring him home for Christmas. And that makes me wonder what Esther will do for Christmas, and whether she'll be spending it with Luke. Christmas doesn't bear thinking about. So I ask Joel about Marion.

'She's got herself a flat in town.'

'Exeter? That does surprise me.'

'So it would me. Marion in Exeter? No way! London's the place. She says she misses theatres and so on, but Marion's no culture vulture. It's the shops, the buzz, the total lack of mud and ponies. Dunno why we stay married.'

'I was wondering that.'

Joel shrugs. 'She's off on another cruise to miss the cold weather. Wouldn't mind some warm weather myself.'

He steps from behind the bar to throw another log on the fire. 'Says she'll come down here in the spring. As soon as it gets pretty. Gambolling lambs and all that.'

I grunt and wonder if I can manage a whole winter up in that barn. Tom's found me an old woodburner and says he'll give me a hand fixing it up with a smokestack. But even so.

255

'So when are we going to see Esther, then?'

It's my turn to shrug.

'Hey, mate. You're not...? I mean, you're all right aren't you? You two?'

'Sure. She's looking after the coffee shop while the manager – you know, Connie? You met her at the trial? While she's taking a break. I'm just thinking, though – Esther may need a bit of space.'

'Space? What's that about? I mean, the girl's nuts about you. It's not because of your daughter, is it? We couldn't help noticing, you know, how she was after the trial.'

Joel won't leave it alone. I've forgotten how protective of Esther he's always been. I end up saying more than I intend.

'This bloke Esther used to know cropped up again. Thought I should back off. You know, give it a chance, give her a chance. Someone younger...'

'Oh, mate.' Joel makes a face, shakes his head. 'What does she say?'

'I haven't said anything to her, not directly. Not yet.'

'I tell you, you mean the world to her. Don't you...'

I hold up my hands. 'Don't worry. I'll do it. I won't let her down.'

I tell him he needs a whisky and hot lemon for his cold, and head off home. I don't want to leave the fire, but I regret telling him all that. He means well, but I don't want his comments. It may come to nothing, Esther and Luke. But in time there will be someone else. I'll write to her. A long, careful letter. Give it a bit of time and I'll do that. Deliver it maybe.

Confiding in Joel is not all I come to regret about that evening. A few days later I realise I've caught his wretched cold. Haven't had one of those in ages. Still, the weather's fine and we're busy, so I think little of it. I pickle it in whisky at night, and pile on the blankets. I'm still getting through a lot of Scotch. It keeps out the cold and it keeps Esther out too.

Meanwhile that ram's been doing a fine job, and we've got a good crop of blue and red bottoms. The day we paint his undercarriage a nasty shade of yellow to mark the remaining ewes, the weather turns.

Tom surveys the sky. 'Looks like snow. Lucky we got that stove fixed. Reckon as you'll be needing it. Plenty wood in the yard. You help yesself. And any time you like, you can move back down to your old room.'

He helps me chuck a load of logs into the pickup as a north-easter howls round the yard.

'Nasty cough you got there. You look after yesself.'

It snows overnight. It's not deep, but a covering. Enough that all the animals need a good supply of hay. It takes all day. It's a struggle. The cough keeps taking over and it's wearing me out. Plus one ewe's slipped and fallen, and I have the devil's job to get her upright and hold her for long enough to find her feet. She keeps going over again. She's so cold, I decide to take her back down to make sure she's properly thawed out. I'm done in by the time I get back to the barn and hit the whisky big time. Anything to fix this cough. The stove's slow to get going as I've run out of dry wood and have to knock the snow off the logs piled outside. I heat some baked beans and spoon them up, shivering beside the stove, thinking of Esther, safe and cosy in the flat. I haven't phoned her in a couple of days and I hope she's not fretting. Probably not thinking of me at all. Maybe that Luke's back down for the weekend.

As if psychic, Tom appears at the door in a gust of wind and slams it behind him.

'That lass of yours just phoned...' He breaks off, stamps his boots and peers at me.

He's carrying a cream churn, wrapped around with newspaper, which he sets on the table.

'Get that inside you. Eric's stew.'

I stagger slightly as I get to my feet and Tom's eyes move slowly from the whisky bottle beside me to the collection of empties by the door.

'I'll get you a glass. Water of life, Tom.'

'No. Not for me.' He gropes in his pocket and pulls out a vintage bottle of "Gees Linctus". 'Thought this might be of use. Give it a try. And by the by, your Esther was phoning to see if we was all okay up here. What with the snow. I told her fine, but I sees I was wrong. Youm not fine at all.'

'Don't you tell her any different.' I make an effort to straighten up and cross my arms to stop the shaking. 'Last thing I want is her up here, fussing.'

Tom grunts and makes towards the door. 'Just you take the medicine and eat that stew while it's still hot.'

Next morning I can hardly climb down the ladder for shaking. My head's pounding, the room's pitching like a ship at sea and I can't face going outside. I pee in the sink, an emergency measure I keep for bad weather. The damn tap's frozen so I can't even wash it away. I down some aspirin with water from the kettle and lurch about to get the woodburner going, which brings on a bout of coughing. Getting back up the ladder is out of the question, so I sink down onto the sofa, pulling the throw round me, unable to stop my teeth chattering. There are ominous pains in my chest and I eye my boots by the door, think about the sheep and try to imagine dragging myself out there, distributing feed. Give it half an hour for the pills to work.

I'm woken by Tom who towers above me like a giant and puts a horny hand on my forehead.

'Must have nodded off.' The words come out in a whisper.

'Best get the doctor to you,' he mutters and is gone again.

Next thing I know, there's a strange man and Tom and Joel amid a great deal of kerfuffle and I'm in Joel's Jeep, being transferred to a bedroom in The George.

Tom's squeezing my shoulder, 'You bain't no good to me in this state. You get yesself looked after. You be better off at The George. Eric baint much good as a nurse.'

I have to rest several times as Joel hauls me up the stairs. Then Pattie's tucking me in and pressing a cold flannel on my head. I never knew it was possible to feel so hot and so cold all at the same time. The shaking starts to subside and I fall deeply asleep.

My memory of what I thought was the next couple of days is pretty sketchy. Voices and figures faded in and out. Pattie was one of them, but mostly I didn't recognise or register them. I dreamt of Esther – who was always turning away or walking backwards away from me, teasing me, smiling her smile, unreachable. When

I finally come to consciousness, I find I've been drifting there for a week and Laura is sitting beside me. Which accounts for the violin I've been hearing. I wasn't dreaming that.

'You know how to give everyone a fright,' she says. 'They nearly took you into hospital, Dad. The first lot of antibiotics didn't do the trick. You were so bad that...' She pauses and looks away. 'They sent for me. And that t...' Her mouth sets in a thin line and she pauses again. 'Pattie's been nursing you.'

I try to make the right noises. It's good to have Laura here, but I'm not quite up to being ticked off for causing a lot of fuss. Evidently, it's all my fault. She's got a plan I'm not ready to hear, so I go back to sleep.

Days pass, and Laura is still here but less with me. I hear Joel complaining to Pattie that she's constantly hogging the landline, chatting to Ed, because she can't get a signal on her mobile. When she does sit by my bed she's always on at me about going back to Exeter. I guess she wants me to be there, so that when she comes at weekends it will be like coming home. I can't blame her. She wants it to be as much like the old days as possible.

The idea of Exeter makes me come out in a sweat. I can't do it. I won't do it.

'You don't have to do anything. I'll take you there. And you'll be warm, and all our old neighbours will look out for you.'

No mention of Esther, I notice.

Next morning I'm just getting dressed for my morning expedition to sit by the fire in the bar when Laura bounces in.

'Last chance, Dad. I'm off today. I have to get back. I've got exams. And Ed's not coping without me. Now you're on the mend...'

I sink back onto the edge of the bed and nod.

'So. I can pack your bag and drop you off at the house. What about it, Dad?'

What a bleak prospect. I shake my head. 'No, Laura, much as I appreciate...'

'I give up! You're so effing stubborn.'

Her fists are clenched and she's fighting back tears. 'Anyway.'

She turns and leaves the room, then runs back in, kisses me clumsily and is gone.

I wait until I hear her car revving and watch from the window as she drives away, before making my slow progress down the stairs.

'So that was Laura, that was.' Joel brings us both coffees and sits opposite me, placing logs carefully in the pale flames of the just-lit fire.

'I'm sorry if she's been a bit...'

'Don't mention it. Just means I get my phone back.'

'How come she was here anyway?' It only occurs to me to ask, now she's gone.

'Well, you were pretty rough, you know.'

'But who sent for her? Nobody knew...'

'Esther insisted she should be contacted.'

'Esther? How on earth did Esther get involved? You mean you rang Esther?'

Joel looks at me strangely. 'What d'you mean rang her? Esther was here. Looking after you.'

'*Esther* was?'

'Certainly was. Sat by your bed three nights and days. Had to be forced to go and sleep. Don't tell me you never noticed?'

I shake my head. I feel an idiot. 'How did she know? Why didn't you tell me?'

'Tom told her. I mean, what was he to say? She kept ringing to find out why you weren't in touch. She came straight up. I met the bus.'

So Esther came. She cared enough to do that. But she left again before I was fully conscious. Back to Luke, no doubt.

Joel reads my thoughts. 'She went as soon as Laura arrived. Said she didn't want to get in the way.'

'Did Laura see her? Did they speak? How were they together?' I'm struggling to get to grips with this news.

'They didn't come to blows, if that's what you mean. Didn't kiss and make up either. But Laura was civil. She was too worried about you to think much about Esther. But they were in there together. In the "sickroom."' He makes exaggerated quote marks in the air. 'Esther was telling her what to do. Not that Laura... I mean, Pattie tended to take over at that point.'

I laugh. 'Laura wouldn't make much of a nurse.' I don't resent that. But I don't like the fact that Laura couldn't even bring herself to mention Esther.

'So what are you going to do, Alfie?' Joel sits back on his bench and looks at me long and hard.

'Well, just as soon as I can walk round the yard… I'm going further every day, you know. I'll be out of your hair…'

'Alfie, that is not what I mean. I'm fed up with hearing you apologise for being here. How many more times do I have to say, you can stay here as long as it takes? No, I mean Esther. What are you going to do about Esther?' He pauses. 'And don't look at me as if you've never heard of the woman. She loves you, Alfie.'

'Rubbish. She did her stuff. I'm touched. I really am. I shall thank her. But then she scarpered before I came to my senses. Can't blame her.'

'Alfie! She left to leave Laura with you on her own. I told you.'

Pattie comes through the door at that moment, shaking her umbrella into the yard and dropping it into the stand. 'Mornin' all. Filthy day! How's the invalid today?'

'Tell him, will you, Pattie? About Esther.' Joel makes a gesture of despair towards me. 'He didn't even know she was here.'

'No, I know. You was right out of it. Didn't know who was who. But Esther, she was so…'

Pattie pauses, and as I look up I'm astonished to see her eyes fill with tears.

'Dear girl, she was so – well, tender – I suppose the word is.' She recovers and continues, 'Couldn't have done better myself. She didn't want to go. I know that. But she just said, "Laura's family, and that's that".'

Yes, that sounds like Esther. I can hear her, sitting up on High Tor watching those buzzards. She's telling me about her Nan, about giving up her degree to nurse her. Telling me that family came before everything else.

'The sad thing is,' Pattie is saying. 'Esther hasn't got any family herself. Not any more. That Auntie What's-her-face didn't work out, did she?'

I shake my head. I'd forgotten all about the dreaded Emmylou. 'That's one of the things about this Luke. You know, Joel? I was telling you he turned up? They used to go out? You see, he remembers her Nan. He knew her. I guess that's important to Esther. It's a link.'

'Funny she never mentioned him.' Pattie gives me one of her looks, reminding me of a particularly stubborn old ewe that always evaded being penned. She starts polishing the top of the bar with unnecessary fierceness.

'Quite,' put in Joel. 'Alfie's being perverse. Talk to him, Pattie.'

'Well, for a start, you didn't half miss her. I guess you was dreaming, but you kept calling out for her. "Esther, Esther." Over and over. Your Laura didn't think much to that.' Pattie grins. It's clear she didn't take to Laura. 'Didn't like it one little bit. But you wouldn't shut up.'

So Laura didn't choose to tell me that either. But you can hardly blame her.

'I told Esther, mind. Sent her a little text.'

Poor Laura. It must have been hard to make the journey and then find your father's lover – ex-lover – in situ. Strange that it should be Esther in my dreams, Esther I was calling out for, and not Meg. Laura would have resented that.

'And for another thing, that girl loves you. No two ways about it. Why else would she sit there day and night?' She turns to face me brandishing her duster. 'I keep her posted. The odd update on how you're doing. So now Laura's gone… Who knows?'

Pattie gathers the beer towels and piles them at the end of the bar.

I shrug. Everyone seems to think my business is their business. Doesn't Pattie have work to do in the kitchen?

'She said she'd had such a weird letter from you. Thought you must have been the worse for wear when you wrote it. Couldn't make head nor tail of it, she said.'

'Is there no privacy round here?'

Pattie cackles. 'Not since I was giving you blanket baths.' Then she sees my face and covers her mouth. 'Sorry, Alfie. No offence. You didn't know I could do those, did you?'

'Hidden talents, has our Pattie,' says Joel. 'Used to be a nurse, didn't you say, Pattie?'

'Oh yes. That was in another life. But Alfie, I have to say, we have to meddle a bit because you do need a bit of sorting out. Oh, that reminds me, Joel. I had a word in a certain quarter and that little matter you mentioned, it's all in place, ready to go whenever.'

Joel nods and taps the side of his nose.

'Oh, for Christ's sake, I've had enough of all this.' I go to get up and am overcome by a coughing fit and have to sink back down. The sweat breaks out all over me, and I feel too weak to protest when Pattie starts saying, "I told you so" and other such remarks, before gathering the towels and heading off to the washing machine.

'Look here, Alfie. I don't think you realise how ill you've been.' Joel's leaning forward, frowning. 'And you're no spring chicken. So don't imagine for one instant that you're going back up to that barn. In case you think you might, I tell you, Tom's put a padlock on the gate. *Just in case he's the bloody fool I thinks he is.* That's what he said.'

'I'm not going back to Exeter.'

Joel holds up his hands. 'No. You're staying right here in the village. Across the road. Holiday cottage. Belongs to Pattie's brother-in-law. You can have it at half the winter rate. Special do. And we can keep an eye.'

You bet they will.

26

I'm lost in the noise of chopping. It echoes in my ears, bounces off the stone walls of the pub car park and fades down the valley. Over and over, I lift the axe and let it drop. A clean split, exposing the creamy flesh of the ash logs as they fall neatly on either side of the blade. The sun's hot on my back. Sweat runs into my eyes. There's more than enough wood now for the evening's fire, but I won't stop, I'm caught in the rhythm, drowning in sound.

Soon I'll go inside, into the smell of woodsmoke and ale. I'll make a coffee and take it to the window. I'll sit in the sun and have another go at yesterday's crossword. My routine. Little things that stop me thinking, keep me going from one day to the next as strength slowly returns.

Engine throb interrupts. Turning in. Joel back already. He'll stop me and I can't say I'm sorry. One more round, four more logs. A door slams, sharp and tinny in the cold air. I raise the axe above my head.

'I bet you didn't ought to be doing that.'

That voice.

The axe comes down, misses the wheel of ash and lodges in the edge of the block instead of travelling on into my leg.

'Christ! You choose your moments!'

I turn, and there stands Esther, eyes grinning, hand over mouth. The sun is catching her hair, giving her a lopsided halo.

'Sorry. I didn't think until it was too late.'

I've straightened up too fast and arc sideways, grab the edge of the porch.

She's there in a second, pushing me back onto the bench. The bench where she sat while Marion had her welcome-home tantrum. Esther in plaster, back from hospital. Esther in love with me. A lifetime away. My head stops spinning, body steadies. I can feel the molecules settling back into place.

'When you've quite finished playing aeroplanes,' she says, 'I've come to see how you're doing. Risen from the dead but determined to get back there, I see.'

I mop the sweat off my face, smile up at her. She's wearing jeans and a black polo neck with a fur-lined bomber jacket. Nothing spectacular, but so Esther. Sexy? Well, yes. But not in an obvious way. Not as if she'd tried for that effect. I can't be a pretty sight, but it's so good to see her.

'Just doing a bit of payback for Joel.'

'You look terrible. But better than when I last saw you.'

'Thanks a bunch.' I make a face. The same Esther. 'And thanks. You know…'

She shifts position, as awkward as I feel. 'Never mind about that. Let's not mess…'

'No. I mean it.' I grab hold of her arm. I want her to stay close where I can breathe her in, the lemony, musky smell of her skin. 'I've meant to get in touch. To thank you. When I found out. They took their time telling me, Pattie and Joel…that you came. I was going to… But I hardly seem to do anything but eat and sleep.'

'And chop wood. Isn't that a bit daft?'

I realise how tightly I'm gripping her arm and let it go.

'I mean, you could have chosen something a bit gentler.'

I watch her step aside to pick up a stray log and place it on top of the pile.

'It's a nice morning. I wanted to get out. And it… Hey, what in hell's name is that?'

I've just caught sight of the crazy vehicle behind her. I suppose I expected to see the Jeep. I assumed Joel picked her up and brought her here.

'It's my van.' She turns toward the thing with a proud little smile.

It's one of those old VW campers, blue and white with huge

pink and yellow daisies painted all over it. I look around for Luke. Is he hiding inside or what?

A pair of rooks caw and jostle onto the shed roof, and I look up to see a buzzard high overhead. The sky is such an intense blue it hurts my eyes.

'Well, not exactly my van,' she's saying. 'I...'

'So you're off then? On a trip.' Honeymoon I suppose. It's good of her to come, but I wish she hadn't. 'Aren't you going to introduce us?'

She gives me an odd look. 'To the van? Well, sure...'

'To Luke, for Chrissakes. Where's he hiding?' I feel angry, humiliated. Why did she have to come with Luke? Why do I have to meet the fellow when I'm at my worst? He'll think I'm a frail old man. I just don't feel up to it.

'Luke? Luke's not hiding anywhere!' She's shrill with indignation. 'Get Luke out of you effing head, will you?'

'But how did you get here?' I seem to be wading through fog in my head.

'Well, I didn't walk. And the van didn't fly. I drove, of course.'

'You never said you could drive.'

'You never asked. Luke taught me...' She holds up a hand. 'Luke taught me *two years* ago.'

'Okay. I won't hold that against him.'

'Look, Alfie. There never was anything – on my side at least – between me and Luke. Not since we broke up – before I came to Devon. I told you all about that. How many more times? What do I have to do?'

I nod. I remember all that, but it didn't mean they couldn't get back together.

'Okay, he imagined he could get me back. But I never had a flicker. He was persistent. I'll give him that. He did come down a couple more weekends...'

'I knew it. I couldn't get him and you out of my head...'

'...But I never let him stay again. Not even on the sofa.'

She puts heavy emphasis on *sofa*. I remember the scene: her stuffing sheets in the washing machine, me wondering whether he really did sleep on the sofa. I'm still not sure.

'It was never him and me, Alfie. If you must know, this is what happened. Just so we're absolutely clear. I had it out with him down in the coffee shop after closing time, and Connie helped. She was there too. She backed me up. And off he went. Ask Connie.'

'But I bet he came back.'

'Sure he did. But I was staying at Connie's – to be certain I didn't see him. And he put a letter through the door of the shop – saying he gave up, basically.'

'And he hasn't been back?'

She shakes her head. 'Let's start again, shall we? As I was saying, I borrowed the van – from Connie and Anne. They're planning a trip in the summer. But until then...'

She leaves a meaningful pause and looks at me. I can't meet her gaze. Summer. Where will I be in summer? Still here? With Tom? Back in the barn? I watch an ant making its way along a groove in the bench. I wonder where it's off to, what...

'Alfie?'

'So who are you off on a trip with? Or did you just borrow it to come up here and visit the sick?' I'm trying to be jokey, but end up sounding petulant.

'That depends.'

'On?'

'You. Whether you're well enough. Whether you really... Well, you see, Joel said you needed some sun. And he knows this guy who's setting up a place. Could do with a bit of help. You know, in return for somewhere to park the van. Because the campsites probably close in the winter. Don't worry, it's not Italy. It's in Spain. It might not look much but it's nicely fitted up inside, and – if you don't like the flower power – we can always paint them out. Connie says she wouldn't mind. Anne doesn't like them anyway. And I've looked up the ferries and got myself a passport...'

All this is pouring out of her in a rush while her fingers clutch at the edge of her coat. I've never seen her so nervous. I'm speechless. I've so convinced myself that her silence meant she was half way to shacking up with Luke. That I might never see her again. And all the time... The dear girl. She's even worked out that I couldn't cope with Italy.

When I say nothing she steps back, turns full circle and faces me again.

'I mean, it's only a holiday I'm talking about. Not that I've booked anything, not until…'

'I don't know what to say. I just can't believe… I thought, you know… I thought…'

'An adventure. It would be an adventure, wouldn't it?'

'Yes. It would be an adventure.' I know she hears the doubt in my voice. I'm staring at that van and thinking, less adventure, more endurance test – which makes me feel old all over again.

She follows my gaze. 'It's got a heater. And we wouldn't go yet. Wait until you're stronger. Now that you're free… In the New Year maybe. That is, if…' Her voice trails away.

The thin cry of a buzzard pierces the air. We both look up. There are two of them now, soaring higher and higher. I wonder if she's remembering. Times we've watched buzzards together. That first time at High Tor. Buzzards and larks. Getting to know each other.

'Of course, it's not "only a holiday". The holiday's the least of it.'

I'm almost surprised to hear her speak. The whole scene feels surreal: the blue December day, the fact that Esther is here at all, the improbable van. I might be in a dream.

'Alfie!' She steps towards me and I refocus.

'Look Alfie, this is last chance country. Just take a look at the last few weeks from my point of view. This is what I've been coping with. You bugger off up here and don't even tell me it's your birthday. Then you don't come back. And I think, okay, he needs some space. I won't hassle him. I mean, there was Meg and coming back to Exeter. And Laura and all her carry-on. A lot to get your head round. So I think, I'll stay away, give the guy some peace.'

I stare at her. 'So you… You were giving *me* space?'

'You certainly seemed happy enough to take it. I mean, the next thing was – you kind of say you're not coming back – by effing letter. Written when you were obviously pissed out of your head.'

'You see, I thought I was giving *you* space. For Luke to… I nearly went off my head missing you.'

She chews her lower lip. 'You did go off your head. If that letter's anything to go by. Next thing is, you get ill and tell people you don't want me to know. And I thought, he's regretting the whole thing. Regretting having a fling with available girl on rebound from losing wife. Wants out. I mean, I got the message, kind of, that day on the bench on the cathedral green. Remember? The Artist and his Model? The play is over. Real life…'

'But that was just…'

She holds up a hand. 'I haven't finished. Then Tom and Joel got on to me. I come and look after you and you don't even recognise me – okay, not your fault. But even so, pretty hard to take. Not to mention having to cope with Laura treating me like something she got on her shoe.'

She pauses for a moment, flapping her hand in front of her face as if waving away the thought of Laura. I want to say that Laura's not like that, really she isn't. But, then again, I know Esther's right. Laura *is* like that. She's not my little girl any more. I can't send her to her room. I can't fix her for Esther.

'Anyway,' Esther goes on. 'Afterwards, everyone says you miss me, but you don't get in touch. And talking of Laura. Even Laura…' She pulls her mobile out of the back pocket of her jeans, presses a few buttons, holds it out to me. 'Read that.'

I cup my hand around the screen to shut out the sun and squint at the text.

Dad still poorly. Needs you. Thought you were a cow.
Maybe not such bad cow. L.

The message is signed off with a scowling face with red devil horns.

I feel my eyes pricking. Signs of a thaw. Aloud I say, 'Not that she's confused or anything.'

'It must run in the family.' Her voice is harsh and she glares at me. 'Anyway, this isn't about Laura. It's about me. Like I was saying, everyone was going on at me – but there's not a peep out of you. What was I to believe? And I thought, there's only one way to find out. So today I swallow my pride to say, one last time, I love you, Alfie Buckland. And I've come up here to see…'

She gives the little shake of the head that shows she's near to tears and I can stand it no longer. I stand up and hold her shoulders. She's quivering. 'Really?' I say. 'You really want this?'

She turns on her heel and walks towards the van jingling the keys in her hand. 'Why don't you come for a test drive? We can go for a drink in Blidworthy. I might even buy you lunch. And if you ask one more totally effing stupid question like that, I'll drive away and leave you there.'

I pick my jersey off the bench. The sweat's clammy on my skin and I'm starting to shake. I extract the axe, chop it neatly into the centre of the block and follow Esther.

Acknowledgements

Thanks are due to my GP, Dr Andrew Eynon-Lewis, for information on medical procedure; to Sally Vincent (rainingsideways.com), Paul Vincent, Stephen Leadbetter and the Dartmoor Whiteface flock of Bramble Torre Farm for initiation into the mysteries of the world of sheep; to the late Steve Widman for sharing his knowledge of Dartmoor; to Margaret Barnes, retired barrister, for advice on legal and court matters; to Anthony Beard of Widecombe and District History Group for information about the Uncle Tom Cobley model; and, as ever, to Hugh for living with it all.

Lightning Source UK Ltd.
Milton Keynes UK
UKOW04f1221211214

243496UK00002B/25/P